WHO NEEDS PARIS?

JOAN MEYERSON

HADLEIGH HOUSE
PUBLISHING

Hadleigh House Publishing
Minneapolis, MN
www.hadleighhouse.com

Cover design by Alisha Perkins

ISBN-979-8-9850576-5-2
ISBN-979-8-9850576-6-9 (ebook)
LCCN: 2023914468

for Mark

Praise for *Who Needs Paris?*

"A deliciously readable page-turner! Meyerson's Kate Miller is a heroine with guts and a charming, self-deprecating sense of humor. I found myself wishing I had a time machine so I could experience the sexy, intoxicating Paris of the 60s and 70s depicted in this book. Alas, the best we can do is read *Who Needs Paris?*"

- Nicole Yorkin, Peabody & Writers Guild Award winner, Writer - Executive Producer *Z: The Beginning of Everything*, *The Killing*, *The Riches*.

"If you know Paris, or if it's just your fantasy destination, *Who Needs Paris?* will take you there. Told through the eyes of Kate, a confident, driven, sexually curious young woman, I gobbled up every juicy experience she has while finding herself. I loved this book!"

- Robin Schiff, Executive Producer, *Emily In Paris*, Screenwriter, *Romy and Michele's High School Reunion*.

"In Joan Meyerson's fast-moving debut, Paris is a city of second chances, of remakes, of do-overs. Join heroine Kate Miller as she navigates celebrities, passion, sex, food, heartbreak, and, of course, wine, as she reconciles the past and accepts the present. Enjoy the City of Lights through Meyerson's loving and attentive eyes. Bon voyage!"

- Mark Sarvas, Author, *Memento Park*, Winner, American Book Award, the AJL Fiction Award.

"A compulsively readable, wise, funny, and sexy tale of one woman's rise, fall, and rise again over two distinct eras of growth and change. A tart and knowing love letter to Paris in all its beauty, promise, and contradiction. An evocative and absorbing ride!"

- Gary Goldstein, author of *The Last Birthday Party*
and *The Mother I Never Had.*

"Who Needs Paris? Apparently, I did! And so will you as you bounce back and forth between the early 60's and late 70's in the City of Lights. It's smart, sexy, and satisfying."

- Larry Wilmore, co-creator, HBO series *Insecure*; creator,
The Bernie Mac Show, Correspondent, *The Daily Show.*

"An American woman's dream that Paris live up to its "City of Love" fame backfires spectacularly in Joan Meyerson's brave, sexy, and compelling new novel."

- Eduardo Santiago, author of *Tomorrow They Will Kiss.*

"The author's use of two concurrent timelines is masterful, pacing the story in an exciting way that hooks the reader ... Meyerson crafts ... a satisfying story of love, redemption and finding oneself ..."

- *Kirkus Reviews*

1964

In the beginning, I loved the darkness,
the oldness, the dirtiness of Paris.
I didn't see grime, I saw a thousand years
of the city's seductive magic.
When the gargoyles of Notre-Dame
stared down at me,
there was no question in my mind.
They were devilish spirits
tempting me into delicious submission.
It was perfect. Until it wasn't.

Because then Paris abandoned me.

PART ONE

"…you should not marvel
if I do not enter that city so quickly."

—*Joan of Arc*

chapter one

1977 July 15
North Hollywood, California

I float through a foggy mist toward a man reaching out to me. His face is obscured in shadow, but I know it's him. My true love. I hunger to drown in him as he envelops me in his arms.

And then he whispers the words I've waited so long to hear:

"Je t'aime."

Our lips softly touch in a slow, tender kiss as a flush of warmth floods my body. He loosens my flowing gown, caressing my face, my shoulders, my breast … Yes, oh yes, yes!

What the …? Ouch!

The dream evaporated along with my ethereal gown as thirty-five pounds of adorable shepherd terrier mix pawed at my Berkeley T-shirt, poking, licking, barking: *Let me out!*

"Okay, Lucy, go chase the squirrel," I murmured, blearily crossing the room and letting her out into the pre-dawn light. She was so-o-o demanding, but I had to admit that Lucy had been my best (okay, only) bed partner for a while. I crawled under the covers, eager to return to dreamland and that heavenly kiss when a ringing phone pierced through my sleep-fog.

I picked up the receiver, ready to hang up, when I heard the words "Kate, it's afternoon in Paris. Time to work!"

A job was calling. I covered the phone with one hand while I blew my nose and took out my dental retainer.

"*Bonjour*, Patrice! It's six a.m. in North Hollywood. What's so fabulous you couldn't wait to call?"

"Kate, you have no idea! TV ratings will explode," he exclaimed in near flawless English, yelling into the phone to make sure his voice carried all the way to L.A. "New studies of human sexuality. We'll take sex out into the open. Forget Alfred Kinsey and Masters and Johnson. Old news. These days it's Louis B. Engler. He's at one of your universities, and he's perfect for the *Cahiers de Californie*— the French need to know!"

I was skeptical that the French needed to know more about sex, but half-listened to Patrice's passionate zeal, imagining him pacing around his office as far as his phone cord allowed, waving a cigarette in smoky circles to punctuate his idea.

That's how it always was with Patrice. I wouldn't hear from him for months, then a call from Paris at some unholy hour, and he's arriving in a week so I need to help produce another documentary for French TV's Antenne 2.

Patrice Carrière had gone from covering the horrors of the Vietnam War to what he enthusiastically called a friendly conflict: "The brave new frontier of California culture will invade France and free it from Old World stultification! And who better than me to record it?"

As far as I was concerned, the '70s in L.A. had gotten out of hand. I wanted more stories of love and commitment—not Patrice's recent focus on male strippers, roller skating discos, and women with guns.

I tried to dissuade him. "Sex studies? It could be difficult to get permission to film."

"Kate, that's your job. Find out where Engler is, what his research is about, and book him. I'm sure you'll do your usual excellent work, as I'm paying your usual excellent salary."

Patrice knew me too well. I was on hiatus (i.e., unemployed), the mortgage payment was due, and he paid in cash. I instantly changed course. "I'll do it, Patrice. Anything for you."

"A wise decision, Kate. Maybe you'll learn something, too," he teased.

"*Oui, Monsieur. A bientôt!*" I hung up and shook away the last vestige of my dream.

I had a job! Lucy came bounding in for breakfast, then took her vigilant position under the kitchen table while I slurped cereal and read her the *LA Times* headlines.

"Hey Lucy, Led Zeppelin's coming to the Forum. Wow!"

Lucy pawed at the paper, eager to sniff out her own dog version. She had the enthusiasm of a young child, and the way things were going, might be my only kid. But at least I wouldn't have to send her to college or pay for a big wedding. In my precarious financial position, I was happy to keep her in kibble.

I'd accepted long ago that documentaries perched on the bottom rung of the Hollywood financial ladder. It was my personal tradeoff: I lived from paycheck to paycheck, but in return the work fed my insatiable curiosity. I learned about everything from savage bees (scary) to alien astronauts (fake). I learned so much I did crossword puzzles in ink and was a whiz at trivia games.

So far I'd made it on my own. I'd scraped up enough for a down payment on an old (but charming!) ranch house, and freelance jobs paid the mortgage. Sure, I lived under a leaky roof surrounded by a wild garden, but there were also wood floors, shady trees, and French doors.

The bad things in my life? Don't let painful memories get you down, right? Better to forge ahead. I'll admit there were a few small details I needed to work on: finding the right man, having a baby, discovering the meaning of life. In that order. But since I vowed not to repeat the mistakes I'd made in my questionable choice of males, the playing field had narrowed considerably. My dating life, along with my other goals, had gone into hibernation.

So what if I was thirty-five and slightly behind schedule? As Scarlett O'Hara said: *I'll think about that tomorrow.*

A few cups of coffee later, the newspaper read, cereal bowl in the sink, and comfy in sweatpants, I sat at my desk (the kitchen table), tamed my unruly brown hair with a barrette, and looked through the sagging French doors at my dog happily digging up the over-grown garden. "Lucy," I called, "dig up some treasure, will ya?" She woofed, and I started dialing. Time to satisfy my curiosity about sex studies. In short order, I found a Dr. Louis B. Engler at UCLA. The operator put me through.

"Hey, Louis B. here."

He sounded young and not professorial, but then the subject was sex. I plunged in with my most potent weapon: flattery.

"Dr. Engler, French Television has heard about your impressive research. They're eager to present it to their viewers."

"*Très* cool," Engler said. "You're talking about my study charting sexual response with thermography?"

"Of course," I said, not having a clue what that meant. "Seems truly revolutionary. Tell me more," I asked, pen poised to take notes.

"It's amazing! We found an asymmetrical vasocongestive pattern in the genital area during sexual arousal."

"Hmm," I said, doodling on my pad, thinking how to tell Patrice it was a boring story.

"Let me put it this way," he said, noting a lukewarm response. "Research subjects masturbate, I chart how hot they get before they climax, and I've got a new emphasis on female subjects."

On second thought, Patrice was going to love it.

Engler agreed to let French TV film his study on the following Saturday, with one caveat. His volunteers performed the research behind a screen, but our filming might skew the results. We'd have to bring our own subjects. He suggested an adult model agency. The idea made me squirm, but who was I to question a professor's methodology?

I did anyway. "Why do we need porn actors if the subjects are hidden behind a screen?"

"Would you be a subject?"

"Well, I ..." I was desperately trying to think of a good excuse when he cut me off.

"I thought not. Get pros."

I agreed to his conditions, hung up, and took out the phone book. Mobile homes. Model makers. Ah, there it was. Modeling agencies ... Exotic Models, Rage Models, Star Modeling Agency. Yuck. Did I really want to do this? Yes, I reminded myself, if I wanted to keep my house and feed the pooch. God help me, I started dialing.

"Star Models," answered a cheery male voice. I only sputtered twice before I got out that I was producing a documentary on human sexuality research. Mr. Cheery Voice was all too ready to help. They were a full-service agency—did I want male, female, black, white, lesbian, gay? I'd covered a lot of documentary subjects, but nothing quite like this. I took a deep breath and reminded myself it was academic research.

"I need a male and female to, um, masturbate so they can be charted by a thermograph machine," I finished low and quick, rushing to get it out of my mouth, then waited for him to reject my request.

Surprise. He didn't care one bit what the job was for. "Sure thing. Blond, brunette, big tits or not? And the guy? Tall, short?"

I assured him it didn't matter since they would be behind a screen, but he insisted I choose. I contemplated my options: going to a scuzzy office in Van Nuys to browse through head, tail, and boob shots, or spending a day watching porno films. I was chewing on a fingernail, trying to decide between bad and worse, when he offered to send a few models to audition for the director himself.

Saved. I arranged a group audition for the day after Patrice was due to arrive from Paris. An L.A. friend had offered Patrice his house in Coldwater Canyon above Beverly Hills for a few days, and the models would meet him there.

A week later, I was on my way to meet Patrice at the canyon house. The plan was that after he'd auditioned the models, we'd go over the logistics and research for the shoot. I turned off Mulholland Drive onto a rutted dirt road marked "Private no access" and chugged my old VW Beetle up to a house of wood and glass perched on the edge of the canyon. I watched as the late afternoon sun cast the scrubby rustic canyon in its golden glow. On a nearby rock a lizard basked in the sun's rays, and in the distance a solitary deer picked its way through the brush. In this wild habitat, nature was at peace with itself. That's what I wanted; to follow *my* nature. But it'd been years since I knew what that was.

I snapped back to reality. I had work to do, money to earn. I breathed in the cool, eucalyptus-scented air. In and out. Mentally preparing for the task at hand. Patrice would be finished with the audition, and we'd get straight to business.

Wrong. I walked through the doorway into a sunken living room carpeted in wall-to-wall orange shag, and "wild habitat" took on a whole new meaning: Not only was the audition still going on, Patrice and his small French crew were lounging on a black leather couch, drinking wine, smoking joints, and comparing the assets of the three Star Models posing for them. It was a veritable smorgasbord: a statuesque blonde, petite brunette, and bouncy redhead. All of them showing off bountiful curves in micro miniskirts and plunging tank tops. Pretending not to notice, I adjusted my floppy peasant blouse, hiked up my bell-bottoms, and walked my flat-chested, angular body into the room.

"Kate, you're early," Patrice called, "or perhaps we are late." Laughing at his own joke, he took a drag, held, then let out the smoke. "These auditions are very intense," he said, grinning widely. "Sit down and take notes. Give us the female POV."

Patrice looked the same as always—craggy, lean correspondent type in rumpled safari jacket, faded jeans, and shaggy brown hair in need of a cut. But the weed, or more likely the girls, had put his demeanor off-kilter. I was about to take a seat on the couch next to the salivating soundman and assistant cameraman, when Patrice waved me over to a man who was older, rather short, with a prominent nose and a curly mane of steel gray hair. In his well-tailored navy blazer and crisp white shirt, he projected a French air of *savoir faire*.

"May I present my friend Jean-Claude Renaud, famous French producer? He's in town to meet with ABC on a co-production deal. I invited him to help with our auditions. He has an eye for talent." Patrice winked as Renaud extended his hand to me.

"Call me Jean-Claude. *Mon Dieu*, Patrice is incorrigible. He said this was a business meeting, yet he seeks my aesthetic judgment," Renaud said in mock amazement, still focused on the floor show. I shook his hand, recalling his name from movie ads. He'd produced one of those movies that made Brigitte Bardot famous.

I couldn't resist. "It wasn't God who created Brigitte Bardot; it was you, wasn't it?"

Laughing in surprise, he turned his attention to me.

"My Bardot film was five years after *And God Created Woman.* However, you may remember—"

"*Eh bien,*" Patrice interrupted, eager to return to the audition. "This is business. I want Kate to take notes. Sit."

Whether or not it was business, as soon as I took out my yellow pad and pen, the meeting escaped into another dimension. With a nod from Patrice, all three of the models pulled off their tank tops, and the Frenchmen pondered the merits of each pair of boobs as if they were comparing fine wines.

"Number One is a bit droopy, but not without character," Patrice observed.

Jean-Claude weighed in, barely containing a straight face.

"Number Two is formidable. I am reminded of an abundant Renoir, or is it a luscious Rubens?"

The assistant cameraman snapped to attention.

"In my professional opinion, the lighting won't be kind to her nipples. They are not the rosy pink the camera loves."

Patrice turned his attention to Number Three, the brunette.

"You have nice melons, *ma chèrie.* Firm and ripe. A bit small, but we can work with them."

This was shaping up to be the most unusual casting session I'd ever been to. It was all in a day's work for these girls, but why did Patrice need to look at their boobs? The study was of the human orgasm. I needed to remind him that he'd be shooting strictly below the belt.

"Uh, Patrice," I whispered, but he ignored me, intent on his directorial vision. I was feeling like an Alice who'd fallen into an X-rated Wonderland, when a nondescript man entered the room and joined the young women.

"I'm Tom. For the audition. Sorry I'm late."

He had a doughy nose, dishwater hair, and a sallow complexion.

His tight T-shirt revealed a pudgy stomach protruding over baggy jeans. I couldn't believe he was a Star Model until he unzipped his trousers and stepped out of them. No underwear for Tom.

"Big Penis," I wrote.

"Do you want to see it hard?" he asked.

I would let Patrice answer that question. My guess was no man there would want to compare himself to this horse.

Patrice glanced at him. "I'll take your agent's word that it's in working order," he said, then turned to me, having his fun. "Unless you have a different professional opinion?"

I'd embraced women's lib and marched for the E.R.A. along with my sisters. But at work I still had to prove that I could be one of the boys, equal to any crew member. If they objectified the women, I would do the same to Tom. As if judging the Guinness World Record for what filled the world's largest jockstrap, I turned to Patrice, deadpan.

"It'll do. Hey, Dr. Engler can finally solve the burning question: 'Does size matter?'"

Patrice laughed so hard he expelled his marijuana smoke. "Kate approves. You got the job," Patrice told Tom. "Saturday, three o'clock at UCLA. Your agent has the directions."

As Tom pulled his pants on and ambled out, Patrice nodded at me in amused appreciation. I'd picked the right agency, he said. He was going to finish the girls' audition at a little pool party on the terrace. There was no reason for me to stay.

"Don't you want to go over my research notes?" I said. "It's a clinical study measuring masturbation."

Patrice didn't take his eyes off the girls. "Yes, yes, but on this shoot, I have to concentrate on visuals. You will interview Engler. Leave your notes. I'll take a look later."

Patrice was a total pro, but I'd worked for him long enough to know when he had an appetite for play.

"You're the boss," I said, glad to leave the party. As Patrice and his crew led the girls outside, I left him the notes and gathered up my purse and briefcase.

Jean-Claude held up his wine glass. "Why not stay, Kate? Tell me more about this study Patrice is filming."

He poured a glass of red wine and placed it on the table in front of me. His ice-blue eyes cut into mine; for what purpose I wasn't sure. Correction: I had a sneaking suspicion, and caution was my keyword. On the other hand, if getting hit on was par for the course in Hollywood, I also knew the town's most important rule: network, network, network. Jean-Claude was an influential man. He had connections in American television. What harm could a drink be?

"Patrice and I never mix business and pleasure," I said, making clear my limits. "But I can tell you a little bit about Dr. Engler's methodology."

While I explained my research notes on thermography, I tried not to look out at the deck as Patrice stripped off his clothes, picked up his 16mm. Éclair camera, and started filming the girls in the pool.

"Uh, as I was saying, Dr. Engler is measuring arousal in terms of Masters and Johnson's four stages of sexual stimulation."

Jean-Claude professed to be fascinated and wanted to know more. While I soldiered on, the show unfolding outside became truly Fellini-esque. Patrice and the girls were laughing and drinking wine in the hot tub, and when the model he called Melon Girl spilled wine on herself, Patrice was there to lick it up. I could deal with the spectacle; that is, until I glanced in the mirror and saw my one-dimensional body in contrast to the girls' fleshy pulchritude. Suddenly it was personal. My anatomy hadn't bothered me this much since puberty, when I'd waited in vain for the big breasts that set the standard for a woman's beauty. The best I could say about my bra-less breasts was they were perky. Perky wasn't much to work with.

To Jean-Claude, the show was harmless background fun. But he could see I was uncomfortable. "Kate, don't let them bother you. Relax."

I gulped down the rest of my glass and tried to make light of it. "It's hard to describe the four sexual stages when who knows what stage they're at in the hot tub."

He'd seen behind my bravado. "I love women. Why don't they understand that men appreciate all forms of beauty? Those women out there, yes, they are architecturally interesting, but in five minutes, boring to me. It's the mind that is endlessly provocative, *n'est-ce pas*?"

I had to admit he hadn't gone out to play with the models. Nor had he tried to get into my pants. Yet. I nodded at his astute observation as he poured me another glass of wine.

Jean-Claude lit a Marlboro and leaned back on the couch. "I have done and seen a lot in my years, and what have I learned about women?" He didn't wait for an answer. "Most women judge themselves by the standards of the day. How should a 'nice' woman behave? What will a man think if she dares to take pleasure in her own sexuality?"

For a split second my mind leaped to a far-away time when I let passion take control. And then I froze.

With both hands, he had taken my long curly hair and lifted it off my face.

"*Très belle.* Yes, blue eyes, chestnut hair, good smile, nice shape of the nose. But that is *ordinaire*. Rather, it is how those mysterious eyes observe and assess life's unexpected moments, as I watched you do during the audition. And as you are doing right now, trying to figure me out." He paused, studying my face. "The language of your lips—what are you thinking when only the ends of your mouth turn up? And that slight movement when you swallow, then push out your tongue so slightly? And then there is the rest of you; I see an adventure to explore in uncharted territory."

As he let my hair fall back down over my shoulders, his hand grazed my neck. It was only a millisecond, but I felt an enticing twinge in the sweet spot between my legs.

He had turned me on. With words.

"Kate, you are smart. You are funny," he continued, smiling with his eyes. "But are you bold, do you dare? Shall we play together?"

"Like out in the pool?" I asked, instantly shaking myself back to reality, his words cutting deep into the layers of distrust I'd built up from too many meetings like this one.

"*Mais non*," he assured me, "something more challenging."

I was sure he didn't mean a game of chess. I had to reset my boundaries, to make light of it. "I'm flattered, Jean-Claude, but my mother taught me never to play with strangers."

"*Ma chèrie*," Jean-Claude said, ignoring my words, "do you have children?"

"Is this your idea of foreplay?" I asked, hoping to shut him up on that subject.

"You are what age? You don't have time for foreplay." He smiled at my poker face, teasing. "Don't you want a baby? I have made *un bel enfant* with one of my favorite stars. I could give you a beautiful child."

It was the most outrageous attempt to get me into the sack I'd ever heard. But strangely enough, he'd hit home. And it stung. I had always assumed I'd have a kid someday when I found Mr. Right. But after too many Mr. Wrongs, my time for "someday" was running out.

Doing it on my own didn't make sense. It might be 1977, but a single unwed mother traveled a rough road, braving gossip, career limits, and financial challenges. Besides, a turkey baster with a male friend's sperm wasn't my idea of fun. But Jean-Claude ... well, that was a new perspective.

I came to my senses; it was ridiculous. "That's a generous offer,"

I said, not even trying to mask my sarcasm. "But you're going back to France."

He quickly recovered from my rejection and turned it on its head. "*Oui, ma chèrie.* Even better. Come to Paris. We'll make a baby there."

Jean-Claude air-kissed me on both cheeks and handed me his business card, as he no doubt had done to a thousand people wanting an audience with him.

"*Quand tu viens à Paris, tu m'appelles.* You can call my office. My secretary will schedule a meeting."

I wasn't sure who was being rejected, but that was the French for you. Just as well.

I'd been to Paris once before, and once had been more than enough.

chapter two

1964 September 17
Paris

I'd come to Paris with my best friend Susan to study at Alliance Française. We were twenty-one, Berkeley grads, and ready to seize our destiny. If we weren't sure what our destiny was, we were certain that Paris would give us the opportunity to find it. Didn't Ernest Hemingway and F. Scott Fitzgerald escape American conformity to find freedom in Paris? Our goal was similar: we were escaping middle-class mediocrity to explore new dimensions of life we'd only dreamed about. And what better place than Paris to do that? For years, while we worked summer jobs to pay for our trip, we gobbled up every movie about Paris, from *Gigi* to *An American in Paris* to Jean-Luc Godard's *Breathless*. And if our experience turned out like that of any of our movie heroines, it would be okay with us.

We got a room at Hotel de Senlis in the student Latin Quarter.

There was a sink and a bidet in the room, a toilet and bathtub down the hall. The heater was temperamental and the beds were lumpy, but at $1.20 each per night, the one-star hotel fit our budget.

Our first night at the hotel, having unpacked but too excited to go to bed, I proposed we search for the hotel's "one star." With lots of laughter and cheap red wine we'd brought back after dinner, we bounced on the sagging beds, shook the dusty bed covers, noted the leaky faucet in the rust-stained sink. And although the bidet held promise for washing underwear, we found no "star" to warrant the hotel's rating. Until we looked out the window.

Silhouetted against the inky black sky, there stood the Panthéon in all its glory—and above it, a cluster of twinkling stars. Susan clinked her glass against mine and we toasted to our "Multitude of Stars" room.

"We did it, Kate," she proclaimed, as she began pulling our scarves and coats off the clothes rack. "Let's go meet Paris!"

We half-ran, half-skipped down boulevard St. Michel and followed a student crowd into a narrow cobblestone street close to the Seine. Wandering past the brightly lit restaurants and shops, we were drawn to music drifting out of a small jazz club called Le Caveau de La Huchette. Blending in with a group who'd already paid admission, we followed them down steep narrow steps into a cellar. A band was playing swinging boogie-woogie, and shedding our coats, we squeezed onto the crowded dance floor, tapping our toes and twirling to music straight from the Jazz Age. We were living our dream, and we couldn't stop grinning at each other.

When the band broke for an intermission, a waiter approached and demanded that we order an expensive drink to cover our drink minimum.

"We can't afford that!" I shouted to Susan, but she laughed and ordered two glasses of champagne. As soon as the waiter left, we grabbed our coats, ran back up the stairs, and escaped into the street, giggling and hugging each other. Drunk on the promise of Paris.

It was cold that September, bone-chilling cold, gray and wet. But we were in the Paris of *Gigi* and *An American in Paris*, so what did it matter? For the first few days, it was a thrill to simply browse the book stalls along the Seine or stroll through the Jardin de Luxembourg on our way to French classes at the Alliance Française.

The Alliance offered French instruction to students from all over the world. We assumed we'd find our *entrée* into a cosmopolitan social life, but our fellow classmates turned out to be a motley group of international hicks from places like Des Moines and Düsseldorf. Susan and I ignored them. Instead, we gazed longingly at the French students dressed in black turtlenecks smoking thick Gauloise cigarettes, eager for the time when we could speak French well enough to engage them.

In the meantime, each day after class I planned excursions to a museum or a Parisian landmark. One afternoon when there was a break in the clouds, we ventured to Montmartre and climbed the hill to Sacré Coeur, with its dazzling view of *tout* Paris. It was dark by the time we found the metro back to our hotel, only to discover the electricity had gone out. We ate a quick meal at a self-service diner and took our homework to the nearest café.

As I sipped my wine and studied French verbs, I told myself we would survive the bad weather and the cheap hotel. After all, we were a team, and if *la vie parisienne* wasn't so great now, we'd figure out how to make it work. Especially if we learned to speak French properly.

"*Je vais boire, tu bois, nous avons bu, vrai?*" Not hearing Susan praise my pronunciation, I looked up to see that she had already finished her entire glass of wine.

"I know we're drinking," Susan said, underwhelmed with my conjugation. "Let's face it: This is not the Paris it's supposed to be.

This is *le bullshit*."

"*La merde*," I corrected her.

"Okay, so what's the word for *Je suis* bored?"

"*Je m'ennuie*," I said with satisfaction. "Why aren't you studying your French?"

"Maybe because we haven't practiced with someone like that doll at the next table." She cocked her head to the right.

"That *jeune homme* is now greeting his *très jolie* French girlfriend," I warned her.

Susan slammed her book shut. "We've been here two weeks and all I've learned is that we're freezing our asses off in a flea-bag hotel."

I tried to make the best of it. "Okay, it's not exactly what we wanted. But look at all the museums we've gone to: The Louvre! The Jeu de Paume! The Grand Palais!"

Susan smiled at me indulgently. "Museums are fine. Beautiful. But did we come here to be tourists or see the real Paris? You know, the sitting-around-cafés, smoking-cigarettes, drinking-wine Paris?" She turned quite serious. "Hanging out. That's what I do best."

"And that's exactly what we're doing. We're hanging out."

"With guys," she said, explaining the obvious.

I had no arguments left. "It's impossible to meet them. We've got to learn more French."

She scanned the room. "How about those two guys in the corner?"

I looked over. One was tall and slender, with pale skin and longish blond hair. Black turtleneck, black blazer, and tight jeans. Very cool, I had to admit. The other one—shorter, a bit stockier, was a study in browns—auburn hair and beard, russet tweed jacket with leather elbow patches, a burnt orange scarf wrapped around his neck. The two were animatedly reading to each other from their respective paperbacks.

"They sound British; we won't learn much French."

"Let's find out how French sounds with a proper English accent."

Susan took off her coat, making quite visible how she filled out a snug sweater and straight skirt. Susan wasn't exactly beautiful, but her bold features framed by long, straight brunette hair came together in one dramatic package. Okay, let's be honest. Guys drooled over her big boobs and tight rear end. But there was also something else about her that men dug. She radiated a take-charge attitude:

I know what you want, and I'll have fun giving it to you.

As if she owned the room, Susan approached the Brits. They looked up from their books as she waved a cigarette and asked the blond one for a light. He took out his lighter, snapped it open, and held out the flame. She leaned over to light her cigarette, her chest in front of his face. In two minutes, all three of them were walking back to our table. Susan gleefully made the introductions.

"Kate, this is Trevor and Colin. And this is their bottle of wine they'd like to share."

"*Enchanté* to meet you and your bottle," I said, moving over to make room. Within five minutes of small talk it was obvious who was going to be with whom. Trevor, the blond handsome one, was focused completely on Susan. That left auburn-haired Colin. I never got the first pick with Susan, but in this instance I didn't mind. His hazel eyes twinkled in tandem with an impish smile. Besides, he was reading something interesting.

"How do you like your book?" I asked.

"*The Doors of Perception.* Aldous Huxley. I might call it an eye-opener."

"How 'perceptive' of you," I said, recognizing a fellow traveler who had fun with words.

He handed the dog-eared paperback to me. "Do you remember in *Brave New World* when people took this drug to lose themselves, to forget? Dig this. Twenty years later in *The Doors of Perception,* Huxley writes about another mind-altering substance—to *find* himself." Colin took the book, searching for one of the passages.

"'I was … in a world where everything shone with the Inner Light.' Bloody brilliant!"

"But that's in the exterior world," I protested, "not about finding what's inside of you."

Colin smiled as if explaining an inside joke. "That's the best part. Enlightenment happens when your own mind expands to include the universe."

"And you know that how?" I asked, then backed off. I didn't want to look like a drug addict. "Purely hypothetically, of course."

"Hypothetically? Drugs are not a hypothetical experience," he smiled knowingly.

Back in Berkeley, I'd heard about Timothy Leary and his experiments with hallucinogenic drugs. Most Americans looked askance at his spiritual "trips." But I was drawn to this new frontier. My "trip" to Paris was to find the freedom to be myself, though I wasn't even sure what that was. It was time to start exploring.

"You've taken them? Mind-altering substances, I mean. Do you have any?" I asked.

"My kind of lady," Colin said. "Bloody shame I don't have any mescaline, but we smoked some hash last week that took us off our trolley."

He turned to Trevor, who had his arm around Susan, showing his copy of *Cahiers du Cinema*, open to a François Truffaut article. Susan was struggling to appear as if she understood more than a few words of French. She had knocked down a couple more glasses of *vin ordinaire* and was definitely in a good-time mode.

"Not to disturb you two, but Kate and I are investigating the spiritual benefits of meditation." Colin held up his copy of *Doors of Perception*.

"You mean you want to get high?" Trevor cut to the chase.

"I thought we already were," Susan said.

"Susan, you are brilliant, but I believe Colin is recommending a trip closer to the stratosphere."

"Not the Eiffel Tower?" Susan giggled at her own joke.

"Did I already say, darling Susan, that you are brilliant? But, I believe it is a visit to Mustafa that Colin is speaking of."

Colin nodded. "Are you girls ready for a tour in search of the black gold of Morocco?"

We looked at each other with that shorthand that best friends read in an instant. Susan closed *Cahiers du Cinema* and stood up.

"What are we waiting for?"

chapter three

1977 July 23
UCLA, Los Angeles

If the audition for Dr. Engler's sex study was like exploring an X-rated wonderland, finding his lab at UCLA was an adventure in a Z-rated horror movie. On Saturday afternoon, deep within the rat's maze of the Psychology Department, my footsteps echoed down a dark, deserted basement corridor. Not even a janitor mopping the floors. Was UCLA purposefully keeping the lab under the radar, hiding whatever nefarious activities might be lurking inside?

By the time I found room B124, the crew was almost finished with prep. A gurney-type hospital bed occupied the front of the classroom; behind it, a large curtained screen.

Patrice grunted hello. "Check out the machine," he said, sending me over to where a skinny guy in baggy jeans, Adidas, and a Led

Zeppelin T-shirt sat in front of a metal apparatus, fiddling with its monitor display of oscillating infrared lines.

"Where's Dr. Engler?" I asked the young man. "I'd like to say hello."

"I'm Louis B," he said, enjoying my startled reaction. "You must be Kate."

My mind was reeling. Who was going to take this guy seriously? "No bowtie like Doctors Kinsey or Johnson?" I asked, hoping he'd take my not-so-subtle hint.

"Aha. I'm not dignified enough? Believe me," he said, pointing to his chest, "Led Zeppelin is serious shit."

When I not so politely suggested he don the lab coat hanging on a peg, Dr. Engler only laughed, picked up a bundle of wires and sensors, and went to prepare his new subjects. Patrice's Melon Girl (known as Brandy) and Tom were undressing at the back of the classroom. As Patrice filmed the process of attaching the sensors to their bodies, I grabbed the lab coat and got it on Engler in the nick of time.

"*Eh bien*, Kate," Patrice at last acknowledged me, "stay out of camera range."

"Okay, but don't forget to put the screen in front of the gurney," I reminded him, "so the models can masturbate behind it."

"Forget the screen. Not good TV. Since we've got the gurney already lit," he directed the naked models, "we'll do the fucking first."

"Fucking?" I was incredulous. "Didn't you read my notes? The study is about masturbation, and you'll have visuals on the thermography machine. You don't want it to look like a porn film," I warned him, certain he'd appreciate my concern.

But Patrice kept checking his exposure. "Kate, I'll take care of the film, you take care of Dr. Engler, and he'll take care of the study. Right, Professor?"

Engler, who was back at his machine, nodded, unperturbed.

I took my position next to him. "I can't believe the university gave you permission to do this," I huffed, barely containing myself.

"Why do you think I scheduled it for Saturday?" He shrugged and a sly smile played across his face. "Too much red tape. Just don't distribute the program in the U.S., okay? But France? Fine. I've got a message to get out, and most people don't read academic stuff. This, they'll watch." He adjusted his dials and gave a thumbs-up to Patrice.

End of discussion. Reminding myself I was a hired gun, I sat down, praying UCLA would never hear about this, fuming at the thought of having to watch porn that I'd unwittingly produced. Then Tom and Brandy got on the gurney, and dammit, my unquenchable curiosity kicked in. As weird and sleazy as it was, when was I ever going to see something like this again?

"Action," Patrice announced.

I wasn't sure if I was saddened or amused at how unsexy sex could be. Brandy's thighs dimpled with cellulite. In the classic missionary position, her boobs splayed sideways under Tom's heaving chest. His ass was white and pimply, and he had a bald spot on the back of his head. It was hard work, and under the glare of the lights, there was nothing exciting about their mechanical performance. Who would write sonnets, build empires, or go to war in the name of this tacky display? What could thermography ever tell us about the mystery of sexual love?

I shook myself back into professional demeanor and motioned to the soundman to start recording Dr. Engler. Patrice wanted sound bites to cover the action.

"Dr. Engler, what are we learning here?"

"Registering thermal changes of both subjects," the professor reported, absorbed in the monitor's artful abstraction of infrared colors.

As Tom pumped away, his body image turned from green to

chartreuse to yellow, then deepened into orange. It was mesmerizing: these images were turning sleaze into science. As if we were watching Tom approach the end zone for a touchdown, we breathlessly waited for red, the sign of orgasm. But the orange plateaued.

Tom's artistic reputation was at stake. A quick hand job and he was back in action. Engler pointed to the deepening colors.

"Hotter colors mean more blood is flowing to the erogenous zone. They're more aroused, excited. Conclusion: humans are hard-wired to have sex for fun."

"Fun? Is that the message you want to get out?" I challenged the professor. "What about love? Or the need to procreate? Isn't that nature's driving force?"

"That's what religion and society want you to believe. But they've confused sex with sin. Why should we punish ourselves for something we're physically engineered to enjoy?"

"C'mon," I protested, forgetting I was an objective interviewer, "how can you say a machine knows when we're having fun? Or even knows what fun is?"

Engler's eyes locked back on the screen, nodding at the fast-changing colors on the thermograph. "Believe me, the machine doesn't lie."

We watched as the images turned fire engine red. Touchdown. Tom and Brandy scored. But did they have fun? I begged to differ with the all-knowing machine.

That evening, Patrice took me to dinner. He had two prerequisites for dining in Los Angeles: a good red wine and New York–style cheesecake. Greenblatt's on Sunset Boulevard was one of those rare places that supplied both—a Jewish deli that stocked the finest wines in L.A.

I followed Patrice through the deli's wine shop as he carefully inspected the stock of French wines, choosing a Pavillon Rouge du

Chateau Margaux. Upstairs in the restaurant, the waiter opened the bottle and the ritual began.

Patrice sniffed the cork, swirled the wine, breathed its developing body, swirled again, took a swallow, swished his tongue, and pronounced it sufficient. As he drank, he picked at his rare roast beef sandwich ("Hold the bread and coleslaw."), while I saluted my Jewish heritage by attacking a pastrami on rye. Patrice watched me eat, enjoying my look of bliss as I got my mouth around the sandwich's thick, juicy goodness.

"Kate, I know you didn't like what happened today, but you got a great interview."

After a film shoot, off the clock with a glass of wine, Patrice and I had been known to indulge in a fair amount of camaraderie and candor.

"I'm glad you got what you wanted," I said, "even though you pulled a fast one on the film set-up."

Patrice shrugged and laughed. "The audition inspired me."

I shook my head in frustration. I was only the hired gun, but that didn't stop me. "I gotta admit, it made me think about a documentary I researched on pygmy chimps. They resolve conflict by screwing each other; because their sex is all about affection and communication." I paused. "At today's shoot, humans seemed a lot lower on the evolutionary scale."

Patrice calmly shoved away his half-eaten roast beef, poured another glass of Pavillon Rouge, and bit into his cherry cheesecake. "Tell me that after the chimps enjoy a good Bordeaux and a New York cheesecake," he smiled wryly. "Kate, it's like this: there's romance, and there's sex. They are both good, even if they don't always go together."

"Don't you want intimacy?" I protested, the wine loosening my tongue to vent what I'd been thinking all day. "That feeling of being so close to someone you want to drown in them? Otherwise, sex is mechanical, like today's performance. It's a turn-off."

"Believe me, Brandy and I had fun the other night. Maybe if I had invited Tom to stay?"

I rolled my eyes. "Pul-eese. I want love and romance. That's what makes my blood flow." I had declined dessert but now eyed his cheesecake as he waved a forkful in my face.

"Why so negative about sex? Look at our stories for *Cahiers de Californie.* They're about the freedom to explore whatever you want." He ticked off the list on his fingers. "Sexual surrogates, wife-swapping key parties, Transcendental Meditation, Werner Erhard and est …" He looked up, challenging me. "Why don't you take est training? Maybe you'll 'get it.'"

"And you? Do you 'get it' in France? You've had fun with Brandy … and now you'll go home to your wife. How can you separate the two?"

He lit a cigarette, and then did that thing with his mouth and eyes that signaled *c'est la vie.* "Christine and I were kids when we married. What did we know about sex? We learned together, but then, okay, there was more to learn separately."

"But you're married," I reminded him. "Don't your mind and body fight each other?"

"There is no conflict. Christine is my family; I cannot imagine my life without her and the kids. But what I do in L.A. has nothing to do with her. Besides, she is free to do what she wants while I am gone."

I studied his face as he put out his cigarette. We would never agree. Time to gracefully change the subject. "Well, one thing's certain. You're not making the usual documentary."

Patrice smiled broadly. "You know me. I never make the 'usual' documentary." He magnanimously offered me a bite of his cheesecake.

Once more the good-natured employee, I leaned over and took

a forkful. "That's what I like about you. So French, yet you adore American cheesecake."

He nodded, back to savoring the cheesecake like a true connoisseur. "Kate, you know me too well. How many years have we worked together now? Five? I call you with very little notice, you find the story, you arrange everything. All I do is show up. It seems you know how to talk to Americans to get the most out of them."

I smiled in silent triumph. "It seems? Look what we got with Engler today. When you go into the editing room, you're going to be very glad you have my interview."

"Precisely." He took another bite. "Besides, you know where to find cheesecake."

While acknowledging my expertise in all things, I gave credit where credit was due.

"You forget one thing that makes all this work. You pay well."

He smiled. "In cash. Yes, we understand each other. I've been thinking … France-Nouvelle wants me to shoot at the American Film Festival in Deauville. I need someone to work with the studio reps in Paris, deal with the movie stars, conduct the interviews, get clips and stock footage from the U.S.—all in English."

I was flattered, but I had to be honest. "That'd be difficult to do in L.A. with the time difference."

"You'll work in Paris. *Tu parles un peu de français, oui?*"

"Yes, I speak some French, but it's a bit of a commute," I said, laughing at his joke.

Then he stopped me in my tracks.

"Kate, I'm serious. I don't know anyone in Paris who has your American sensibility, can work so fast, and yes, who will put up with me as well. You will make my life easier."

"But what about my life?" I asked. *First Jean-Claude, now Patrice, calling me to Paris, exactly where I didn't want to go.*

"Of course, your weekly salary," Patrice said, as if reading my mind. "For as long as it takes. And I've got an extra one-way Air France business ticket to Paris. Sound good?"

The truth was I had avoided Paris for a long time. But this was a job, a well-paying one. I searched my mind for an excuse. "And where would I stay?"

"You'll have to pay your own living expenses in Paris, but I'll cover everything when we're in Deauville."

I must have looked dubious, because he sweetened the pot.

"And who knows, maybe more work after that. France-Nouvelle is a big agency and I'm head of TV production."

I, who always had an answer, had none. I stalled for time, my fork poised over the last of Patrice's cheesecake with the cherry on top, but he swooped in and took it.

"Hey, I was about to take that last piece!"

"So I'll buy you a chocolate éclair if you come to Paris," he said.

Éclair au chocolat. A delicious taste memory sprang out of no-where, then anxiety erupted, and the sweetness turned bitter. *Paris. Who could say no to that? Me.*

I looked for a gracious way out. "I don't know, Patrice. I've got responsibilities here. There's my house; and I don't know if I could leave Lucy."

"Lucy?" Patrice teased. "I didn't know you were that way."

"Lucy is my dog, Patrice."

He stifled his laugh; then said once more, "Paris, Kate. A job."

There was nothing left to tell him except the truth. "I haven't been to Paris since my student days. It was a difficult time. I, well, you know … " *No, I can't tell you the truth, and we'll leave it at that.*

Patrice shrugged a Gallic shrug. Pursed lips, head tilted to one side, raised eyebrow. Where did the French learn that? Maurice Chevalier movies?

"Kate, you're so American. Whatever happened in the past is over. *Fini.* What is there to be afraid of?"

chapter four

1964 September 17
Paris

Our first adventure in Paris!

Trevor grabbed the bottle of wine, Colin tucked away the books, and we donned jackets, scarves, and gloves before leaving the warm comfort of the café. The boys warned us that the "black gold of Morocco" was found in a Parisian neighborhood where tourists didn't venture. We shivered with delight.

During a long metro ride to the northern edge of Paris, we learned they were on holiday after graduating from Cambridge. Trevor was to begin post-grad film school in London; Colin planned to write poetry while exploring the Big U (the big universe, he explained).

Most of the passengers left at the Gare du Nord train station. In the deserted car, rattling through dark tunnels, I wondered if this was a good idea after all. The next stop, we were the only passengers to get off at Chateau Rouge. Up on the street, I saw no "red castle," only two men hanging out in front of a seedy-looking bar who followed us with their eyes. I had a sinking feeling that we'd made a big mistake.

I went into survival mode, trying to remember our route so we could retrace our steps back to the metro. But the streets all looked the same. This was not going well. When Trevor led us down a gritty narrow alley, my heart palpitations began. I nudged Susan to get her attention, but she was oblivious. In Susan's world, there was no reason not to have absolute faith in two Brits we'd met an hour before.

I had to warn Colin. "There's nothing open. This can't be right."

"Don't worry, I think Mustafa's café is around the corner."

"You *think*?"

I was about to grab Susan and run back to the metro (but where, how?) when we turned a corner out of the alley and saw a group of men loitering outside the entrance to Café Tunisien. I wasn't sure whether to be relieved or scared. The men looked suspiciously at Trevor and Colin, leered at Susan and me, and said things in French and Arabic that I was glad I couldn't translate. Inside the brightly lit café, men in blue denim work clothes clustered around cheap Formica tables, smoking, drinking, talking loudly.

"You girls can wait out here while we go in," Colin offered.

"Not on your life. We're all sticking together," I said, stuffing down an image of the American embassy notifying my parents their daughter had disappeared into white slavery. The four of us entered the noisy, crowded café and made our way through the sea of rough male faces. I cursed my stupidity for coming.

A big, bearded, scary-looking guy approached. He didn't look happy to see us, but when Colin held out a wad of francs, he handed over a small plastic bag in exchange.

"*Allez-vous en. C'est pas bon ici pour les filles!*" he said, gesturing at Susan and me, gruffly warning the boys we shouldn't be here. It was time to get the hell out of Dodge.

Trevor grabbed Susan, Colin took my arm, and we split. I was too frightened to look back, certain that someone was following, ready to mug us for whatever money we had left.

Once in the safety of the train, I broke out laughing with the others, instantly forgetting how scared I'd been. We had scored!

It was midnight by the time we got back to *boulevard Saint-Michel*. Under a full moon, we walked along the *quai*, the specter of No-tre-Dame looming across the Seine. The boys stopped in front of a bookstore. When I peered into the window, a tabby cat draped on top of a pile of books stared back at me, luminous green eyes aglow. This cat knew all.

"Follow me, ladies." Trevor fished out a key and opened the door. "Welcome to Shakespeare and Company," he whispered. We tiptoed past bookcases crammed with books in English to the back of the store and up a narrow staircase to the second floor.

"Is that you, boys?" a voice called from behind a door with a sliver of light underneath.

"Yes, George," Trevor softly answered. "It's Trevor and Colin."

"Carry on, then," the voice said, and the sliver of light disappeared.

"George owns the store," Colin explained. "We help him out, and he lets us stay here."

We entered a small, dark room. Trevor switched on the light. From a dangling bulb with the wattage of a single candle, I made out the outlines of a room that had existed for centuries. Thick slabs of white paint were peeling off the plastered walls. Rickety shelves were jammed with books, a lumpy mattress covered with faded silk pillows sat on the floor, and an unraveling wicker day bed was positioned to look out onto the Seine. I carefully walked on the cracked, uneven hexagonal floor tiles over to the window and peered out across the river to Notre-Dame.

Susan squeezed my arm. "*Now* we're in Paris!" she whispered.

"Maybe we shouldn't smoke the hash," I said, scared that what I had asked for was actually about to happen. "We might lose control."

"I hope so," she giggled, taking my hand.

Underneath my fear, I felt something more powerful rising: my need to explore a new world; to break through that middle-class curtain of conformity that had closed me off from the rest of the universe.

"Your chariot awaits, m'ladies." Trevor plopped down on the bed beside Colin. Susan and I followed suit. I watched, riveted, as Colin carefully unwrapped the small square of hashish and placed it on a plate. Trevor handed him a penknife and pipe. Colin sliced off about a third of the hash and put it in the pipe. Trevor flicked his lighter. No luck. Out of lighter fluid.

"Got a match?" he inquired.

With a solemn nod, I dug around in my purse and handed him the Venus de Milo matchbox that every *Tabac* sold with its Gitanes or Gauloises cigarettes. Colin got the pipe going and passed it to me. I took a tentative drag, trying not to inhale too much, but also not wanting to look uncool. The smoke went down. I passed the pipe to Susan, who took a drag, passed it on to Trevor, and then back to Colin. Quiet, businesslike, we passed it once more, then waited for the hash to take effect.

In a few minutes, I noticed we were sitting on a blue velvet bedspread. I felt it, brushed it, petted what suddenly seemed a plush and luxurious fabric. The sagging bed turned into a soft billowing cloud. I decided to ride it. Floating above, I watched a slow-motion movie of Trevor as he took his camera and led Susan over to the moonlit window. With benign detachment, I saw Susan respond innately to Trevor's direction as he arranged her hair, adjusted her sweater, and took pictures of her. I heard soft murmurs of "too much," "far out," as they traced the contours of each other's faces. Their voices trailed off as he put down the camera and kissed her. Their arms moved tighter around each other, and soon they slipped to the floor and were lost from view.

Through the window, the ghostly Notre-Dame beckoned; its gargoyle beasts braying at a full moon. What did it mean, this place of worship that spouted menacing creatures from its roof? What secrets did they hold?

I shivered and turned my attention to a light show on the wall and ceiling. Colin put a record on an old phonograph, and the intricate pattern of shadows shifted and danced to the strains of Ravi Shankar's sitar. I moved inside the music, separating each note, riding with the rhythmic beat as it wove in and around itself.

My mind was expanding, or was the room growing larger? The keys to the universe dangled right beyond my reach, taunting me to grasp them.

My cloud bounced as Colin lay down next to me. "May I enter the music with you? We'll transcend into the sitar," he whispered.

"I don't want to be in a sitar," I whispered back. "I want to be myself. How can I plan my life if I don't know who I am or where I should be?"

"Kate, you're in Paris. You're where you need to be. Remember, 'There are things known and things unknown, and in between are the doors of perception.'"

I relaxed with this bit of wisdom. We lay close to each other, connected, warm, gliding on the pulsating sitar note that swirled around the room.

"You're so smart, Colin."

"It's bloody Huxley, not me," he said, caressing my cheek. "But this is me."

He reached over to embrace me. We were touching groin-to-groin when my brain separated from my body, and I knew it was not to be. I sat up.

"Colin, I don't know you, but I do know you are going to be my true friend."

He smiled and massaged my back. Slow, gentle circles that freed my anxiety. "Don't worry, sweet Kate. Friends have time."

We heard low moans near us on the floor, then the sounds of clothes coming off.

Colin drew me up. "Let's give them some privacy. I'll walk you to your hotel."

As we tiptoed down the stairs and out of the bookstore, the cat stared at me from her perch. She knew all, but it was not her business to enlighten me.

The next morning, I woke up in our hotel room to see that Susan's bed had not been slept in. I wasn't too worried, sure she'd be back by the time I returned from class. But at 2:00 p.m. there was still no sign of her. I fell asleep, and it was almost dark when I woke up. Alone.

I didn't know whether to be mad or worried. What had she and Trevor done? Or worse, had he done something to her? What did we know about these guys? Susan could be at the bottom of the Seine by now. I had just put on my coat to go back to the bookstore when she walked into our room and threw herself on the bed.

"Kate, he's the one!"

Susan was glowing. I wanted to hug her and be mad at the same time.

"That's nice. But you could've left a message at the hotel desk. I was worried."

She sat up, oblivious of my concern. "I know it sounds weird, but Trevor and I spent the whole day walking around Paris, planning our lives together."

I couldn't believe what I was hearing. "Come on, that's the hash talking. We had a great experience. But planning your life with him? Trevor's going back to London."

Susan was always impetuous, but this time she floored me.

"Kate, he wants me to come with him! He wants to be a movie director and he's starting as an intern tomorrow on an American film. When he's finished with grad school, we'll go to L.A. after London, and I'll get a job in the movies too!"

"Tomorrow?!" I tried to process this information, to share her enthusiasm, be happy for her. But my heart sank. What was I supposed to do in Paris by myself? I knew about museums; Susan knew about life. She had the ideas, and I organized them.

"But we're a team," was all I could say. It should have been enough.

"Then come to London with us. It'll be fun." She looked at me as if she were trying on a third arm.

This could not be happening. She wasn't being fair.

"We planned Paris together. We were going to be students; maybe even live here! How can you give it up?" I implored, desperate that she not throw our dream away.

She collapsed back on the bed. "If I don't go, I'll lose Trevor and my chance at the kind of life he wants. I'll just be the cute American girl he remembers from his Parisian trip."

Her romantic notions were always rooted in tough pragmatism. Susan instinctively knew when to switch her priorities. I was no longer one of them.

She looked up at me and smiled. "Kate, I know you'll make your dream come true. I'll come and visit."

I couldn't believe it; Susan was deserting me. I would be on my own in Paris.

chapter five

1977 July 23
North Hollywood

Driving through Laurel Canyon after my dinner with Patrice, Steely Dan's "Reelin' in the Years" shot through the car speaker with its unwanted truth. I'd been "stowing away my time, gathering my tears" ever since my student days in Paris. Would that city never let me go?

In 1964, Paris had thrilled and seduced me. Until my dream turned into a nightmare. At first it was romantic to suffer from a love gone wrong. But as the years dragged on, I built a protective armor around my broken heart. I tried to bury the grief, and told myself it didn't matter what I'd gone through. I'd leave it behind and wait for a new beginning.

I was still waiting.

I felt worse as my Beetle rattled over Mulholland and descended into the Valley. How could I have condemned myself to the low-rent wasteland of North Hollywood?

Driving through the gauntlet of tacky mini-malls and cheap apartment complexes, I escaped down a dark lane where my house hid behind trees and overgrown ivy. Collecting the letters from my country mailbox, I pushed open the creaking gate and braced myself for the attack waiting on the other side of the front door.

Sure enough, thirty-five pounds of love and eagerness almost knocked me down as I stepped inside. I dumped the mail and got her leash. Lucy's walk came first.

It was the same every night. After the sheer relief of emptying her bladder, Lucy slowed down to read the evening smells as if they were the latest newspaper headlines. Then, straining at the leash, she chased squirrels. She never caught any, but that didn't stop her from trying. What beats the thrill of the chase?

Lucy always stopped to greet dogs behind the gates that held them captive. These inmates threw themselves against the picket fences, barking, baring their teeth, mad to get to her. She wasn't scared; she pitied the poor fools who were condemned to their square of manicured grass.

Yes, Lucy relished a life well-lived, and nothing beat dinnertime. She didn't worry if something was good or bad; she went for the gusto in front of her nose. Watching her lick the last crumbs from the bowl, I was struck by her absolute wisdom. Did she turn up her nose at a Milk Bone because she'd prefer a ham hock? Nope! She gobbled it up and asked for more.

Damn if I didn't want to be Lucy. While I waited for the perfect job, the perfect husband, and the perfect kid, I was missing out on life. I'd condemned myself to my own little square of grass and built a fence to keep the world away. Which included Patrice's job offer.

What was I so afraid of? Paris was calling me, and I'd be a fool not to answer. If it turned out to be no more than a job for a few weeks, a visit to the Louvre, and a walk along the Seine savoring a Nutella crépe, it would be better than what I had now. I would live.

To quote my most enlightened literary hero, Auntie Mame, "Life is a banquet and most poor bastards are starving to death." I'd fasted long enough. I was hungry and eager to find my place at the table. Lucy would love to stay with her boyfriend Barney, my neighbor's dog. Nothing could stop me!

Until I opened the pile of mail. Bills. Mortgage statements. Late-fee notices. Was I crazy? Pay my own living expenses in Paris in addition to a mortgage back home? And if Patrice didn't give me more work, go into debt, lose my house? Risk everything for a shot at an uncertain future? Fear burned through my mind, feeding on itself until I was a powder keg a spark away from exploding. I could only imagine disaster.

I needed advice. There was only one person I knew who always told me the unvarnished truth, even if I didn't want to hear it. Susan Goodman Wells, aka "my former best friend, the bitch." Yes, the Susan who'd abandoned me in Paris all those years ago.

After we both ended up back in L.A., Susan and I reconnected. It was like the good old days, but she and now-husband Trevor soon jumped on the showbiz merry-go-round. Susan garnered friends in her new status circle, then in the higher circle she wanted to move into. As they became one of Hollywood's Golden Couples, my best friend grew less available, abandoning me all over again. After too many times when she promised to return my calls and never did, I'd been too proud to call her. But these were desperate times. When I picked up the phone, it was almost ten o'clock.

"Hello." Susan's voice was preoccupied, rushed. I heard a baby's wail in the background.

"It's Kate. I need to talk to you."

"What are you waiting for? Come over."

This from a woman who told me last Thanksgiving she'd check her calendar and get back to me.

"It's late," I said. "If you're busy, we can talk on the phone."

"No, no. Come here. Now." And she hung up.

It took twenty minutes to go over Beverly Glen and enter Bel-Air off Sunset Boulevard. In the hushed darkness of Stone Canyon Road, I glided past high walls and mansions protecting privileged lives. And one of these lives belonged to my old friend from the plebeian suburbs.

We'd discovered each other in high school. Susan and I were the oddballs who didn't want to be cheerleaders or date football stars. Rather, we dated foreign exchange students, auditioned for high school plays, snuck out at night to crash Hollywood pot parties, and swore each would be the first to know when the other had lost her virginity.

We, the proud misfits, understood each other. Unlike our other friends, we weren't going to be teachers—a worthy profession, but in 1959, also one of the few acceptable jobs for nice middle-class Jewish girls. After all, wouldn't we soon marry (preferably a Jewish doctor or lawyer), have babies, and quit work? Once the children had grown, we could look forward to playing bridge and doing charity work. Maybe a Mahjong game with "the girls" every Thursday. Like our mothers, life would be comfortable, secure, predictable. In other words, boring.

No thank you. We wanted more.

By the time we got to Berkeley, we were plotting our escape. When Susan realized that a Hollywood glamour job was unrealistic, we agreed our dream should be Paris, the legendary City of Lights. We would breathe in French culture, open our eyes to new ideas, and spend hours in a café discussing philosophy, art, and life. We'd find our place in the world.

Dammit, I still felt that precious link between us, and by the time I made it to Susan's gate. I was ready to erase "bitch" from her name.

The gate swung open and I drove through a small forest of trees to a house that Frank Lloyd Wright could have built. Susan stood at the open door, the huge glass walls dwarfing her, jiggling her toddler in her arms. Even from this distance, I could tell something was awry. Her hair unkempt, she was dressed in baggy sweatpants and T-shirt. Not her usual tight-in-the-ass designer bell-bottoms, revealing silk shirt, and the celebrity stylist haircut of a Charlie's Angel.

"Thank heaven you're home. I'm so stressed," I said, slamming the car door against a thick oak tree as I got out.

"I'll show you stressed." Susan thrust her now-screaming daughter into my arms. "Hold Amanda. I've got to check on Jeremy." She sprinted back into the house.

"Is Mommy being silly?" I whispered to Amanda and waltzed her into the house. She stopped crying and burbled in delight.

Susan's 1930s Art Moderne home, with its white walls and floor-to-ceiling windows, smelled of all the success and money needed to buy good taste. No sign of children's toys or clutter, only the clean lines of Mies van der Rohe furniture set off against museum-sized abstract paintings. Baby in arm, I walked into my favorite room: the library. The desk's polished teak wood surface was bare save for a phone, the latest Selectric typewriter, and two stacks of scripts: TV episodes Susan had written, and screenplays her husband Trevor had directed. At the well-stocked bar, I poured myself a Rémy Martin with one hand and sank into one of the deep leather club chairs. Amanda curled up against me and fell asleep on my lap.

Sipping my cognac, I thought of how times had changed in the past thirteen years. Susan had a fabulous house, a movie director husband, two adorable munchkins, and a TV writing career. And what did I have?

"Don't talk to me until I've got a drink," Susan announced when she walked in. "I had to read *Where the Wild Things Are* twice before Jeremy would let me leave."

She poured herself a Rémy, took Amanda, and collapsed at her desk. I politely waited for her to take a sip and relax before I would open my floodgates. But her words spewed out first.

"Trevor's on location until the end of the month, my *Love Boat* script's due in two days, and the nanny left me this afternoon. You've gotta take care of the kids while I work."

Instantly my fond memories curdled, and I flushed them down with the cognac. Susan hadn't changed. It was still all about her. Something in my fragile state snapped.

"Susan, it's a shame you're having a bad day, but am I missing something here? I need a friend, but you only want a babysitter? Call your agency."

She didn't miss a beat. "Kate, no offense, but what the hell crisis could you have that beats mine?"

I reinstated the "bitch" label. "Forget it. This was a mistake." I got up and headed for the door, turning around for one last look at my dead-to-me friend.

"All right, what's so bad in your life?" she said, glancing over the page in the typewriter to make a quick notation.

One of Susan's great talents was her ability to defuse a volatile situation. Even one she created. I did what I always did with her: surrender. I collapsed back into the cozy chair and spilled out my guts in an incoherent mess.

"Patrice offered me a job in Paris. He can be a challenge; I won't even tell you what we filmed today. I have to give him an answer to-morrow. Besides, I still haven't found Mr. Right. Who knows, maybe he's waiting for me in the produce section at Safeway right now. And my dog … the whole thing is a mistake. Should I be going to Paris at all?"

Susan wiped drool from Amanda's face. "How about if I go in-stead of you? Even a bad time in Paris sounds good to me. There, problem solved. Now it's my turn: Ask me what my loving husband is doing with his leading lady. Or why I haven't met the deadline for my new script."

She dabbed at a spot of spit-up on her T-shirt. Refilling her Rémy, she sat down on the couch next to me, growing quiet while she patted Amanda's back. In the darkened room, she reminded me of the young Susan, when she was my best friend. Fuck it. I needed to try again.

"You're having a tough time," I empathized. "Let's both of us take a breather. Remember when we told our parents we were going to a slumber party and escaped to that coffeehouse in Topanga Canyon? We should do that again. Only this time your parents can babysit."

Susan yawned; memories bored her. "Well, we did go to Paris. Wasn't that great?" She plucked *Architectural Digest* off the coffee table and leafed through the pages. It was the issue that featured her and Trevor with their interior designer.

"Great, until you met Trevor," I said, "and went back to England with him."

"But you stayed in Paris, and if I remember correctly, you did very well on your own, French boyfriend and all. *Ooh-la-la!* What was his name? Pierre? Jacques?"

"François, his name was François," was all I could manage, as embarrassment welled up inside me. Anything not to talk about him. "Susan, you're the only one who gives me the truth. Should I go to Paris?"

She tossed the magazine back on the table. "Kate, the truth is you can do anything you want. But you're paralyzed by what might go wrong. You worry too much."

That was the good and the bad about Susan. If I asked for the truth, I got it. Not only about Paris, but why she'd ignored me for so long. I wasn't an A-list friend taking her to the Polo Lounge for drinks; I "worried too much." I didn't do the celebrity circuit;

I "worried" about house payments. In Susan's rich-person universe, no one ever admitted to money problems, but I blurted out my deepest fear. "If I go to Paris, I might not get another job; I could lose my house."

Without acknowledging the financial chasm between us, she picked up the *Hollywood Reporter* and turned the pages until she got to the real estate section listing "Star Properties." Was this her version of telling me to eat cake? She tapped her finger on an ad at the bottom of the page.

"House rentals. Sublets. You have a house. Make use of it."

"Rent out my house to a stranger who might burn it to the ground? Who knows what kind of creep answers ads in the *Hollywood Reporter*?"

She was unfazed by my protest. "Make sure it's a creep who pays in advance, with a large security deposit." She picked up the phone and handed it to me.

"Here, call Patrice. Tell him you'll take the job. Tomorrow morning, call the *Reporter*. Place the ad. What do you have to lose?"

"Shall I give you the list?"

"Do it anyway," said Susan.

So I did.

It was a bad idea. As soon as the ad ran in the *Reporter*'s weekly Real Estate section, my mind raced with everything that could go wrong. All day Friday I prayed nobody would answer, so I could call Patrice and beg off. No such luck. When I checked my answering machine at 6:00 p.m. there was a message from a Rob Greene. He was coming to see the house at noon the next day. What kind of name was that? Had to be an alias. He'd ruin my home. Skip the rent. Or worse, stalk me after I returned, breaking in and raping me while Lucy cowered in a corner.

I had a very active imagination.

The next morning at 11:45 a.m. I noticed for the first time the messiness to which I'd become blind: mounds of dog hair on the wood floors, books and magazines strewn everywhere, my kitchen table covered with work papers, yesterday's clothes hanging off chairs. At 11:46 a.m. I started throwing the clutter into a laundry basket while I vacuumed from room to room. Lucy growled at the noisy machine, then ran out the French doors to escape the monster.

"Lucy! Get back in here!" I turned off the machine and shouted again.

Only then did I hear the footsteps. A man entered through the open French doors, Lucy close at his heels, herding him inside.

I prided myself on my instant evaluation of strange males. But this picture wasn't clear. He wore the L.A. showbiz uniform of jeans and T-shirt, but they were better fitting than most. I wondered if his lean look came from exercise or too much cocaine. Was the short brown beard fashionably stubby, or was he too lazy to shave? Were his alert eyes assessing the house or casing the joint to see what he could steal? Age and good looks were the only things I'd bet on: appropriate.

"Oh, I didn't hear you!" I said, gesturing to the vacuum. "You're the one that's interested in the house?"

"Yeah. Rob Greene. And this is Debbie," he said, referring to a woman following him inside. Younger, blonder, and skinnier than me.

I shook their hands. "Kate Miller. Excuse the mess, my cleaning lady's off today," I fibbed, stuffing the detritus of my life into the basket as Debbie departed to look around the house, and Rob sat on the couch, testing it out. Which Lucy interpreted as a sign to push her rear-end into him. I gave up on tidying and pulled her away.

"This is Lucy. She has no shame. Nothing she likes better than a pat on the rump."

Rob gave her a teasing scratch. "Lucy, we'll start out slow. Then we'll get into the rough stuff." She turned toward him, and he held her face in his hands. His hazel eyes warmed and crinkled as he smiled in pure delight at Lucy's welcome.

Debbie returned from her house tour. "It's not bad, Rob. I'll check out the garden," she said, walking through the French doors onto the patio.

Rob scanned the living room. He took in the peg-and-groove oak floors, the brick fireplace, the bookshelves stuffed with books. "It reminds me of my apartment in New York. I'll take it," he said, barely looking at me.

Decisive, no chitchat. I was immediately suspect. Who would rent a house without looking at all of it? Hoping I didn't sound too suspicious, I suggested he see the other rooms. While Lucy and I trailed him, Rob walked quickly around the bedrooms and bathroom and back into the living room.

"I've seen it. I'll take it."

He had a sincere if impersonal demeanor, but bottom line, did I really want to do this? If I said yes, I'd have to go to Paris. I stalled for time.

"What about the kitchen? You haven't seen the kitchen."

I led him into my disorganized kitchen, quickly piling the dirty dishes in the sink. He took in the old stove, the noisy fridge, the butcher-block table.

"Okay, I'll still take it."

I thought fast. "That's great, but don't you want to talk to your wife first?"

"Why? She's got her own apartment in New York. We're separated."

I recovered quickly. "But Debbie … she'll be here?"

He laughed, looking at Debbie zoned out on the patio chaise lounge.

"I'm getting divorced. Debbie's a friend, helping me find a place."

The most important question. Did he have a job? "What brings you to L.A.?" I asked.

"My company transferred me. Seaboard Records. I'm a producer there."

Again, the straightforward, precise answer. But unsettling. Music business. A rock 'n' roller? Wild parties, trashing my house? Wait a minute, my house was fairly trashed already. What more could he do to it?

Rob looked over the jumble of old pots and pans hanging from their hooks on the wall. He took one very bent frying pan off its hook, running his fingers over the pan's dented bottom.

"I love garage sales," I explained, embarrassed. "Don't worry, I'll pack up all my old junk and store it while I'm gone. You probably won't be cooking much anyway."

He slid the pan's bumpy surface on the burner, trying to keep it even. "No, leave them here; I like the challenge. Cooking is my way to relax."

For an instant, I envisioned the two of us cooking together; then in the glow of the fireplace, our arms entwined as we toasted each other.

I came to my senses. "Um, I'm glad you're interested, but I've got one more person to show it to," I lied, stalling for time.

"Look, there's a lot of shit out there. Malibu has rockslides and traffic jams on PCH. There's stilt houses in Laurel Canyon about to fall off a cliff. I need a comfortable house until I can find something permanent. I'll pay you a hundred dollars more a month."

He'd do what it took to get what he wanted. If I said yes, I was going to Paris.

"Cash in advance, and I'll throw in the dog," I joked, hoping that would give him pause.

He reached down to pet Lucy, his face softening as he scratched behind her ears. "I always wanted a dog. You've got yourself a deal."

"Wait a minute," I said, not expecting that answer. "That was a joke. I might let you rent the house, but not Lucy." I knelt down beside her.

Rob sat down on the floor, and Lucy turned over on her back, giving herself to this alpha male.

"I'm a New York City boy," he said, rubbing her belly, his face softening. "Lived in apartments all my life, and none of the women in my life wanted a dog. Not even my mother."

His genuine emotion was endearing. The little boy with his first dog.

"She's a great dog. But she sheds a lot, and even farts," I said, giving him the downside of canine love.

"Don't we all," Rob said philosophically.

I laughed in spite of myself.

"Seriously." He looked me straight in the eyes. "I promise to take care of her."

This man was no ax murderer. But he was still a stranger.

"Sorry, I've made arrangements with my neighbor Linda, but I'm sure she wouldn't mind if you visited Lucy." I reached down to Lucy. "What do you think, sweetie?"

Lucy was too busy playing with him to answer. She had sealed the deal. I made sure it was airtight. "I'll get a lease for you to sign, starting August 15. As we agreed, the first three months payable in advance, with an option for more, depending on how long I'm away."

"Sure. Bring the lease to my office and I'll give you a check."

Both of us back to business, concise, impersonal. We shook hands and he collected Debbie; he went on with the rest of his life. I reminded myself that his rent money meant my freedom.

I was going to Paris.

chapter six

1964 September 22
Paris

You could count on Susan to follow her best interests. And so the night after our hashish-fueled adventure, she left Paris on the train ferry to London with her new love Trevor. Or depending on one's viewpoint, deserted me to follow a guy she barely knew.

Without Susan, I was alone and lost. I worried I couldn't afford even a cheap hotel room on my own. Too anxious to think straight, I dropped out of the Alliance Française to save money. For two days I wandered the streets, wallowing in self-pity, obsessing on what to do with my life. I couldn't imagine living alone in Paris, but I hated going home to the predetermined future I'd just escaped from. I saw the future so clearly: Grad school, then marriage to a nice Jewish boy and a life I didn't want. It was inevitable. No way out.

By the third morning, I was ready to give up and book my open return ticket home. I bought a crépe from a sidewalk stand for breakfast while I walked up boulevard St. Michel toward the travel agency. Nibbling on the delicious Nutella crépe in the open air, I noticed the change in the weather. The late September sky had turned blue, and the trees along the sidewalk flamed golden red. Across the street, students were having a lively conversation in the Sorbonne's sunny courtyard.

Impulsively, I slipped in with a group entering the university's main building and walked down the old corridors, peering into the lecture halls where students on wooden benches were taking notes from a professor rattling on in French. At the end of the corridor, I stopped at a bulletin board filled with notices. Among the flyers, I spotted an announcement for a course on French civilization for foreigners. History, culture, language! Why had I not known about this? This is where I should be. I read further. The semester's tuition cost as much as my hotel room. No way.

As I moved down the corridor, I noticed another bulletin board covered with notes from professors looking for au pair girls. I'd heard about au pairs in America. They were cute French or Swedish girls who lived with a family, helped out with the kids, and didn't pay rent. Plus, they met rich American boys. Wow.

I took one of the au pair ads and walked out into the courtyard. Sitting under the shade of a chestnut tree, watching the everyday world of Parisian students, I remembered an expression I'd learned in my college French class: *savoir faire*. The literal definition was "to know how to do things." But it meant much more: Parisians with *savoir faire* knew how to live well. They surrounded themselves with beauty, art, ideas, and fine cuisine. They savored life itself.

With a new goal brewing, I began to think rationally for the first time in three days. If I could live rent-free with a French family as an au pair, I'd learn about French life *and* I could afford to study at the Sorbonne. What better way to acquire Parisian *savoir faire* and follow its path to a life well lived?

Besides, I was damned if I was going to give up my Paris dream because of Susan.

The name on the ad was Professor Charpentier. He lived near the Latin Quarter in Montparnasse and needed a tutor to help his four children with their English and Spanish lessons. (Who knew my high school Spanish would help me in France?) I walked to the nearest café and called him from the *téléphone public*. Professor Charpentier asked me to meet him at his apartment, 149 Rue de Rennes, that afternoon at 5:00 p.m. The concierge would let me in.

Rue de Rennes was a bustling shopping street leading up to the Montparnasse train station. Sandwiched in between a dress boutique and a shoe repair shop, I found a plaque labeled 149 on a black wooden door. I pushed the entry button, and the door clicked open onto a cobblestone courtyard that must have been used for horse and carriage.

As soon as I walked into the foyer, I heard "*Bonjour*" and looked through an open doorway to see a hefty middle-aged woman in a faded blue housecoat seated at her kitchen table. She was knitting while watching a French TV soap opera. From this perch, nothing or no one could get past her. She had to be the concierge.

"*Bonjour*, madame. Monsieur Charpentier?"

She pushed aside a lank piece of dark hair escaping from her bun and scanned me with x-ray eyes.

"*Quartième à la gauche*," she said, holding up four pudgy fingers. She'd already determined I was an illiterate foreigner.

"Elevator?" I asked, motioning with my hand.

"*Non*," she responded, enjoying my disappointment. She went back to her knitting, and I immediately dubbed her Madame Defarge, the woman who knitted while heads rolled off the guillotine.

I instinctively knew I better be on good terms with this woman.

I climbed four flights of stairs and knocked on the door at the landing's left side. A thin, gray-haired man in a tweed jacket and sweater vest opened the door and stared at me.

I forced a smile. "Monsieur Charpentier?"

He nodded curtly and led me through an antique-filled living room into his book-lined study. Sitting at his desk, I was left to stand awkwardly in front of him. He squinted through rimless glasses, speaking without regard for niceties of polite conversation. I tried desperately to follow him, already sure I'd failed the test.

"*Mademoiselle, j'ai besoin d'une tutrice qui peut aider mes enfants avec la langue anglaise. L'accent britannique est préféré, mais si vous pouvez enseigner l'espagnole aussi, j'accepterai votre accent américain. Nous vous offrons une petite chambre de bonne, souper quatre fois par semaine, et un bain hebdomadaire. D'accord?* Okay?"

Except for the "okay," I had no idea what he said. But it sounded positive.

"*Oui* or *non?*" he pressed.

"*Oui,*" I said. I had a 50-50 chance this was the right answer.

"*Bon. Vous commencez demain, dix-sept heure.*"

I wasn't sure what I'd agreed to, but I was afraid to ask for fear he'd change his mind. I needed this job. "*Merci,* Monsieur Charpentier."

"Tomorrow, five o'clock," he said in English, and waved me to the door.

I floated down the stairs. In two minutes, I'd landed a job, a place to stay, and my own French family. If Susan could see me now! In my mind's eye, I fantasized about the coming weeks. In the afternoons, teaching children and shopping with Madame Charpentier. In the evenings, intellectual conversation with the professor, then games around the fireplace with the children. Madame would teach me how to cook and introduce me to her handsome young cousin.

I would learn the art of *la vie Parisienne*, and I didn't need Susan to do it. *Formidable!*

The next day at 5:00 p.m., I arrived with my suitcase, ready to move into the Charpentiers' spacious apartment and start tutoring.

"*Bonjour*," I said to Madame Defarge, now chopping vegetables at her kitchen table. She finished guillotining the carrots from their leafy green tops and handed me a key.

"*Votre chambre. Au sixième, nombre dix.*"

"*Mais Les Charpentiers, ils sont au quatrième étage,*" I answered. The Charpentiers lived on the fourth, not the sixth floor. There must be a mistake.

"*Votre chambre, Sixieme.*" She went back to her slicing and dicing.

I dragged my suitcase up the wide curving staircase, stopping at each landing to relieve my aching thighs. On the fourth floor, I looked longingly at the Charpentiers' front door. But I had two more flights to go. The staircase to the sixth floor was narrow, dark, and steep. Step by painful step, I hauled the suitcase up.

Heart pounding, I emerged at the end of a long, windowless corridor and dragged what was now my ball and chain to No.10. By the time I inserted the big iron key into the lock and opened the door, I was ready to collapse and claim my prize: my very own charming Parisian room. Inside, I found what I can only describe as a closet.

Faded, peeling wallpaper covered the walls of the tiny space. An old wooden armoire anchored one end of the room. At the other end—a three-step walk—a table held a washbasin, pitcher, and an electric hot plate. A single bed covered by a thick duvet took up the entire side of the third wall. Across from the bed, a gas heater sat in front of dusty red chenille curtains that covered what must be a huge window. I cheered up; at least I'd have a view of the famous Paris rooftops. Ha! I opened the curtains and stared into an airshaft.

It got worse. I heard a flush and peeked into the hallway to see a man emerging from the next door with a newspaper under his arm. He grunted *Bonjour* and shuffled down the hallway. I knocked on the door to be sure it was vacant, and then opened it to an even smaller closet: the WC. Holding my nose, I looked down at a hole in the floor. On either side of the hole were porcelain footrests. A chain hung from a big water tank. At least it flushed.

I returned to the room, collapsed on the bed, and stared out at the airshaft. This room made our crappy hotel look like a palace. Susan would never have put up with it. Why should I?

I dug into my purse for the emergency chocolate bar I'd taken to carrying. If I was going to leave, I'd need energy. But where to go? Back to the hotel? I couldn't afford it.

As I munched, I noticed birds and butterflies flying through the wallpaper's flower garden. I admired an old-fashioned water pitcher and bowl straight out of a Degas painting. I looked in the oval mirror of the antique armoire and saw the room reflected behind me.

If I'd come to France to escape American materialism, to be inspired by great artists and writers, this was the room to do it in. Montparnasse was where the young Picasso, Hemingway, and Modigliani had lived. And now Mademoiselle Kate Miller. This wasn't a servant's room. It was the garret of every starving artist and writer who'd come to Paris to find their destiny. Here in my *petite chambre*, I could live the life of *La Bohème*.

So what if I couldn't see the rooftops of Paris? I was in one.

PART TWO

"The past is prologue ..."

—*William Shakespeare*

chapter seven

1977 August 16
Paris

I waited for Lucy's wet doggie nose to nudge me out of bed. Until I remembered I wasn't home, and she was six thousand miles away. Eyes half-shut, I turned off the buzzing alarm, dragged myself out of bed, drew open the heavy brocade drapes, and squinted out at rooftops against an impossibly blue sky.

I was in Paris.

The day before, my anxiety about returning to Paris had increased as the plane descended into Charles de Gaulle Airport. By the time I'd gone through passport control and baggage collection, the fear of facing those dark memories only grew worse.

I was in the taxi thinking about how I would tell Patrice I couldn't stay, when the driver, an immigrant from Cote d'Ivoire, cheerily told me he'd escaped from the death squad of a repressive world and made a new life in Paris. Compared to what he'd been through, what did I have to fear? *Grow up, Kate!*

As we entered the city, it was as if Paris had read my mind. An army of workers was pressure-washing the historic monuments, releasing them from their ancient dirt-stained shrouds. The old buildings sparkled in the sun, ready to meet the future. Notre-Dame's gargoyles grinned wickedly, dancing on the parapets, beckoning me to a city of boundless promise.

I was headed to Passy, a neighborhood in the quite tony 16th arrondissement, a world away from Montparnasse and old student memories. Here was wealth and privilege. I had neither, but I'd scored an affordable short-term rental on a quiet street of classic 19th-century apartments.

From the outside, No. 1 Ave. de l'Abbé-Roussel looked perfect for my new life. Then I opened the door to a dim narrow lobby with no elevator. I struggled with my suitcase up creaking wooden stairs, just as I had to my old *chambre de bonne*. Dammit, I was trying to follow the light, and this apartment was going to take me right back into my youthful vulnerability. I opened the door, dragged my suitcase straight into the bedroom, and crashed.

I'd deal with it tomorrow.

Yes, Scarlett, tomorrow was another day.

In the morning, I shook myself awake, prepared to demand a change from this small dark apartment. But *voila!* I walked into a spacious living room, morning light spilling in from huge French windows illuminating stark white walls topped with elegant Art Nouveau molding. Memories of my '60s maid's room faded as I sat on a black leather sofa that contrasted nicely with the antique marble mantelpiece. There were glass and chrome tables, a black ceramic lamp, and even a good bottle of Bordeaux that the owner left to welcome me.

It was perfect. Only the empty bookshelf seemed out of place. Bare save for a forlorn telephone directory flopped over sideways. I flipped through the pages, put it back on the shelf, stared at it, and pulled it out once more. It was a game, I told myself. Okay, maybe I was just a little curious about what happened to him.

I thumbed through the phone book more slowly, stopping at the G's.

Granier. There were at least ten listings for François Granier. Which one? As my finger slid down the list, I realized this phone book was leading me back to the sadness I'd tried to forget all these years. *Kate, stop it! Remember why you're here. A new life.* I slammed the book closed and shoved it back on the shelf. I had a meeting with Patrice in two hours. That was real.

A shower and a cup of coffee were the priorities. I padded into the kitchen and found enough pots and pans to cook a gourmet meal. Even condiments and another bottle of wine. But no coffee. I had better luck with the linen closet, which yielded a stack of clean towels and several bars of French milled soap. The French handheld shower was a challenge, but I finally tamed it to spray on me instead of the entire bathroom. Within thirty minutes I was dressed in my business uniform of good jeans and tailored silk shirt, but my head still screamed for coffee. I headed toward a *bar-tabac* down the street.

As soon as I walked in, I breathed in a sense memory: tobacco smoke mingling with a strong coffee aroma and the faint stink of beer and wine. With every cell in my body, I knew—in the most existential sense—I was in Paris.

A man behind the bar with a white apron tied around his waist approached me.

"*Bonjour,*" he said, a Gauloise dangling from his lips. It was not so much a greeting as a command: Don't waste my time, tell me what you want.

"Un café au lait et un croissant, s'il vous plait," delighted that the words came out so easily. I watched the barman as he worked the espresso machine; tamping the grounds and sliding them in, letting the coffee drip out, watching as the steamed milk hissed into the large cup. As the ash from his Gauloise was about to fall into my coffee, the barman flicked it away and placed the cup in front of me. He was a pro.

The mundane details of Paris continued to assault my senses at the metro—giant posters lining tile walls, the rush to catch the train before the doors clanged shut, and above all, the faint scent of urine mixed in with fuel exhaust. Ah, the *parfum-de-Paris.*

Exiting at Trocadero, I glanced across the Seine. One look at the Eiffel Tower and my heart jumped out of my chest. What was this city's magic, its power? Could Paris be bigger than any fear? Dammit, it felt right to be here. Then came the epiphany, a flash so instinctual I had to believe it: Not knowing how or why, something here would set me free.

Thirteen years ago, I'd dared to start that path to self-discovery. It had been scary, but also exciting, even rapturous. I saw flashes of the person I wanted to be. Then the dreams shattered. I left the city, shut down, unfinished.

Now here I was, with the opportunity to walk again that path of discovery, but this time away from the past and toward the person I was supposed to be. There was but one question: How could I afford to stay? The answer was easy. Earn enough to buy the time I needed. But actually doing that would be a challenge. I'd have to become indispensable to Patrice so he'd keep me on for the next job, and the next.

France-Nouvelle was one of the largest photo agencies in France. I expected to see a modern skyscraper. But I found myself in front of a 19th-century apartment building, the agency's presence announced by a discreet, polished brass plaque. Inside, walls had been knocked down and the space divided into cubicles. A receptionist directed me to the fourth floor, where Patrice's TV division was in one of the original large apartments. Following the sound of voices down the hall, I peered into what must have been a master bedroom, now an editing suite. Shutters were closed tight against the light; racks of film cans lined the walls.

Patrice huddled with his editor at a Steenbeck editing machine, barricaded in by overflowing bins of 16mm. work print labeled "UCLA *Sexe*." On the viewing screen, I saw a shot of Brandy the Melon Girl performing in her natural glory.

I knocked on the open door. "Bonjour, Patrice, Mademoiselle Kate reporting for duty."

The editor paused the footage as Patrice turned around with a smile. "Kate, bienvenue! We were waiting for you. Meet Bernard. Like all good editors, he hardly leaves his room or talks, but when he does, he can speak English quite well."

Bernard was a pale thin youth with a shock of mousy brown hair hanging down to his thick wire-rimmed glasses. He did the French equivalent of snorting at his boss's comments, then shook my hand. "Patrice says you researched the UCLA sexuality study. Good subject. Well covered."

That was one story I didn't want to take credit for. "Merci, but it was Patrice's idea. He's the master."

"Don't be modest, Kate," Patrice said. "Perhaps I had the idea, directed and filmed it, supervised editing and wrote the narration, but you found our superb research subjects."

If making myself indispensable to Patrice meant inflating his ego, so be it. I assured him the program would be brilliant, that he was blasting into a new frontier of science, and redirected the conversation back to my new role as faithful handmaiden.

"I'm glad to be here, Patrice. It'll be a privilege to help you with this film festival documentary. I'm sure you'll outdo yourself."

"The Deauville Festival is two years old and has no character," he said, focusing on the freeze frame of a reclining Brandy that reminded me of Manet's Olympia. "But the TV station Antenne 2 wants the program, so we will deliver an hour of PR *merde* and movie trivia. That does not make me happy."

"Don't worry, Patrice. It's a festival of American films. And this American," I pointed to myself, "is going to track down a great story hiding there, waiting to be discovered."

I had no idea how, but I would deliver a film proving my worth a thousand times over.

"Yes, Kate, make me glad I brought you here." He smiled, but his gray eyes challenged me, calling my bluff. Daring me to come up with something better than he could.

"To your new office," he commanded, and I hurried to follow him.

"Voilà," he said, opening the door to what might have been the apartment's storage closet. Crammed into the space were a desk, phone, two chairs, and stacks of press kits. He spread the piles of folders across the desk, rattling off subjects in no particular order.

"Tributes to Gregory Peck, Vincente Minnelli, Sydney Pollack. We'll interview them all. Especially Pollack. He's screening his new film, *Bobby Deerfield*, set in the Grand Prix racing world. He's a must. Plus we've got the French premiere of *Star Wars*. A sensation in the U.S., but will France like it?" He flipped through more press kits. "Independent filmmakers—Andy Warhol, John Waters, and Henry Jaglom—isn't that Orson Welles's friend? We'll throw in Orson if he comes. Yes, we have famous people. But is that enough for a film?"

With all this glitter, there had to be gold. I'd have to track down each name, score private interviews, secure film clip rights, deal with agents and studios. I pushed down my jet lag and pulled out the press kit on Gregory Peck.

"Shall we start with the best?"

"Yes. Lunch."

I was glad to see some things had not changed.

"Ah, with the chocolate éclair you promised if I came to Paris?"

"Better. Around the corner, there's a quite good Vietnamese restaurant."

I had no idea what Vietnamese food tasted like, but if it took us away from sex studies and the *merde* of the film festival, I would love it. Besides, Patrice had never told me about his experience as a war correspondent in Vietnam. He'd be flattered that I wanted to hear his war stories.

"Violent. Deadly. As you saw on TV. As I filmed. Not interesting."

I couldn't believe Patrice so casually responded to my questions, as if the Vietnam War was not worth talking about. As the waiter served the *beignets de crevettes sauce Mekong*, I seized the moment to ask Patrice about action on the Mekong River. He said he'd never been there, drained his wine glass, and suddenly rushed through the rest of the meal, claiming he was too busy to work with me, and anyway I should sleep off my jet lag so I could work twice as hard the next day.

Something wasn't right; I wanted to reach out to Patrice, but clearly Vietnam was not a subject to be discussed. Not if I wanted to remain on good terms with him. I reverted to my handmaiden role and promised to be at work bright and early the next day.

With the afternoon to myself, my jet leg went into hibernation. It was mid-August, when every Parisian worth his Bordeaux has fled to vacations in Provence or Normandy or Grenoble.

Most of the city was empty, but not the nearby Champs Élysée, which bustled with tourists and the few remaining locals.

I walked past a sidewalk café where an old woman dressed in layers of lavender toile was sharing tidbits of *croque monsieur* with her poodle. Lucy would definitely like this city. Across the street, beneath a giant poster of Roger Moore 007, a line of people at a movie theater waited to see *L'Espion qui m'Aimait*. At the corner, I paused where another crowd had gathered in front of a news kiosk, reading the headlines: *La Mort d'Elvis Presley: Le Demon du Rock.*

Elvis Presley dead! I joined American tourists to mourn in a little pocket of home as we shared memories: from a young Elvis on "The Ed Sullivan Show," to the recent sight of a bloated Elvis.

I bought a copy of *Le Figaro* that announced "*Elvis Presley est mort—pour avoir voulu maigrir,*" Elvis dead because he wanted to lose weight. But I knew what killed him: The empty calories of American superstardom. He was starving for love. I was sorry for poor Elvis, yet his death made me realize how alive and grateful I was. How my own heart was filling up with love. For Paris.

As I walked down the Champs, past Concorde and along the Seine, the city's magic drew me back into its mystery. Was it the buildings garnished with wrought iron balustrades and elaborate cornices? The quaint book stalls along the Seine? Or the *gendarmes* with their cute caps directing cars every which way? Yes, Paris, take me. I'm yours!

I crossed the bridge to the Left Bank, where Paris present was instantly complicated by memories of Paris past. In the bookstore window of Shakespeare and Company, an old tabby cat lay curled on a stack of books. Could it be the same cat? I pushed open the door and entered. The man at the cluttered desk looked familiar. Same gray goatee, green corduroy jacket, and floppy poet's tie. If older and a bit frayed at the edges, it was George Whitman, the owner. George looked up absentmindedly from his book, stroking his goatee.

"Can I help you?" he asked, peering over his reading glasses. Looking at the books filling up the shop and the view of Notre-Dame Cathedral across the Seine, my thirty-five-year-old self disappeared and the shy twenty-one-year-old student answered.

"I was here in 1964 when I was a student at the Sorbonne. My friend stayed upstairs."

"A tumbleweed, was he? They roll into Paris and stay until the wind changes direction."

"Yes, he was one of those," I said. "I loved coming here. You'd let me read the new books as long as I didn't mess them up. I read the first two chapters of *A Moveable Feast* in that old stuffed chair."

"Good book. Must be a copy back there. Look in the Hemingway section."

I maneuvered through the warren of books piled high on the floor, spilling off chairs, jammed into the rows of shelves. I found a copy of *A Moveable Feast*, then climbed the narrow staircase past the Staff Only sign to the small room in the attic. It was exactly as I remembered. Bookcases lined the walls with barely enough space for a window facing Notre-Dame. A bed in the corner almost filled up the room. I swear it was the same old blue velvet bedspread, now even more faded. I sat down on the bed, caressing the threadbare fabric, inhaling its musty smell.

This room was my own time machine, eternally set to 1964.

chapter eight

1964 October 8
Paris

By the time the cold, gray gloom returned, I was well into my new Paris life. I'd burrowed into my *chambre de bonne* at 149 rue de Rennes, and embraced the weather as part of my daily adventure. When I woke, I stuck a hand out of my cozy duvet, turned on the heater, and waited for the room to warm up. Then I got out of bed, heated the pitcher of cold water, made a cup of tea, and poured the rest of the water into the basin for a sponge bath. From the window ledge—my "Parisian fridge"—I retrieved yogurt and juice. As for the weather forecast, I leaned out the window, craning my neck to see if the patch of sky was gray or grayer. I dressed accordingly and clambered down six flights of stairs, carrying my trash to throw in the courtyard *poubelle*.

Out on the street, I joined shoppers, schoolchildren, and office workers rushing to various destinations. Mine was the Sorbonne. In the morning, I attended difficult-to-understand lectures on 17th- and 18th-century French literature and history. Slowly, by osmosis, something of French civilization penetrated my brain. Then in the afternoon, it was French grammar and phonetics, where I learned how to move my lips, curl my tongue, and give that lilt to my voice until my accent was passable.

After class, I walked the cobblestone streets of Montparnasse, doing errands and practicing the art of *savoir faire*. The etiquette of shopping was all-important: "*Bonjour*, madame," I spoke in my sing-song voice whenever I entered a shop, and "*Merci*, madame. *Au revoir*," when I left. *Savoir faire* also required a certain look, so I found discount boutiques and stores like Monoprix that sold cheap versions of the latest fashions. I dressed in knee-length straight skirts, poor boy sweaters, and pointy-toe heels. My American clothes and sensible shoes took their last trip to the *poubelle*. I would never be caught dead in them again. One inspired afternoon, I got my long curly hair cut into the short pixie style that Jean Seberg wore in the movie *Breathless*. When I left the salon, I looked like every Parisian girl on boulevard St. Michel. Mission accomplished.

Four times a week at 5:00 p.m., I reported to the Charpentier apartment to tutor the children in English and Spanish. Afterwards, I shared supper with the family. They were polite but distant. I was still *l'étrangère*, the foreigner.

On a Thursday in October, I took an opportunity to enter their lives. I started my session in Veronique's room. She was seventeen—a tall budding beauty with blonde hair and a radiant, no-makeup look that American teenagers had already lost. I sensed she hid her thoughts from her parents and thirsted for freedom from the bourgeois rules of the older generation. Needless to say, I liked her a lot.

That afternoon Veronique didn't bother opening her book, but turned on Radio Luxembourg, the station that played the American and British pop songs. Chubby Checker's "Let's Twist Again" was playing. She began dancing, looking like a stork flapping her wings in a mating dance. I stifled a laugh; she reminded me of my own adolescent gawkiness.

Veronique stared at me, desperate. "Mademoiselle, I do not need language practice today, but can you learn me to dance?"

I leaned toward her, as if we were co-conspirators. "Your father must not see us dancing when we should be studying."

This was true, but I also saw my chance to create the family time I craved. I quickly demonstrated a few snappy Twist movements and threw in a Funky Chicken. "I'll teach you these steps tonight after supper," I promised. "I know the latest American songs."

Veronique turned off the radio and walked to the door with a look of horror. "In front of my parents? Are you insane? I leave you now, Mademoiselle. Marc will profit from your lessons more than I."

As she stomped out of the room, I felt for this girl. The first step in teenage rebellion is hiding your life from your parents. I was an expert on that one.

A few seconds later, thirteen-year-old Marc entered. With his floppy hair and lingering baby fat, he reminded me of a big playful puppy, eager to please. He should be amenable to a friendly overture.

"*Buenos tardes*, Marc," I said. "I was going to review your Spanish grammar, but how about a game of Scrabble in English instead?"

Marc apologized that he couldn't stay; he had to prepare for a mathematics exam. Veronique and Marc had disappointed me, but I had hope that the young Charpentier twins would wants to have fun. Clarisse and Danielle were freckle-faced, pigtailed nine-year-olds; eager to learn, enthusiastic, not yet affected by youthful rebellion.

I went over their homework; in Spanish and English, they told me the time, the days of the week. As the aroma of lentil soup began wafting through the apartment, I asked them to tell me in English if we had time before supper for a walk in the *Jardin du Luxembourg*.

"We have one hour! It is seven o'clock in one hour!" Clarisse answered, triumphant.

"I ask Maman," Danielle cried, and ran down the hall. I was planning our excursion when she returned, deflated. Maman had said no; however, I was free to take my bath early.

Thursday was my day for a bath in the Charpentier apartment. With six in the family, that meant one night in the week was left for me. If I needed another bath, Madame Charpentier instructed me to go to the rent-a-bathtub rooms at the Montparnasse train station. The rule seemed harsh until I saw the tiny water heater above the tub. It provided barely enough hot water for one shallow bath.

I turned on the spigot, undressed, siphoned off a bit of Madame's *bain moussant*, and lay as flat as I could in the small tub so the water covered me. I had my best ideas in the bathtub, especially if there were bubbles. Today was no exception: I'd struck out with the kids, but at tonight's supper table, I would engage the parents with my improved French and new *savoir faire*.

At 7:00 p.m., we convened in the dining room. The everyday blue and white checked tablecloth covered the polished mahogany table. Silver cups engraved with each child's name marked their places. Madame sat nearest the kitchen, Monsieur presided at the head, Veronique and Marc on one side, and I squeezed in between the twins on the other. As Madame Charpentier ladled out the soup, the professor passed me that day's edition of *Le Monde*.

"Your student *camarades* have made the news, Mademoiselle. The University of California, no? *Quelle horreur*," he said, tapping an article on the bottom of page one.

Le Mouvement pour la Liberté de Parole, The Free Speech Movement, the headline proclaimed. A blurry photo showed a huge crowd surrounding a police car with a student inside. How exciting!

My fellow students demanding change, creating a new world.

For good or bad, it was the first time the professor had taken an interest in me. Here was my moment to impress him with my knowledge and university pedigree.

"Monsieur, the fight for *la liberté* and free speech is in both of our great traditions—French and Americans together. Don't you agree?"

"This would never happen in France," sniffed Monsieur. "Our students respect the government that provides education. Rebellion is chaos."

I looked to the family for support. "George Washington and the Marquis de Lafayette, brothers together!" I cried, rallying the troops. Astonishingly, Veronique started singing "La Marseillaise."

> *"Allons enfants de la patrie,*
> *Le jour de gloire est arrivé!"*

Marc and the twins chimed in, beating out rhythm with their spoons against plates and cups. Their father groaned "Ça *suffit!"* He'd heard enough. Madame, who'd been smiling in approval, looked at me apologetically and passed the cheese. But the professor was not through with his lecture.

"Mademoiselle, have you no regard for law in your country? Witness your actions in Vietnam. And what happens if Barry Goldwater wins the election for president? He thinks America can do whatever it wants, with no concern for Europe or the rest of the world. Since Kennedy was killed, we've mourned the loss of reason in America." He sliced a piece of camembert, tore off a hunk of the baguette, and took a savage bite.

I was desperate to agree with him, to smooth things over and to do it in French.

"*Oui*, Monsieur, we must follow in Kennedy's tradition. I am voting for the first time, and *bien sûr* I support Lyndon Johnson."

He was not moved. "As you wish, Mademoiselle. It makes little difference. It is Mr. Johnson who sends more troops to Vietnam."

He turned to his wife. "The camembert is not ripe."

Discussion over. We ate in silence. Ironically, I understood why he was angry with the Americans. My country had started a war I could not defend, and held on to a racism I could not abide. But to the professor, I would always be a symbol of what was wrong. My heart sank. It was not a good time to be an American in France.

After supper, the children disappeared into their rooms and the professor and Madame retreated to the TV. That was my signal to go. The Charpentiers treated me like a governess in a 19th-century novel. I ate at the table and afterwards, like Jane Eyre, I was expected to discreetly disappear. There would never be any parlor games or walks in the park. My newly acquired *savoir faire* had worked no magic. They would always see me as "the American girl." Whatever that was.

Back in my *chambre de bonne*, I read Voltaire's *Candide* in French, but the cozy room began closing in on me. There was no phone, TV, or even a radio to connect me to the outside world. I needed to escape. I threw on my coat and scarf and took the metro to the Latin Quarter. Chances were Colin would be at Shakespeare and Company. He'd stayed on at the bookstore to work and write poetry, and because he was British, he escaped my embargo on Americans and my vow to speak only French. Besides, he understood me. And I often needed understanding, which he generously dispensed along with a joint in his now private room.

The lights were on inside the bookstore. I briefly locked eyes with the enigmatic tabby cat, then plopped down next to George, the owner. He looked up from his crowded desk and peered over his glasses at me.

"Kate, right? You're Colin's friend. He's finishing an inventory. He'll be down soon."

I wandered over to a display of new books, the latest from John le Carré, Terry Southern, John Lennon. Plus Ernest Hemingway's *A Moveable Feast*. I gazed at it longingly. It cost a week's worth of lunches.

"Go. Sit. Read Hemingway," George said. "But don't mess the book up or I can't sell it."

"Cool. Thanks, George."

I walked through the maze of bookshelves to a small reading room overflowing with books. Curling up in a shabby overstuffed armchair, I opened *A Moveable Feast* and entered Hemingway's Paris. With a thrilling shiver, I realized it was also my Paris. I shopped at the same market on rue Mouffetard, walked through the Jardin du Luxembourg as Hemingway did, and I too had a hole-in-the-floor toilet with "two cleated shoe-shaped elevations." I was lost in the book when a voice intruded.

"'For you are call'd plain Kate, And bonny Kate and sometimes Kate the curst; But Kate, the prettiest Kate in Christendom, Kate of Kate Hall, my super-dainty Kate. Kiss me Kate, we will be married o' Sunday.'" Colin finished his Shakespearean proposal with a hand flourish and bent down on one knee in front of me.

I was never sure about Colin. Sometimes I thought he wanted more than friendship; more often I figured he was gay and not ready to admit it. Either way, we had fun teasing each other.

"Colin! I know you're happy to see me, but no need to go to such drastic measures."

"I'm always up for new experiences. Follow me."

He led me up the stairs to his room. Throwing my coat on the faded velvet bedspread, I peered out at Notre-Dame. The cathedral was silhouetted against the darkness, its ghostly presence inscrutable. Too bad there was no mystery in Colin's room. Only Colin.

Reaching behind the pillows on the bed, he pulled out a small paper packet. "C'mon, luv. This grass is brilliant."

I sat down on the bed and settled in against the pillows. "You went back to the casbah and lived to tell the tale?"

"Easy-peasy. And our good mate Mustafa personally guarantees the goods." He took a cigarette paper, rolled a joint, lit it, took a drag, and passed it to me.

"So Kate, what brings you here? Had enough of the kiddies?"

"Tonight, Monsieur Charpentier gave me his message loud and clear: You are the hired help. Give your lessons, have your supper, get out of my apartment. *Merde*, is one bath a week all I have to look forward to at 149 Rue de Rennes?"

"Your knickers in a twist, are they?"

I took another toke. The marijuana was smooth, the kind that lifts you up the mountain and gently places you on a scenic plateau so you can look down on your life with a new perspective.

"My knickers have never felt comfier, thank you, but I do have one question: How do I decide what to do with my life?"

He took a deep drag from the joint. "First off, come to India with me and explore new realms of consciousness."

"I'd be giving up on Paris. Besides, my parents would kill me," I said. "They think I'm coming home to become a teacher, then find a nice Jewish husband."

Colin choked on his laughter as he took a toke. "Bollocks. That really sounds like you."

In defiance, I took another long drag, thinking what I couldn't say: Colin, my dream for Paris also had room for love and romance; and I'm sorry, but it's not with you.

I went back into safe territory. "I thought Paris would show me how to live. My new French veneer fights off the bourgeois demon, but as it is, my life is spiraling out of control."

"Which makes it difficult to stay on a straight path," Colin said, putting the stub of the joint in a roach clip so he could continue to smoke.

"C'mon, wise guy, is the universe drawing me into its chaos—or its infinite wisdom? Then again, maybe it's female hormones. What do you think?"

Colin took my head in his hands and forced me to look into his eyes. "The chaos of wisdom, the wisdom of chaos; take your pick. But I do know one thing: the best way to meet the universe is with— are you ready? A back massage."

His hands moved to that place between my neck and shoulders that was always tense and began loosening the knots.

"I say, with no false modesty, you are feeling the hands of the best masseur in Paris."

Even in my altered state I knew it might lead to trouble. "Colin, you're changing the subject. I need to be serious."

"I said I would give you a massage, not a fuck. You need this. Trust me."

Colin's fingers stroked from the base of my neck down to the small of my back, up over my shoulders and down my arms. I should've protested but it felt too good. I was putty in his hands.

"Colin, you have magic fingers."

"Told you." His hands were kneading deeper. My mind floated outside my body.

And with that, I entered nirvana. Or fell asleep.

When I woke up, Colin was folding a piece of paper. He handed it to me.

"Something I wrote while you were zoned out. Read it when you get home."

I barely made the last metro. As I trudged up the six flights of stairs to my *chambre de bonne*, I wondered why I'd rushed back. There was nothing here for me.

I unzipped my boots, left my coat on the floor, and crawled under the heavy duvet. Only then did I pull out the folded piece of paper Colin had given me. It was a poem he'd written.

A small tree
helpless,
needs only a support,
which by being there
strengthens,
and the tree grows straight.

How well Colin knew me. It was true. I needed a support. But that support wasn't Colin.

chapter nine

1977 August 16
Paris

I flicked the dust off the old blue velvet bedspread along with my time-machine memories. My life in Paris had started in this room. But all that was left was the same sagging bed and nostalgia for those long-ago dreams. *C'est comme ça*, it's like that, as the French say. I descended into the bookstore, paid George for *A Moveable Feast*, petted the cat, and slipped out of of Shakespeare and Company into the Latin Quarter.

Thirteen years later, the neighborhood was the same: Medieval buildings crowded together on narrow cobblestone streets. Ethnic restaurants advertising cheap prix fixe meals. Tourist stalls selling University of Sorbonne T-shirts. Here too were my memories of a youthful Kate, so thrilled to be walking in Hemingway's steps, so fervently searching for meaning in her life. If that notion had evolved, one thing remained the same.

I was alone.

I sat at an outdoor café, ordered a *café noir*, and looked at the people around me. After a few minutes of feeling sorry for lonely me, it was time for a pep talk. After all, I'd taken the leap and left L.A., determined to take charge of my life. I'd faced the anxiety of coming back to Paris. I even had a job.

I knew how to get things done. If I was producing a documentary on Parisian cafés, I'd have already introduced myself to the people around me. But as mere Kate Miller, without the cover of an assignment, my self-confidence plummeted. That's why Susan and I had worked so well together. If I was too cautious, Susan could realize my idea with abandon, taking me with her. I was the yin to her yang. I almost wished she was here with me; we'd have made five friends by now.

I knew only one other person in Paris besides Patrice: Jean-Claude Renaud, my ready-to-be sperm donor. I rummaged through my cluttered purse for his business card. Was I crazy? Not if he was the last person in Paris did I want to see Jean-Claude Renaud.

I appraised the purse trash laid out on the table. Out went the collection of half-used tissues, the no-ink pens, a chewed-up pencil, the coupons and business cards I would never follow up on. Back into the purse went lipstick, Afro pick for my curly hair, working pen, key to my apartment, wallet, and my calendar/address book.

My tidy purse now held indisputable proof of my left-brain prowess. Logically speaking, then, why not handle my personal life in the same way I produced a documentary? Why not indeed?

<u>Step one: Research</u>. I flipped through my address book, looking for anyone with connections in Paris. By the time I got to S, I wished I hadn't produced so many wildlife programs: the closest contact was a stork refuge in Holland.

Under T, I first ignored the name of Annette Tessier. The ink was faded, the name crossed out. Annette was a French film editor who'd worked next to me years ago. She'd come to L.A. to work on the Jacques-Yves Cousteau TV series. But when Cousteau moved his production company back to Paris, I'd lost contact with her. Maybe they'd know where she was.

Step two: Pre-production. I purchased a phone jeton in the café and clambered down the stairs to the *sous-sol,* where the public telephone and phone directory resided next to the *toilettes.*

I found a listing for the Cousteau Society, dialed, and when I heard "Société Cousteau, *bonjour,*" inserted the jeton.

"*Bonjour.* Annette Tessier, *s'il vous plaît,*" I said.

"*Un moment,*" a receptionist answered. And then, "*Oui,* Annette *ici.*"

A hole in one. But would she remember me?

"*Bonjour,* Annette—*une surprise du passé,*" I said, not remembering how much English she spoke. "*C'est* Kate Miller, *nous nous sommes recontrées à* Los Angeles …"

"Kate? Of course, you were in the next edit bay."

Her English sounded as good as mine. This was going better than expected.

"Yes, and now I'm in Paris to work with Patrice Carrière on one of his projects."

"But why are you working with him?"

"Don't you remember? You recommended me to him five years ago."

"I did? I am so sorry."

"But I thought …"

"I'll explain later. I go into a screening in two minutes. How about a drink tonight at my club? Meet me at the St. Germain metro stop at ten o'clock. *D'accord?*"

"*Formidable,* see you then." I hung up, dazed but triumphant.

Step three: Wardrobe. Dressy chic or casual funky? Monoprix used to be my favorite store for cheap knockoffs. It was a few blocks up boulevard St. Michel. I found a simple black dress, sleeveless, with a bit of a flare in case there was dancing. Then downstairs to the food hall to stock up on essentials. Coffee, milk, bread, and cheese went into my basket along with a bottle of champagne, a serviceable Cabernet, a tin of foie gras, and a jar of Nutella.

<u>Step four: Production</u>. Back at my apartment, jet lag was hitting. I took a power nap, downed a cup of very black coffee, stepped into my basic black, and caught the metro to the Left Bank. Action!

At the St. Germain metro stop, I searched the crowd, hoping I'd recognize Annette. I had only vague memories of a rather frumpy woman hunkered over her Steenbeck editing machine. So I was startled to see a chic female dressed in what looked like a Chanel suit, with her copper hair swept into a French twist, waving at me. Unbelievable. It was Annette.

"Kate! *Je m'excuse*—Cousteau is a charming man, but the screening went on forever." She kissed me on both cheeks. "It's wonderful to see you."

"And you, Annette, you look so … so Parisian!" Perhaps the dumbest thing I've ever said, but her appearance was a total shock. She had to be nearing fifty and her face boasted a few laugh lines, but she was vibrant, self-possessed. Beautiful.

"That is what happens when you live in Paris." She shrugged and took my arm, leading me past Les Deux Magots and down rue Bonaparte, where we stopped at a nondescript building. A small sign with the English words "King Kong Club" was posted on its plain wooden door. Annette pushed the buzzer, and the door opened.

"*Bonsoir*, Madame Tessier," the doorman said. "*Bienvenue*."

We entered a marble foyer lined with potted ferns and faux palm trees. "My ex-husband has a membership for his clients," she explained. "The club thinks I'm still married, and the bills go straight to his business manager for payment."

She smiled conspiratorially and took my arm. We descended a spiral staircase to the disco, where murals of Henri Rousseau-like gorillas, lions, and elephants stared out of a jungle, daring the human animal to expose its own wild nature.

It was early by disco standards; the French version of elevator music serenaded an empty dance floor. We sat down at a table and Annette ordered two kir royales.

"Tell me, what film are you working on with Patrice Carrière? He's had a reputation in Paris for strong documentaries, powerful journalism. But the last few years he has been doing, how do you say it, 'fluff'? Those bizarre stories coming from America."

"Those stories are what you recommended me for," I admitted. "Didn't you know what *Cahiers de Californie* was?"

"Of course not, or I would have warned you. I'm sorry—I only knew Carrière by his earlier work. You were next door to me, you needed a job, and *voilà*."

"Well, fluff or not, that first job with Patrice led me back to Paris. I thank you."

"Yes, Paris is a wonderful place to be." She took a sip of her kir royale and leaned back against the banquette. "I took the job in Los Angeles to escape. Not from Paris. From my marriage."

"I sensed you were unhappy."

"Happy, not happy, what does that mean? I was healing. In that little dark editing room, I was remembering who I was."

"It looks like you succeeded." I took in her elegant coiffure, her simple but expensive Chanel suit.

She laughed. "You know the French expression, *comme il faut*, as it must be? When I was thirty-eight, my life was not *comme il faut*. My friends thought it was time for me to marry; I ignored them. Finally, one friend invited me to a dinner party. Ha! The only other guest was Alexandre, a director of an international shipping line. He was obsessed with his work; perhaps that's why his wife left him.

He would show her!"

"What did he do?"

"He made the rush for me. Three-star Michelin dinners, a trip to Japan to meet his clients. I thought maybe my friends were right. We married. For four years, I lived the life Alexandre wanted."

"Sounds glamorous."

"It was horrible. When you are a certain kind of woman, you must not work."

"A certain kind of woman?" I asked.

She ran her fingers through her auburn hair until its sculpted waves fell free. "A woman from Vésinet. Like your Bel-Air *quartier*, only *plus riche*."

Annette signaled for two more kir royales. "Our house was very correct, very formal. It fit well the personality of my husband," she acknowledged with a hint of sarcasm. "My life was *comme il faut*. I went shopping, took the train to Paris for lunch with my friends, prepared beautiful dinner parties."

"Sounds like a good life. A lot of women would love it."

"Except I was forty-three years old and dying inside. When I wanted to go back to work, Alex scolded me, 'Your job is to be my wife.' I could not breathe. When I ran into Cousteau at a party, it was like finding a life raft in the ocean. I took his job offer and moved to L.A."

I thought of Susan who had everything and was desperate to hold on to it. And here was Annette who had thrown it all away; yet she was confident, even radiant.

"I fell in love again with film." Annette beamed. "When I returned, we finalized the divorce."

"But don't you worry about being alone?"

Annette looked at me as if I were an innocent child. "We are all of us alone. But that doesn't mean lonely. In the editing room, I am with my film, my creativity. And I have friends—male friends, yes, and sometimes they spend the night." She smiled broadly at the couples dancing. "Who knows, maybe there is someone here."

Loud pulsating music blasted through the speakers. Annette pulled me up, leading me to the dance floor, her arms outstretched, growing wings, flowing with the beat.

The Euro-flavored beat entered my system thumping, insistent. I, who analyzed every word and thought, began to move to my own muse, untethered to all but the music. It felt good, more than good, to let go. I barely noticed when Annette shouted she was going to *la toilette* and disappeared.

The DJ switched to American disco. I was dancing to Donna Summer's moans of "It's so good, it's so good," when I noticed a man a few feet away, his back to me, dancing alone. We were both moving to the throbbing rhythm, and without realizing it, I began to mimic his movements. When he turned around, I saw he was young, deeply tanned with short black hair and dark eyes shining out of a face with classic features. His eyes locked into mine. Donna was singing what we were feeling: "You and me, you and me, you and me."

As if in answer, his slim body gradually moved closer until we were dancing together, swaying in harmony as if we'd known each other for years. I wasn't thinking of anything but how much fun we were having, both of us grinning at our mutual surprise at being in perfect sync. In our own world, we danced closer and closer until we were almost touching.

A slower song started. I turned away, teasing this beautiful stranger. He moved up against my back. Moving together in unison, our bodies acquainted themselves in a private, wordless conversation. He caressed my shoulders and arms, kissing my neck. Then his hands slid down around my hips and thighs. As he pressed himself against my back, I felt him hard against me. He took my hand and we half-hid behind a column, kissing with open mouths, tongues moving together in their own sensuous dance.

There was no hesitation, no concern of us being in a public space. But in the recesses of my mind, a thought sprung to the surface. How could I be doing this? Thirty-five years of cultural and parental mores objected to what my innermost self craved. In that moment, all the "Don't be trashy!" messages collapsed, powerless against my feelings. What was happening? I wasn't in love; I was in heat. I didn't have to think, only feel. If this was the power of Paris, bring it on.

He took my hand and whispered his first words to me. "*Vien avec moi*," come with me.

I replied with the first words that came to mind. "I don't know you."

He smiled broadly. "*Américaine. Superbe.* My name is Armand Assas. I came here alone, with some friends." He motioned to two couples dancing, looking toward us and smiling. "Believe me. I will be your taxi. Wherever you want to go."

"I have to talk to my friend," I answered. "I'll be right back."

Annette was sitting at our table, watching me, smiling. I sat down and gulped the rest of my kir royale. "Do you know this guy I've been dancing with?"

"He looks familiar; perhaps a member."

"He said he'd take me home."

"You are safe, I think."

"Annette, I can't leave you alone."

"Of course you can. In any case, I must go soon. I have work early tomorrow."

"Are you sure? I've never done anything like this before."

She smiled. "Then it's time you did. Live your life! Go!"

Without speaking, Armand and I walked out of the club onto the street. Waiting for the valet to get his car, he pulled me aside, staring intensely into my eyes. "Who are you?"

For a split second, I thought to keep it all a mystery. Who needed names? But it was time to be me.

"My name is Kate Miller. I'm here to work on a documentary at the American Film Festival at Deauville. I'm not married. Your turn."

"You know my name. Armand Assas. I work in a bank. I also race rally cars. I was divorced six months ago. I have an apartment across from Parc Monceau, with not much furniture—my ex took most of it."

"I've never been to Parc Monceau."

"You can see it from my apartment."

The valet pulled up with Armand's car, and we got into his silver Jaguar. He turned to me, his hand resting lightly on the polished wood gearshift knob.

"Where to? I will drop you off at your apartment, or you can come with me to the Parc."

He spoke quietly, politely, making clear it was my choice. My old self told me it was absurd to even consider it. But this new self didn't hesitate. I put my hand on top of his.

"I want to see the Parc."

The apartment was old-style luxurious, with parquet wood floors, high ceilings, lots of molding, and large windows overlooking the now dark park. No matter. I hadn't come for the view. I walked through the spacious furniture-deprived living room to the fireplace, where photos were displayed on the mantle. Armand in front of a racing car, Armand scuba diving, Armand with a young woman on skis.

He opened a cut-crystal decanter on the bar and picked up a glass.

"Have you ever had a brandied apricot? You must taste."

With a crystal spoon, he fished a plump apricot swimming in brandy nectar into the glass. I reached for the glass, but he held it away from me.

"No, this is how you drink it. We share."

He took the apricot along with the amber liquid into his mouth. Then he bent down and put his lips on mine. Before I knew it, with his tongue he had passed the apricot along with the brandy into my mouth. The taste of his tongue erotically lingered as the apricot, round and juicy, swam around in the brandy. I swallowed everything together, the voluptuous fruit, the succulent juices, the essence of Armand. It was splendid.

He unzipped my dress and drew it down until it fell to the floor. Whoosh. No awkwardness about my state of undress; he instantly picked me up and effortlessly carried me into the bedroom. No one had ever attempted that before.

When he lay me on the bed, I looked up to a ceiling painted a robin's egg blue with white puffy clouds scattered about. I was staring at heaven.

He quickly stripped off his own clothes, sat on the bed and kissed me, this time slowly and softly. The kisses continued down my neck and onto my breasts. Unhindered by any distracting inner voice that lectured, analyzed, or questioned, I was aware of every taste, feeling, touch, whisper. No words. None needed. None wanted. Without the messiness of egos and mind games, we communicated by the urgent contact of bodies.

He slid off my panties and kissed his way down to my growing wetness. How long had it been since I felt this free, so sure of what I wanted? I sat up and it was my turn, my hands and mouth exploring the electric lightness of his skin, feeling the lean muscles underneath, moving down until our bodies were exactly where they wanted to be. Then he moaned and pulled himself away, gently laying me back down, lightly stroking my breasts until it was almost too pleasurable to bear.

How joyful it was to move in tandem as we had on the dance floor; this time to the murmurings of our own song. He took my head in his hands and stared into my eyes, watching me with the immense satisfaction of knowing that with each movement, he was bringing me closer to the crest of the wave, until the tsunami broke and ran through each nerve in my body, flooding me with tingling joy. He waited until I calmed, then with his last moves a punctuation mark to my own, he collapsed on top of me.

The torrent subsided; we were spent. After a while, resting in each other's arms, we attempted a conversation of words—what kind of racecar did he drive, who was I going to film at Deauville— but the reality was neither one of us cared. Armand fell asleep, his breathing soft and regular. I lay there quiet, as the afterglow began to fade. A joyous, unexpected experience, but I instinctively knew it could only go downhill from here. The magnetic, sensual mystery of a beautiful stranger had been magnificent. But the stranger had turned into a nice but rather ordinary young man whom I had little in common with. The more I knew him, the less attracted I would be.

Better to end it now.

It was after midnight when I quietly dressed, kissed him lightly on the cheek as he slept, whispered *au revoir*, and tiptoed out the door.

chapter ten

1964 October 14
Paris

"Mademoiselle! *Téléphone—on vous appelle.*" Veronique stuck her head in the door, interrupting my tutoring session with Marc.

"Miss Kate, the telephone waits!"

I hurried down the corridor, running through my mind who could be calling. After my recent debacle at the Charpentier dinner table, I was sticking to rules, and Monsieur made it clear personal calls were not welcome.

As I rushed past her, Madame called out, "*Mademoiselle. Limite de téléphone! Cinq minutes—c'est tout!*"

"*Oui, Madame!*" I shouted back as I picked up the phone.

"*Non, je ne suis pas Madame,*" said the voice on the other end. "See, I remember some French."

"Susan!"

"You recognized my voice with its veddy British accent?" she asked, oblivious to the shock she'd created to my system. We'd exchanged a couple of polite but short letters since she left. But a long-distance call was serious. My heart sang: *She misses me! She's coming to Paris!*

"When will you be here?" I eagerly asked. "I can't wait!"

"Sorry, Kate. London is where it's at. Guess what? I've been helping Trevor scout locations for Otto Preminger's new movie."

My heart sank. "Sounds like you're having fun," I said, trying not to sound wistful. I waited for her to ask me how I'd been, so I could tell her how much I missed her. But she kept babbling on about whom she'd met and the glamorous spots she'd been to.

"One of the Stones came to this cool party in Soho, and Trevor got so jealous when I danced with him!"

I wanted to be happy for her, but pride got in the way. I needed Susan to think I'd succeeded as much as she had, and like Ginger Rogers dancing backwards, I'd done it in French. And by myself.

"Glad everything's worked out so well for both of us," I said. "*Je suis très française,* living *chez* Charpentier. *J'aime* my Jean Seberg hairdo. And my French is getting *très bon.*"

Madame Charpentier shouted down the hall. "*Mademoiselle! Cinq minutes!*"

"Susan, I can only talk for five minutes."

"I'll be quick. I'm glad your French is good because I've got a job for you."

"A job? In London?" *You do miss me!*

"No, silly. Preminger wants to shoot his next movie in Paris, and he insisted on location photos for one scene. Trevor got the name of a set designer in Paris who can shoot them with a theatrical eye. We need you to translate and make sure we get the film ASAP."

It sounded exciting, but my hurt feelings spoke first. "Sorry, I've got my job and classes, and, you know."

"No, I don't know." Susan was never one for excuses. "Kate, I need you. Tell Madame you've got a friend on her death bed—and I will be, if you don't help me. It's at Père Lachaise something. His name is François something. He's got a car, and a list of what we need. He'll pick you up at two o'clock tomorrow. Oh, and we can pay you twenty dollars."

Twenty dollars—I could eat out every weekend for a month. But dinners aside, the truth was that where Susan led, I wanted to follow. *She needed me!*

"Okay, I'll reschedule my tutoring. Tell the guy to pick me up in front of the Montparnasse train station. But how will I know him?"

"He's got a blue Renault. He's French. You can't miss him."

The voice from down the hall again. "*Mademoiselle, s'il vous plaît. Le telephone!*"

The next afternoon at exactly 2:00 p.m., I was outside of the train station waiting for a blue Renault. I was almost glad when at least ten of them passed me without stopping. If "François something" didn't come, I could go to the movie across the square: *Dr. Strangelove* in its original English version. I'd take Kubrick over Preminger any day. I had fifteen minutes before the showing when a beat-up blue Renault passed, screeched to a stop, and backed up.

"Kate? *Venez vite!* Get in quick, too many cars rushing."

I hopped in, closed the door, and the car sped off. Only then did I get a good look at who was driving. What can I say? François definitely had that *je ne sais quoi*. The soft brown bedroom eyes and beguiling crooked smile of Belmondo. The slightly messy black hair and lithe frame of Alain Delon. All this young man needed was a cigarette dangling from his lips.

"*Bonjour*," said the vision.

I stared back, unable to think of anything to say.

"*Je m'appelle* François Granier." He took one hand off the wheel and shook my hand vigorously, removing it barely in time to turn the wheel and avoid an oncoming car.

"*Ooh la la!* We go to Père Lachaise now?"

I nodded dumbly, then muttered under my breath, "In one piece, *s'il vous plaît.*"

"*Le trafic est fou*, crazy," he said. "But I have too much photo equipment to take by the metro. It's on the other side of Paris, not a good *quartier*. You know the cemetery?"

Oh, lord, it's a cemetery. The way he's driving we'll end up in the cemetery ourselves.

As he played Parisian car roulette, we kept up a running dialogue in a weird mix of French and English.

"How did Susan find you?" I asked, hoping for reassurance that he wasn't insane.

"Ah, they know someone who knows someone, who knows my boss at Antenne 2. Last month," François continued, "I designed a haunted cemetery in the TV studio. The director loved it." He leaned toward me. "*Ou-ooo-ou*," he moaned in a stage whisper, a portrayal of what I presumed was a French ghost. "Very scary."

"Watch out!" I pointed frantically to a bus that had stopped to let out passengers.

He changed gears rapidly and missed rear-ending it by inches.

"Yes, very scary," I said. He was brash, a little out of control, and I wasn't sure his good looks made up for it. I tried to be calm. "What kind of film will they shoot at Père Lachaise?"

"A *policier*. Perhaps a shoot-out in the cemetery?" He pointed his index finger at me like an imaginary gun. "Bang, bang," he said, holding his finger to his lips to blow off the imaginary smoke. He sped up again, changing lanes three times in a single block.

I laughed in spite of myself. He looked in his early twenties but acted like a kid. Somehow we got through the Left Bank and drove across the bridge toward Bastille.

"I like a good cemetery, and Père Lachaise is the best," said François.

"I'm afraid I'm not a connoisseur of the dead. What's a 'good' cemetery? A scary one?"

"*Mais non!* A good cemetery does not frighten. *Pas de tout.* For me, they are ghost villages filled with the spirits of their residents. And Père Lachaise is a village of spirits *extraordinaire.* The best of France. Delacroix, Balzac, Collette, and now, Edith Piaf. *C'est triste,* only one year since our little sparrow moved there."

He took a deep breath, collecting himself. "You will feel their presence, I promise you."

"I like the French spirit," I said. "But so far I've only met the living kind."

"I remember the first American I met. It was the end of the war, I must have been four years old—how you call it, a G.I. soldier? He gave me an orange." He slowed down, remembering, and the manic guy turned into a vulnerable young boy.

"The first orange I ever tasted. I will never forget him. Or that orange."

"*Je suis désolé,*" I said, "I don't have any oranges today."

François laughed. "That's okay. I liked the chocolate bar he gave me even more."

I reached into my purse, pulled out my emergency ration, and offered him the weeks-old Nestlé's bar. "Now you won't forget me," I said.

He took the bar, tore open the wrapper, and broke it in two. Gave me half and devoured the other. "You are not what I expected," he said between bites. "American tourists in Paris are so, so ..."

"I am not a tourist," I corrected him. "I'm a student."

François was now careening around Place du Bastille, changing lanes as if he were playing a pinball machine. If we crashed, at least I'd die in Paris.

Ten minutes later, François parked next to a high wall separating the cemetery from the rest of the blue-collar neighborhood.

"Our village of the dead," he dramatically announced.

I looked down the shabby street. "France's illustrious citizens wouldn't be caught dead here," I joked.

"It's okay, they are beyond all earthly concerns," he answered, leaving me to wonder if my pun had made it through translation. While François gathered his equipment, I looked over Susan's list of graves and started to translate it into French, but François took the paper and stuffed it into his pocket. "Don't worry. I read English better than I speak. You keep track of where we're going. And carry the tripod."

I shouldered the tripod, surprised yet somehow pleased by his lack of chauvinistic etiquette. He bought a cemetery map from a flower seller, and we began our trek through the crowded jumble of graves and tombs.

Vous êtes ici. You are here, the map said. But whichever way I turned, I was lost. I waved the map at him. "It's got no resemblance to where we are."

It didn't seem to bother François. "We'll walk, and we find them. I think Oscar Wilde is up this path."

I trudged after him, carrying the tripod that was getting heavier by the minute.

While François took photos of the gravestones, he introduced me to their inhabitants. At Chopin's grave, he told me to close my eyes and listen. Damn if I didn't hear the faint strains of a Polonaise.

"Do you know if George Sand is with him?" I asked with one eye open, catching François humming Chopin.

"Of course, and she is smoking a cigar." He blew an imaginary smoke ring.

At Georges Bizet's grave, François whistled "The Toreador Song." I plucked a rose from a flower arrangement, clenched it between my teeth, and swept an imaginary cape. François fake-charged me like a bull.

I placed the rose I'd taken from Bizet onto Gertrude Stein's headstone. "Miss Stein," I whispered in what I hoped was proper respect, "did you ever consider a rose is a carnation is a chrysanthemum?"

As we walked down the rows of graves, I was struck by how many famous Americans and other foreigners were buried in Père Lachaise. "Did they love Paris so much they wanted to stay here, even in death?"

"Of course, because their spirits became French. They are singing 'Le Marseillaise' now. Close your eyes again; you will hear them."

I closed my eyes and heard the echo of "*Allons Enfants de la Patrie*" from François's ghostly repertoire. This community of dead spirits was rather lively after all. We had given up finding Oscar Wilde's resting place when we turned a corner and there it was: a marble tombstone covered with lipstick kisses and a naked angel showing his genitals quite nicely.

"Looks like he had the last laugh. Do you know what Oscar Wilde said on his deathbed?" I asked François before delivering my favorite quote: "'My wallpaper and I are fighting a duel to the death. One or the other of us has to go.'"

François didn't laugh but simply nodded, straight-faced. "French wallpaper can be like that." He said no more and motioned me to follow him down a dirt road toward an old brick wall, half-covered in ivy. Nothing on it but a simple plaque, *Aux Morts de la Commune*, To the Commune Dead. Not much for a photo, I thought. It certainly wasn't on the list.

"This is not for Preminger," he explained. "This is to share with you. France brought back the monarchy a hundred years ago. It was a terrible time. Some brave Parisians protested and set up their own government with free schools, no death penalty, and most radical of all, equality for women. It was called the Paris Commune."

"So progressive!" I marveled.

"Or treasonous, if you believed the new French government. They sent the military to crush them. But the Communards resisted until the streets turned red with their blood." François drew a finger across his throat. "Seventeen thousand killed. A few escaped, but the rest made their last stand here in Père Lachaise."

He ran his hand against the rough-hewn stone wall. "Almost a hundred and fifty of them executed against this wall. They are buried where they fell." As if his fingers could feel the tragedy of the Communards, he scooped up a handful of dirt, letting it run back through his fingers to the earth. "I have taken their spirit into my heart."

Who was this person? Drawn to the lessons of the dead yet full of life. With a kid's sense of play and an old man's soul.

He quickly crossed himself, then handed me the tripod. "We are losing our light. It's time to go."

I glanced at the list. "One left. Colette. My favorite."

"Then we shall find her. She's on the way out."

Ici repose Colette. Here rests Colette. The polished black stone marker was like a headboard on a queen-sized granite bed. I could envision her looking at me with a slight smile, as if daring me to … do what? Colette had followed her own instincts with no apologies. She'd ignored attacks from the bourgeoisie and took her revenge by writing international bestsellers.

"Colette, you weren't afraid to live your life," I called to her spirit. "That's what I want too."

"That's what we all want," François said. "But how do we know the right way to live?"

"It's what I've come to Paris to find out."

"*Ma chère,* that is what the best Americans have done. I wish you success."

"And the French?" I asked. "Where do they find the right way to live?"

"For me, I'm not sure it is Paris. But perhaps you and I are on the same quest."

François was like nobody I'd ever met. How could we possibly have the same goal?

None of that mattered, however, because I couldn't turn down those warm brown eyes and crooked smile.

He tilted his head to the right. "There is a bar down the street. I propose we watch the sunset, take a glass of wine, and discuss this in more detail."

chapter eleven

1977 August 17
Paris

Was it the disco dancing, the brandied apricot, or that beautiful stranger and his heavenly ceiling? Here's what I did know: I'd been in Paris one day, and it was definitely not the Paris of my student days.

It was six o'clock in the morning, the sun piercing my eyelids, when I realized too late that I hadn't closed the bedroom drapes. No hope for returning to sleep. I rose as if from the dead, and in the quiet dawn, sipped coffee and nibbled on a baguette and cheese. No need to analyze, overthink, or regret. Sex studies, bah humbug! Someday I'd understand why I experienced such pure delight without romantic love attached. This morning, it was enough to know that the barriers I'd knocked down freed me to find that pleasure.

I imagined Armand waking up without me. I didn't want to repeat our evening, but I also didn't want him to think I hadn't enjoyed it. I hated it when men left me hanging, disappearing after we'd had a great date. I would write a note to him with no return address. I went over to the bookshelf and picked up the phone book. Under the A's, I found *Assas, Armand*, and jotted down his address. But then, like an addict who can't say no, my fingers took a walk of their own back to G for *Granier, François*.

Despite my powerhouse evening with Armand, one man still had a hold on me. Why couldn't I accept the past was over? I had to face it once and for all. I opened the phone book to the list of *Granier, François*, and in a moment of false courage, I dialed the first number.

"*Allo?*" A sleepy male voice answered as I realized it was 6:30 a.m. I slammed down the receiver and shoved the phone book back on the shelf. Screw it, I might as well go to work.

At 7:30 a.m. the France-Nouvelle office was closed, but the security guard let me in. On the fourth floor my closet office was as I'd left it the day before, cramped and overflowing with research material. I sat at the desk, staring at the pile of press kits, PR releases, and correspondence. Took a deep breath and plunged in.

On top of the pile was a press kit for *Star Wars*. I flipped through the 8x10 glossies of Luke Skywalker, Princess Leia with her curious hairdo, and Han Solo piloting his spaceship with hairy sidekick Chewbacca. Han Solo was definitely cool, but it was Chewbacca, with the furry face of a giant terrier, who did me in. Looking at the Wookie, I saw Lucy.

My Lucy. Oh, I missed her. She was probably having the time of her life with my neighbor Linda and her pooch Barney. I looked at my watch: 10:30 p.m. in L.A. I had a free phone line, no questions asked. Linda was probably watching the evening news. I pushed the stack of papers to the side and dialed her number.

"*Bonsoir*, Linda," I said when she picked up.

"Are you back already?" she asked.

"I'm in Paris, Linda," I said. "How's Lucy? I'm missing her so much. Is she sleeping with Barney now? What's it like walking with the two of them together?"

"I don't know. She's been walking with Rob."

"What do you mean? She's supposed to be with you."

"Lucy's fine. Actually, she's fine now, because she's back in her home. With your tenant."

I started to hyperventilate. "Rob? You let her stay with that rock 'n' roller? If anything happens to her … !"

"Kate, calm down. You should be mad at Lucy, not me. After you left, I was taking the dogs out and we bumped into Rob coming home. Lucy was crazy to go with him, digging under the fence to get into your backyard. I finally took her over there for a visit but then she refused to leave—she kept doing that stick-her-butt-out thing so he'd scratch it. They're in love!"

"C'mon!"

"Seriously, she won't leave Rob's side. He swore he'd check in daily if I'd let him have a trial run. It's only been two days, but so far, he's a man of his word."

"I can't believe it!"

"Believe it. When Rob walked Lucy this morning, she sniffed my Barney for two seconds, then followed Rob like he's the Pied Piper."

It was now 10:45 p.m. in North Hollywood. I called my home phone number, betting my showbiz tenant was in the shank of his evening. He picked up on the second ring. "Hello?"

I heard clanging in the background. "Rob? Kate Miller."

"Kate! *Bonsoir*, or I guess it's *Bonjour* for you."

"It's 7:45 a.m. in Paris." My voice was friendly, if business-like. "Hope I didn't call you too late. I just spoke with Linda. She told me about Lucy."

"We didn't want to worry you. Seriously, it's all good. Lucy's in her home with all your smells. Don't worry, I can't smell them. But I do love taking care of her."

"So Linda says," I answered, hesitation in my voice.

"Everything's cool, Kate. We just got back from a walk. She's eating her supper; I'm having fun with your pots and pans."

"A little late, isn't it?" If Lucy didn't get dinner until almost midnight, it was time for Rob to hand her back to Linda. I'd play the concerned landlord; give him an out. "You sure she's not too much for you? Linda will be happy to take her back."

"I had a night recording session, so made a trip home for a tea-time snack and walk, right, Lucy?"

I heard Lucy panting, which signified her pleasure with someone thumping her rear end. Damn, Linda was right. Lucy was happy with Rob. I fought my base instincts and rose above my jealousy.

"Give her a hug for me." Hearing something sizzling in a pan, I added, "Sounds like you're finding everything you need in the kitchen."

"Your kitchen is an adventure in improvisation. Reminds me of Boy Scout camp." He directed his voice away from the phone. "Sherry? That's the wrong knife for bread. Use this one."

A pause, then back to me: "Oops, my sous-chef needs a little help."

I ignored the smooch I heard him give Sherry. "Sure, go back to your cooking. I'm at the France-Nouvelle office in Paris in case you need to reach me."

"France-Nouvelle? I'll remember. I might come to Paris myself someday. *Au revoir.*"

I hung up and stared at the phone. Rob was not only taking good care of Lucy, he was enjoying my kitchen with a female. Why should that bother me? It was good news. If Rob Greene was happy with the house, he might renew his lease. With his rent money covering my mortgage payment, I could keep my Parisian apartment and have Lucy flown here. That is, if I got more work after Deauville.

One more call to make before getting down to work. I dialed the Cousteau office, remembering Annette said she had to work early. She came on the line immediately.

"Kate, I was beginning to worry. I shouldn't have encouraged you …"

"No, I wanted to thank you for a most lovely evening."

"Another Franco-American *rapprochement*? *C'est génial.*"

I knew Annette was working, but as a thank-you, I invited her to lunch. Turns out no matter how busy a French person is, a proper lunch is essential. She would pick me up at one o'clock.

"*Parfait. À toute à l'heure!*" I said, feeling very French.

I dug back into work, setting up a tentative production schedule and making a list of possible interviewees. I was engrossed in a press release about Andy Warhol's *Bad* when Patrice knocked on my open door. "You look well-rested. No more jet lag?" he asked.

"A night in bed does wonders," I said, as if reporting a scientific study. He smiled knowingly, winked, and I went back to work.

At 1:00 p.m. on the dot, the office phone rang. Bernard called back to me. "Annette Tessier to see Kate Miller."

"I'll meet her downstairs," I shouted back, but he'd already sent her up.

A moment later, I heard Annette's voice in the edit bay.

"Bernard! I haven't seen you since you were an assistant at Pathé."

I grabbed my purse and rushed to the edit bay, hoping to get Annette out the door before Patrice accused me of disrupting his work. Too late. Patrice was shaking Annette's hand with a big smile.

"*Oui*, Pathé has the best training for editors," he said. "I'm Patrice Carrière. Have we met?"

"Annette recommended me for *Cahiers de Californie*," I cut in, smiling at Annette, who looked effortlessly elegant. The white linen sleeveless dress showed her curves and set off a turquoise squash blossom necklace. The laugh lines around her eyes only enhanced an aura of sophisticated beauty. She was comfortable in her own skin.

"I would have remembered you, I'm sure," Patrice said.

Oh yes, he was interested. It wasn't like when he ogled Brandy. This was different.

"You only heard my voice," Annette said. "I was in L.A. and you were calling from Paris. But, I know your work. Your coverage of Vietnam was *exceptionnel.* You made me feel the humanity of those boys living the nightmare of war; it compromised them forever."

Patrice stared at her, as if someone finally understood the horrors of what he himself had experienced.

"Merci," he said. "And I do know your face! Where? A Cousteau screening. That film on the killer whales."

"Could be. I was the editor." Annette smiled at Patrice, their mutual attraction clearly evident.

"How wonderful you know each other's work," I chimed in, wanting Patrice to know I was responsible for his meeting Annette. "Shall we let Patrice and Bernard get back to editing?"

"*Bien sûr,*" Annette said. She shook Patrice's hand again, boldly straightforward. "I'm almost finished with this season's Cousteau episodes. If you need an editor, I may be available."

"Yes," Patrice said, "that could work very well."

Out on the street, I broke out laughing. "Annette! There is something you like about Patrice!"

She shrugged. "He's a good filmmaker, that's all. More important, I recommend for your first lunch in Paris, the Café du Trocadero. The cuisine doesn't rate in Michelin, but I give it three stars for the view of *Le Tour Eiffel.*"

While Annette and I enjoyed a quiche, a glass of sauvignon

blanc, and the iconic view of the Eiffel Tower, I recounted an edited version of my night with Armand. Then, acknowledging the importance of all of life's pleasures, Annette insisted on dessert.

I cracked the thin caramel crust of my crème brûlée with a spoon, mixing together the crème and the caramelized sugar. Each bite was custardy and crunchy. I reveled in its sweetness.

"Okay, Annette, your turn to share. I thought you'd written off Patrice as a person who made fluff."

She took a bite of her *sorbet de cassis*, licking her spoon as she reflected on the question. "You're right. Then I remembered his earlier programs. They were powerful; they could be again. With you there, perhaps Monsieur Carrière will become more serious."

Should I warn her about his very unserious experience with Brandy? No. If anyone could handle herself around Patrice, it was Annette.

"I'm afraid we are back to fluff, or would the French say *banal*? An *entire* program on the Deauville American Film Festival."

"Perhaps not so bad," Annette reflected. "Truffaut and his friends love American films. There is fertile ground now between French and American cinema. Patrice was smart to hire you."

I hoped so. But if Patrice didn't like my work, I needed an option. And I wanted Annette's take on it.

"Is it the same for television? Is that why Jean-Claude Renaud is looking for a U.S. co-production deal?"

"Renaud is a powerful man; his movies do well on French TV. *Oui*, it makes sense he wants to expand into American television. But why do you ask?"

"I met him in L.A. when he was visiting Patrice. He told me to get in touch when I came to Paris," I said, careful to not show any expression. I wanted her unbiased opinion.

She looked at me as if I were stuck on a railroad track with a signal flashing bright red.

"Renaud has lots of fingers in the pie, as you say. That includes his reputation as a playboy. Be careful."

Why was I not surprised? "Of course," I assured her. "Business is my only interest."

Over the next two weeks, I thought of nothing but the Deauville Film Festival and our production, enduring eighteen-hour days to make connections in different time zones. I cajoled movie studios to send clips of their film entries. I confirmed director David Lynch for an interview about his film *Eraserhead*; François Truffaut to opine on the *nouvelle vague* of American cinema; and an exclusive for Patrice about *Star Wars*'s revolutionary special effects. I even scored private sessions with Gregory Peck and Vincente Minnelli. Director Sydney Pollack was the only holdout. I couldn't get past his agent, who would only say he'd pass the message on. Two minutes after I hung up, the phone rang. It must be Pollack! I picked up.

"Mr. Pollack? I'm so glad to hear from you!"

"Pollack? Kate, It's Rob," he said in a rushed, nervous voice, "and I was outside, but your phone cord isn't long enough, and your house was shaking, and books were falling off the shelf, and I see a broken cup on the floor. What should I do?"

"First, you should calm down. Rob, what's happening?"

"Earthquake, Kate! What do I do? I'm from New York."

I smiled to myself. A sophisticated New Yorker meeting his first earthquake.

"Is the house still shaking?"

"Not now, but where should I go? The electricity's off. "

"If it starts to shake again, stand under a door frame. Where's Lucy?"

"She's under the bed. Maybe I should join her?"

"Don't worry, Lucy will come out when she wants to. So what's the damage? To the house, I mean."

"I can see a lot of books fell on the floor. *Ulysses, War and Peace.* Hey, you've got some great books! Hmm. *Lady Chatterley's Lover.* Pretty sexy, right?"

Rob was shook up, and he needed to get his mind off the earthquake.

"You gotta have some fun reading, right? Feel free to borrow it."

He laughed. "So my landlady likes to have fun. And how else do you have fun?"

"I'm just a bookworm. When I was a kid, my favorite thing to do was curl up in an armchair and spend the afternoon reading."

I heard shuffling. "Hey, here's some Oz books! I loved those books when I was a kid."

"Me too. That's why I can't get rid of them. Feel free to read them again."

"Do I need a library card?"

My turn to laugh. "Don't worry, I won't charge for late returns."

"That's a relief." He paused. "Shit. I just felt a new tremor." He paused again. "No, it was a truck rumbling by."

"You sound a lot calmer now," I reassured him. "The electricity will come back any minute."

"Yeah, I better take Lucy out for a little walk before I head into the studio. It's really been great talking to you. I've never had such an understanding landlady. And certainly not one with interesting books."

"A pleasure talking to you, too. And now I have to get back to work. Got to track down Sydney Pollack."

"And I've got a recording session. But let's stay in touch."

"Sure thing. *Au revoir.*"

"And she speaks French, too! *Ciao.*" And Rob hung up.

I smiled at the thought of a New Yorker's first California earthquake. Rob was a nice guy, fun to talk to. Once again, my vision of us with Lucy appeared. I pushed the thought away and reviewed my schedule for Deauville—with Sydney Pollack still in pencil. Patrice would understand. I'd find another director to interview. It wouldn't be a big deal.

Wrong.

"Good job, Kate," Patrice admitted, as he handed the schedule back to me. "Except for Pollack. His films are iconic: *The Way We Were, They Shoot Horses, Don't They?* And now his *Bobby Deerfield* film about the Grand Prix. France loves that action. He's a priority."

Patrice looked straight at me, challenging. "Kate, you have a job. Do it. I don't care if you have to go to Hollywood—or Timbuktu—to find him. Do it. Get Pollack."

"On a silver platter." I pasted a smile of ultimate confidence on my face. Back in my office, I collapsed at my desk, head in my hands, ready to panic. I had no idea what to do. Pollack's agent had stone-walled me. My only hope was a personal contact. I sped through the Rolodex in my mind, coming up empty … until I remembered that Susan's husband Trevor had worked on *Three Days of the Condor.*

Why not? Everyone in Hollywood took advantage of personal contacts. About time I did as well. It was 10:30 a.m. in L.A. I picked up the phone and called Susan, remembering how clear she'd made it to me that I was not a member of her elite world. True. But I was in Paris. What the hell. As soon as she answered, I couldn't help myself.

"Paris calling," I said.

"Kate!" Susan screamed. "I don't believe it. Tell me all! Wait a minute, I've got to wipe up spit. My nanny quit and I'm waiting for a new one."

"Unfortunately, I'm a little far away to help. Give the kids a hug for me," I said.

"Sure, you're living the glamourous life while your friend Susan changes diapers on one kid, ferries another to daycare, and sees her *Love Boat* script die in rewrite hell."

"Wow, you've got a lot going on," I lamented, feeling a bit guilty for my twinge of schadenfreude. I tried to empathize, be casual about my own problem. "I've been busy too, setting up all the celebrity shoots for Deauville. Which reminds me. Sydney Pollack is coming for the French premiere of *Bobby Deerfield*, and I'd love to interview him, help promote his film. Isn't Trevor friends with him?"

"Trevor's on location. To be honest, I don't give a flying fuck if he ever comes back."

"What's wrong?" I asked, mentally erasing Trevor's name as a contact.

"He's shagging his star as we speak. That's Brit-speak for fucking." Susan spilled out the whole rotten mess. "He actually told me he's in love with her. What horseshit, coming from him. Wait until he comes back, ready to make up. He's going to pay. Big time."

Susan was putting up a tough front, but it was a lousy thing to happen. "That's terrible. I can see why you're upset."

"Upset doesn't begin to describe how I feel. Yes, I performed a supreme act of self-annihilation yesterday."

"Oh, no!" I feared the worst.

"I cut my hair."

Well, it wasn't on the level of slitting her wrists or sticking her head in an oven, but Susan's hair was her glory.

"Your *Charlie's Angels* hair? Why would you cut it?"

"Massacred would be more like it."

I wanted to be sympathetic, but my unspoken thought was something else entirely: *If you hadn't ditched me in Paris for Trevor, none of this would have happened.*

"What are you going to do?" I asked instead.

"Other than buy a wig? Divorce the bastard, what else? Or maybe first, I'll come to Deauville and visit you. I've met Pollack. I could help you out—and you'd have a free assistant."

Did Susan ever do anything unless there was something in it for her? How would she screw me up this time? *God help me.*

chapter twelve

1964 October 14
Paris

Away from the ghostly spirits of Père Lachaise cemetery, François and I were suddenly strangers, awkwardly sitting together at a small table, watching the sun disappear behind growing clouds.

It was all a mistake. Why had Susan insisted I take the job with François?

The waiter brought a carafe of *vin rouge*, and François offered me a Gitane cigarette. Holding the match for me, he averted his eyes. Then he fiddled with his camera, unloading the rolls of film, labeling the small 35 mm. film canisters. One by one, he placed them on the table in front of me.

"*Merci*," I said. He nodded. The silence continued.

"Your quest?" I finally ventured, trying to break the ice. "You were going to tell me."

He seemed unsure. "Normally I don't talk about this, and then, you are *américaine*, after all." He earnestly searched my face as if gauging whether I could be trusted.

"Please, I want to hear." My heart fluttered as he met my plea with a hesitant smile.

"Today we were with the spirits of Père Lachaise, *oui*? Chopin, Colette. Oscar Wilde. If they could commune together, what would it be like?"

"The greatest dinner party in history?"

François laughed enthusiastically. "Imagine a *communauté* of people working and living together, each for the other. That is more than a dinner party. That's a full and happy life!"

"Like the Paris Commune? Is that your quest?"

"One for all, and all for one!" he exclaimed with joy, waving an imaginary sword like one of the Three Musketeers.

In his exuberance, he took my hand in his; I felt a small shock as we made contact. Could François be the person to support my quest to find the right way to live? I was swept up in his ardor, ready to fight alongside him for a better world, when he threw me a fast curve.

"Do you know about the Israeli kibbutzim?" he asked.

Uh-oh. Time to come clean. In this Catholic country, best to let him know now. "Yes, it's a community where everyone works and shares together. I'm Jewish," I explained, throwing out the footnote as if it had little significance.

If he was surprised, he didn't show it, but grew *more* enthusiastic in his passion to create a better world. "Then you know when people help one another, each of their lives improve. Of course, there must be an underlying faith in common."

"You mean Catholic?" I asked with a sinking heart.

"I love the Church, but it is faith in the *communauté* that I speak of." He gently took one of my hands. "What do you think, Kate?"

At his touch, a warm feeling washed through me. But before I could speak, my stomach growled. He laughed and pulled me up. "*Ma chère*, we have fed our spirits; it's time to feed our bodies."

Not far from the Bastille, François parked the Renault on a dark, quiet side street near a small Chinese grocery store. We walked down a stairway in the store to a basement café, with room for only a few tables. All but one were occupied by Chinese patrons, busily shoveling noodles into their mouths with chopsticks. For me, this tiny café was better than any fancy restaurant – the hidden, real part of Paris I was longing to discover.

We sat down at the empty table, and a waiter who looked like Confucius with his wispy white beard brought us a small blackboard menu. François glanced at the menu and ordered *Riz au Crevettes* and *Pâtes aux Porc*. It sounded so exotic. Ten minutes later, the waiter served us fried rice with shrimp and pork chop suey.

With my chopsticks, I plucked out a shrimp and popped it into my mouth.

"I cannot compete with an expert," François said, picking up a fork and twirling noodles.

"I learned how to use chopsticks when I was at the University of California," I explained between slurping up noodles. "It's near our Chinatown in San Francisco."

"That is the university where the students are fighting for free speech, yes? Chopsticks and free speech. A good education."

A tease or a compliment? I needed to investigate.

"I see you know your way around cemeteries. But what about your education, Monsieur Granier?"

"After *lycée*, what you call high school, it was the army. Algeria. Lucky me, the war was winding down. I was assigned to information services and learned to shoot photos instead of guns. On my days off, I'd take my camera and wander into the villages." François paused, remembering those days. "Do you know how these people survived the war? They had each other. And slowly, they made me a part of their *communauté*." Again, the crooked smile. "After the army, no university—my father had died, I had to work. Got a job at the TV station as a photographer, and now I'm a set designer. I create my own world."

"A world of communities," I noted.

He took my hand and lightly kissed it. "Kate, how do you know my answer before I even pose the question?"

It was as if I'd known him for years, not hours.

"I will take you to your door," François insisted, as he parked on rue de Rennes. We walked in silence to No. 149. In front of the entrance, he kissed me, and without thinking, I passionately returned the kiss. In the foyer, we tiptoed past Madame Defarge nodding over her knitting as a TV presenter delivered the late news. As if one body and mind, we quietly climbed the six flights of stairs to my *chambre de bonne*, stopping only to furtively kiss on each landing.

At my room, François took the key from my hand and opened the door.

"*Bonne nuit*," he said, giving me back the key.

"*Bonne nuit*," I repeated, waiting for more, knowing there would be more. But he said nothing. With one last caress of my cheek, he walked away and disappeared down the stairs.

I couldn't believe it. He must have felt our connection; how could he leave like that?

I shut the door and turned on the heat in the ice-cold room. "*Merde*," I muttered, my insides feeling as if they'd been dropped down an express elevator chute. All I had left was disappointment and hurt.

Then a knock on the door. I opened it a crack. François stood there sheepishly.

"Kate, I must confess. I did not want to leave. But it is only two months since I ended a very bad affair. I swore I would be celibate and do penance."

It was a novel rejection. "Okay," was all I managed to say.

He held my face in his hands. "But your eyes, I cannot forget them," he said, "or what we talked about. It is too important to me." He sighed. "Perhaps I have done penance enough."

He stepped into the room, looking around. "Or perhaps the wallpaper is my penance."

With that crooked grin, he drew me to him, and we sat on the small bed, laughing, kissing, hugging.

"Too many clothes," he murmured.

We eagerly helped each other slip off jackets, socks, and shoes, pulling sweaters over heads. For the first time in my life I wasn't pretending to be a reluctant good girl. I was Kate without shame, doing what I wanted with an urgency I didn't question. I needed to be as close to him as possible—and that meant having him inside of me.

The room fell away. There was nothing but us together in a place where the world and its troubles could not touch us. I'd heard about seeing stars or hearing bells when one fell in love. For me, it was electromagnetic—my skin tingling next to his, his body pulling me ever closer, until we joined together and became one.

chapter thirteen

1977 September 9
Deauville

There were no old memories here to cloud my mind. After weeks in Paris of pre-production for the film festival, I was glad to finally be in Deauville. On my early morning walks along the empty beach, I'd turn my face into the ocean spray, inhale a lungful of sea air, and step into a Monet painting.

En plein air, the artist's touch was everywhere: cloudless azure sky, aqua sea, furled red umbrellas lined up in soldiers' precision on the pristine sandy beach. In this luminous spot of harmony, I had my precious moments alone to focus on the day's work ahead. Because in just a few hours, the town would transform into a circus, starring that weird American subspecies called Hollywood.

It hadn't been easy navigating through the crowds during the *Festival du cinéma américain de Deauville*, but I'd come prepared, and I kept Patrice on schedule. While he shot press conferences and the festival ambiance, I searched for the serendipitous moments that would earn me extra brownie points. Not only did I get Patrice into the Playboy dinner at the casino, but I arranged *entrée* to candid, behind-the-scenes Bunny action. I was a bit surprised that he didn't hang out with the girls afterwards. Could this be a new Patrice?

I should have congratulated myself on my stellar work; instead, I was frantically trying to avoid all-out failure. We had two shooting days left, and they were reserved for private in-depth interviews with Gregory Peck and directors Vincente Minnelli and Sydney Pollack. I was nervous about interviewing icons Peck and Minnelli, but it was Pollack who had me on the verge.

Patrice was determined to make Pollack and his film *Bobby Deerfield* a focal point of our documentary. But I had one small problem: After two weeks of trying my damnedest, I still hadn't booked him. I also had a big problem: Patrice didn't know.

Patrice and I understood each other. He expected me to deliver—and I did. But if I failed, he wouldn't trust me for his next project. The French equivalent of "Don't take it personally" would be the first words out of his mouth, then "*Au revoir*, you can buy your ticket home now." I couldn't let that happen. In a strange way, I sensed Paris was giving me the freedom to be myself. I was back on that path to finding the person I was meant to be. A place where I didn't have to prove anything to anybody. Except Patrice. Because who else was going to give me a job and a paycheck so I could stay?

I had one card left to play if I could only find Pollack: my weird talent to flatter anyone into believing a documentary interview could change their career, their life, or even the world. While the crew took its lunch break, my secret plan was to track down and speak to the great director himself.

I saw Patrice and the crew at the entrance to our hotel. Gulping one last breath of sea air, I brushed the sand off my feet and stepped into my work high heels.

"*Bonjour*, Patrice!" I called as I crossed the street and put on my Good News face. "I persuaded the casino to give us their private terrace for our interviews. I'll show you where we can set up."

We walked next door to the casino, showed our press passes, and a security guard unlocked the glass doors leading to the terrace. Patrice assessed the view of the ocean with his director's eye.

"We'll shoot Peck with the beach in the background. And then we can face the other way for Minnelli—reveal the casino behind him, especially when he talks about his films *An American in Paris* and *Gigi. Très bien.* This will work. And where do we film Pollack tomorrow?"

I forced myself to smile and act cool.

"Definitely not here." I improvised on the spot, impressing even myself. "I'm seeing Pollack on the road in a sports car, in action."

"Get away from talking heads," Patrice said, nodding.

"Yes, Pollack living his movie, knowing in his bones why Bobby Deerfield risks death: racing in order to feel alive."

"I'd have to ride with him, use film with a mag track. No space for a soundman," Patrice said, considering the possibilities.

"Of course, your camera right in his face. Fabulous!"

"Might work," he said. I could tell that Patrice was dying to be in that car.

"You'll love it." Fuck, I prayed, don't let this be a lie.

Gregory Peck stepped out of a black Rolls-Royce limo, a stunning vision of American male charisma in his white linen suit, brown-checked shirt, and knit tie. Forever linked with his compassionate portrayal of moral courage in *To Kill a Mockingbird*, he walked through a surging crowd of paparazzi and news crews as if he were Moses parting the Red Sea.

I pushed through journalists tossing out questions that floated away unheard and unanswered, and dodged past the cameramen jockeying for a clear shot. Nearing my end zone, I held up my press card, calling out, "Mr. Peck! France-Nouvelle TV!" It was a sweet moment when he motioned me over and grasped the lifeline of my outstretched hand.

"Mr. Peck, I'm Kate Miller with France-Nouvelle. We have your interview set up on the casino terrace, if you'll follow me."

"Kate, get me out of here and I'll follow you anywhere." His eyes crinkled, flashing a clear message: *I'm kidding, but isn't that fun.*

"Anywhere?" I joked as I led him into the casino's side entrance. "How about I find a motor scooter and spirit you away like you did with Audrey Hepburn in *Roman Holiday*?"

"One of my favorite movies and dearest actresses." He squinted at me. "I do see a slight resemblance."

I was sure he was referring to my flat chest, but for a nanosecond I saw us making a break for it on a Vespa to an isolated Normandy beach. Until I remembered his beautiful French wife was joining him that night.

How do you interview a legend whose career spans thirty years, who starred in the unforgettable *To Kill a Mockingbird*? I told myself Gregory Peck put on his pants one leg at a time like everyone else, but I didn't believe it. He was so humble yet so aware; so plain spoken yet so eloquent. I wasn't sure if I was talking to Gregory Peck or his character Atticus Finch.

"Are you Atticus Finch? He's a universal symbol of justice, yet you made him so human."

"I felt very close to Atticus," he admitted. "It's gratifying when your character sends a message you believe in."

He paused, as if debating whether to reveal a secret. "But it's not easy. I absorbed so much of Atticus, it was like carrying the weight of the world on my shoulders."

He leaned toward me conspiratorially. "I wish directors didn't see such serious characters in me. I confess some of my favorite roles have been comedy, when you can have fun being someone else."

He then asked himself a question I'd never have thought of: "Why couldn't I have been Cary Grant or Jimmy Stewart?"

"Even movie stars wish they were someone else," I said to Patrice as we watched Peck walk back through the crowd of paparazzi to his car.

"And why not? In every movie, they have the opportunity to play a different character, to experience life with someone else's fears and desires." Patrice lit a cigarette and exhaled as if he were Bogie. "We all should pretend a little in real life."

Patrice sometimes said things I truly wondered about. "But that's being phony. Isn't the goal to be yourself?"

"In America, perhaps. But here is my philosophy: I believe in playacting. Sometimes you find your inner self that way."

"I really don't follow you, Patrice. Sounds like a contradiction to me."

He blew a smoke ring. "What is the real you? Your daily life, your habits? If you take a vacation from them, indulge in a bit of fantasy, you will explore parts of yourself you never knew existed." He put out his cigarette. "But now is reality. Go get Minnelli."

Wearing a butter-yellow linen jacket with a natty silk handkerchief sticking out of his breast pocket, Vincente Minnelli was ready for his public. Now he was better known as Judy Garland's former husband and Liza Minnelli's father. Yet his glory days had been magical.

"*Lust for Life, The Bad and the Beautiful, Some Came Running,*" I ticked his films off on my fingers. "Classics of American cinema—and all dramas. So why are you remembered for your musicals?"

He looked at me astonished, as if I were the first person to ask him.

"I do like musicals," he said. "We all like characters that must choose between the real world and fantasy. And what better way than in a musical?"

"*An American in Paris*?" I asked.

"Kelly's dance scenes carry him into his imagination, and it's there that he finds the courage to make his dream a reality."

"And what about *Gigi*? Isn't that a fantasy through and through? The happy courtesans, the rich and handsome suitor?"

He thought a moment. "Yes, but even though Gigi loves Gaston, she turns him down because she doesn't want fantasy. She wants marriage."

"But is she choosing the reality of marriage or a fairy tale of happily-ever-after?"

The camera continued to roll as he pondered. "I don't know," he said at last, "but isn't the question so interesting?"

As Patrice and I walked back into the casino lobby for the lunch break, my brain was whirling with ideas that had bubbled up from that day's interviews. For so long, I'd been the straightforward, nose-to-the-grindstone Kate who made a living turning facts into films. And where had it gotten me?

"Patrice, I don't understand," I said as he lit a cigarette. "Isn't playacting only for the movies? How can you ever escape the real world? Dreams are empty; you always wake up." It was all rather existential, but then this was the land of Sartre and Camus.

"Let's take a more immediate example," he said. "Lunch. The reality is we must fuel our bodies. But our dream is to savor the meal, indulge our senses. Right now, I am dreaming of *un plateau de fruits de mer*." He kissed the tips of his fingers. "We say 'fruit of the sea.' Is that not already a fantasy? Yet it makes the lobster and the oysters taste even better. That's reality. Why don't you join me and experience for yourself?"

I was tempted. But the reality of a missing Pollack intervened. "I would love to, but I have a few last-minute details to arrange. I'll meet you later at the *Star Wars* reception."

"You will miss the best oysters in France."

"Maybe tomorrow?"

"Seize the moment, Kate. Who knows about tomorrow?"

Tomorrow I'd be fucked if I didn't find Sydney Pollack today. I said goodbye and sprinted out of the casino back to our hotel, pushing down my fear of failure and plotting my strategy. This wasn't Cannes. The Festival was centered around two hotels and one casino. Everyone ate at the same restaurants, walked on the same boardwalk. If Pollack were here, I'd find him.

Hôtel Normandy housed the studio reps and journalists. Since *Bobby Deerfield* was a co-production, the Columbia rep sent me to the Warner rep, who sent me back to Columbia. I checked the press room on the ground floor. It was buzzing with French and American journalists, but no one knew the whereabouts of Sydney Pollack.

Hôtel Royal catered to the American stars and directors. I ran into its *haut* bordello-style lobby. But as sweetly as I smiled at the desk clerk, she would not divulge Pollack's room number or even if he had checked in. He wasn't in the bar or at the swimming pool. In the elegant restaurant with its white napery and red and gold carpet, Patrice was savoring his *fruits de mer* and *blanc de blanc*; but no Sydney Pollack. I rushed through the hotel boutiques that were giving out promotions to festivalgoers. I scored some cool sunglasses but no Monsieur Pollack.

Cursing my high heels, I jogged through Deauville's *centre-ville*, oblivious to its quaint Norman-styled timbered buildings. Festival-goers were streaming out of a screening, and a nearby brasserie was filling up. I pretended to search for *la toilette* while I checked out the patrons, spotting Orson Welles under the red and white striped awning. But no Pollack.

I hurried back past the hotels and crossed the street to Ciro's, an elegant beachside restaurant. As I rushed into the foyer toward the dining room, the impeccably dressed maître d' stopped me, staring at my jeans, disheveled hair, and sweaty face.

"You have a reservation, madame?"

I waved my press card. "I'm meeting Sydney Pollack," I said, trying to sound casual. "Perhaps he's already arrived?" The maître d' scanned the reservation list. "I do not see his name."

"He uses an alias," I coolly responded and started to walk into the main room.

"You may wait at the front door," he sniffed, and retreated to his desk to greet a couple that was obviously more important.

I was tired, hungry, and my feet hurt. But I was desperate. I walked around the restaurant to its beach side and peered through the huge windows into the dining room. Several people looked at me like I was stalking them. None of them were Sydney Pollack.

I jogged the boardwalk until a blister made the heels unbearable. I stopped to adjust the straps.

"*Très bien* for a woman in heels," I heard a man shout. Out of the corner of my eye, I saw a young and good-looking guy approaching. Shit, it was Armand, my one-night Parisian stand.

"Armand, what the hell are you doing here?"

He grinned and patted me on the bottom. "After you left my bed so abruptly, I remembered you were working at the Deauville Festival. I thought we might have another dance."

"It was a most exceptional night, and I won't ever forget it. But I'm working now, and I've got to find Sydney Pollack."

"Forget Sydney. He must be over forty. I am in better shape."

I grabbed his arm. "Armand, do you know Monsieur Pollack? Is he here?"

"I'm sorry, Kate, I haven't seen him. My rally club visited the Monte Carlo Grand Prix when they were filming his new movie, and Mario Andretti's pit man got us tickets for the premiere."

"Aha, you didn't come here to see me?" I said, teasing him.

He shrugged. "Why I came is not important. Have I not been looking all over Deauville for you? I can get you an extra ticket to the film."

"That's very sweet of you, but it doesn't do me any good."

Armand would not give up. "My friends are meeting tonight at Regine's in the casino. About ten o'clock. I invite you for a drink."

Armand seemed so earnest, so friendly. But I had no time for romance. Or even sex.

"I'll try." I blew him a kiss and dashed onward, only stopping to take off my heels once I hit the sand. I tripped over children's sandcastles, tried not to gawk at the topless women, and skirted the fat men lying on their lounges. Like Inspector Clouseau, I even surprised a few secretive lovers tucked inside their private cabanas.

No Sydney Pollack. The beach had been my last chance. I walked to the water's edge and collapsed onto the wet sand. It was hopeless.

I'd have to tell Patrice at the press reception that I'd failed. He would no longer trust me to get what he needed. It was over.

Just as Paris was opening its arms to me, bringing me back up to bat, I was doomed to strike out just as I had so many years before.

chapter fourteen

1964 November 1
Paris

November descended on Paris. The days grew shorter, the nights longer, the rain more constant.

I reveled in the darkness, especially as my *chambre de bonne* had become a cozy nest where François and I basked in our passion. If François was free during the week, I'd finish my tutoring, beg off supper with the Charpentiers, and meet him across the street at the local càfe, L'Horizon. Along with a carafe of *vin ordinaire* and *soupe à l'oignon*, we'd feed each other ideas, philosophy, and dreams about how we'd live our lives.

François always came up with new thoughts on his *communauté*. It was a beautiful concept, I told him, but I wasn't sure I was ready to have the collective good prevail over my independent spirit. I wanted to explore every dream and opportunity. If I stayed in Paris, maybe I'd even get a job at the American Embassy! François was more focused; he liked his creative work at the TV studio, but his main goal was to create and live in his *communaté*, away from the contamination of a big city. We argued, and then we laughed and gloried in finding each other. The discussion always ended with a kiss, and we'd hurry across the street, climbing six floors to our little hideaway, taking one article of clothing off at each landing, the faster to get in bed.

If he could leave work early, we'd meet at my *chambre de bonne*. After our passion was quenched, we'd head to the Latin Quarter to eat and see a movie. François introduced me to his favorite French film auteurs. One night after dinner at the Brasserie St. Jacques, he was browsing the weekly Paris guide for movies, and his eyes lit up. He slipped on his jacket and handed me my scarf and hat.

"You must *faire le connaissance* of Louis Malle. It is essential to know his films. *The Fire Within* is playing at Le Champo in twenty minutes!"

"Then we better hurry," I said, and we raced each other up to rue des Ecoles. The usher showed us to our seats, and François bought chocolate bars from the girl walking up and down the aisle with a tray of candy and ice cream.

"I might one day embrace your *communauté*," I whispered as the lights dimmed. "But I will never accept that French movie houses don't sell popcorn!"

We ate our candy and held hands as we watched the renowned actor Maurice Ronet portray the raw emotions of a man who planned his suicide and was spending his last day on earth walking the streets of Paris. Revisiting his life, rejecting beautiful women like Jeanne Moreau, disdaining rich friends who reached out to him. He could find no *raison d'être*, no reason to live.

After the movie we walked arm and arm down St. Michel, my mind overwhelmed with Malle's existential drama. "That man had so much to live for, but he couldn't find a meaning to his life," I said. "The scary part was that I understood his pain of not having a purpose."

He stopped in the middle of the street and held me close. "*Ma petite* Kate, that's what happens when you cannot touch others, when all is empty inside you. That is not you! Don't worry. You will find your own direction, your own power; I know it."

I melted into his arms. I was finding my *raison d'être* right here. With François.

The weekends were ours. It didn't matter what we did, as long as we were together. One Saturday morning we made a foray to the Porte de Clignancourt flea market. François needed props for a TV series set in a blue-collar apartment, and his budget was miniscule. It was raining, but that didn't stop him from zipping his beat-up Renault through the downpour into an illegal parking space. As if the sky knew we'd arrived, the rain stopped and the vendors removed the plastic sheets covering their wares. François's eyes lit up like a pirate who had discovered a buried treasure.

I was skeptical. "You're going to find props here?" I loved a bargain, but this was junk.

"You have to know how to look. Pick a stall," he offered.

I pointed to one with piles of broken crockery, rusty locks, stacks of old white shirts, and paintings that rivaled the black velvet art I'd seen in Tijuana.

"You cannot find something more difficult?" he asked with a sly grin. In less than a minute, he had sorted through stacks of dishes, pulling out plates, cups, and bowls with no cracks or chips. A stack of old white shirts turned out to be surplus French navy uniforms. He picked a white middy with classic blue trimming, and held it up to me along with a scarf he said matched my blue eyes.

"*Tu es adorable. Très á la mode.*" François had good taste; the shirt was very cool. "Perhaps I change from set decorator to costume designer? I have a beautiful model." He caressed my cheek and tousled my hair.

He gestured to the woman at the stall. "*Combien pour tous? Cinq francs?*"

Eyes narrowed, she scanned the merchandise. "The shirt for the mademoiselle. That alone is worth *cinq* francs." She was right. One dollar was a steal.

"*D'accord.* Then I give you another two francs for everything else."

"*Ah, non,*" she muttered, regarding us with disdain, her lips curling in the French version of *You are an imbecile and beneath the dirt under my feet.*

François put the shirt back on the table. "*Tant pis,*" never mind, he said, and took my hand. We got about ten feet away before the woman called after us.

"Okay, okay!"

Five minutes later, the stuff packed into his string bag, I admitted his shopping prowess.

"I would not have paid so much, but I wanted to buy you that sailor shirt," he said.

He smiled widely, giving me a hug and the most beautiful long kiss in front of everybody in the market. I was embarrassed until I remembered we were in Paris, and that's what lovers did. Yes, we were lovers, and my heart swelled as I breathed in the essence of François.

We spent the next hour buying towels, a lamp, a frying pan, and a saucepan. It was as if we were furnishing our own apartment. But as we moved from stall to stall, I knew we needed one more thing that wasn't on his list. And I couldn't avoid it any longer.

We were not using protection. He didn't wear a rubber, or as the French called them, *préservatif.* And I wasn't sure why. When I had asked him before we made love, he just murmured, "It's not a bad time of month, is it?" As he smothered me in kisses, I buried the worry and entered the bliss.

I should have known better; in fact, I did know better. But talking about it was embarrassing and clinical, and the truth was I didn't want to think about it. I just wanted to be in love. I'd gotten my period once already and convinced myself that I was in a safe time of month. After that passed, what then? Would we have to stop having sex? God help me, no!

It was lunchtime, and perhaps after a glass of wine, I'd have the courage to bring up the subject. François led me to Chez Louisette, a crowded bistro squeezed in between the market stalls. He ordered the specialty, *moules marinière*, as a man wearing a beret started playing the accordion. A woman channeling Edith Piaf walked among the tables, singing "Je Ne Regrette Rien." François chimed in, beaming as he squeezed my hand, singing about how the joys of life began with finding me.

How could I bring up *préservatifs* now? I was in Paris with François, living my dream. There was nothing to regret. At least not yet.

François smiled at me as the song ended. "You must meet my mother. She has asked about you."

That was a lovely surprise. Meeting mothers was a sign, a serious one.

"She will be pleased I have found such a beautiful, smart woman … even if she is *amèricaine*." He laughed and leaned over to kiss me. "How do you say? *Ma belle amèricaine*; very liberated, very free." He kissed me again, and I felt the familiar, delicious twinges in my body, his magnet pulling me closer. Wanting him. But hesitant still to bring up what I had to say. I told myself he would understand; that *préservatifs* would be best for both of us.

I downed the rest of my wine and caressed his cheek. "François, that song is right; we should not regret anything."

"*Bien sur.* Especially not that kiss!"

I took a deep breath and tried again. "Yes, not any of our kisses. But there is something else I don't want us to regret. François, can we talk about … about *préservatifs*? Wouldn't it be a good idea to get them?"

He looked straight into my eyes. "I do not use those things."

I must have misunderstood. I tried again. "But what if I got pregnant?"

"Haven't you been douching?"

For a split-second I was speechless at his naivety. "François, douching doesn't work. Those sperm are very fast, very determined. They find their way in."

"Then we will have a baby." He said it so easily, as if that were the only possible answer. "You know my religion."

I couldn't believe it. Now my words spurted out with an urgency I couldn't stop.

"François, this isn't about religion. This is about you and me. About being careful. We're just beginning our lives. We're not ready to be parents."

He lit a cigarette, took a deep drag, and exhaled directly into my face. Staring at me like I was an unwelcome stranger.

"You are an atheist? You have no beliefs, no faith at all?" he asked incredulously.

How could he be so strict to the letter of an outmoded rule? I tried to reason with him.

"I know the Church opposes birth control; it also opposes pre-marital sex, divorce, and eating meat on Friday. And yet French Catholics get divorced, don't have babies every year, and eat what they want. Maybe not everything the pope says makes sense."

"*Incroyable!* Now you say my religion is *merde.* What is wrong with you?"

A pit in my stomach opened up like a sinkhole.

What was happening? Was he a stranger, or was he my François? With trembling hands, I took a cigarette from his pack and tried to strike a match. He took the matchbox and the cigarette from me, lit it, and gave it back to me.

I inhaled, slowly let it out, and controlled myself. "I'm sorry. I don't understand."

He poured wine into my glass and drained the rest of his. He spoke quietly, evenly.

"There are several reasons why I believe the pope. But the most important is my faith. Don't you see? Without faith there's no hope, and nothing to live for."

How could I argue against faith? "François, I have a religion too. But I don't follow all the laws from the Old Testament. Like eating pork. A no-no for Jews. But does eating pork make me a bad person? Well, maybe the pig thinks so."

That brought a chuckle from François. He took my hand and kissed it.

"Kate, we have such a good time together. Let's not think of the future. Who knows? Next year, you'll be back at Berkeley. I will be in my *Communauté* in the Auvergne. We must enjoy each other now."

I froze, my brain shattering into shards. "Is that what you want? To never see me again?"

He looked away, quiet for a moment. "Kate, it will work out. That is why I have fallen for you. I can talk with you. We can discuss. We can even argue."

He took the scarf he had bought out of the bag and draped it around my neck.

"You are so beautiful. We would have a beautiful baby." He wiped away a stray tear, then gave me his handkerchief. I blew my nose. One minute he was ignorant and prejudiced, sending me back to California, and the next he was saying the words that made me love him. I entered his fantasy as a naïve child might, hoping in some crazy way that he was right.

"Yes," I said, "you in Paris, me in California. We'll meet in New York to transfer *le bébé* back and forth."

François was caught up in the image. "At the Empire State Building. Like that American movie—"

"*An Affair to Remember*? Yes, you are definitely Cary Grant."

He turned up his collar. "*Oui, c'est moi.*"

It was growing dark when we left the market and drove back to the Left Bank. We had just crossed the Seine when François pulled into an empty space on the street. "Let's walk down to the river. The sunset is magic on the water."

We descended the steps to the Seine's embankment, where I expected to see lovers in the shadows, but under the bridges were the *clochards*, the homeless who had their own kind of *communauté*. Sharing friendship and forgetfulness, this is where they came after begging enough francs to buy a cheap bottle of wine. I impulsively put my hand to François's cheek, drew his face down and brushed his lips with my own. But François did not respond. His eyes were focused beyond me as we heard a splash, a yell, a rush of footsteps. One of the *clochards* at the end of the bank shouted, "*Il est tombé! Au secours!*" He fell, help him!

François pointed toward the black water. "*Ma chèrie*, there! Don't you see? Something in the river."

I made out what looked like a bundle of clothes floating in the murky water. A hand poked out of the clothes, struggling. Then nothing.

"He's not moving!" François said, as a few other people stopped to look down, horrified at the drama playing out in front of our eyes.

"*J'appelle les gendarmes!*" One of the men shouted and ran away to call the police.

"It will be too late!" Françoise blurted, and ran down the bank toward a ladder descending into the river. "*J'arrive!*" I'm coming, he shouted into the cold, dark water, pulling off his jacket and shoes.

"What are you doing?" I cried after him. "It's too dangerous. Wait for the police."

"He'll drown by then." He climbed down the ladder into the Seine.

"François, this is insane. Come back!"

My heart pounding, I ran after him along the embankment as he swam toward the man. The river's current pulled François forward, but also swept the drowning man out of reach. Meanwhile, a crowd had gathered on the bridge closest to Notre-Dame. They cheered as François reached the man and got his face out of the water. Now, swimming against the current, dragging him, François strained to make his way back toward the embankment.

More people had run down to the river, and one of the men climbed down the ladder to pull François and his human cargo up from the rushing water. Two other men dragged the drowning man onto the embankment.

The police and ambulance arrived as I was helping François out of the river. The ambulance driver performed artificial respiration, but the poor man was gone. The driver expressed his condolences and draped a blanket over François's shoulders to warm him, but François threw it off and placed it on the corpse, as if he could some-how bring the man back to life. He shook and shook, as I tried to comfort him.

"I could not save him," he repeated. Over and over.

In fits and starts and with much grinding of gears, I drove François's stick shift Renault back to No. 149. By the time I got him up the six flights of stairs, he was shaking all over. I lit the gas furnace while he collapsed on the bed in his sodden clothes. As the room heated up, I pulled off his sweater and got his shirt off. Unbuckled his belt and pulled off his pants, his socks, his briefs. Then I took a towel and rubbed him down, massaging his shoulders and back.

François looked up at me, squeezing my hand, quieting down. His breathing grew slow and regular. We did not speak. I covered him up with the duvet and tried to pretend that everything was normal. But it was not. He had risked his life for a total stranger. I could not refute this new evidence of his courage and compassion. It was information to be processed, weighed, added to the complex mystery that was François. This young man was full of faults and imperfections. But yes, also full of virtue.

I undressed, put on my flannel nightgown, turned out the light, and climbed into bed with him. He could stay the night; I would keep him warm. Under the duvet, my fingers lightly traced his smooth skin, down to his hips. No further. We would be chaste.

Then François groaned, a primal need reaching out from his subconscious. He took my hand and guided it to where I could feel him getting hard, stiffening. He half-opened his eyes and looked up at me, almost begging.

"J'ai besoin de toi." I need you.

From deep within came my response. I took his hand and placed it on my heart. My heartbeat grew wild from his touch. He encircled my breast and I strained against his hand, closer, closer.

I knew I should stop. This was not safe. This was not smart. And yet I could not stop the wetness, the warmth spreading down through me, equally as insistent. Maybe he was right. What would be, would be. He rolled over, placing himself in between my legs that opened willingly. Moving up and down with each thrust, I received him further into me. I closed my eyes and entered that ultimate state of completeness. As we came together, we both let out a cry that was at once exquisite passion and overwhelming relief.

It was real. It was a dream. How could it not be right?

chapter fifteen

1977 September 9
Deauville

What could save me this time? Was it time to believe in miracles?

Try as I might, I had not conjured up Sydney Pollack for an interview. I dragged myself off the Deauville beach, struggling to come up with a way to tell Patrice I'd failed. Not that it mattered. The shoot was almost over and I needed another job. But Patrice did not hire people who didn't do their job. I was now in that category. It would be the end of Paris for me.

When I arrived at the *Star Wars* reception, it was packed. The event was limited to celebrities and journalists, but wherever there was free booze and deals to be made, showbiz wannabes invariably found a way inside. Armed with my press pass, I watched would-be producers flash phony business cards, and cute young things in skimpy outfits sashay in with a smile.

I made my way over to Patrice, ready to confess all, but he was busy shooting *cinema verite* and waved me away. Staying out of camera range I tried to look busy, but mostly I unburdened the waiters of champagne flutes as they passed through the crowd. Swallowing the false hope of bubbly, I continued my fool's errand: waiting for Pollack.

The crowd wasn't yielding up the elusive director, but I scored in the game of people-watching. I saw Claude Lelouch, the famous French director whose Club 13 manor we were shooting at the next day. Fifteen-year-old Jodie Foster was speaking excellent French to Leslie Caron, who'd been discovered in *An American in Paris* when she was about Jodie's age. Orson Welles was chatting with a Hollywood producer, no doubt trying to charm him into a deal.

After I'd unsuccessfully scouted the entire room and patio for Pollack, I retreated to a corner to mope and drink. The more I drank, the more entertaining the action became. Bunny Banks, the aging D-list star of "King of the Nudies" Russ Meyer movies was on the prowl. Encased in skin-tight leopard-print capri pants, her butt shook in syncopated rhythm with her boobs, which were covered by a tight pink sweater, its neckline ending right above her nipples. One of those nipples kept peeking out like a puppy's nose as she teetered along on four-inch heels.

Oh no. Bunny was making her way toward Jean-Claude Renaud, the producer who'd offered to make me a baby in L.A., and who was walking in my direction. I ducked behind a column as she bumped into him. No way could I deal with Jean-Claude—even though he did cut an impressive figure in his paisley ascot and tennis sweater casually draped over his shoulders. I'd have loved to spy on Bunny's flirtation with him, but champagne bubbles were bursting in my brain. I needed to sop them up with caviar. I headed for the hors d'oeuvres table. As I reached for the last canapé, I bumped elbows with the actor I'd loved in *Star Wars*.

"It's yours," he offered graciously and speared a shrimp instead. He looked uncomfortable and out of place. The press was ignoring him, and I thought he could use a compliment.

"Excuse me," I said. "I wanted to say how good you were in *Star Wars*. You're going to be big. I've got a sixth sense about these things; I felt the same about James Dean when nobody knew who he was. I'm sorry, what's your name?"

"Harrison Ford," he smiled and shook my hand. "Thanks. Very kind of you."

"I don't suppose you've seen Sydney Pollack?" I said.

"No, is he here?" He was about to say more when a publicist broke through the crowd and dragged him off for photos.

Patrice was busy filming Bunny trying to engage Jean-Claude, so I returned to my people-watching. Who were all these would-be and has-been seekers of fame and fortune? Those like Bunny were sadly desperate, but I was more concerned with the young women who still had a choice for their future. These poor girls were desperate to let a horny middle-aged producer fuck them, hoping for a walk-on part in exchange. And how many times did their investment in wardrobe, makeup, plastic surgery even get them that? But they saw no other way. Put out or give up.

Not ten feet away, their backs to me, I spied a prime example: a sexy girl with her arm around a male target. The tight pants, stiletto heels, and long blonde hair cascading down a bare back gave her away. Although I had to admit she had a cute butt.

As I drained my champagne flute, the man turned around to wave to someone, and I saw his face.

Sydney Pollack!

Merde. He was here, and I was shit-faced. I willed my inner being to take control.

"Excuse me, Mr. Pollack?" I interrupted. The girl next to him turned around and her eyes opened wide. Mine opened wider.

"Susan!"

"I knew I'd find you!" she shrieked.

I was instantly sober. "What a pleasant surprise. You're here."

She laughed and patted Sydney's cheek. "Yes, and look who I found. Sydney, meet my best friend, Kate Miller. She's working with French television on a wonderful documentary. Kate, why don't you tell Sydney about it while I fetch more champagne?"

Susan's technique was admirable, leaving me alone with Sydney and enough time to make him believe in the utter importance of my documentary.

"It's a privilege to meet you, Mr. Pollack. Yes, I'm with France-Nouvelle. I was hoping to find you at the reception."

"Here I am," he said, politely disinterested. "Susan talked me into coming. I was going to hide out until my film premiere and disappear as soon as the credits ran. I'm not much of a festivalgoer."

"Me either," I responded, with my most elite of invitations. "Our prime-time TV special focuses on something more interesting: the synergy between American and French films. We have interviewed François Truffaut, and a short talk with you as an American auteur exploring French cinema is the perfect counterpart."

Pollack stopped scanning the room and started listening. Time to ramp up my pitch.

I knew nothing about his film except the trailer, but I told Pollack how brilliantly he'd visualized the world of Grand Prix racing, how powerfully it illustrated the film's theme: That death exists in order to appreciate life. I complimented him on his artful adaptation of *Heaven Has No Favorites,* the Erich Maria Remarque novel. If Remarque's *All Quiet on the Western Front* was an iconic war film, *Bobby Deerfield* would be a classic exploring the human condition.

"Kate, you're impressive," Pollack admitted. "You know who Remarque is; that already puts you on my favorites list."

He became my captive audience, and I went in for the kill.

"You've got one of America's biggest stars, Al Pacino, wrestling with European sensibilities. It will be our privilege to launch your film in the biggest market on the continent. And we'll take very little of your time."

Sydney sounded almost wistful. "You've given a lot of thought to this but—"

"We'll put you in a sports car of your choosing and interview you while you're driving."

Susan was back with the champagne, and Pollack was weakening.

"You could do it on your way to the Claude Lelouch luncheon," she added helpfully.

"That works," I said. "We're going to film there as well."

Pollack shrugged. "In a sports car? Interesting notion. I'd love to drive an Alpine Renault. It won the world rally championship."

I'd get him a Renault. There were lots of Renaults in France.

"It will be outside the Hôtel Royal at noon tomorrow waiting for you."

He snagged the bait. "Kate, you've got a deal. See you then."

Inside I was howling. Outside, coolly professional. "We look forward to it."

Pollack turned to Susan. "Susie, I'm late to a meeting. Great to see you, though. Why don't you come to Lelouch's with me?"

Susan kissed him on both cheeks. "Of course. Trevor would want me to take care of you."

"Tell him he owes me a lunch." And with that, he was off.

As soon as he was out of hearing range, Susan giggled. "Told you I'd come!"

I was still in shock. "I didn't recognize you. Your hair, your clothes! Why didn't you call? I've been running around Deauville all afternoon looking for Pollack!"

"Kate, I was lucky just to get here. First, I had to get the new nanny settled in. Then Sydney's people had to find out where he was staying. Plus you, my dear, were filming who knows where. But most importantly," she paused dramatically, "I was not about to be seen in France with massacred hair."

She fluffed her wig. "Like it? Frederick's of Hollywood."

"I love it! I love you!" In truth, I was blown away. Susan came five thousand miles to help me. Okay, she came for herself, but she'd delivered Pollack. I flashed on our old school days. Making a plan, turning a dream into reality.

"Susan, you saved my ass. Now all I have to do is get a Renault before noon tomorrow. Do you think Hertz is open?"

"Sweetie, Sydney said that the Alpine Renault was a champion rally car. I don't think Hertz has them."

My mind went into sixth gear. I was too close to give up. Hmm, a rally car? Yes!

"Susan, I've got an idea. Meet me tonight at ten in the casino, near the entrance to Regine's. I'll explain everything later. *Tout a l'heure!*"

Susan patted me on the behind. "Bet your bottom dollar!"

People were leaving so they could dress for the French premiere of *Star Wars.* I jotted down a few notes for the Pollack interview and found Patrice as he was packing up his camera. He was in great spirits.

"I got good stuff—Bunny Banks auditioning for Minnelli! That new actor in *Star Wars,* what's his name? Producers trying to sell me their movies. All the showbiz *merde* that makes up film festivals. Where were you?"

This time I didn't have to lie. "I was confirming Sydney Pollack. You'll interview him in a sports car while he's driving to Lelouch's for lunch. Here are some questions for you to ask." I casually handed him my notes as if I'd not performed a miracle. Better for Patrice not to know how close I'd been to failure.

He nodded, glancing at my interview questions. "Looks good. Now I'm going to see *Star Wars* and find out what all the fuss is about."

Back in my room, I panicked that I'd never pull off my plan to get the Renault for Pollack. I needed to soak. Once in the warm bath, my mind drifted to the interviews with Peck and Minnelli. Hmm … could I become a character in a movie of my own life, confident and daring? No. I'd always been true to myself; minimum makeup, no flashy glitz.

Then I remembered the dress that was in my suitcase.

The day before I left Paris for Deauville, I'd met Annette for lunch in Saint-Germain des Près. Over croque-monsieur sandwiches, I teased her until she confessed she was seeing Patrice.

"He is an interesting man," Annette allowed, then in her no-nonsense style, directed the conversation back to me. "Tell me about your schedule in Deauville. Any special events? A premiere?" she asked. "Do you have the right clothes?"

"I'm working. It doesn't matter what I wear."

She looked at me with x-ray eyes. "Do you want to be a success in France or not?"

Before I knew it, we were at Le Mouton à Cinq Pattes, a designer outlet known only to savvy Parisians. Annette worked her way through the dress racks lining the small shop as if she were flipping through a deck of playing cards. About halfway down the third rack, she pulled out a jade green chiffon dress. It was a '30s style that would have clung to Jean Harlow in all the right places.

"Don't bother with anything else. This is the one. Buy very high heels to go with it." She pointed to a pair on the shoe rack, and then like a fairy godmother, she kissed me on both cheeks and was gone.

When I packed for Deauville, I almost didn't take the outfit, sure that I'd never wear it. At the last minute, fearing that Annette would ask me about the dress, I zipped it into the suitcase's top pocket, and forgot about it.

What the hell. Tonight was do or die. I took a breath and slipped on the dress, pulled up my pantyhose, pushed my feet into the heels, and walked over to the full-length bathroom mirror.

I saw myself in a parallel universe. I looked confident, elegant—maybe even grown-up. The chiffon hung gracefully in folds and even showed off a few curves. The jade color changed my blue eyes to green. The heels made me sway as I walked. When I entered the casino, no one would guess I was a documentary filmmaker.

Fantasy, reality, who cared? I was ready to make my stage entrance.

chapter sixteen

Casino de Deauville

At ten o'clock, my green dress and I floated into the glistening white palace of the Casino de Deauville, swept up the curving marble staircase, and glided past red silk curtains into the gaming room. This was no Las Vegas joint with beer bellies, flashing lights, and clanging slot machines. Here was the civilized hum of players in evening dress clustered under crystal chandeliers, playing *les jeux traditionnel* of roulette, baccarat, and *vingt-et-un*, blackjack. Making my way past the genteel sound of chips raked across deep green felt, I stopped for a moment at a *chemin-de-fer* table.

"*Neuf à la banque,*" the croupier called to the Beautiful People gathered around the table. Was that Agent 007 drawing cards from the baccarat shoe? And was I ready to be a Bond girl, shaken, not stirred? You bet. But I had work to do.

I found Susan at one of the blackjack tables. She had changed into a classic black sheath cocktail dress, low cut with a glittering pin set in the middle of her impressive cleavage. Twirling strands of her long blonde wig with her fingers, she concentrated on the cards, ignoring the martini beside her.

"Hit me," she said to the dealer, brushing her cards against the felt.

"Is that what they say in French?" I whispered, leaning over her shoulder to look at her hand. She had an eight and a four.

"A universal language," she muttered as the dealer flipped a card in front of her.

It was a three. Now she had fifteen. Stay or go for it? Of course Susan went for it. The next card was a seven. One too many. Susan shrugged as she watched the dealer rake away the last of her chips.

"Easy come, easy go. Or is that what they say about husbands?"

It had been a long time since I felt the need to help Susan, but despite her sexy camouflage and glib remarks, I'd never seen her look this vulnerable. I guided her to an empty table where we could bond together like two high school girls again.

"Trevor's a bastard," I consoled her. "Don't beat yourself up. You deserve better; Deauville will give you a new perspective."

Susan downed the rest of the martini and reapplied her lipstick with a trembling hand.

"Damn it, Kate, this isn't the first time that miserable piece of shit lied to me and I didn't want to know the truth. Especially when his dick was otherwise occupied." She looked into her compact mirror, willing herself to smile. "That's what you do in Hollywood. Look the other way, hang onto your rung of the fucking social ladder. Turn your life into one big fat lie."

I felt a rush of sympathy for her. She was being honest with me, and even more importantly, with herself. I knew too well how hard it was to own up to one's life.

"Hey, we did good today. We're on third base—ready to go for a home run?"

"Sure, but no picking up young men and looking for hash. That didn't work out well."

"This is going to be better. I know I'm better," I said.

Susan eyed my dress. "You're learning—that dress is smashing on you. And at least my hair is better."

"I thought you massacred your hair?"

"Hey, I paid for this wig—so it's mine. Now what's the plan?"

I thought again of our teenage selves, plotting our future. But this time, I was in charge.

"Follow my lead. We'll have fun."

Susan tossed her hair and grabbed her purse. "You're with a blonde. We'll have more fun."

The disco's gatekeeper looked us up and down, barely scanned his list, and waved us through into the private club. We walked past the gold and black lacquered walls and toward the small dance floor, where more Beautiful People were letting loose to the funky rhythm of the American hit, "Car Wash."

"Let's keep those cars a'coming," I whispered in Susan's ear, as I spotted Armand in a group of young men standing around the zinc bar, laughing and drinking.

He waved me over. "Kate!"

"Kate!" The other men yelled in unison, holding up their glasses in a rally cry.

Armand gave me a wide smile, clearly approving of my dress, reminding me that he already knew what was underneath. "*Comme tu es belle ce soir*," you are beautiful tonight, he whispered as we air-kissed.

"Like you," I said, stroking the fabric of his well-tailored black suit, made casual with an open collar shirt, no tie, and white loafers without socks. I could feel his hard, slim body beneath the suit, but I wanted something other than a sequel to our night together.

Susan, however, lit up in the way that meant I like what I see, and I'm open to more. I pushed her in front of me.

"This is my good friend, Susan. We were in Paris together a long time ago."

He took Susan's hand and kissed it. "*Enchanté.*"

"*Oui, moi aussi.*" Probably the only French words she knew. With Armand, that might be all she needed.

"Champagne?" He motioned to the bartender to open one of the Moet et Chandon bottles stacked behind the bar. The French national drink, it seemed. More than enough reason to consider citizenship.

I took a sip and made my play. "Armand, I know you wanted to meet Sydney Pollack. Guess what? Susan is a good friend of his."

"*Oui, oui.* Sydney *et moi,*" Susan chimed in.

"Super!" Armand said. "He is here in Deauville? We are very excited about his film."

"Susan has helped arrange my interview with him tomorrow." Susan nodded as if she was humbly accepting a Noble prize.

"Then you found him! *Parfait.*"

"Yes, but not exactly perfect," I said. Now for my big gamble. "There's a condition. He wants to be filmed while driving an Alpine Renault."

Armand did not blink. "Of course. It's the best rally car there is. Even more perfect."

I paused. "It would be, if I had an Alpine Renault. It's not as if I can go to Hertz."

He laughed. "*Pas de tout.* The Alpine is a very special car."

"It must be if Mr. Pollack wants to drive it," I agreed. "Susan and I would love to see one."

"*Oui, oui,*" Susan chimed in.

"I don't think anyone has an Alpine here. Let's see." Armand turned toward his friends, who were several champagne glasses ahead of us.

"Marc! *Tu as ton Alpine Renault ici?*"

"*Non, c'est la Porsche,*" was the slightly slurred answer.

"Too bad, Kate," Armand said. "Pierre has a Lancia, Roland the Alfa Romeo, Michel, the Ford."

"Sydney wants a French car," I said, not wanting to appear ungrateful.

His eyes brightened. "Then you are in luck! Guy has a Citroen." He was about to call Guy over when I stopped him.

"*Non, non, je suis désolé,* it must be the Alpine Renault."

"There is only one other in the club, but Jean is not here. He had to work tonight. And even if he came, he would probably not drive his Alpine."

My heart sank. There wasn't any time for Plan B, even if I could think of a Plan B. After I'd come this far, I wasn't going to reach the finish line.

For the next half hour, I sat on a red leather banquette, playing my part, laughing with the others, drinking champagne, while I ran through all the ways I might pass off a Citroen for an Alpine Renault. Not a chance. My mind was so consumed with defeat that I didn't take notice when a slim young man with thick blond hair ambled over, a bit unsteady on his feet, drinking straight from a bottle of Moet et Chandon.

"Armand, you keeping these beautiful women to yourself!"

Armand looked up in surprise. "Jean, how can you be here? You were working tonight."

"I had to come in support of *Bobby Deerfield.* My Renault made the trip very fast."

"Your Alpine Renault?" I interrupted. Could life be worth living again?

Armand drew me in. "Kate, may I present Jean Boucher, a World Rally Champion. Driving his Alpine Renault."

I shook his hand. "*Enchanté.* I hear it's a beautiful car."

"*Bien sûr*, it's not Formula One, but it does not disappoint on Route A-13," Jean said. "200 *kilomètres* from Paris. Ninety minutes." He took another swig from his champagne bottle and offered it to me. I politely declined, as Armand came to the rescue.

"Kate wants to give you the honor of lending your car to Sydney Pollack, director of *Bobby Deerfield*!"

Jean squinted out of his alcohol-induced fog. "You are speaking about my Renault? You think Monsieur Pollack will not crash it? *Absolument pas!*" He turned back to me, all smiles. "However, if Mademoiselle Kate is interested, I would be happy to show her my beautiful car."

"*Sensationelle!*" I said, returning his flirtatious smile. *You're drunk enough to talk into anything.*

Bleary-eyed, he refueled himself with champagne and held out his arm. "*Allons-y*, let's go, it's right outside."

Electric blue, low to the ground, graceful aerodynamic curves flaring out over the wheels. Gorgeous. Even I was in love. We walked up to the car and the valet gave Jean his keys.

"A little drive?" Jean offered, opening the passenger door to what looked like a space capsule cockpit. The soft black leather seats beckoned. I couldn't resist.

"No driving, but I'll sit for a minute," I said, and folded myself into the seat as if I were an astronaut preparing to blast off. He climbed into the driver side, smiled broadly, and started the motor. My body reverberated with the burst of power straining to be unleashed.

"No!" I yelled, but we were already off, screeching down the road along the beach.

For a moment I was transfixed, becoming one with the speed and power of the Renault. Until we came to the end of the divided highway and, looming ahead, a roundabout.

Jean accelerated, driving in his drunkenness as if he were on a racecourse, rounding the circle at 120 kilometers, tearing over the gravel on the edge of the road, barely missing a concrete-walled flower bed. He was out of control. Tires screeching, car swerving, he roared down the road back toward the casino.

My adrenalin pumped into overdrive. "Slow down. Stop at the next corner," I said calmly as if I were the instructor for a driver's test. But he only smiled and continued at racing speed, turning the wrong way up a narrow one-way street. A car's headlights were coming toward us. Jean froze, unable to move.

"Goddammit, I said stop!" This was insanity. I wanted the car, I wanted Patrice to give me more work. But was it worth risking my life?

In desperation, I reached over, pulled the key out of the ignition and grabbed the wheel. As the Renault slowed, I steered it into an alley a second before the oncoming car passed us.

The car now stopped, Jean peered at the dials, rubbing his eyes, banging his head on the steering wheel. The alcohol had turned him into a weeping child.

"*J'ai honte*, I'm ashamed. I beg you, don't tell anyone. I'll make it up to you, I promise."

Should he be barred from racing because he almost killed me? Not when I could help the poor boy. "Jean, it will be our secret if you allow Sydney Pollack to drive your car in celebration of *Bobby Deerfield*."

Jean had already forgotten his conversation with Armand. "The director of *Bobby Deerfield* wants to drive my car?" he asked. "It will be an honor. But first ..." He opened the door, crawled out, and bent over. I listened to the sounds of retching, the champagne bubbles pushing up his dinner. Minutes later, he turned his back to me, went to the gutter, and peed away the rest of it. Then he climbed back into the car.

"Now I take a rest." Eyes closed, he lay his head on the steering wheel, patting the car's dashboard, muttering "*Je m'excuse, ma petite Alpine*, I will not abuse you again."

I waited until I heard the regular breathing of sleep. Then I crept out of the car, taking the key.

Back at the casino, I took a quick trip to *la toilette* to freshen up. I was trembling, but the face that stared back at me in the mirror was flushed with excitement, cheeks rosy, eyes bright. Had I gone completely bonkers or was all that adrenaline a beauty aid?

Susan was at the bar, downing J&B shots in a drinking match with one of the young men. I found Armand at the other end of the bar and handed him the car key.

"But where is Jean?" he asked.

I resolved to keep my pact. "He said he would be honored to lend Monsieur Pollack his car. He's sleeping in his beloved Alpine in an alley off rue Blanc. Perhaps one of your friends can drive him to his hotel?"

"Yes, we'll get him to bed. *Malheuresement,* this is not the first time."

"Armand, I don't know if he'll remember he offered me the car."

"Don't worry, we make sure Jean doesn't want to drive tomorrow. We only borrow the car for a few hours." He refilled my champagne glass, drawing me closer, his body lightly touching mine. "And now, a dance before we work out the details for tomorrow?"

The visceral memory of a magnificent night in Paris shot through my body, but then I remembered what was behind those bedroom eyes. A nice but rather boring guy.

I was debating how to answer when I had my best idea ever. Susan and Armand had both done me a great favor. Why shouldn't I offer them a small reward in return? I kissed Armand's cheek and took his arm off my shoulder.

"I would love to, but I have to work tonight. Anyway, Susan

knows more of Monsieur Pollack's schedule than I do." I waved her over. "Susan, I hate to impose, but would you help Armand deliver the Alpine Renault to Sydney tomorrow? The Hôtel Royal at noon."

She glanced sideways at me, lips upturned, with the slightest of nods. After thirteen years, our radar still picked up each other's signals. I loved offering Susan something she might not get on her own. I felt so generous.

She appeared to hesitate, then gave in. "I suppose I can help out. Sydney does want me to go with him tomorrow."

"*Formidable!* Now I really have to run. Patrice is in the casino."

As I gave Susan a hug, she whispered in my ear, "I won't let him out of my sight until we deliver the car."

Patrice was my excuse for leaving Regine's, but I was ready to call it a night. I walked past the players at the gaming tables. Exchanging wads of francs for piles of chips, their eyes filled with dreams as they watched the wheel spin, the baccarat shoe pass, the dealer flip a card. Then, with frozen faces, they watched the croupier raking their dreams away. The odds were always with the house. There must be a better game to play.

A waitress offered me a martini. "*Non, merci,* I didn't order anything," I told her.

She motioned over to the next table. "The gentleman sent it."

Among the crowd at the roulette table I saw Patrice raising his glass to me. At his side, Jean-Claude Renaud. Damn, I could not escape that man. Then again, maybe I shouldn't. Jean-Claude liked games. I was ready to play for higher stakes—a job. In my green dress, he wouldn't dare touch me.

I approached them as Patrice was polka-dotting the roulette table with chips.

"*Merci* for the martini. How did you like *Star Wars*?" I asked.

"The force is with me! I will cause the roulette wheel to stop on 14. Or 21. Or 7."

He sliced the air with an imaginary lightsaber and turned to Jean-Claude. "You remember Kate, my colleague from Los Angeles?"

Jean-Claude looked at me. Really looked at me.

With a slight smile, I took the enigmatic charm offensive. "So nice to see you again."

He took my hand and raised it to his lips; his clear blue eyes boring into mine, exactly as they had in that house off Mulholland Drive. "Please refresh my memory," he said. "So many people in that enchanting house floating on top of the canyon."

My green dress armor weakened, and my stomach tightened. For a man who wanted to give me a baby, I hadn't made much of an impression. Still, I showed no emotion. In this game, weakness was a penalty.

"Allow me to remind you: The casting session for the UCLA sexuality study. And no, I was not one of the actresses." I smiled provocatively.

Strangely enough, his seeming obliviousness spurred on my competitive spirit. I smoothed the chiffon folds of my skirt, restoring their power, remembering I was not that uncertain girl he first met. I had assumed the character of an accomplished producer.

"We discussed games that night. You must be doing something right in this one," I said, nodding to his pile of chips. "Perhaps I'll join in." I gave the croupier a hundred franc note. Twenty dollars. I could manage that. I pointed to the color of the chips in Jean-Claude's biggest stack.

The croupier handed me one chip.

"*Faites vos jeux!*" Place your bets, called the croupier. I held the chip over the roulette table waiting for a number to call to me. Might as well blow it all on one roll; the odds were only thirty-seven to one.

I looked again at Jean-Claude's pile of chips. "What's your lucky number?" I asked him.

He took my chip. "A proposition. We go fifty-fifty." He added the chip to his stack, divided the stack in two, and gave me one of them. "You will give me luck."

He placed half of his stack on odd. "A safer bet and you stay in the game," he said, smiling at me … or was it leering? I put half of my new stack next to his.

"*Rien ne va plus*." No more bets, the croupier announced, and he set the wheel spinning.

Mesmerized, I watched the little steel ball whirring around the edge of the wheel as it spun, slowed, and bounced on the slotted numbers. After several of these near landings, it came to rest on seven.

Jean-Claude grinned. We greedily picked up our winnings, and with Patrice at our side like a chaperone, we played for an hour more, not really talking, simply enjoying the roller coaster ride of the roulette wheel.

Clearly, Jean-Claude knew how to stay in the game. Despite his cavalier memory of me, he projected a charisma I couldn't ignore. He wore his tux as if it were a second skin. Yes, he was short, but his mane of curly steel-gray hair made him a lion. In his world he was king, and the other roulette players merely members of his pride.

It was after midnight when Patrice pocketed his few remaining chips. "I'm done."

"I'll walk with you back to the hotel," I said to Patrice, intuitively knowing my game with Jean-Claude had to be played out slowly, keeping the anticipation alive. I cashed in half of my chips, giving the other half to Jean-Claude, plus one.

He gave the chip back to me. "Your original stake."

I flipped it back to him. "No, it is yours, a gift to my teacher."

Without skipping a beat, he kissed the chip and put it in his pocket. "*Merci* for bringing me luck. You must come with me to Claude Lelouch's for lunch tomorrow."

Jean-Claude had made a new move. I wasn't sure what the game was, nor how I would counter. But if tonight was any indication, whatever obstacle presented itself, I could turn it into opportunity.

I'd done it with Sydney Pollack, hadn't I?

chapter seventeen

1964 November 2
Paris

How glorious it is. That moment when you know with certainty that you are living exactly the life you want. It was the morning after François's heroic attempted rescue in the Seine, and everything—from lying in bed with him, to the petite wallpapered room I lived in, to the breakfast yogurt on the windowsill—was perfect. François wrapped his long, warm body around me, brushed his messy hair from his eyes, and kissed me. "Bonjour, ma petite fille." We savored a few more hugs, then he reluctantly pulled himself out of bed, dressed, bent down for one more kiss, and rushed off to work.

I went through my morning routine humming "Je Ne Regrette Rien." In my tiny chambre de bonne, the world was as it should be. I was in love; I was invincible. I floated out of No. 149, waving to Veronique as she left for school. "See you at five o'clock for class!"

But as I began to match the pace of the busy people around me, reality set in. I was hurrying to the Sorbonne, impatiently waiting for a light to change, when I noticed a woman grabbing the hand of a small child who had jumped off the curb into the busy street. Worries about pregnancy invaded my mind. I'd had unprotected sex again with François. I could not keep doing that. It was time to enlist help.

Colin spent his afternoons selling the *Herald Tribune* near the Champs Élysée. I had a break between the Sorbonne and tutoring, so I hopped the metro to the Right Bank.

La Rive Droite wasn't my Paris. It was different. It was rich. In front of the famous George V Hotel, bellboys pushed me away as they unloaded luggage from a Rolls-Royce, escorting guests in fur coats and fancy clothes. Embarrassed by my Monoprix rags, I quickly crossed the street. But rue Marbeuf was worse. Well-dressed customers were going in and out of elegant shops showing the latest fashions. One of the store windows displayed custom-made shoes with soles so finely stitched you wouldn't want to ruin a pair by walking in them. I swore I'd never be a slave to blatant materialism.

It was a relief to see Colin on the corner, his curly russet hair and beard setting off his old Navy peacoat. He walked up to me, waving the *Herald Tribune*, shouting in his clipped British accent, "Extra! Extra! *New York Herald Tribune!*"

As he gave me a hug, I whispered in his ear. "Extra, extra. Girl needs to find rubbers."

Colin looked at me and grinned. "It's not raining."

"You know what I mean," I said. Colin knew about my feelings for François and accepted them. My only punishment was merciless teasing.

"You mean Frenchies?" he asked. "For your Frenchie, I presume."

It was embarrassing, but I had no idea how to get them on my own. They were illegal in France, but like marijuana, there were ways to find them. Colin was my only hope. I assured him that once I got them, *if* I could get them, I'd talk François into using them. Colin lifted a skeptical eyebrow but kept his thoughts to himself. "You are in luck, my bonnie Kate. Your Army's got a PX down the street that sells all things American … and I've got a friend's entry card."

32 rue Marbeuf was classic 19th-century Paris, but inside the PX it was pure 20th-century America: Velveeta cheese, Cheerios, and Chef Boyardee filling the shelves. *Life* and *Look* magazines piled on a counter. Beach Boys, Barbra Streisand, and Dean Martin albums stacked in the record racks. Could I spend the rest of my life in France without all this?

Except for Barbra Streisand, an unequivocal yes.

Sandwiched between the Kotex and the Kleenex, we found "The pleasure you want, the protection you trust." At least that's what the Trojan package promised.

"How many?" Colin asked, holding up packages of twelve and thirty-six.

"Let's go for the big one," I whispered, hoping the army wives shopping nearby didn't hear. I took a deep breath and gave him twenty francs, about four dollars. I'd be eating lunch at the student cafeteria for the rest of the month.

At the cash register counter, I noticed a display of Zippo lighters. I picked one up and flicked it open. François would love it. But I'd shot my wad with the Trojans, so to speak. Colin noticed when I reluctantly put the Zippo down.

"We get the PX discount. You've got enough."

The cashier handed me fifty centimes back, which I returned in exchange for two Hershey's chocolate bars. François could not resist me now.

Two nights later, as I clambered down the staircase of No. 149, on my way to meet François, I almost ran into the concierge. Madame

Defarge, as I'd dubbed her, was actually named Madame Just. Even more appropriate. She knew exactly how everyone should act, and dispensed justice accordingly.

"*Bonsoir*, Madame Just," I greeted her in the lilting voice I'd learned in my phonetics class.

"*Et vous, Mademoiselle*," she answered with a hint of a smile as she swept the stairs. She still treated me like a stupid American, but her response was at least a step in the right direction. Until I tripped on her dustpan and the debris scattered back onto the stairs. She looked at me with disdain.

"*Je m'excuse*," I apologized, scrambling to help her clean up and making it worse. I started to explain in bad French that I was rushing to meet my boyfriend for an important dinner.

"*Faites attention*," she said, cutting me off. Excuses didn't interest her.

At our favorite basement Chinese restaurant, François had already ordered, and the food arrived as soon as I sat down. He'd gone home to get his clothes cleaned after the river experience, and two nights of his mother's cooking were enough. He was starving for *Chinois*. As I watched him stuff an eggroll into his mouth like a little kid, it was easy to imagine his mother sniffing her son's clothes after their soaking in the filthy Seine, scolding him, stripping them off like when he was a child.

"She said I smelled like a sewer. What could I do?"

"What did she say about risking your life, trying to save a drowning man?"

"That I was foolhardy. But was glad you were there. She invited you for dinner."

"Oh la la," I said, already debating if I should bring flowers or candy. Both, I decided. I'd advanced to the semi-finals. This was the crucial test.

After dinner, François took out a cigarette and his box of Venus di Milo matches.

"Wait," I said. "I have something for you." I took the package out of my purse and handed it to him. "A little present."

When he saw the Zippo, he let out a whoop. Clinked it open, clunked it shut, clinked it open again. He kissed me on both cheeks, then a long, slow, tender kiss on the mouth.

"I'll be like my American GI heroes!"

"Exactly. I got it at the U.S. Army PX. It's the real deal."

He dangled the cigarette from his lip, thumbed down the flint wheel, and presto, the flame appeared. He offered me the cigarette and lit one for himself.

"You are special, Kate. You know me so well. I will always use it."

"It has a lifetime warranty, so perhaps you will," I said, with an image of him, old in a Humphrey Bogart way, lighting my cigarette.

"What else did you get? Elvis Presley records, maybe Hershey chocolate bars?"

"You'll see." I took his hand, teasing, enticing. "It's another gift for you. Well, really for us. It's in my room."

"Allons-y, let's go!"

Back at No. 149, he dragged me up the six flights. I opened the door and led him to my bed.

"I have been thinking about this for two days," he murmured, unbuttoning my shirt.

"Then you can wait two more minutes." Making sure he was watching, I slowly took off my clothes. Clad only in bra and panties, I bent over, opened the bottom drawer of the armoire, and took out the Hershey's bar and one of the Trojans.

Hiding the Trojan in one hand, I held up the Hershey's and tossed it to him.

"Hershey's! *Je suis tout à fait américain.* One hundred percent!"

I got into bed, the Trojan in my hand. Between the Hershey's bar and my striptease, I hoped he'd be excited enough to do anything.

He pointed to my cupped fist. "A package of Lucky Strikes?"

"No, it is something the GIs carried. Also one hundred percent American. I'd love to try one right now." I handed him the Trojan. François looked at it. He was calm, collected. I had to say that much for him.

"If the GIs used them, they can't be bad," I whispered. "They were heroes, like you."

He handed it to me and put his shirt back on. He looked so sad and disappointed. "I thought you accepted my beliefs."

I could have pointed out that we were already violating the church's rule of sex out of wedlock. But I didn't want to fight. And I didn't want him to leave. What other option did I have?

Capitulate.

I unbuttoned his shirt and pulled it off. I hated myself, but if his sperm hadn't hit bullseye yet, I was probably safe for the next three weeks before I ovulated again.

"Okay, not tonight," I said. "Maybe when it's a bad time of month again."

"*Ma petite américaine*," he whispered in my ear. "You are persistent, not a quitter." He drew the covers over me and unhooked my bra.

"Neither are you, François," I said as my hand slid down his briefs.

"Okay, we talk about it another time," and he slipped my panties off.

I dropped the Trojan on the floor and let the magnet of his body draw me in.

chapter eighteen

1977 September 10
Deauville

Stationed underneath the red canopy of the Hôtel Royal entrance, I waited for Sydney Pollack and pondered life's what-ifs: Thirteen years ago, what if François hadn't been so Catholic? What if Susan hadn't left me in Paris? And what about today's what-ifs: What if the Alpine Renault doesn't show up and Pollack bails? What if Patrice cuts me loose and I have to slink back to L.A. knowing I'd failed a second time in Paris?

I'd be okay. But did I want "She had an okay life" on my tombstone? I couldn't bear the thought. It wasn't only a job; it was my life I was fighting for. I was exploring new parts of myself I'd forgotten or never knew existed. Something inside me was liberated. But all I'd done to keep Patrice happy and ensure my stay in Paris could still fall apart.

I called Susan in the morning to confirm. No answer. Sydney Pollack's room wasn't accepting calls. Armand was not listed at the hotel. Jean-Claude Renaud—who knows? My only constant was Patrice, with his soundman and assistant, who arrived at 11:55, ready to go. While we waited for Pollack to arrive, Patrice had his fun with me.

"You gambled with Jean-Claude Renaud. Be careful. He makes awful movies."

"But they are successful," I said. "If you don't have more work for me, maybe he will."

Patrice wouldn't let go. "I'm sure he has other plans for you."

I was about to make a sassy feminist retort when an electric blue vision of grace and power appeared: the Alpine Renault. Even Patrice's usually unflappable demeanor cracked.

"*C'est chouette, non?* Very cool."

It was happening. Like clockwork. The car rolled up to the valet stand. Armand hopped out and directed Susan, who was driving his Jaguar, to stop behind him. She got out, waved to me, took Armand's arm, and they walked over to Pollack, who was emerging from the hotel.

"There's Pollack," I said to Patrice. "Let's go."

I shook the great director's hand as if we actually knew each other, and introduced Patrice. Pollack nodded courteously, but his eyes were locked on the car. "Let's do it!"

The soundman put a wireless mike on him, and Patrice started filming as Pollack slid behind the wheel. Like a little boy with his first toy car, he couldn't keep his hands off it, touching the controls, stroking the fine leather, running his fingers over the polished wood dashboard.

Still filming, Patrice climbed into the passenger seat. As Pollack put the car in gear, Patrice asked questions I'd given him in my notes.

"Why do men love speed? Why do they defy death?"

And they were off, followed by the film crew and Susan and Armand in the Jaguar. *Unfuckingbelievable.* I was floating on air, congratulating myself on how brilliant I'd been, when I realized I was still standing at the valet stand. Alone. And Jean-Claude was not there to pick me up. Instead of obsessing over another what-if, I asked the doorman to call me a taxi. Five minutes later, just ahead of the taxi, Jean-Claude drove up in his Porsche.

"Am I late? Business. Always business," he said, leaning over to open the passenger door for me.

Yeah, monkey business, I thought, all smiles as I hopped in the Porsche. My instincts snapped to attention, alert to every move. I was back in the game.

As it had for five hundred years, the Normandy stone manor house stood majestically in a sunlit clearing at the end of a private road. If it wasn't destroyed by two world wars, I supposed the manor would survive today's action at what was now Claude Lelouch's home.

Jean-Claude escorted me through the living room with its stuffed chintz armchairs and oak tables piled high with scripts, pointing out Lelouch's two Oscars for his hit film *A Man and a Woman*. Out on the patio, tables were set up under white umbrellas, and servers with drinks and hors d'oeuvres circulated among the mix of celebrities and French elite. Since Patrice was busy filming, I was free to accept the champagne Jean-Claude handed me from a passing waiter.

"These events can be entertaining," he said, turning to me with those x-ray eyes. "However, I am more intrigued by what I see before me. Let me be frank, Kate, last night you were a different woman than you were in L.A."

"You recovered your memory," I said.

"Yes, I remember our talk as the sunset glowed over those mountains of Mulholland. Solve the mystery, Kate. Who are you?

What are you?"

I shrugged. "A Gemini."

He stifled his laugh, narrowed his eyes, and dared me to confess. "But what do you really do in America, Mademoiselle? Do you write, do you direct, do you produce? Do you know Norman Lear?"

"All of the above," I said, lying only about Norman Lear. "And I met Gregory Peck yesterday," I boasted.

"I don't care about Peck. I make television programs. I've signed with your ABC network to remake some of my French Movies of the Week."

Aha. His Hollywood deal had gone through. He really could be a backup if Patrice didn't keep me employed. I changed directions, stretching the truth only a tiny bit.

"Since I produce programs for both American and French TV," I said, "you'll be interested to know I'm exploring job opportunities, looking for that right person who values my international expertise."

Jean-Claude looked at me as if he were a detective sizing up a suspect. "I might have something for you. Come to my office next Wednesday. Five o'clock."

I wasn't sure if I believed him any more than when he'd offered to make me a baby. But he was an influential man, and a meeting could be a first step toward a business opportunity.

"Five o'clock it is," I said, offering him a handshake to seal the deal.

He took my hand and kissed it. "We do it American and French Style."

"International relations are so edifying," I agreed.

Jean-Claude then excused himself to chat up the movers and shakers. I found Patrice and ran interference for him until he was finished with Pollack. Then we sat down to lunch. As Patrice always said, work should never intrude when it came to a good meal. And this lunch was one of those towering seafood platters—oysters, clams, periwinkles, crab, lobster—complemented by a delightfully crisp Chenin Blanc.

Patrice slurped an oyster. "You are a lucky person—life offers you another opportunity to taste *les fruits de mer*."

"Yes, and I'm not passing it up this time." As I worked a lobster tidbit from its shell, I prodded Patrice into praising my fabulous skills. "The Pollack interview went well?"

"That Alpine is *superbe!*" He took a giant crab leg and cracked it open. "Pollack was alive at the wheel. He was feeling the movie. I make him and *Bobby Deerfield* our lead story: An American auteur caught in the romance of European racing, in a flirtation with death. What do you think?" He sucked on the crab leg with relish.

"I think I delivered for you." I smiled, popped an oyster in my mouth, savoring its essence of the sea, and brought the conversation back to my agenda. "What's next for us after Deauville?" I waited for the new job offer. Maybe even a raise.

"As expected, you did a great job, Kate. A pity I don't have anything coming up that suits your talents."

My mind went into freefall, thinking up something he would like. "Patrice, I have a great program for France-Nouvelle. It's French-American and right here in Normandy. I could scout before I return to Paris."

"Oh?" he said, halfway interested.

I leaned in and whispered conspiratorially. "The Yanks were heroes on D-Day, but what about all the French who lived here? After four years of horror, how did they survive that fateful day? You know how good I am at finding subjects—you'll get firsthand, uncensored stories!"

Patrice put down his crab leg. "Did I not tell you I hate war?"

"But that was Vietnam," I protested weakly.

"It's all the same. No American cemetery. No survivors weeping about that bloody landing." His face expressionless, he delivered his final edict. "Forget it." He picked up an oyster, swallowed it, and smiled at me as if we'd never had the conversation.

I savagely split open the last crab leg and smashed the claws. Patrice had to know he couldn't keep me dangling. I was about to lay into him when Jean-Claude made a brief appearance, apologizing for missing lunch, but he had to go back to Paris *toute de suite*.

"I understand," I told him. "We'll talk more next week."

I watched him leave, and then turned to smile broadly at Patrice.

"I must thank you for introducing me to Jean-Claude. I'm meeting with him about a job next week."

"Oh?" He laboriously picked out a periwinkle from its tiny shell, examining it before swallowing the *petit* morsel. "The best part of eating the periwinkle is the sport of extracting it from its shell. But you must have patience."

"Is that all you can say?"

"Patience in all things. If you really need work, I can get you an under-the-table job translating captions in our photo division."

The word "prick" came to mind. But as Patrice would say, why spoil a good meal?

While the crew packed up, I took a last walk on the beach to clear my head. I wasn't sure if I should be anxious or excited. Patrice didn't have a new job for me, but Jean-Claude was in the wings. And then there was Susan.

After our great adventure last night, I'd invited her to stay with me in Paris for a few days. Eat bistro dinners, drink wine, and have all the girl talk we'd been missing. But it turned out I still wasn't on Susan's A-list of friends. Such a shame, she lamented, but she had to meet a producer for drinks at the Beverly Hills Hotel. It was like the first time in Paris—she had a better offer. Some things never changed.

I sat on the sand near the water's edge, mesmerized by the waves rolling onto shore. It was an endless cycle, the old wave creating the foundation of the new, the past always part of the present.

As I walked through empty streets back to the hotel, a fog floated in from the sea. In the dusk, I didn't notice a man rushing past me until he almost knocked my bag off my shoulder.

"Hey!" I shouted, convinced he was trying to steal my purse.

The man turned around in the gathering darkness. "*Pardon, je m'excuse!* You okay?"

"*Oui,*" I said, making sure my bag was intact. As the streetlights turned on and illuminated his face, he hurried off. I stared at his receding figure. The way he walked, the gesture of his hand through his hair, all so familiar.

François? No, I told myself, it couldn't be.

Driving back to Paris with Patrice, the man's phantom image returned to the darkroom of my brain, slowly developing into sharper memories of François. Memories I didn't want to have but that had invaded my mind for years—even more so now that I'd returned to Paris.

Back in my apartment, I sipped wine and had a conversation with myself.

I'd come a long way from that little cubby hole of a maid's room. Here I was, in a beautiful apartment, working in a profession I loved. So why couldn't I move on and forget François? Just as I was finding my voice, building the confidence to go after an independent life in Paris, the past once again had reached out its ugly claw and held me captive. It had been thirteen years, and I was still obsessed with those damn memories.

Yes, I'd been afraid to return to Paris. Afraid I might see François and that I wouldn't like what I found. But dammit, I had to admit I was curious. I did want to know what became of him, to know the truth of him. At this point, the truth had to be less painful than my failing attempts to stuff the heartache away.

I took the phone book down from the bookshelf.

Fingers tingling, I found the list of *François Graniers*, took a deep breath, picked up the phone, and dialed the first number.

As the phone rang, my resolve wavered. What if he answered? What if a woman answered? Or worse, a child? I slammed the phone down. There had to be a way that wouldn't leave me so exposed.

I would write a casual note to his mother's address. It would be forwarded to him. If he didn't answer, I'd at least have taken action. It took me an hour to write three sentences:

Dear François, Hello from the past! I am in Paris and send my regards. You can call me at 45-25-91-30.

Before I could change my mind, I walked to the *bar-tabac* on the corner, bought a stamp, and in homage to the past, a pack of Gitanes cigarettes. I sat down at a table, sipped a *vin rouge*, and smoked a cigarette.

The mailbox was outside the café. It was a powerful feeling when I shoved the letter through the metal slot … until I panicked and immediately wanted to retrieve it. But it was gone.

As I walked back to my apartment, I told myself once again the long-ago shattered dream of love belonged to that naïve young girl. Not me.

chapter nineteen

1964 November 12

The Rolling Stones in Paris!

It was the Stones' very first concert in Paris, and I helped Colin sell New York *Herald Tribunes* for a week to pay for our tickets. I was just as glad François was away on location; I needed space to sort out my dilemma in the *préservatif* department. An evening with the Rolling Stones was exactly what I needed.

While selling newspapers, I'd had to skip a few of my tutoring lessons. But Veronique, who adored the Stones even more than the Beatles, came up with such creative excuses for my absence that Monsieur Charpentier never even questioned me. In exchange, I swore to my willing accomplice that I would share every detail of the concert.

Colin and I arrived at the Olympia Music Hall ready to push through a frenzied line of teenage girls. Instead, we encountered a rowdy group of young men—rock 'n' rollers in black motorcycle jackets who looked like Marlon Brando in *The Wild One*. They called themselves *Les Blousons Noirs*, the black jackets. They were rebels, *le type* Monsieur Charpentier could not abide. I loved them.

Inside the Olympia, known for legendary Edith Piaf and Jacques Brel concerts, the fans were clapping and screaming for Mick and his bad boys. When Jagger finally appeared, he was casually dressed in a tweed jacket and black T-shirt, but he shot out more electricity than all four Beatles in their mod suits.

Mick grew wilder with each song, grabbing the mike stand and playing it like a guitar, shaking his long unruly hair, dancing like no one else I'd ever seen. Mick was a bad boy all right, and he shouted out DEFIANCE! in the face of betrayal. TRIUMPH! over rejection. FREEDOM! from a love gone wrong. I was dancing in front of my seat, his lyrics merging into my own thoughts—I loved François but felt boxed in by his beliefs and his refusal to wear protection. By the time Mick got to "It's All Over Now," it was as if the song had been written for me. If François wouldn't be reasonable, would I have the nerve to say "It's All Over Now"? You're damn right!

By show's end, the black leather guys were so jacked up they rushed the stage trying to get to the fleeing Stones. Colin grabbed my hand and we pushed our way through the theater packed with squirming bodies. One of the guys grabbed me, shouting *"Tu es mignon, vien avec moi,"* Cutie, come with me! I was suddenly dizzy, woozy. My knees were buckling and everything was going black when Colin shoved the guy away, holding me up as I collapsed into his arms. I came to, indignant that I had lost control.

"You fainted. Are you okay?" he asked anxiously.

"I can't breathe. I need fresh air."

Out on the street, the rock 'n' rollers were running down the boulevard des Capucines smashing windows with rocks, bottles— anything they could get their hands on. I should have been scared, but it was strangely thrilling. Adrenaline spiking, we ran past the wailing police sirens, the cops spilling out of their cars, and slipped down a deserted side street, exhilarated by the Stones and our brush with mayhem.

"I was itching to pick up a bottle myself and send it crashing through a window," I confessed to Colin.

"Is this the real Kate?" he said, picking the broken shards of glass off my coat. "A bird who wants to be like Mick and the bad boys? What would your François say?"

"C'mon, Colin. I want love *and* freedom."

"Yes, but your beloved France isn't ready for that. Especially for women, who only got the vote twenty years ago. Catholicism is strong. Abortion is illegal. And what about your beloved François? Love yes, freedom no."

I thought of François, who tried to follow the strict rules of his religion; of Veronique and the other Charpentier children, whose lives were strictly regulated by their parents. I suddenly realized why French parents kept their teenage daughters from the Stones— all the girls would want to escape the boundaries of their lives.

Like me.

The next evening Monsieur Charpentier came to supper with the newspaper once again tucked under his arm. "Here in *Le Monde*," he brandished the headline in front of his children, "'Police Break Up a Riot After a Rolling Stones Concert. 75 Arrested!' These Stones with their long hair and songs of rebellion? They want the false dream of *américain* indep`endence. It is not a dream, it is a nightmare!"

I stared up at him, agreeing with grand indignation. "My father would share your opinion, Monsieur Charpentier. He always said I must not break the rules of society."

After supper, I took my homework to the café L'Horizon across the street. While I nursed a *café noir*, my books unopened, I took out my journal to write my thoughts about the concert.

I stared at the last entry, and my stomach dropped.

More than two weeks ago I'd noted "period due." I was always irregular and assumed it would come in a few days. A week at the most. But two, impossible!

I did the only thing that would make me feel better: I ordered a chocolate éclair. Creamy custard encased in flaky pastry covered with drippy chocolate always cheered me up. I filled my mouth with its rich goodness, but after a few bites, my queasy stomach fought back. One look at the rest of the éclair and I wanted to gag.

I flashed on my fainting spell after the Rolling Stones concert. Coincidence, that's all it was. My period would come. Probably tonight or tomorrow. I paid my bill and returned to No. 149.

Walking past Madame Just's window, I forced a smile as she looked up from her TV.

My queasiness turned into nausea. I felt my insides pushing up. I'd never make the six flights up to my room. I looked around for the dustbin, but Madame Just had already cleaned up. I headed for the *poubelle* in the courtyard, scarcely getting there in time. While I was heaving into it, I heard footsteps approaching.

"Mademoiselle!" Madame Just handed me a towel. "*Êtes-vous malade?*" Are you sick? she asked.

I wiped my face clean of vomit, dabbed at my coat, and smiled weakly. "*Non, non, c'est rien.*" It's nothing, I replied.

"Come with me." Madame Just led me by the arm back to her little room, took her knitting off the table, and sat me down. She carefully placed a porcelain, hand-painted rose teacup in front of me and poured a cup of tea.

"The tea is freshly brewed. You must let it steep for a moment." Her stern eyes bored into my face. "Mademoiselle, I have seen you with a young man. I have seen him come and go late at night."

"He is only a friend," I weakly protested.

"Do not lie to me." She pointed to her eyes, her ears, then to me. "I see, I hear, I know everything that goes on in this building. You are fortunate I am not speaking to Monsieur Charpentier."

"Please don't tell him," I begged. "I'll be fine."

I took a sip of tea. She closed the curtain on the window that looked out into the foyer and sat down at my side.

"We are private now. It will not go beyond this room."

She sat down at my side. "Mademoiselle, either you have eaten a bad oyster, or you have a problem."

I didn't know if I could trust her, but I was desperate to talk to someone. "It's a little problem with my period. That's all."

Madame Just was stern, ready to dispense her justice. "This is a proper building," she said, "and it is my duty to keep it that way. But I also know what happens to women," she continued, "and sometimes men do not understand."

My nausea subsided. "You're right. It's a difficult world for women."

"I know. It happened to me." Her tone softened. "We must do what we must do."

Madame Just rummaged through papers in a drawer. "Where is that name?" she muttered, dumping the disorganized scraps of paper onto the table, fishing out a card. Placing it in front of me, Madame Just spoke slowly to ensure I understood. "I helped a girl in the building keep a secret from her parents. She told me the doctor's name: Marcovici. He is a good doctor."

Madame Just gave me a pen and opened my journal to a blank page.

"Do it," she commanded.

I wrote down the name. "Thank you, Madame Just. But I will not need it."

"Even if ignorant men make bad laws, you cannot allow them to decide your fate. Go to bed. You will feel better tomorrow."

As I stepped through her door and walked up the stairs, she opened the curtain and leaned out the window. "Mademoiselle, we do not speak of this ever again," and she disappeared into her lair.

The following three days, no blood. Nothing. I was consumed with worry. I had to know. I made an appointment with the doctor. But what kind of doctor was Madame Just sending me to?

chapter twenty

1964 November 17

I got off the metro at L'Opera, each step taking me deeper into my nightmare, positive I'd find the doctor in an alley behind perfume shops and fancy cafés. There would be a rusty door with a hand-scrawled sign screaming *Avorteur*, Abortionist!

I was still suspicious when no. 16 Rue Auber turned out to be a well-maintained office building across from the Opera House and American Express. In the marble lobby, a directory listed Dr. Daniel Marcovici, *Gynécologue*, fifth floor. I entered the elevator, certain the other passengers knew where I was going and why. Certain they were nodding to each other in disapproval as I got off at five, walked across the corridor, and opened the door with Dr. Marcovici's name prominently displayed.

Surprise. It was not a small dark room with the soiled, threadbare sofa I had imagined. Instead, pale green velvet couches lined the sunlit room, and delicate floral prints in gilt frames hung on the matching green walls. There was no receptionist, and I sat down across from two well-dressed matrons who silently waited for their appointments.

My mind was racing. Was this a cover? Did Dr. Marcovici masquerade as a respectable doctor, while making money off girls who were in trouble? I shouldn't be there. I got up to leave, but the nurse called my name and I followed her into hell.

Dr. Marcovici sat at his big mahogany desk, the window behind him framing the green opera dome a block away. He was small and wiry; I guessed in his late forties. With his horn-rimmed glasses and white lab coat, at least he didn't look like the devil. Flicking ashes off his Gauloise into an overflowing ashtray, he motioned to a chair in front of the desk.

"*Oui, mademoiselle?*" He waited for my response.

I had to say something non-incriminating, but in a code he'd understand.

"My period isn't regular," I told him. The doctor waited to hear more. I forced the words out. "I want to know if I'm pregnant."

He shook his head, resigned. "When is your period due?"

"I'm almost three weeks late," I said.

He shrugged. "It's probably too soon to tell."

This was not going well. Didn't he realize the urgency of the situation?

"But I must know," I said, afraid to divulge more.

He motioned to the adjoining room. "Go into the examining room and remove your clothes from the waist down. We shall see."

The room was small and bare, almost entirely filled up with an elevated table to which strange metal stirrups were connected. I'd never been to a gynecologist before; I really couldn't imagine how they would work. I took off my skirt and panties, looking in vain for something to cover me. Draping my coat over my knees, I sat on the edge of this torture-chamber device and waited.

After a few minutes, Dr. Marcovici entered. He motioned to me to sit at the end of the table and lay down. Taking my feet, he placed them in the stirrups and spread them apart. I felt exposed and vulnerable as his fingers poked. And then I felt him push what must have been a hard, cold instrument even further up. Paranoid thoughts ran in spurts: He was getting a weird enjoyment from this. He wasn't even a doctor. I wanted to push him out of me, to get up and escape. But I had to know.

An eternity passed until the instrument came out. He stood up and placed it back on top of the cabinet.

"Get dressed and come into my office."

With the comforting formality of a desk and my clothes back on, I calmed down. Dr. Marcovici lit another cigarette and offered one to me. His face remained a mask.

"There is a swelling. It's too soon to be certain, but from what you tell me, it's probable. Congratulations." He smiled at me for the first time.

Why was he saying congratulations? Was this a horrible trick Madame Just played on me? Didn't he know I wouldn't be here if I wanted to be pregnant?

I looked past his eyes, focusing on the opera dome in the window behind him. What could I say that would leave no question of what I wanted?

"I'm not married."

He wasn't giving up. "What about the young man? Do you love him?"

Why was he asking me this? I wasn't going to tell him I was scared, that I loved a boy I shouldn't love, who might not love me.

"Yes, but we cannot get married … not now, anyway." That was easier than saying all I felt was fear. Fear that I hadn't figured out my life, fear that François wouldn't marry me. I grasped at straws. "We are not the same religion. I'm Jewish." That should do it. Now he'd have to be sympathetic.

"So am I. And I married a woman of a different faith. So what?"

Years of listening to parents and friends gossiping about unwed mothers took over any rational thoughts. I'd be branded a pariah. I panicked.

"But it's my life! I need to have a choice, that's all there is to it. Can't you help me?"

I waited for him to order me out of his office, but his face softened, almost as if I were his daughter who had messed up. "Have you told the young man yet?"

"Not yet," I admitted. "I'm afraid of what he'll say."

The doctor sighed and put out his cigarette. "Okay, we will see. I can give you a treatment and pills for a few days. If you are not pregnant, they may start your period."

"What if that doesn't work?"

"It means you are pregnant," he shrugged.

I was on the verge of tears, begging. "But a friend told me about you …"

"France is no different from America. Abortions are illegal." His tone was even. It left no room for doubt. "I can't break the law."

"But she said—"

He stopped me in mid-sentence. "Listen closely. If a girl starts an abortion herself, it is legal to finish it to safeguard her health. Do you understand?"

I left Dr. Marcovici's office, wandering blindly through the crowds on the rue de Le Paix, as if trying to feel my way out of a suffocating closet. Why should François and I be pushed into a life we weren't ready for? If I was pregnant, the logical solution would be to do what it took to get back to normal. I'd have my parents wire the rest of my savings so I could do some "shopping." No one back home need ever know.

And yet. Hadn't I come to Paris to explore new dimensions? I'd learned the French *savoir faire* that makes life worth living. Then there was François's idealistic vision of a *communaté* to investigate. And now, totally unexpected, unplanned, and even unwanted, fate had presented me with another possible direction: François will hug and kiss me and say without hesitation, "I love you. Marry me. We will have a baby."

The fantasy grew and blossomed. François and our adorable *bébé*. A life in France. As Saturday approached, the big night for dinner with his mother, I began to think maybe François was right. If I was pregnant, it was meant to be. He didn't yet know about my fears or my visit to Dr. Marcovici, and I would not say anything that might ruin our evening with Maman. If she liked me, anything was possible.

The little village of Villeneuve-le-Roi was only fifteen miles outside of Paris, but it might as well have been another country. François drove slowly down the main boulevard, excitedly pointing out the landmarks of his childhood. The small church where he was a choir boy. The Hotel de Ville, the city hall which seemed the grandest building on earth. He turned down a quiet street with identical gray stone houses lined up next to each other, and drove until we reached the railroad tracks, where a few small stores clustered next to the train station.

"My mother's store," François said, proudly pointing to a tiny shop next to the *boulangerie.* In the window, a mannequin draped in bolts of fabric stared at me with unknowing eyes. Across the street, he parked in front of a boxy two-story stone house that stood alone on a small knoll. "*Bienvenue chez nous.* My mother was born here; her mother before that."

I grabbed my candy and flowers and followed him up the steps, with fleeting thoughts of future visits holding a *bébé.* The door opened, and welcoming us was a woman with delicate features, smooth skin, and silver-gray hair drawn into a bun. She was dressed in a well-fitting, simple black dress, with the excellent posture of the model she had once been.

"Maman, *je te presente* Kate." I gave Madame Granier flowers and chocolates. "*Je suis très content de faire votre connaissance*," I said, hoping I'd remembered the correct way to say "I'm pleased to meet you."

She kissed me on both cheeks, then looked at her son, laughing. "Mademoiselle Kate knows how much you like chocolates, *n'est-ce pas?*"

"But they are for you, Madame," I insisted, as François took the box, opened it, and popped one in his mouth.

Madame Granier led us into the living room filled with dark, heavy furniture from another époque, the walls lined with cabinets and curio displays.

"Sit down. The chicken is roasting, and dinner will be soon."

"Please, Maman, I want to prepare the mayonnaise," François announced, and led me into the tiny kitchen, built in a century when a single sink, a two-burner stove, and a small chopping block were all that was needed to make a three-course dinner.

"Make mayonnaise?" I questioned. "Doesn't it come in a jar?"

"Sit down," he pulled out a kitchen chair. "No jar, only nature's miracle of creation."

Françoise expertly broke two eggs, separating out the yolks into a small mixing bowl, added a dash of vinegar, and a bit of what he explained was dried mustard. Then he slowly drizzled oil in the bowl, drop by drop.

"You see how important it is to keep *le courant* going at an even flow?"

I watched breathlessly as the oil merged with the eggs, and magic! Mayonnaise was born. He gave me a taste, and my tongue swirled around a thick, creamy, intensely flavored richness. This was not white stuff from a Best Foods jar. This was the miracle of creation.

It was an everyday family meal, but each flavor was distinct, each food just as it was supposed to taste. The roast chicken, flavorful and juicy. ("Make sure the butcher has one with *pate noirs*, black feet," counseled Madame Granier.) The potatoes, oven-roasted with the chicken, a touch of mayonnaise making them creamy and crunchy at the same time. The *salade*, dressed with simple vinaigrette, served after the main course. The camembert cheese, proclaimed ripe as François pressed his thumb into the middle of the round. Dessert was a pear, which we carefully peeled and ate with a fork and knife.

Around the dinner table, François's mother and I grew comfortable with each other. Madame practiced her English, confessing she had not spoken the language since she was a schoolgirl. She was interested in my family, and I compared my father's stationery store to her sewing shop. I did not say she might have something else in common with my father: Both would be horrified if I was pregnant.

After dinner, she took us back into the overstuffed living room and turned on the television. We watched a French variety show with singers, jugglers, a ventriloquist, and a comedy sketch I didn't understand, but laughed anyway. If the French excelled at *le cuisine*, they had a ways to go when it came to *le télévision*.

When the evening was over, it was with genuine emotion that Maman and I hugged and said, "*À bientôt*, see you soon."

The rain started on our drive back to Paris, the methodical thumping of windshield wipers punctuating our conversation.

"My mother liked you very much," François said, happily beating out his own rhythm on the steering wheel. "She approves!"

"I'm glad, François. I liked her too."

"Her English is not bad, yes?"

Meeting his mother had taken my mind off my condition, but now the anxiety came flooding back. If I was pregnant, it might be worse telling Maman than my own parents. But she liked me! And if we got married … ? This was the time to tell him.

"François, do you know what the English word 'period' means?"

"For the woman? Of course."

"I haven't gotten mine."

He continued driving, placing his hand on mine, but kept his eyes on the road.

"I'm late, François," I repeated.

"Perhaps it's because you are excited, worried," he said.

I searched his face for more of a reaction. Nothing.

"I went to a doctor. He thinks it's possible I am pregnant."

"But not for sure? Don't worry, it will come." He squeezed my hand.

"But if it doesn't?"

I waited for him to reassure me. But he kept his eyes on the road, his face turning to stone. I had to break the silence.

"What should we do?" I pressed. Again, nothing.

The rain was growing heavier; in the distance, a clap of thunder. He pulled over to the side of the road and turned off the motor. I could hear my own heart pounding and the rain flooding the windshield. There was only him and me. I saw the tiniest of tremors around his mouth, as he fought not to show any emotion.

"What do you think, Kate?"

I didn't want him to say that. I wanted him to tell me he loved me, and we were in this together. But he needed to say it on his own. Not because of any guilt.

I forced myself to say it aloud. "If I'm pregnant, should I get an abortion?"

And I waited for François to tell me not to.

He stared out the car window. A flash of lightning illuminated the anguish on his face. Finally, he spoke.

"To have a baby now, maybe it's not a good idea."

I hadn't heard right. How could he be saying this?

"Even though you're a devout Catholic?"

He continued to stare out the window; his eyes guarded, opaque, his hands gripping the steering wheel. Battling with the rules of his faith against his own emotions. He said the next words quietly, evenly.

"Can the doctor help you take care of it?"

The words cut like a knife. He'd given me my answer.

PART THREE

*"There is but one Paris …
however hard living may be here, and
if it becomes worse and harder even—
the French air clears up the brain
and does one good—a world of good."*

—Vincent Van Gogh

<h1 style="text-align:center">chapter twenty-one</h1>

1977 September 14
Paris

I really didn't need another reminder of François. But here on rue Marbeuf, thirteen years ago, was where Colin had taken me to the Army PX to get condoms. What were the odds that Jean-Claude's Élysée Films would be two doors down from where I bought those damn Trojans?

I said a silent prayer of thanks for the enlightened '70s; especially for the six months' supply of birth control pills I'd brought with me. I'd taken charge of my own life, and I was glad François hadn't responded to the "casual" note I'd sent him. His lack of a reply had given me my answer. There was nothing left to mourn. Besides, I had a much more interesting prospect, the very reason I was on rue Marbeuf: my five o'clock meeting with Jean-Claude Renaud.

In Deauville, I'd made it clear to Jean-Claude that I was looking for a job. Period. I was determined to keep our meeting focused on work, to dazzle him with my professional expertise. I knew budgets, scheduling, legal clearances, who to contact and what to say. I'd even researched his production slate and had casting suggestions. He'd be so impressed he'd hire me on the spot.

As I rode up to the fourth floor, I checked my appearance in the mirrored elevator. I was selling Artsy French/Glitzy Hollywood and had dressed accordingly. Black leather boots covered my tight jeans almost to the knees. My burgundy corduroy blazer was stylish but professional. For the latest Parisian look, I'd draped a knock-off Hermes scarf around my neck, and topped my long curly hair with a newsboy cap. I examined my French makeup. Minimalist. Barely enough that the blush looked real and my blue eyes sparkled.

I was ready.

Elysée Films looked like any TV production office in Hollywood: leather couches, coffee tables stacked with trade magazines, framed posters of recent productions. It might be Paris, but it was still an office, I told myself. Nothing to worry about.

The receptionist took my name; I sat down and flipped through an old weekly *Variety*. I was soon directed to Renaud's office. Jean-Claude sat behind his desk, listening to someone on the phone. When he motioned me forward, he seemed surprised. He covered the phone with his hand.

"Who are you again?" he whispered.

In a flash, I knew this was now our little game—pretending not to recognize me. Okay, Jean-Claude, *les jeux sont fait*. I rolled the dice.

"Who would you like me to be?" I asked. "Gambling partner? Hollywood producer?" I gave him a smile that promised nothing. "How about your American liaison?"

"Sit down where I can see you," he commanded, then ignored me as he returned to his call. In rapid-fire French, he maneuvered his way through release dates, publicity, and plastering *les affiches* all over Paris. After five minutes, he hung up and looked at me as if I were the only object in the universe.

"One thing for sure about you," he said, "you're a gambler." He shuffled a few papers on the desk, found a casino gambling chip, and tossed it at me. "The chip you gave me at Deauville."

I caught it and tossed the chip back on his desk. "You invested in me; a deal is a deal. It was a profitable evening, and I'm glad you want to discuss another business opportunity. Strictly business." I smiled again, ready for the next move.

"Everything in life is profitable for me. Even if it's not business." He returned my smile, flipped the chip, and watched it land.

"Tails," he announced. "My favorite."

I ignored the comment. "As a businessman, you know what a wise move it is to have an American liaison for your TV remakes, someone who networks in both countries."

He watched me for a long moment. Leaned back in his chair, thinking. Looked at his watch. "Tell me, Kate, can you act?"

"I'm not here to act," I said, determined to keep the focus on business. "I'm here to talk about enhancing your TV presence where it counts. I know the VPs of development at all three American networks, and I'm also working with the publisher of the *Hollywood Reporter*. Bottom line, they answer my phone calls. You know how important that is." Not a lie. I'd say I was calling from Paris.

He held up his hand. "If you want a job, then *I* do the interview, ask the questions. *N'est-ce pas?* I ask once more, can you act?"

Aha! A new game. I took a breath and played my move.

"Shakespeare said it all," I announced. "'All the world's a stage; the men and women merely players.' What do you have in mind?"

"I have an appointment with an apartment manager to look at a rental, and I'm late. Let's have some fun. Make a movie."

"Do you have a script?" I asked, ever the producer.

"We are in love. We are getting the apartment for our secret love nest. We have stopped by quickly because we are meeting Georges and Marthe at Castel's for dinner. That's the setup, but I want you to improvise, show me your creativity." He led me out of the office. "Can you do it?"

"What about your wife?" I cautioned. "If you take the apartment, it could be a problem."

"No problem. I am separating from my wife. That's why I need an apartment."

Uh-oh. I could almost read his mind. He was planning a new game: "Get the Girl into the Bedroom." But I could handle it. The apartment manager would be there. I smiled and blew him a kiss. "Of course, Jean-Claude, *mon amour*."

The apartment building was only a few blocks away on avenue George V. As Jean-Claude pulled his Porsche up to the canopied entrance, the doorman and car valet snapped to attention, and a third man in a black suit materialized to lead us into the building.

"Henri Treves, property manager," he said, introducing himself. "We are delighted to show you our penthouse, Monsieur Renaud."

"Yes, and this is *mon amie*," Jean-Claude said. He put his arm around me. "We insist on strict privacy."

"*Absolument*," I added, shaking Treves's hand with a devilish smile.

Treves led us past the doorman and to the elevator, whisking us up to the fifth floor. There were two doors. "Maintenance access," he said, dismissing the first one, and unlocked the carved mahogany paneled door.

"*Voilà*," Treves announced with a flourish. We walked into a foyer, its walls covered in gold satin damask, past an antique round table with carved claw feet and topped with a huge bouquet of fresh flowers. Treves stopped in the living room overlooking avenue George V and waved his hand in a grand gesture.

"Entirely furnished," he said. "Everything from bed linens to kitchen utensils to fresh flowers. Mademoiselle will be very happy."

"Of course, if there is good maid service," I warned Monsieur Treves.

Jean-Claude took my arm and we stepped out onto the balcony. You could see the Arc de Triomphe in one direction, and in the other, *le Tour Eiffel*.

"What do you think, *mon amour*?" He drew me close, blocking the manager's view, and bent over for a kiss.

I placed my fingers on his mouth. "I do great sound effects," I whispered, making a loud smooching noise on the back of my hand before stepping away, smiling in full view of the manager. Then, more loudly, "Oh, Jean-Claude, the view from the balcony is so romantic!" As I took his arm, he shook his head in admiration.

"What about the *salle à manger*?" Smiling sweetly, I led him back through the door into the small but formal dining room. "We'll be having dinner parties," I explained to Treves as I walked around the table, pacing off its size.

"*Oui, ma chérie*," Jean-Claude affirmed. "But we'll have our big parties at Maxim's. This room will be very *intime*, for our favorite people."

"*Oui*, like Georges and Marthe, and of course your mother," I said. "She'll love the view."

"So far, I am interested," Jean-Claude told Treves. "But what about the most important room, the bedroom?"

"Yes, the bed must be firm. He has a fragile back," I explained to Treves.

"If you'll excuse us," Jean-Claude said. The manager looked at us approvingly as my lover led me down the hall into the master bedroom.

With its own balcony overlooking the avenue, the room was dominated by a king-sized bed covered in a purple fluffy duvet.

Satin pillows leaned up against a thickly padded toile headboard. A velvet chaise lounge was placed to view the leafy chestnut trees lining the avenue below. Jean-Claude playfully flopped down on the bed, pulling me down next to him.

"*Mon amour*, do you think the bed is big enough for three?" he said, loudly enough for Treves to hear.

"The cozier the better, *n'est-ce pas*? We'll take turns with Georges and Marthe," I answered for Treves' benefit. Then I whispered to Jean-Claude, "And now for a little improv."

I began to moan. "*Oooh, aah*, oh Jean-Claude, aah, that's so good." More heavy panting, then I breathlessly added, "I can't wait, *mon amour*. Let's take the apartment right now!"

"An Academy Award performance," Jean-Claude whispered before getting off the bed and walking down the long mirror-lined corridor into the marble bathroom.

I had to admit I was having fun. Yes, Jean-Claude Renaud could be cocky and more than a little full of himself. Yet in his brashness, he was more playful than aggressive. If my intent was a job, I could bring him back to business after the game.

I followed Jean-Claude into the bathroom. He was sitting on the side of a Jacuzzi tub big enough for at least two people. There were mirrors covering every wall. *Mon Dieu*, I realized, one's body would be on view from every angle. Taking the bottle of bubble bath from the tub's edge, I turned on the water, poured in the contents, and watched as the bubbles burst forth.

"I think this will do beautifully," I said, scooping up bubbles and blowing them into his face. Jean-Claude laughed as he splashed bubbles back at me. The manager must have heard the water gushing forth and ventured into the bathroom. Jean-Claude thanked him for his discretion, and announced the apartment was to our satisfaction. He'd take it.

In the growing darkness, the Porsche swept smoothly down the Champs.

"We must celebrate our 'movie without film,'" Jean-Claude said, "and my new apartment. I propose a drink."

"I accept, but be prepared to pay residuals."

We drove through Place de la Concorde, crossing the Seine while Jean-Claude enthused about the apartment. I told myself to be patient. We'd get to a job offer over drinks. It was all going to work out. We were on the Left Bank, driving down boulevard St. Germain, when he turned up rue Princess, a narrow street lined with nondescript old buildings.

"*Tu connais Chez Castel*, you have been there?"

"Yes, of course," I lied.

Chez Castel was the most exclusive private club in Paris. *Très branché*, very "in." Admittance required more than mere money. You had to be "known," and Jean-Claude was known. When he stopped the Porsche next to a paneled red door identified only by the number 15, the valet took our car, a chic woman opened the red door, and we were ushered into the inner sanctum.

"*Bonsoir*, Monsieur Renaud," she said. "My favorite guest."

"Hugette, *charmant* as always," he said, kissing her on both cheeks. We ascended a lacquered gold staircase to a jewel box of a dining room: Red-flocked damask walls, tables covered in fine white linen napery and crystal stemware, waiters in tuxedos hovering over dinner guests. I had stepped into a scene from Vincente Minnelli's *Gigi*—and I happily slipped into character.

The maître d' stood at attention. "*Bonsoir*, Monsieur Renaud. Your regular table?"

"*S'il vous plait*, Michel."

Michel escorted us to a soft white leather semi-circle of a booth, enfolding us into a cozy personal space.

"A bottle of Dom Pérignon from my stock, Michel."

Michel nodded and disappeared. Two minutes later, he was back with a serving cart bearing the champagne bottle in a silver ice bucket and a selection of *amuse gueules*, tasty tidbits to "amuse our mouths." Michel poured the champagne as Jean-Claude ate a pastry shell stuffed with foie gras.

"Yes, your tongue will be delighted," he said and picked up his glass.

"Mmm," I nodded, unable to speak as a mound of black caviar burst inside my mouth with a buttery, briny flavor.

"To my gifted actress," he toasted. "Apartment hunting is boring. You made it amusing."

As we took a sip, I subtly guided the conversation toward my business agenda.

"And you, Jean-Claude, are a natural. Tell me, do you find acting an asset as a producer?"

"I have acted since I was six years old," he said, "when little Joshua Cohen became Jean-Claude Renaud, and Paris was my stage."

He paused dramatically for my surprised reaction, which I gave as soon as I'd swallowed a mouthful of foie gras.

"Joshua Cohen?" He'd gone so far off script, I had to follow through. "What happened?"

"I don't usually talk about it, but you, Mademoiselle Kate, make documentaries. Perhaps you will be interested."

He poured more champagne. "What happened? Hitler happened. I was born in Germany, but when the Nazis took over, my Jewish parents could see the future. They escaped to Paris, but it turned out Paris wasn't friendly to Jews either."

He took a sip of champagne, savoring the taste. "Maman didn't trust the French, but she loved Paris, and had a flair for theatrics. She gave me a stage name and taught me to playact. My first big role was as a Catholic schoolboy." He laughed, remembering. "Confession was the best. The priest must have been quite entertained.

"When you're six years old," he continued, "pretending is a game. I was Jean-Claude. I was also something called a Jew, but it had no meaning for me, except I couldn't talk about it. Or reveal the one proof of my Jewishness." He winked.

I smiled knowingly. "I can't compare what you went through, what you had to risk; but I know what it was like to grow up Jewish in America, and yes, life was easier if I didn't announce my religion. When I learned to 'pass,' as we called it, it was amazing how people treated me differently."

He clinked my glass once more. "Then you'll understand. By the time the war came, I knew if I wanted to survive, I had to hide my religion."

For him, the Nazis weren't an abstract evil from history, but real monsters that killed Jews named Joshua Cohen. There but for the Grace of God, the mantra of the American Jew, leapt into my mind. "How scary it must have been when the Nazis invaded."

"After France was defeated, my parents wanted me to leave Paris, but I wouldn't go without them. By '42, it was getting bad. A neighbor told the SS about my family, and we were ordered to report the next day to the Vélodrome d'Hiver. My parents made me leave Paris that night. They couldn't go with me; they knew their accents would give them away. But my French was flawless, and my school registration paper listed my name as Jean-Claude Renaud, Catholic. I escaped to the south of France where the Nazis had set up a puppet French government, and I joined the resistance. I was seventeen, I didn't know about guns, but I did know how to playact. I became a courier, disguising myself as a bank clerk, a janitor, a shopkeeper. I played all the roles for almost two years."

"You were never caught?"

"Ah, when you're young, you think you're invincible. On my last trip, I traveled to Avignon dressed as a priest. At the city walls, I blessed the security policeman for allowing me to bring my bibles to the faithful. Of course, he wanted one. Underneath the bibles were the guns and the false documents. My reward for good acting was the city jail."

The lavish restaurant, the champagne and hors d'oeuvres, had faded away. There was only Jean-Claude and his story.

"What happened?" I asked breathlessly.

"I wrote Christian poems for the warden, so he'd have no reason to question my religion. Then toward the end of the war, the Nazis came through, cleaning out the jails. I was about to be taken to a labor camp when the Americans arrived, and we were liberated." He shrugged as if it were nothing, as if he had not escaped a close brush with death.

"And you found your parents after the war?"

"They had been shipped off to Auschwitz. It was the end for them."

He took a long swallow of champagne, as if he could wash away the tragedy of their deaths.

"I'm sorry, Jean-Claude." And I was. He was either a very good storyteller or one hell of an interesting man. Probably both. "You should have become an actor after the war. On-the-job training, as we say."

"I did for a while, but it was the producer who held the power, who made the decisions," Jean-Claude said. "The business side seduced me. Now *I* control the script."

"As we did tonight at the apartment?"

"That was a game, not business."

I took the plunge. "You're a smart man, Jean-Claude. A survivor. If your films are as creative as you are, you are the kind of producer I would like to work with."

I took a sip of champagne to fortify myself. "I'm looking for the right situation, a 'good fit' as we say in the States. Why not the American liaison for your co-productions? I've already produced programs in both America and France for Antenne 2. I arranged the entire Deauville shoot."

He took a long look at me. I waited, stuck out on that proverbial limb.

"Kate, I am impressed with what you tell me. You are intelligent and *charmant*. Patrice was fortunate to have hired you."

I waited for him to say he had a position begging for a person with my skills.

"But negotiations with the American networks are in a delicate balance; my reps cannot be replaced."

My stomach sank. "But you said in Deauville you might have something for me."

"Here in Paris? Perhaps you know documentaries, but not the kind of movies I produce."

I wouldn't give up. "Producing is the same process whether it's a doc or a feature."

"You would be happy with a low-level job? I regret that even for a production assistant, your French is good but not good enough."

He was brutally honest. No playacting; no room for negotiation. I'd struck out again. First with Patrice and now with Jean-Claude. I mustered my remaining strength. I would not let him see me in tears. I gathered up my purse and jacket. Cool. Calm. Collected.

"Then there is nothing more for us to talk about. *Bonsoir*."

He put his hand on my arm. "Wait."

He refilled my champagne glass; handed me a cracker liberally spread with caviar.

"Since that night on Mulholland, I saw something in you waiting to be explored, ready to blossom. It is captivating."

My calm exterior collapsed, as disgust came roaring in. "I knew it! You set up this meeting so you could offer again to make me a baby. You are *dégueulasse*, disgusting."

"*Calme-toi*. I apologize about that night. I was how you say—off my game?"

"I'll say," I agreed, putting on my jacket. I'd had enough.

"Kate, one favor, please. You like stories. Please listen. Then leave if you want."

Barely containing myself, I kept my purse on my lap, ready to make a getaway.

"There is an actress I often hire. Wonderful to work with: she's a true professional, never *égotiste*. But, she is not as successful in her personal life. Three marriages; all catastrophes. But she wanted a child. We had become friendly, and she asked me to do her the favor—"

"Okay, Jean-Claude, that's heartwarming," I cut in, "but nothing to do with me."

"*Au contraire.* That night on Mulholland—your intelligence, your no-nonsense attitude, your age—it all reminded me of Isabelle. I thought, it worked quite well for her … why not again?"

The memories of that night flooded back. Deep in my mind, my biological clock had fleetingly considered his offer. But I'd never tell him.

"No excuses," I challenged him. "You only wanted sex."

"Yes, but never say 'only' sex, *ma chèrie*. Sex is an art, an adventure, one of the great pleasures of life. And that night I saw in you a most worthy partner. Oh, the games we could play, that is, if you are willing?" With a gentleman's flourish, he took my hand and kissed it. "This is my honest invitation to you. Will you accept?"

Unbelievable, this courtly proposal for *sexe sportif*. As if he were wooing Madame Pompadour. I couldn't help it. I burst out laughing. "At least you're creative in your approach."

He grinned. "That's why you excite me. You see the humor—and you're not afraid to take a bet. Believe me, it does not interest me to have sex one night and then I'm bored. Kate, I am talking about sex that engages the mind as well as the body. The best kind."

He put his hand under the tablecloth, holding my hand still

clutching my purse, and locked his eyes into mine. His manner and style, his intellect, his body still in good shape, even his big nose, suddenly came together into one charismatic package.

"You are beautiful, but you can be more," he said, as he lightly stroked my hand. Without thinking, I responded to his touch, and our fingers played under the table.

This wasn't love, so why did I feel so alive?

He dipped a finger into his champagne glass and gently touched my lips with the wet finger. Without realizing what I was doing, I opened my mouth, wanting to lick it. He smiled, handed me my champagne, and regarded me seriously. "Kate, yes, let's play games, let us enjoy the sport of sex. We'll see where it leads. What do you say?"

I took a gulp of champagne and tried to absorb the meaning of it all. I'd been hell-bent on rejecting him. How could I be considering this?

Jean-Claude noted my confused look, and turning his attention to the menu, gave me a reprieve. "Take your time. It is up to you, of course. But you should know I am a man of many appetites—let's order dinner!"

While he read the menu, I pondered the pros and cons. I wasn't in love with Jean-Claude, but I couldn't deny my attraction to him. It had been fun matching wits and improvising with him. And the honest-to-God truth was that I'd enjoyed his flirtations, his ability to arouse me.

Was I shameful? Immoral? Thinking of sex as only a sport? So be it.

I recalled my night in Paris with Armand. The handsome, sexy Armand. I'd followed my own inner self and let go of those old rules I'd been taught. That enchanting experience had begun to break down the wall I built so long ago. That wall had protected me from the hurt of the past, but as Auntie Mame would have reminded me, it also shut me off from the banquet of life.

Jean-Claude presented me with a tempting appetizer; perhaps his proposal would continue my liberation. If nothing else, unlike with Armand, I would never be bored. Jean-Claude had made it clear I had no hope of a job. So much the better. I'd be an equal player.

I dismissed the cons and was left with my bottom line: *Sexe sportif.* A new world to explore.

Besides, he was Jewish. I looked over his shoulder at the menu. "What's for dinner?"

chapter twenty-two

1977 The following night

Jean-Claude had demonstrated his impeccable taste in ordering dinner, and by the time we were swooning over the delectable petit fours, I'd agreed to help him "inaugurate" his new apartment the next night. He had a business dinner meeting first, so I was to arrive at 11:00 p.m.

"Almost my bedtime," I'd protested.

"Even better," he'd replied. Facing this new twist in my life, my pre-*sexe sportif* jitters were running rampant. By 9:30 p.m., I'd changed my outfit three times. What was the dress code for this game—pants, skirt, dressy, informal? Then again, if one is quickly disrobed, why should it matter? I settled on a gypsy-style long skirt that Annette claimed was *très à la mode*. Fifteen minutes later, as I was debating whether I should wear a bra under my tank top, I knew it was time to get out of my apartment.

The evening was mild and breezy, and I decided to walk to Jean-Claude's apartment, following avenue President Kennedy along the Seine. At Trocadero, I looked wistfully at the young people strolling arm in arm against the backdrop of the Eiffel Tower. How romantic; how different from what I was about to do. Second thoughts flooded my brain. It wasn't too late; I could be true to my principles, blow him off and wait for Mr. Right. Then came a stunning moment of insight: Fuck that. In s*exe sportif*, there wasn't the inevitable agony of rejection, disappointment, or broken heart.

I began plotting my moves.

#1. Keep him waiting. I turned up Avenue George V, lingering at each boutique window. He'd be getting anxious, wondering if I was going to stand him up. At 11:20 p.m., I entered the elevator of Jean-Claude's new apartment and was swept up to my fifth-floor destiny.

His door was ajar. I tapped lightly and walked in. Jean-Claude was on the balcony in shirtsleeves, tie loosened, looking out over Paris. Master of all he surveyed. He walked toward a table set with a bottle of J&B, two glasses, an ice bucket, and a portable cassette player. He hit the play button and the mellow sounds of Dexter Gordon's saxophone filled the air.

"Whisky?" he asked.

#2. Be cool. "On the rocks," I answered, hoping I sounded like Lauren Bacall with Bogie. I watched as he tossed ice cubes into the glasses and poured, handing me one. He brushed a stray curl off my forehead, looking at me as if he were about to paint my portrait.

"Yes, much better. *Très jolie. Salut!*"

I took a long swallow. The scotch was strong and smooth, its warmth sliding down my throat and into the rest of my body.

#3. Uh-oh, I had no #3. Time to go with the flow. He took my hand and led me inside to the couch. "What are the stakes?" I asked, sitting down. "If it's a game, shouldn't we bet?"

He pondered. "We'll start slow. The stakes will increase. The goal in this game is to give—and get—the most pleasure. Is that not a competition *formidable*?"

I pondered back. "As long as I'm not playing with the Marquis de Sade."

I caught a glimpse of disgust. "It's true, Kate. I have colleagues who boast of their conquests. That is no fun. You and I, we can do better than that. Here's my first bet," and he kissed my hand.

I took another long swallow of scotch and upped the stakes with a two-cheek kiss. "I'm new at this," I admitted. "You choose the game."

Jean-Claude stroked his chin. "You called me your teacher when we were at the casino. Why not call this game The Professor and the Student?" He stood in front of me. "Yes, we start on our feet."

I stood up. He took off my blazer and pulled my tank top over my head, revealing my braless breasts. He nodded in approval, but did not touch.

"Turn away from me," he instructed, directing me. I couldn't see him, but there was something strangely exciting about this. The anticipation increased along with my heartbeat, wondering what he would do next.

The answer came as he reached under my skirt, and slowly slid my panties down.

"Don't move," he whispered in my ear. I was already wet, as my body responded to his instruction. But my mind? Well, my mind was on the ceiling, looking down as if I were watching a movie, alert to the action, curious. Where was he going next?

The tip of Jean-Claude's finger teased its way up my inner thigh and found its way inside me, searching deeper. I was disappointed when he withdrew, but the yearning for more was exciting. Jean-Claude turned me around, facing him.

"An excellent student," he beamed in approval. "Kneel down and take a look. See what you've done. It may be time for you to teach me. What say you, Professor Kate?"

For a moment, my body froze. He had given me no guidelines for this new character. Was I a nurturing or naughty professor? Should I act like a street walker at Place Pigalle, or pretend I was Madame de Pompadour having her way with King Louis XV?

Then the most surprising thing happened.

My out-of-body mind floated back inside me and a united Kate took charge. I knelt down and took a good look.

"Poor guy, I think he needs air," I said, unzipping his pants, taking out his growing erection. In my hand, it took on a life of its own. There was no hesitation, no soul searching, no emotional pull, no neediness for love. It wasn't like with my beautiful stranger Armand and our briefly romantic, sensual connection. Instead, Jean-Claude and I read each other's movements, focusing on the fun of the game, fulfilling the craving sensations of lust. I was having a helluva time as I instructed him to lie down on the couch as I got on top.

"Now, Professor," my student said, grinning up at me. "What is my next lesson? Are you going to teach me how you like to be fucked?"

Until Jean-Claude, I had made love. Had sex. Slept with someone. Screwed around. Gone all the way. Done it.

But I had never fucked.

It was time.

I drew him into me.

At three o'clock in the morning, I slipped out of the big purple bed, drew on Jean-Claude's warm robe and walked out to the balcony. I dug into my purse and found the pack of cigarettes and matches I'd bought when I sent my letter to François. As far as I was concerned, he was now from another world; another time. I was glad to be here and now, in control of my own body.

I pulled a cigarette from the pack and started to light it, but a gust of wind blew out the match. "Oh fuck," I said to myself, and laughed out loud at all the "fucks" I'd said in my life. *Fuck it. Don't fuck with me. Where the fuck is it? How the fuck would I know, fuckface?*

I'd said it when I was mad, upset, angry. But none of it had been about fucking. I was going to have to reassess the word. I looked out over the rooftops of Paris and smiled. Now I was fucking Paris. Well, Jean-Claude, anyway.

Yes, fucking could be a beautiful thing.

chapter twenty-three

1977 September 16

"You know how to give a good workout," I murmured as Jean-Claude kissed me awake at eight o'clock in the morning. I squinted up at him. He was showered, dressed, and ready to leave.

"You went beyond my instructions," he said. "Its's the sign of an innate talent, building on what you are given. A-plus."

"My teammate rose to the occasion," I answered, only realizing my unintended pun when Jean-Claude took my hand and placed it where I could feel a bit of action.

"We'll schedule a rematch when I return from Zurich."

I was instantly awake. "Zurich? What's in Zurich?"

"Bank loans." He put his hand under the covers and lightly caressed my breasts. "Investment deals." The hand moved down slowly, lightly tracing my skin until it reached my inner thighs, and found its way inside my growing wetness. "Equity partners."

Who knew business talk could be erotic? I pulled the sheet down. "How about a short co-production right now?" I asked.

He blew me a kiss. "Soon. But relax, stay as long as you like. I insist!"

And with that *Monsieur le Producteur* was out the door.

I had the apartment to myself, but first things first. I filled the Jacuzzi tub with water, poured in half a bottle of *bain moussant*, and watched the jets create bubble magic. For an hour I lay in the warm bath, turning the jets on and off, contemplating my existence and where to go from here.

I reran the film festival in my head: Gregory Peck and Vincente Minnelli inspiring me to act out my fantasies. Working my game with Susan. Snagging the Alpine Renault for Pollack. Playing Bond Girl with Jean-Claude at the casino. All in service of my goal to stay in Paris.

At first, it was blind instinct, this need to stay in Paris. But as the weeks passed—as I lived my life—the reason to stay had turned laser clear. *Oui*, Paris was beautiful, the cuisine divine, the lifestyle so civilized. A superb way to live. But what was most important in Paris was the freedom to be myself. In America, as a 35-year-old woman I was considered on the cusp of middle age, past my prime. In Paris, however, experience and a mature beauty were valued, and I sensed a growing confidence in myself and in my work. I wasn't judged or ignored. Here, I believed in myself.

The only thing missing was Lucy. If I got more work, I'd send for the pooch. But so far, I was still teetering on the brink of success. Patrice recognized my expertise but hadn't committed to another project. Jean-Claude, my Plan B, hadn't offered a job. Yet. So now what?

I scooped up a handful of remaining bubbles and blew them to smithereens. Strangely enough, bursting bubbles always made me think of Dr. Teller and his physics class at Berkeley.

Edward Teller, the so-called father of the H Bomb, the man who was the inspiration for *Dr. Strangelove*, had walked up and down our packed lecture hall with a bucket of water and a bubble-making wand. Wiggling his giant bushy eyebrows, he dipped his wand into a pail of water, waved it energetically in the air, and created bubbles that immediately burst. Then, with a magician's flourish, he added soap to the water and made more bubbles. This time, the bubbles floated above our heads! Why? The soap softened the air's natural tension and helped the bubbles last longer. Conclusion: Too much tension makes bubbles burst.

And thus I devised my Bubble Bath Principle of Life, or BBPL: Each romantic prospect or job opportunity equaled a new bubble in the bathtub of my life. Case in point: According to the BBPL, my long-ago love bubble with François had been too intense. I'd been too serious. No wonder it burst.

It was time to create a new bubble: my extracurricular activity with Jean-Claude. To keep that bubble afloat, I'd stay cool and avoid tension, especially in the throes of passion. If I stayed calm I could follow my own instincts, my own desires.

Only as I was blissfully drying off did it hit me: I hadn't checked in with Patrice since we returned from Deauville.

Jean-Claude thoughtfully left coffee in the pot and a croissant on the kitchen table. I poured a cup, took a bite of the flaky pastry, and called the office. Patrice came quickly on the line.

"Kate, I've been calling you. Where have you been?"

"I stepped out for a minute to get breakfast."

"The last of the dailies are here. They're all logged and synced up. I assume you'd like to see the footage?"

"Of course! What time?"

"Eleven o'clock. Sharp."

I looked at my watch: 10:15 a.m. No time to waste. I slipped on my wrinkled gypsy skirt and imagined Patrice's sly smile if I walked in wearing it. A quick search of the apartment yielded no iron. Did every Frenchman send his clothes to the dry cleaners? No time to go back to my apartment and change. It was a twenty-minute walk to France-Nouvelle via the Champs Elysée. A Monoprix was en route on the corner of rue La Boetie and the Champs. I walked out of the store wearing a new pair of jeans, my rumpled skirt stuffed in a bag, and entered the office at 10:58 a.m.

Patrice was slouched in the one comfortable leather chair in front of the Steenbeck, the glow of the editing screen lighting his face as he stared at Sydney Pollack driving the Alpine Renault. I pulled up a stool and sat down, yellow pad and pen ready.

He barely acknowledged me. "*Génial!* I was right to do it this way," he said. "Pollack racing the car, living his movie, turning a dream into reality. It's not Chinatown. It's Hollywood."

"*Chinatown* was Roman Polanski, but it's an interesting mix of metaphors," I said, stuffing down the fact that it was I who had made it all happen. I stayed calm, even smiled. "You're a genius, Patrice. I always knew it."

"I wouldn't say that." He turned to me for a fleeting second. "You can, however." Then he laughed, acknowledging my work. "Good job, Kate. Thanks for making me look good."

"My pleasure." Maybe I could squeeze one more paycheck out of him before editing started and I was no longer needed.

We spent the next two hours choosing the scenes Patrice wanted to start editing. We'd gotten the gold I promised. From François Truffaut to Playboy bunnies, we had high art and low comedy. I felt again the thrill of shaping *cinema verité* into a compelling story. It wasn't simply a job; it was what I was meant to do. But no matter how good I was, it was the boss's film. I was the hired help.

A thought flitted through my brain. I had the ideas, knew how to produce, and yet I took it for granted that a man would be in charge. Hmmm, who wrote that rule? While we watched the Deauville footage, the bubble of a new idea started to brew.

We took a break for lunch, walking to Lac Hong, the Vietnamese restaurant Patrice had taken me on my first day. In the entryway, passing by the golden Buddha with its belly rubbed shiny by patrons wishing for good luck, I added a rub of my own. It was worth a try.

I was anxious to talk to Patrice about my idea, but I remembered he'd been upset at the restaurant when I asked him about Vietnam. I'd have to be extra careful and stay calm—I didn't want my new bubble to burst. I was lost in thought when Patrice broke the silence as he was enjoying his first glass of Beaujolais.

"We have a problem," he said. "Antenne 2 has moved up the airdate. We have only one month until delivery."

"We?" I looked at him in mock shock.

"Kate, Bernard can't edit it by himself. I've brought in Annette as a second editor. She's been screening the footage. You will work with her on half the sequences and supervise post-production."

He, the great provider of jobs, raised his glass to me. "To Kate, and another month of employment."

I was ecstatic, but I wouldn't give him the satisfaction of saving me from overdue bills.

"I have to check my schedule," I said, taking out my calendar.

"You have another engagement?" he joked.

I shrugged, meaningfully.

"*Zut alors*, you saw Renaud?" Patrice smiled broadly. "He wants to steal you from me? That old bastard. We'll see about that."

I'd let him stew for a moment.

"Jean-Claude and I are negotiating, working on a game plan." I flipped through the calendar, not letting him see the empty pages. "Patrice, you are in luck. I can fit you in."

Fortunately, the food arrived and Patrice switched his attention to the chef's culinary art. But it wasn't long before he returned to his favorite dish: getting my goat.

"If I know Renaud, he has different work for you than making films."

I bristled at the innuendo, even if it was true. "Sex isn't work for Jean-Claude. It's a sport," I said, immediately regretting what I'd revealed.

Patrice didn't miss a beat. "Good, it will keep you in shape for those long hours in the editing room."

Deflecting his comments, I went on the offensive.

"And for Annette too?" I teased. "She told me she's seeing you. Is that sport for you?"

He sipped the wine, contemplating his answer. "No, Annette is different," he admitted. "But then, I'm no longer that interested in gymnastics."

"You were quite athletic with Brandy that night in L.A."

He nodded, thinking. "Yes, Annette is more than a sport. She's a strong, independent woman, and when we have sex, we are equals. Okay, I admit it. She is a new kind of passion."

He looked strangely vulnerable, "This connection with Annette, it is unusual for me. We think alike, we feel alike. She understands me. Perhaps if I had met her when I was young, we would have married."

He was mellow, no tension in the air. Perhaps that fermenting bubble would be safe if I floated it in his direction.

"I have found a new passion as well."

"Yes? Another man? You will be very busy."

"Is that all you can think of?" I joked. "No, the passion was born this morning as we screened the dailies. Minnelli was talking about *An American in Paris*, and I thought of all those American artists who came to Paris in the '20s, Hemingway, Fitzgerald, Josephine Baker. But what about Yanks who come here today for the freedom to create? They are the stars of *New Americans in Paris!*"

Patrice watched intently as I pitched my vision.

"Patrice, your *Cahiers de Californie* shows the French what they're missing out on in the U.S. Let's turn the tables. Wouldn't your French audience like to know what Paris has that Americans want? More fantasy? More liberty? More camembert? What?"

He was thinking, not saying no. He actually seemed attracted by my proposal.

"Making this film is your passion?"

"Patrice, I understand these people because I'm one of them. Or I'd like to be—to live in a liberating culture that a lot of Yanks never experience at home."

"Kate, don't you remember? You wanted nothing to do with Paris."

My bubble grew taut. How to release the tension? Admit the truth.

"I blamed the city for my pain," I confessed. "I was afraid to face my own past. It wasn't Paris; it was personal. And now Paris has helped me see that."

That sentence, once impossible to say, relaxed the bubble and I floated back to my proposal. "Patrice, I'm very close to this subject, but stories with an emotional connection make the best films, yes? Like your *Cahiers de Californie*."

Patrice nodded, weighing the possibilities. "Interesting idea. But who are the Americans?"

"I'll tell you when I have it all together. But they're here."

I didn't have a clue.

"Come back to me with a proposal after we finish Deauville. I might be able to sell this film to Antenne 2."

I tried to hide my excitement. Bargaining time.

"Deal. If I'm the director," I said flatly. Silence. "With you as Executive Producer," I added.

He shrugged. "Show me how good you are in the editing room. Then I'll think about it."

In Patrice-speak, that was almost a yes. I really might have the chance to make a film on my own terms. I gave Buddha another rub on the way back to work. I needed all the luck I could get.

Too much had gone wrong the first time I was in Paris.

chapter twenty-four

1964 November 25

For the second time in a week, I was back in the stirrups.
Dr. Marcovici's bald head between my legs, his instrument probing, investigating. After what seemed an eternity, he withdrew, peeling off his surgical glove, taking a cigarette from his packet of Gauloise, fumbling through his pockets for a match. Finally, he looked at me, almost apologetic.

"Mademoiselle, the swelling is more pronounced. You have not your period. There is nothing more to do."

He pulled my legs together and stood up. "Get dressed and come into my office."

This surreal nightmare could not be happening. I was not a girl who got pregnant and ruined her life.

When I entered the doctor's room, he'd found a match and was smoking his cigarette. He watched the tears stream down my face.

"Sit down, have a cigarette."

"That's it?" I said, sinking into the chair in front of him, taking the cigarette he offered, as if it would calm me down and stop my tears. Instead it made me nauseous. I ground it out in the ashtray.

"I'm sorry it's not the answer you wanted." He handed me a piece of paper.

"Read the instructions. If you want to terminate, the sooner the better. Come back tomorrow morning after you've done it."

I shoved the paper into my pocket. I couldn't bear looking at it. Not yet. "Thank you, Doctor," I whispered, and walked out the door in a daze.

It was a gloomy day, the damp cold penetrating through my wool coat straight to the bone. In my own fog, I somehow survived the metro ride from the doctor's office back to Montparnasse and No. 149. I was about to click open the front door, but couldn't face the knowing eye of Madame Just spying on me from her concierge window. She'd helped me once, but swore she'd never speak of it again, and I believed her.

I crossed the street to L'Horizon. It was three o'clock; after-lunch, before-aperitif hour. That lonely time when everyone else is busy at work or school. Busy living their lives. I sat by the café window, my frozen hands wrapped around the comfort of a hot tea, watching the gray day darken and scattered raindrops grow into a steady rain.

"The sooner the better," the doctor had said. I told myself I was glad François was busy with work. I didn't even want him around. My heart had already snapped in two.

As the water pounded against the café window, I unfolded the paper from Dr. Marcovici. His directions were brief and concise. Purchase rubber tubing, gauze, Vaseline, antiseptic. Sterilize the tube, lubricate it, then stick it up the vagina past the cervix and leave it there. I was to see him the next morning at ten o'clock and he would finish it off.

In a moment of false courage, I set myself in motion, banishing any thoughts but the task ahead. A microscopic sperm and egg had gotten together inside of me. They were quickly replicating and I must remove them. I unfurled my umbrella and stepped out into the heavy rain. Around the corner, rue du Cherche-Midi was lined with all the shops one needed for daily life—including a *pharmacie* and a small hardware store where you could buy a light bulb … or a rubber tube.

I loved to shop on this street, but today it offered no relief. With impersonal clerks too busy to answer a question—*What's the most flexible rubber tube? Do I sterilize with antiseptic?*—I felt more and more isolated, helpless.

The City of Lights had turned into a dirty old world filled with rude people attending to their own selfish lives. I thought about going to Colin. But then I remembered tomorrow was Thanksgiving. George Whitman was closing Shakespeare and Company, cooking a turkey dinner for stray Americans, and Colin had gone home to London for the long weekend. I could call Susan, but she was busy in London leading her wonderful life. Just as well. I didn't want Susan to know I was in this mess. I didn't want anyone to know. It was embarrassing, shameful.

I would do it myself and forget about it.

chapter twenty-five

1977 September 16

My parents taught me early that to get things done, you can't count on strangers. They always scolded, "Do you think trash magically disappears? Clean it up yourself!" At the restaurant with Patrice, it had been fun to rub Buddha's belly for luck, but that wasn't going to get my documentary *New Americans in Paris* made. I'd have to rely on my own resources.

I returned from lunch to my little office, where a huge pile of paper had accumulated in my absence. Near the bottom of the signed agreements, bills, and production sheets was a letter from my tenant. I'd been checking in with Rob on a regular basis, but between shooting schedules and time differences, I hadn't been in touch for a couple of weeks. I tore it open, scared that something had happened to Lucy.

Greetings from North Hollywood,
Lucy says woof, or in translation,
"I'm having a lot of fun. I love your tenant!"
Your office said you were in Deauville, hence this note.
The stove isn't working. Can't cook.
> *Best regards, Rob Greene*

p.s. Coming to Paris in two weeks for a recording session.
Lucy will be hanging with Linda and Barney.
p.p.s. I'll be at L'Hotel. Stop by for a drink.

Damn, the letter was postmarked ten days ago. Which meant he'd be coming to Paris in a few days. It was now 8:00 a.m. in Los Angeles. Maybe he was home. I dialed my number.

"Hello?" The voice was huffing and puffing.

"Rob? It's Kate Miller, your landlady."

"Hi, Kate, I was bringing Lucy back from her walk." Another pause while I heard in the background, "Good girl! Breakfast is *tout de suite.*" Then, in a kewpie-doll falsetto voice, "I peed and pooped for you, and now you make me wait for breakfast!"

My goodness. Rob was really getting into Lucy.

"Hello again," he said into the mouthpiece. "You know, Lucy can be quite demanding."

"Give her a hug for me and tell her to cool it, that Uncle Rob is taking her on lots of walks!"

"Oh, I've been promoted to Uncle Rob?! I do love my walks with Lucy—she takes me away from all the work bullshit."

"So true. I miss her a lot. I'm sorry I wasn't able to get in touch earlier about the stove—I only just got your letter."

"Yeah, it's been a lot of takeout and cold cuts."

"At least that sick stove survived the earthquake," I said, trying to keep it light. "And you did, too?"

"Yeah, as well as most of the dishes. I guess they liked staying on the shelf."

"Good news! Because my dad can't mend broken dishes, but he is a genius at fixing appliances or calling a repairman."

The vision of Rob and I cooking in the kitchen once again popped into my head; along with a new one of taking a walk with him and Lucy. He was a good guy. He deserved a good landlady.

If it's not working before you leave," I offered, "I'll cook dinner on my stove in Paris when you get here."

As soon as the words were out of my mouth, I wanted to pull them back in. I was sure Rob was busy with his new girlfriends. Anyway, I had too much work to do.

"It's a deal," he said enthusiastically. "By the way, I'm getting to know your house. And I like it. Stove or not."

"Does that mean my garage sale addiction hasn't destroyed the décor?"

He laughed. "You are too much, Kate. Hey, I'm flying to Paris next Thursday. If I have time, let's meet for a drink. I'll have my secretary set it up."

Sure thing," I said, quickly reverting to my gracious landlady role. "À bientôt!"

Now I had to call my parents about the stove. The folks would be thrilled to hear from me, eager to help. I could depend on them, but their support came with an expensive emotional price tag. They didn't say anything negative, but I heard every unspoken word. I could even translate their pauses and inflections. *It's a good life in L.A., why did you leave us to live halfway around the world? Come home, marry a nice Jewish boy. Be like us.*

It had been like that since my student days. The message was in their genes; they couldn't help themselves. I took a deep breath and dialed halfway around the world to Sherman Oaks, California.

The suburb I'd traveled thousands of miles to escape. After four rings, just enough time for my mother to get from the kitchen to the den, she picked up.

"Hello?"

"Bonjour, Mom."

"I don't believe it, Kate, it's you! From Paris? Gosh, what time is it there?"

"It's 5:15, Mom. P.M."

"Harold! It's Kate, all the way from Paris!" I could hear her calling out to my father, and his reply, "What does she want?"

"It must be important! I can't even imagine how much this call costs."

"Mom, I'm calling from the office. It's on their dime. How are you? I've gotten your letters. Sounds like everything's okay."

"Of course, dear. We had the family over last Sunday. Grandma baked her apple strudel. Your sister brought that green bean dish she makes. The one with the almonds and the can of, you know …"

"Cream of mushroom soup." I cringed.

"Yes, that's the one. Everyone's asking about you, Kate. What you're doing in Paris. When you'll be home. I don't know what to tell them."

Why couldn't you be like everyone in the family? Find a husband. Give us grandchildren.

"Mom, I told you, I'm working for a French producer on his documentary. I love living here. Ernest Hemingway wrote a book called *A Moveable Feast* about living in Paris. I highly recommend it."

"French food is too rich for me. But I know you liked Paris that time you learned to speak French and stayed with a family."

"Learning French back then helps me in my work now. And I get paid too."

See, Mom? I'm a responsible person.

"That's nice. You always paid your own way. Even that time in Paris when you asked us to send more money from your savings." I could hear her silent questions: *Why did you need that hundred dollars? What did you throw your money away on?*

I'd never told my parents about François. Better to keep it to what they could understand and accept. Back in 1964, there was a lot they didn't understand or accept.

Sex before marriage? You'll be ruined forever. Existential crisis? Nonsense. Go to a therapist? We'll tell you how to be happy and not charge you all that money: Stay home and find a nice Jewish boy.

I quickly changed the subject. "Mom, I've got to get back to work, but I have a favor to ask. My tenant says the stove isn't working. Can you and Dad take a look and see if it can be fixed?"

"Hold on, darling." Again, the calling out to my father. "Harold, can we go over to Kate's house and check on her stove?"

"I told her that stove was no good," my father shouted in the background, then the sound became muffled as my mother put her hand over the mouthpiece.

"Of course, Kate," Mom said, now back on the phone. "Don't worry, sweetie, we'll take care of it."

Her comforting maternal voice catapulted me back into little girl mode, sheltered from the unknown dangers of the world. Even my father's gruff manner was part of a familiar behavior that told me he cared. I would always have a place at the table, even if they never understood me. At least not the part of me that was me—my dreams, my hunger to go beyond their limited horizons.

"Kate, did you hear me? When are you coming home?"

"Soon, Mom. I've got to go now. It was wonderful to hear your voice," I said, surprised to really mean it.

"Goodbye, sweetheart. Don't worry. We'll get the stove fixed."

I hung up and looked around my office, reassuring myself that I wasn't at my parents' house in Sherman Oaks. Yes, I was still in

Oz, aka France. But unlike Dorothy, I was in no hurry to get home. Besides, there was work to do.

I was struggling to type thank-you letters to Peck, Minnelli, and Pollack on the French keyboard (It was a pleasure came out It zqs q pleqsure) when Annette stuck her head in the doorway. She'd changed from her casual editing garb into a simple black sleeveless dress. She looked fabulous as usual, her auburn hair swept off her face into a smooth bun. A Hermes scarf was draped around her neck, the outfit set off by black leather pumps and a Gucci bag. She was so classy, I couldn't figure out why she was with Patrice. Why be the mistress of a man who'd never leave his wife? A mystery yet to be solved.

I waved her in. "Isn't it great? We're going to work together!" I said, gathering up my purse and jacket. "Let's have a drink and celebrate."

"How about the George V?" she said. "I've got a quick meeting in the hotel bar. Then I'm yours."

Thirteen years ago, George V bellboys had dismissed me. Tonight, I was one of the elegant hotel's privileged guests. Life was interesting indeed.

We entered the bar—not dark like an American bar, but rather a library in a private French chateau. We walked past paneled wood walls, tapestries, and wingback armchairs in which the clientele in designer clothes drank cocktails and chatted in a sophisticated French hum. There were even the showbiz types in jeans and satin shirts to make me feel at home.

Annette spotted an empty table. "Why don't you sit down? I'll join you in a few minutes."

I sunk into one of the sumptuous velvet armchairs, and watched Annette approach a Catherine Deneuve lookalike sitting by herself on a love seat. Blonde hair, classic features, wearing a form-fitting dress revealing promising cleavage and very long legs. As Annette talked to her, she listened intently, nodding, sipping her glass of wine.

I was too far away to hear what was said, but I saw Annette take an envelope out of her purse, hand it to the woman, and shake her hand. It seemed a strange place to conduct business, but then I was still getting to know the French.

The waiter approached as Annette came to our table and sat in the chair across from me.

"*Un* Pernod, *s'il vous plaît*," she told the waiter. "*Et toi*, Kate?"

"*Oui, le même.* Pernod." I'd never had the drink, a traditional French aperitif. Time to get acquainted.

Annette shrugged off her jacket and leaned back in the chair. "Tell me, how was Deauville? Most importantly, did you wear that exquisite green dress?"

"Mere words cannot describe the festival, which is why you are going to love editing its images. As for the green dress, I have one word for it: magic."

The waiter arrived, setting in front of us two glasses with a small amount of yellow liqueur. He placed a pitcher of water on the table and disappeared.

Annette took the pitcher. "Water?"

"Same as you," I said.

She poured water into each glass, and the yellow liqueur instantly turned milky white. We clicked glasses, and I took a sip. A strong licorice flavor masked the alcohol. Delicious. I took a bigger swallow.

Before I knew it, I was ready to tell all. "Can you keep a secret? This is not for Patrice."

"Don't you know about film editors? They don't talk to people; they work alone and in the dark. Think of the editing room as a confessional. We are in my editing room now."

The room disappeared; the crowd's noise turned into an echoed whisper. I leaned toward her confidentially.

"Putting on that green dress was like pouring water into Pernod. Alchemy. When I looked in the mirror, I saw another person. A character I could play."

She nodded. "In that green dress, you could be anyone you want to be."

"Annette, you waved your wand and conjured up that dress. You are my Fairy Godmother."

"Then who was your Prince Charming?"

"That was the real magic." I raised my fist in triumph. "I didn't need a Prince Charming—I was the hero of my own story."

Annette was somehow not surprised. "Kate, it was as I always saw you. What sorcery did you perform?"

The images of that magical night lit up my brain as I finished my fairy tale. "When I saw Jean-Claude Renaud playing roulette in the casino, I transformed myself into a woman very different from the one he'd met in L.A. And the more I acted, the more I believed I was a powerful Hollywood producer."

"Did it work? Did he offer you a job?"

My voice fell. "He had an interesting proposal … but not for work."

"Is it confession time?" Annette raised her eyebrows, already knowing my answer.

"Okay, okay, you warned me that first day at lunch," I admitted. "You said he was a playboy … and, well, we played."

"Yes, Renaud is a bit notorious. But don't you see? Your dress worked; the power you projected was an aphrodisiac to him. If that is what you want."

I shook my head. "No, not romantically. But I have to admit the sex was great fun."

She smiled and made the sign of the cross. "Don't worry, I won't make you say three Hail Marys. If you're enjoying yourself, what's wrong with that?"

I held up my hand. "Patrice is always teasing me about Jean-Claude, so you must swear not to tell him."

Annette downed the rest of her glass, then raised her hand to swear. "Don't worry, we are in the confessional. But now that you've told me your secret, may I share one with you? Patrice can't know this one either."

"I swear."

"I'm bringing Patrice here on his birthday. The woman I spoke to? She's a surprise for him. A very expensive dessert."

"What do you mean?" I asked, fearing I knew very well what she meant.

"Patrice and I will enjoy our dinner. Perhaps foie gras, lobster, champagne. Then that beautiful dessert will arrive at the table. I will wish him a happy birthday and give him the key to a room I've booked here. I'll stay at the table, have my own dessert—my favorite profiteroles, then a *café*, and after that, a liqueur. He won't have to rush."

I couldn't believe my ears. I didn't know what to say. But my face gave me away.

"You are shocked?" she asked.

My friend was gifting a beautiful woman to Patrice. A hooker, no less. I didn't want to be judgmental or provincial but …

"Annette, I'm trying to understand. You're helping Patrice cheat on you? Aren't you shutting yourself out?"

"Of course not. I'm keeping the excitement alive. Because after my dessert, *café*, and liqueur, I'll join them."

I gulped.

A smile played around her lips. "He'll have fun with his present, but I know what he likes."

When I didn't smile back, she shrugged. "Kate, don't be such an American. You know the French look at things differently. When it comes to matters of the heart—or the body—everyone makes their own rules. It's a private affair."

"But you're already sharing Patrice with his wife." I was sad, thinking about Christine, all alone.

"Kate, I know they have a strong marriage. He is not 'cheating' with me, as they say in the States, because they have an agreement, an open marriage."

"Then you also know that he will never leave her."

Annette was unfazed. "Kate, I have no interest in marrying again or ruining his marriage. Besides, Christine is the one who deals with his daily worries of life. I get the part of Patrice that he is free to give."

"You will not grow old with him."

"I had breast cancer two years ago. Perhaps I will not grow old at all. Or he will fall off a cliff as he's filming a documentary."

I'd run out of arguments. Whatever Patrice and Annette chose to do was their business. I'd entered new territory, a world where independent and liberated people did what they wanted. I had to admire Annette's strong spirit, but as I followed her into the dining room, I wondered if Jean-Claude was going to come up with any similar games.

And what would I do if he did?

chapter twenty-six

1977 September 20

Elizabeth Taylor and Richard Burton. Frank Sinatra and Princess Grace. Salvador Dali and … Rob Greene?

A few days after my drink with Annette at the George V, I found myself in an even more exclusive hotel. L'Hotel was a Left Bank haven for elite literati and showbiz types, and apparently my tenant Rob was one of them. We were to meet at 6:00 p.m. He was late, so I amused myself by walking around the very French *classique* red-walled lobby, admiring photographs of the hotel's legendary guests, wondering if one day, Rob Greene (famous for being my tenant?) might join this rogue's gallery.

Off in a corner of the lobby, I deciphered the French scrawl of a framed letter written by none other than Oscar Wilde:

> *I've received your charming letter*
> *I would be very happy to have the*

joy to see you again, but where?
Your place? Or in a café? Send me a note.

It was eerie—exactly the letter I'd hoped to receive from François in response to the note I'd sent. Then I read the bio next to the letter: Oscar Wilde had lived in this building, back when it was a fleabag hotel called L'Alsace. It was in room No. 16, the bio stated, that he'd written on his deathbed:

My wallpaper and I are fighting a duel to the death.
One of us has got to go.

Oscar's words were like daggers. My heart pounded wildly, intense fear and nausea invading my body. I was living my nightmare again.

I'm entombed in my chambre de bonne. Clawing at the
wallpaper's stains and rips. My body is convulsing with pain.
Blood is caked on my legs, staining the sheets. Nothing matters
but escaping that room with its disgusting wallpaper.

I stumbled blindly out of the hotel, gulping deep breaths of air, but the beery smell of a sidewalk café with boisterous drinkers made me want to vomit. I started to cross the street as a taxi pulling up to L'Hotel screeched to a stop in front of me, honking.

"*Mademoiselle! Attention! Etes-vous aveugle?*" Are you blind? the driver shouted.

"*Excusez-moi,*" I said, tears running down my face, as none other than Rob Greene got out of the cab. He looked tired, rumpled, but he rushed up to me.

"Kate! Are you all right?" He took my hand, his concerned hazel eyes peering out above a scrubby beard.

"Yes, I'm fine, the taxi startled me." I forced myself to smile. In his Dodger baseball jacket and bell-bottom jeans, he looked so, well, American. I'd forgotten how comforting that could be. I found my ground and pushed the nightmare away.

"*Bienvenue à Paris.*"

He nodded and gave me the two-cheek French air kiss. "Lucy wanted me to lick you; but I told her no, I must do my first 'French kiss.' Unfortunately, I also had my first Parisian traffic jam. The plane was delayed two hours; we landed in time for rush hour."

"That's okay, I was going to take a little walk while I waited," I said, putting on a cheery face.

He glanced at his watch. "I don't have much time, but we'll have a quick drink."

"No, no. You've got a lot to do. I'll take a rain check." *Please, let me out of here.*

"We'll make time," he said, guiding me back into the hotel. "We can both use a drink. While I check in, why don't you order for us? I'll take a Chivas on the rocks, *s'il vous plait.*"

The bar was down a narrow curving staircase into the cellar. At least there was no wallpaper on its stone walls. Five minutes later, sipping a vodka tonic, I had pushed the darkness back inside of me. By the time Rob appeared, I raised my glass with only a small tremor.

"I tried for Oscar Wilde's room, but it isn't available," he said, taking a large swallow of his scotch.

"Ah, the importance of being Oscar's room." With a slightly forced smile, I took a deep breath. The more normal I acted, the more normal I'd become. "Tell me, what are your plans in Paris?" I avoided the issue of the broken stove, hoping he wouldn't recall my offer to cook him dinner.

"I'm here to help with a new album. Barclay Records is recording a live performance of Memphis Slim at his regular gig, Aux Trois Mailletz jazz club, and my company's thinking of distributing the album in the States. Eddie Barclay made jazz musicians like Dizzy Gillespie and Quincy Jones popular in France, so I'm hoping he'll do the same for Slim."

I couldn't believe my ears. Memphis Slim, legendary blues artist, could be one of the *New Americans in Paris*!

I spoke casually, like I was doing him a favor. "I love Memphis Slim, and my boss adores all things American. France-Nouvelle might be interested in a photo spread, or even a TV segment." I threw in a *petit* shrug. "Publicity for your album. It couldn't hurt."

I watched the wheels turn in Rob's head. He shrugged. "Sure, why don't you come with me to the show? You can talk it up to your boss."

Aux Trois Mailletz was a small restaurant. Rather inauspicious until a waiter led us down steep stone stairs into darkness, as if we were the Count of Monte Cristo condemned to Chateau D'If.

"Lumiere!" the waiter shouted. A sudden blast of light revealed that we stood in a long, narrow vault lined with tables. At one end was a small stage, bare save for a piano and a set of drums.

"Rumor has it this was once a medieval torture chamber," the waiter confided with a gleeful smirk. "Thirteenth century. I've heard the diabolical instruments are around here—"

He was interrupted by footsteps clambering down the steps. A young man appeared, not in an iron mask, but draped in cables and wires and carrying lots of mikes. Rob got busy with the soundcheck, and as I watched, I was already imagining how to shoot this set-up scene for my documentary. A waitress came in with a carafe of vin rouge and two pizzas. They were probably for Rob and the sound guy, but I grabbed a slice before anyone could stop me.

"Who's eating pizza without me?" a voice bellowed. I looked up to see a very tall Black man in a pinstripe suit walking down the steps into the cavern. Heading straight for the pizza, he bent over, flashing his huge diamond pinkie ring, and scooped up a slice with long slender fingers. Only then did he notice me staring at the top of his head, where, as if painted on, a white stripe of hair ran smack down the middle. He rolled his eyes upward.

"They say it's the skunk in me." He put down the pizza, smiled, and extended his hand. "Peter Chatman," he said. "*Enchanté.*"

"Kate Miller," I responded. "But aren't you—?"

"Yeah, I'm that, too. Memphis Slim." He gave a little pat to his mid-section. "Though I ain't in Memphis and I'm not so slim any-more." He chuckled and took a generous bite of the pizza.

Rob materialized and reached for his own slice. "Hey, Slim, great to see you! This is Kate. She's working with France-Nouvelle, but we need to get ready for the show. Can she talk to you during the break?"

Slim looked at me with a smile as wide as his face, as if to say, I may be the center of my world, but you're definitely invited in.

Showtime. The cellar was jammed … and jamming. Slim was bob-bing his white stripe of hair up and down and side to side. His long, elegant hands flew over the piano keyboard, his fingertips pointing up against gravity as they danced an infectious boogie-woogie beat.

"I got to tell you like it was," he told the audience, "but first I must have a drink of my *jus de pomme*," and he took a sip of some-thing that looked like apple juice. Thus fortified, he sang the stories of his life; how he'd started out in Memphis, then moved around, "boogin' and bluesin'" until he ended up in Paris.

I felt his songs in my bones: the flat-out joy and pure sorrow of the blues with its defiant cry of freedom breaking through the heart-aches of life. Without a shadow of a doubt, Memphis Slim was my key to *New Americans in Paris*!

At the end of the set, I found Slim upstairs in the restaurant at a small table in the back, pouring himself a drink from a bottle of Johnny Walker Red. He motioned me over.

"Sit down, little lady, and share my apple juice." He poured me a glass of the scotch.

I took a swallow. "That's some juice," I agreed. "Rejuvenating."

"You're right about that. Hey, little lady, what can I do for you?"

"Slim, I need to know. Your music is so true, so American. Don't you miss home? Why do you live in Paris?"

"Here's the 'true' of it," he said, lighting a Pall Mall. "When I toured Europe, the shows were packed, and me and the band were treated good. Then I'd go back to the States and have to scramble for gigs the rest of the year. It was worse in the South, my own neck of the woods. Even when you had cash in your pocket, nobody gave you a good hotel room, or let you eat in their restaurant."

He downed the rest of his scotch and gave me a broad smile. "One year when I stopped off in Paris for a show, I plumb forgot to go home. That was in '62."

"But a lot happened since you left the States! The whole Civil Rights movement. Didn't that make life better?"

Slim took a drag on the Pall Mall and laid on some more truth. "In Paris, I drive my Rolls-Royce from my very nice house in the suburbs, do the gig, and then go home to my beautiful wife. We eat in restaurants like Maxim's and the Tour d'Argent. When I can do that in Mississippi, I'll go back."

Oh, how I wished a camera was rolling. A hundred years after the Civil War, the City of Light appreciated what the U.S. ignored: their own Black artists.

"Hey, little lady, do I have to spell it out? Paris doesn't care about my color. It's the music that's important."

"Slim, I'm planning a documentary about Americans who've found freedom and equality in Paris …"

I got no further, as Rob appeared and interrupted with recording questions. By the time he was finished, Slim had to head down for his second set. I tapped Rob on the shoulder as we got up from the table.

"Thanks for letting me come. I loved it. Memphis Slim deserves a TV story."

Rob lit up in agreement. "Great. I'll call before I leave Paris."

"Lovely," I said, knowing he would not.

I floated to Place St. Michel and the metro, oblivious to the traffic and crowds of people.

I was on to something good. Yes, a great personal story, but also a saga revealing a profound insight into American society. I wasn't Black. I wasn't a man. I wasn't a musicologist. My problems were small compared to artists like Memphis Slim. But I was invisible in my own way: A single woman in her thirties, no kids, no husband, no regular job. Something had to be wrong with me. The story of an American not understood in their own country resonated deep inside me. I had to tell this story.

Riding the crowded metro, I noticed a young couple kissing, moving their bodies to the rhythm of the train. A soundtrack came to mind, but it wasn't a romantic song. It was Slim's "Every Day I Have the Blues." *Every day, every day,* pounded in my head. And yes, today all it took was Oscar Wilde's quote to bring me back to that night in my *chambre de bonne* and its horrid wallpaper. I'd pushed it down for thirteen years, but the pain was still there.

chapter twenty-seven

1964 November 25

The moment of truth. I notified Monsieur Charpentier that I was coming down with *la grippe* and taking to my bed. I assured him I would stay away until I was contagion-free so as not to infect the family.

Back in my room, I opened the shopping bag and pulled out my strange selection of purchases, queasy at the thought of what was about to happen. I went over and over in my mind if I should wait until François came back. Even if he didn't change his mind, I could go ahead with the pregnancy and maybe he'd marry me.

The deeper truth, however, was that I wasn't sure myself. I loved him, oh did I love him. But we were from different worlds. His strict Catholicism, his desire for a communal life, was beautiful but daunting. It was too soon to tell if we could manage a life together.

None of that made a difference now. Because if we didn't marry, it was out of the question to go home and face the stigma of being an unwed mother. I was drowning in hurt and rejection, shame and fear. There was no other way out.

I heated a pot of water on my electric burner, put in the tubing and scissors, and let them boil. I undressed and put on my nightgown. I was ready.

First, a little reward: a fresh baguette, a big chunk of Port Salut cheese, and a few slices of saucisson. I was in France and would eat well before I performed the deed. I carefully swept the crumbs away and took a bite of good chocolate.

Then, in an out-of-body experience, I became my own nurse. Methodically, I unwrapped the package of surgical gauze, washed my hands with the antiseptic, and took out the sterilized scissors and tube. I cut a square of gauze, which I wrapped around the end of the tube and slathered with Vaseline. Holding the other end of the tube, I sat on the bed. As if it were a Tampax, I parted my legs and stuck the tube up inside me. It didn't go very far. I gently tried to maneuver it until it could make its way through my cervix. Nothing was happening. Oh lord, was I doing it right?

In a fit of anger at François, I gave the tube a strong push, daring it to resist me. It fought back with a sharp stab of pain. I doubled over, eyes tearing, regretting what I had done. It was too late. I'd condemned myself.

Then a reprieve. The pain subsided. I sat still, waiting for something. Blood? No. Fluid? No. This was loony. I'd see Dr. Marcovici in the morning, and soon it would all be over.

I had fifteen hours before my appointment. Fifteen hours to think about the inferno I'd put myself in. How could I have done this? It was hopeless. I sobbed and sobbed until there were no tears left.

Exhausted, I crawled under the covers and dozed off.

I woke up late and realized my class at the Sorbonne had already begun. I ran down the six flights of stairs, but Madame Just had mopped the floor, and I slid down the last flight, banging my knee. As I hobbled into the street, a crowd of people gathered around two cars. François was wildly gesticulating at a woman who kept pointing to her dented fender. He was showing her his own bashed-in headlight when he saw me and waved me over. As police sirens approached, we jumped in his car and he drove me to class, but as soon as I got there, we were having an exam and I had forgotten to study. Everyone else was prepared. Not only that, I looked down and realized I didn't have any clothes on. I froze in embarrassment, as it dawned on me that I'd been naked all day. I was looking around for something to cover me up when I felt a gush between my legs.

Consciousness came slowly as I realized I was in my bed, and I'd woken up from a nightmare. But being awake was worse. The pain was real. A tightening metal vise was pushing together the soft flesh inside my abdomen. I turned on the light, and as if in a horror movie, I saw sticky blood in thick clots oozing between my thighs. I gingerly pulled out the tube and lay in the blood-soaked sheets, unable to move. Doubled up in agony, I waited for the pain to pass; instead, it grew intolerable, unlike anything I'd ever endured. The vise would not release; a knife found its way inside me, stabbing, pushing.

Three a.m. Seven hours to go before my doctor's appointment. I needed to focus on something. I stared at the old wallpaper behind the brass rails of the headboard, where the seams of the paper were separating. The pattern had seemed so charming when I first moved in, an enchanting garden of faded pink roses and chartreuse leaves. But now I saw the truth: it was a disgusting garbage heap. Scrawny birds were struggling through rotting vegetation and splotchy water stains. It matched the hellhole of my insides.

I thought of Oscar Wilde. He was right. Either that wallpaper goes or I do.

I began to tear off the frayed paper. As if on an archaeological dig, I uncovered the room's previous eras. Behind the fetid roses was a patch of garish red wallpaper dotted with fleur-de-lis; underneath, a shit-brown paper with tarnished circles of gold. I wondered if any maids in this *chambre de bonne* had gone through the same as me, and which layers of wallpaper they'd stared at. There was nothing but this small tomb of a room sealing me in with the ghosts of those poor girls.

At four o'clock in the morning, I became sure I was going to die. And there was nothing I could do about it. I had no phone, and I didn't have the strength to crawl down six flights to Madame Just. I couldn't even manage two flights to the Charpentiers—not that I had the nerve to wake them up in the middle of the night.

In my fevered state, I thought of the horrifying coat hanger and knitting needle stories of the girls who didn't know better. I was a Berkeley graduate, but in reality I was the fool, so stupid I deserved to die.

Why wasn't Susan here? If Susan had stayed in Paris, she would've helped me get through this. She would've talked François into using contraceptives. Damn it, if Susan hadn't left me, I wouldn't have even met François. None of this would be happening.

I was going to die in a foreign country, alone in a tiny garret. My body wouldn't be discovered for days. Not until someone smelled a decomposing corpse, or the Charpentiers decided to investigate. When my parents found out, they'd tell everyone at home about their poor daughter's burst appendix, and that would be that.

The light of dawn broke through the airshaft about eight o'clock. The knife-stabbing agony was now a dull ache; the bleeding mostly stopped. I'd entered a different world—a growing fever taking me beyond the pain to somewhere outside myself. I tried to sit up. I saw an arm curl, a leg slowly fall over the side of the bed. If I moved incorrectly, the pain jabbed back sharply.

But I had not died.

Sitting on the edge of my bed, I sponged off the blood caking my legs. Then even more carefully, I pulled on clothes. Warm, loose clothes. Two scarves, a hat, wool gloves. The hardest part was the boots. After what seemed like an eternity, I left the room and made my way down the six flights of stairs. Madame Just had not yet opened her concierge's window, so I walked out into the sunlight, and began to cross the street to L'Horizon.

Step. Step. Step.

The signal turned red before I could reach the other side. The drivers, usually so anxious to roar down the street, waited for a poor old woman, huddling under a heavy wool coat, knit hat pulled down on her face, bent over, walking ever so slowly and carefully.

Step. Step. Step. They waited for me.

I entered the café. With that supreme Gallic indifference I was now grateful for, waiters went about their business, putting out ash-trays, cleaning tabletops. Eventually one waiter must have decided I wasn't a ragged *clochard* trying to get in out of the cold and asked me what I wanted. I ordered a cup of tea.

The café grew crowded with its morning rush. Cigarette smoke swirled around me, making me want to throw up, but I stayed, not able to move, waiting for my ten o'clock appointment. I thought of going in earlier, but that would have meant walking down to the *sous-sol* to telephone.

I needed to be strong, to not give in. I had made my mistake; I would fix it myself. The worst was over. I was strong enough to endure.

But not on the crowded metro. I took the bus.

chapter twenty-eight

1977 September 23

Work in the editing room was intense. But the more exhausted I was, the less my mind took me to past places I didn't want to go.

I was glad Jean-Claude was away on business, since Annette and I sometimes worked until almost midnight. The morning after one of these late-night sessions, I'd overslept and was rushing out the door when the phone rang.

It was Rob Greene on his last day in Paris. My stove in North Hollywood was waiting for a new part, so he was taking me up on my offer to cook on my Parisian stove.

"You'll get off easy—lunch," he cheerily announced.

Dammit, you remembered.

I was trying to impress Patrice so he'd greenlight my new dream project. Being late was not a way to do it.

"I'd love to, but I'm already late to work."

"My plane doesn't leave until nine o'clock. Are you condemning me to wander around Paris by myself for eight hours?"

"There's a great exhibit at the Louvre," I said, trying to be helpful.

"No museums. Hmm, do you know where E. Dehillerin is? The cookware store? C'mon, we'll try a new pan on your stove. I always wanted to cook a meal in Paris. Why don't you meet me there? Can't you think of it as a long lunch?"

I was about to politely decline when my mind switched gears. Rob might know of other American musicians living in Paris for my documentary. Change of plans.

"I could use a good spatula," I said. "I'll meet you there in an hour."

I called France-Nouvelle and asked Annette to cover for me. She was working on the opening tease for the film. Annette was a true artist when it came to editing glitzy montages with wild quick cuts. She could work a whole day on a forty-five-second title sequence.

"Patrice won't even notice you're missing," she told me, a bit curt, preoccupied.

"*Merci*, Annette. I'll try to get in this afternoon."

"Don't bother," and she hung up.

What was that all about?

Rob was waiting in front of the E. Dehillerin window display, wearing a wide-wale green corduroy jacket, like those in the designer shops on boulevard St. Germain. I guessed he'd squeezed in some shopping time.

"Are you ready for the 'Cook's Tour'?" Rob asked, opening the door and escorting me into a crowded space packed with cookware. I followed him down the narrow aisles as he browsed through the *gadgets de cuisine*.

"This is a must," he said, picking up a sturdy small knife with a bent tip.

"But it's bent. What good is it?"

"Try opening an oyster without one." He took the knife and mimicked the motion of prying open a shell.

I held up a small pitcher with a spout on either end. "And this? For the Mad Hatter's Tea Party?" I asked, not entirely in jest.

Rob looked at me as if I was an extraterrestrial to whom he had to explain the obvious. "One side for pouring gravy; the other for separating out the fat."

Who knew there was more than one kind of spatula? Rob did. He chose one for me that could flip a pancake or a fish. Then we got into the serious stuff. He checked out every frying pan from the smallest saucier to the giant paella pans, picking out a gleaming copper gratin pan that I would have used as a wall hanging.

When he asked for an omelet pan, a clerk led the way down a narrow staircase into a basement-like cellar with pots and pans lined floor to ceiling. The clerk climbed a ladder to the top and brought down several pans.

"You want a pan for omelets only?" I asked Rob.

"It's the right size for two eggs. Sides slant at the correct angle so the spatula lifts what's cooked and the rest runs underneath. Small enough so it's easy to fold the omelet."

He held up two pans, feeling the heft, tucking one under his free arm.

"I'm ready," he said, and we carried his bounty up the stairs to the cash register.

Once we were out on the street, I confessed. "I've got a stove, but nothing to cook."

"There must be a supermarket near here," Rob said.

I looked at him with mock disdain. "Your pans can't be touched by packaged food from Monoprix. My neighborhood market is open today."

Without skipping a beat, Rob stepped out into the street and hailed a taxi. "New York training," he explained.

Even though I didn't cook much, I loved walking through the open-air *marché gros*, mingling with the shoppers as they studied each stalk of broccoli or debated the freshness of the fish. I led Rob to the seafood stall.

"Met any oysters in Paris yet?" I asked him.

"Not with my new knife to greet them."

In two minutes, with a dozen Spéciales de Claires in a shopping bag, we moved on to the cheeses. I wanted to taste them all. But the *fromagère* did not give samples, only offered those we dare not refuse: Port Salut, triple crème St. Andre, and Crottin de Chavignol. Dairy was next: a half-dozen farm fresh eggs and crème fraîche.

"Crème fraîche is my big discovery," I explained. "It's not sour cream; it's not whipped cream. I call it heaven."

"What do you use it for?" Rob asked.

"Everything. Maybe even a facial."

We passed by a gorgeous display of produce, and I picked out a lovely frisée, its leaves opening like a flower. Nor could I resist delicately fragrant *fraise des bois*, those tiny wild strawberries, with crème fraîche.

With a quick stop at the corner *boulangerie* to buy a baguette, we arrived at my apartment, panting as we lugged our purchases up two flights of stairs. As soon as I opened the door, he dropped his shopping bags in the entryway and walked to the French doors that led out to the small balcony. It was a gray day, but nothing can spoil a view of Paris rooftops.

"How about a sublet of your sublet?" he asked.

"My landlord is a stickler for leases," I smiled.

We deposited our purchases in the kitchen, and I presented the two-burner stove. "Not much better than my broken one in North Hollywood, I'm afraid."

"No sweat. We've but two omelets to make. Damn, we forgot the wine!"

I pulled a good Sancerre from the refrigerator.

"Wine I am never without. This is perfect with oysters." I opened a cabinet and took out a Burgundy. "And this for the cheese. The omelets go both ways."

"To work," he said, taking out the oyster knife and handing me the omelet pan. "While I open the oysters, you season the pan."

I had no idea what he meant. "Season? With salt and pepper?"

Rob laughed. "No, but almost as easy. Warm the pan on the burner, pour a little oil on it, and then put it in a heated oven."

"I can do that," I said with utter confidence.

In five minutes, the pan was in the oven, and Rob had shucked two oysters and scraped himself three times. It was comforting to know that even Rob could have a kitchen accident. I retrieved Band-Aids, antiseptic, and doctored his battle wounds. He went back to the oysters with determination, while I made the salad and set the table. We worked silently, companionably. Like a team who knew each other's thoughts. Like the image I'd had of me and Rob cooking when I rented my house to him. I shook it away. I wanted Rob to be a business friend, not a boyfriend . . . didn't I?

"Oysters first," Rob pronounced, admiring his dozen on the half-shell adorning a large platter. "Then we'll have intermission and make the omelets."

Sitting at the table overlooking the street, I poured two glasses of Sancerre. With a beatific smile, Rob picked up an oyster, sipped its liquor from the shell, slurped the oyster into his mouth, and let his tongue savor it before slowly chewing.

Rob was in a good mood. It was time to ease into how we might collaborate. Starting with Memphis Slim.

"The recordings went well?" I asked. "It was such an honor to meet Slim."

"He's a true gentleman. Not like TR, that punk rocker I'm working with now."

"You don't mean TR Melville?" I loved his songs; he was a rebel.

"He doesn't have to be a gentleman. He understands what life's all about."

"Ha! Try being in the recording studio with him when he's hoovered a small mountain of cocaine, and he doesn't like the sound mix. He makes you record take after take, all sounding the same. Then when you delicately suggest he take a break, he pulls out a gun." Rob slid another oyster into his mouth, seemingly unfazed. "Loaded."

I was horrified. "Not my idol! I don't believe it!"

"Believe it. He pointed the fucking gun right at me. I ducked a second before he pulled the trigger, and the idiot blasted a Pepsi can on top of the mixing console. The soda shot out and splattered all over the board. But at least it wasn't my brains."

"Scary. What'd you do?"

"What d'ya think? We did another mix. I gave him a joint so he'd calm down, then I played the first mix we'd done. He loved it."

Rob slurped another oyster, savored it and swallowed. "Hey, all I want to do is produce good music. But now it's either disco or punk rock. TR Melville aside, they're not my thing."

"And Memphis Slim is?" I asked.

"Need you ask? I talked my boss into Slim as a low-cost way to try a partnership with Barclay Records. The biggest budget item is my hotel room."

"You could have done worse than L'Hotel."

"I would have recorded Slim if I had to stay at the Holiday Inn. Fortunately, there aren't any in Paris."

"I think there's one out near the airport," I teased.

"Shhh, don't tell my boss," he said, popping the last oyster into his mouth.

"So why did you move to L.A.?" I asked, still looking for that entry into how we might work together.

"Seaboard had a spot open in the Westcoast office, and TR hates

L.A. I was hoping he'd stay in New York. No such luck."

He shrugged. "Also, personal reasons."

Being polite was never my strong suit. "You mean your divorce?"

Rob poured more Sancerre. "Let's say it was the right time to change my life. Now it's time for omelets."

While I watched the master chef, he made the first omelet. Eggs beaten with a whisk, a *soupçon* of water added. Next, a generous pat of butter sizzling hot in the pan before pouring in the eggs. Then the fun began, lifting the edge of the mixture, watching the egg run underneath and cook.

I made the next one. Soft on the inside, a bit crispy on the outside. When I turned it onto a plate, he grabbed it.

"Perfection. This one is mine."

"Beginner's luck," I smiled, and we started our second course.

"I'll remember Paris every time I cook an omelet on your stove in North Hollywood. The stove that your father assures me will now last forever."

"You met my dad?" I asked, not thrilled at the news. I'd assumed my parents had gone to the house when Rob was at work. Now that he'd met them, he had proof I was just a nice middle-class Jewish girl trying to act like a showbiz producer.

"And your mom, who said the house was the cleanest she'd ever seen."

I put a dollop of crème fraîche on his omelet, hoping to change the subject.

He took a bite. "Forget housekeeping. You're a natural when it comes to omelets. Just like my wife."

"I'm not sure what to say," I said. "If you don't want to talk about her—"

"It's okay. I talked about her for seven years. Started therapy a month after we got married. And stopped the night I was offered the job in California." Rob took another bite of his omelet, as if waiting for more questions. I obliged.

"Didn't your wife want to go to California?"

A small smile appeared, as if he had decided to divulge a secret.

"When I was offered the job, an image popped into my mind: driving a convertible in Malibu with a long-legged, blue-eyed, blond-haired girl. Living the California dream."

"Yes?" I asked.

"Nancy is short, with brown eyes and brown hair."

"Oh." Wow. Rob was certainly honest. Maybe too honest.

"I know it sounds harsh, but if nothing else, therapy made me face the truth. The night I got the news, we cooked a celebration dinner—fantastic meal, a great bottle of wine. As we were eating, I realized that unless I did something, our life would be like this for another fifty years. Great buddies. Good cooking partners. Terrible lovers. 'Nancy,' I told her, 'I want passion in my life.' Nancy looked straight at me, taking her last bite of risotto. 'We're passionate,' she said. 'That meal was to die for.'"

I burst out laughing. "You gotta admit she has a sense of humor."

"I'll give her that. She was also quite the planner. We were clearing off the table when she said, 'We'll need two cars in L.A.' That's when I knew I couldn't live a lie one minute longer. I gave it to her straight: I wouldn't need two cars."

I gasped at this new revelation. "That's how you told her?"

Rob sighed. "It wasn't one of my better moments. But she wasn't surprised. For years, we both knew we shouldn't be married. Now that it was out in the open, she didn't skip a beat. I could leave, but everything else stayed. I left that night with nothing but my clothes, my Cuisinart, and my California dream."

I visualized Rob alone on a street corner, facing the unknown, with a Cuisinart under his arm. If he had to be brutally honest to get his freedom, at least he'd done it.

"I have a dream too," I said, ready to tell him about my idea with Memphis Slim.

"Yeah, Kate, what about you? I feel like I know you from your house, but there's no evidence of husbands, lovers, or otherwise."

I told myself I'd never see Rob again after he moved out of my house. Besides, I sensed he might even understand. Plus I'd had two glasses of wine and was feeling a little chatty.

"I'll give you the *Reader's Digest* version: It was the sixties, when anything seemed possible. It wasn't."

"C'mon, it's got to be a better story than that."

"Okay, a few gory details. After college, I came to Paris. Did what you're supposed to do in this city—fall in love. Only problem was the collateral damage—a broken heart." I tossed the remark off as if it was simply another adventure. "So I came home, ended up working in documentaries. I did meet other guys, but nothing ever panned out. There was always something not in sync. And that's how I learned that committing to a bad relationship can be worse than none at all."

"Like you said," Rob concurred, "it was the sixties. That totally explains everything."

"And now, I've got Lucy … and my documentary jobs. But, I'm back in Paris, and there's something here that makes me want to stay."

I cleared away the plates, glad to have busy work. It felt good that Rob hadn't freaked out at my story. That he accepted me as I was. I gave up trying to talk about Memphis Slim; not the time for business. As I brought in the cheese, the sun was struggling to come out. Shafts of light pierced the clouds, exposing luminous blue-sky patches. Time to leave the doom and gloom.

"Now that you made your break," I said, pouring two glasses of the Bordeaux, "how's your California dream going?"

"Instead of a convertible, I got a BMW with a sunroof," he said, slicing a hunk of each cheese onto our plates. "And the blondes were fun."

I nodded, remembering. "When I talked to you on the phone the first time, you were telling someone named Sherry how to cook something."

"She's gone. Along with serveral other blondes. You know, dreams can change . . . I thought my California dream included a Malibu condo or Laurel Canyon retreat. Then I rented your North Hollywood house. Worst of all, in the Valley suburbs. No offense," he said hurriedly.

"None taken," I smiled. "There's a certain charm to the slums, isn't there?"

"C'mon, I love it. There are my walks with Lucy, and on the nights I hang out just the two of us, I'm never lonely. You've got all this stuff. It's like you're still there."

We fell silent, tasting the cheese, nodding in contentment..

"Remember those Oz books I discovered during the earth-quake?" he asked. "I loved those books when I was a kid."

Maybe my clutter wasn't so bad. "Did you want to be Dorothy, too?"

"No, but I went through a Flash Gordon phase," he said as he brought out the strawberries. "Then there's your eclectic record collection: Beethoven's Seventh, *My Fair Lady*, *Sgt. Pepper's Lonely Hearts Club Band*. The biggest surprise was the John Lee Hooker album—great blues artist. I feel like I've gotten to know you right in your house!"

"And Lucy, too," I added. I was glad we had similar likes, but I still wasn't sure who he was. A rock 'n' roll music producer who liked blonde California girls? Or a nice guy who liked to cook, walk my dog, and who believed in the truth?

Then came the surprise. While we spooned up the heavenly *frais des bois* with crème fraîche, he told me stories about Slim and his music—and agreed what a great idea it was for his company to be involved in my documentary.

We only noticed the time when the lengthening shadows stretched across the table, darkening the room.

Rob looked at his watch. "Five o'clock. Shit, I've got a plane to catch."

I gave the dirty omelet pan a quick swipe with a paper towel, bundled it up with his other purchases, and we rushed down to the corner to hail him a cab. With a quick hug, he was off.

I'd forgotten how pleasant it was to hang out with someone I could be myself with. Rob was a nice guy. A cute guy. Still, maybe it was better if he was into surfer girls. It was easier to be a business associate if there were no hormones in the way. I'd forget the fantasy visions of me and Rob, and he'd help me with Memphis Slim and my documentary. A win-win.

As I climbed the stairs back to my apartment, I heard the phone ringing. Probably Patrice wondering what I'd been up to all day. Or maybe Jean-Claude, back from his business trip and ready for a new game. In a rush, I tripped over the entryway rug as I lunged for the phone.

"*Bonsoir!*" I answered, catching my breath.

A pause, then a male voice responded. "*Bonsoir,* Kate."

A stranger's voice, no one I recognized. "*Qui est-ce?* Who is this?"

"*C'est* François Granier."

This was not the voice I'd heard in my head for thirteen years.

"*Je n'y crois pas,*" I don't believe it, I blurted out. Then as the blood drained from my face and my body turned numb, I realized it was the voice of a grown-up François, a stranger François. My knees buckled and I sank down on the couch.

"Fran ... Francois?" I stammered, waiting for him to say something. Silence. Then I heard someone talking in the background.

"You got my letter?" I finally asked.

"Yes," came the businesslike response. "Can I call you back?"

He was the one who'd called! After less than two minutes, the bastard was hurling me into another torrential void, abandoning me again. What kind of a cruel joke was that?

I had some dignity left. "I'm busy right now. Can you call me back in an hour?"

"Okay" was his impersonal reply.

I hung up, my head buzzing as if the universe had made a huge left turn and taken me with it. I had an hour to figure out what I would say. One hour became two, then three. At midnight, I was still by the phone. Still waiting. François was doing it to me all over again. Present and past merged together, as if thirteen years had disappeared.

chapter twenty-nine

1964 November 26 – Thanksgiving Day

Dr. Marcovici took one look at my sweating face, fresh bloodstains on my skirt, and ordered me into the exam room.

"What did you do? How far up did you go?" He spread my legs and poked around. "You went too far," he answered his own question, shaking his head, muttering to himself. "I've seen too much, too many girls … when will the French bastards change the law?!"

His words floated by me in a fever-fog. "Is it done?" I asked, too weak to even be scared.

"There's infection, maybe more. You must go to the hospital at once."

My logical side illogically surfaced. Abortions cost money, paid up front.

"But I don't have any cash for the hospital. I'll have to go to the bank."

I was astounded when he took 200 francs out of his desk drawer and shoved the money into my hand, along with the address of the hospital.

"The hospital will expect you. Don't waste time; take a taxi. Give the rest of the money to the hospital. You'll pay me back later. I'll meet you there."

It had to be serious if I couldn't even take the bus. Back on the street, I hailed a cab, positive everyone was looking at me, knowing I was about to have an abortion. I was supposed to go straight to the hospital, but I made the taxi driver take a ten-minute detour to No. 149. With faltering steps, I entered the foyer and went up to Madame Just's window. As soon as she looked up from her knitting, she knew something was wrong.

"Mademoiselle, what happened?"

"I have to go to the hospital," I told her, trying to stay calm. "The Charpentiers think I have the flu. They won't bother me until next week. If my friend François comes by, please tell him that I am at Notre-Dame des Bons Secours, rue des Plantes."

"Don't worry, I'll take care of it. Now go."

With every cobblestone the taxi passed over, every bump in the road, I felt a corresponding wrench in my stomach. In my fevered state, it came to me that today was Thanksgiving. In America, families came together, grateful for their blessings. There would be love and warmth and good cheer.

What was I thankful for?

I'd always believed an unwanted pregnancy was an accident, easily rectified by an abortion. For everyone else. But not for Kate Miller, the girl who did everything right. Such a smart, good girl would never be in that position. Then I remembered that I wasn't a good girl. I had slept with a boy who wasn't committed to me. It was my fault. I deserved whatever happened.

I, the promiscuous slut, laboriously walked up the steps of the hospital, pushed open the heavy wooden doors with what strength I had left, and made my way down the echoing marble hall past arched windows. Was this a hospital or a convent? A nun dressed in the traditional black and white habit hurried past me, pointing out the reception area. Behind the counter, in front of a plain large wooden cross on the wall, another nun in starched white coif and black habit motioned me forward. Now I was really going to be punished for my sins. Or they'd find out I was Jewish and make me leave. But Dr. Marcovici was Jewish, so it must be all right.

"Dr. Marcovici sent me," I said, pulling out the rest of the money, placing it on her desk.

"Yes, we know. Sister Monique will help you."

Sister Monique, with a round unlined face and rimless glasses, materialized and led me down the corridor into a large room with six beds. As if in slow motion, while the other patients watched, she undressed me, helped me into a hospital gown, and gave me a sedative. I listened to her pre-op questions, her voice reaching me through a wall of cotton. She didn't ask what was wrong; she didn't make judgments. After all, I was at Notre-Dame des Bons Secours, Our Lady of Good Help. Whatever her thoughts about this infidel, she kept them to herself.

She helped put me on a gurney and an orderly wheeled me into an operating room. The last thing I remembered was Dr. Marcovici leaning over me on the operating table, smoking a cigarette.

"Don't worry; we fix everything," he said, the cigarette dangling from his lips. I had a fleeting thought that the French definition of sterile conditions wasn't the same as in America.

And then it was black.

I slept for hours, occasionally waking to an incredible soreness, but with an overwhelming sense of gratitude that these hovering nurses, these angels of good help, were taking care of me. I remembered it was Thanksgiving. That night I did indeed give thanks.

The next day, groggy from the anesthetic, I barely heard the chit-chat of the other patients in the room, women who were having such procedures as hysterectomies or gallbladder surgery. They were sympathetic and friendly; they assumed that I had miscarried, that my husband was out of town on business.

As far as I was concerned, François could stay out of town for the rest of my life.

And so that night I was surprised when an apparition covered by flowers, a stuffed animal, fruit, and candy appeared before me.

"Kate, *ma chèrie*," said François tenderly as he deposited his presents on my bed. I picked up the oranges, the chocolates, the flowers, the teddy bear, wanting to throw them back at him. *You bastard, did you think you could get rid of your guilt by giving me presents?*

But if my anger and hurt ran deep, my need for his love in that moment was even deeper. I had to believe he was concerned and loving; that he cared.

He touched my cheek. "*Ma chèrie*, what happened? Why didn't you wait for me?"

"The doctor said the sooner the better. But something went wrong. It was awful. An infection, I guess."

I couldn't go into detail; nuns and doctors and Catholic morality infused the very air. I wanted him to tell me how much he loved me, how he felt my pain. But I accepted something less.

"Don't worry, it'll be for the best, you'll see." He smiled with that endearing, crooked grin I never could resist. Gently kissing me goodnight, he assured me he'd come back the next day and the next.

On Monday, François was to take me home from the hospital during his lunch hour. That morning, I distributed to the other women in the ward all but one of the bouquets that François had brought, and what was left of the oranges and nuts. I picked up the teddy bear, gave it a squeeze, and put it in the trembling hands of Madame Binot, the elderly patient with a broken hip who occupied the bed next to mine. I wouldn't need any toys for a long time.

François arrived with his typical burst of energy. "Madame Binot, that bear becomes you!" He picked up my bundle and kissed me.

"I'm parked in an ambulance spot, let's go, *ma petite* Kate." He was all smiles and good cheer as he led me out of the room and past the nuns scurrying up and down the corridor, these ladies of Good Help.

I braced myself as I opened the door to my little *chambre de bonne*, dreading the bloodied sheets and blood-stained carpet. But the bed was made up with freshly ironed sheets, the carpet scrubbed clean, the half-eaten cheese and *saucisson* gone. Even my nightgown and robe had been washed and folded neatly in the armoire. François helped me get undressed and tucked me into bed.

"You must rest, Kate, and I must go back to work. I will come tomorrow night." He took my hand, kissed it, and was gone.

When I woke several hours later, I put a coat on over my night-gown and took the bouquet of flowers I'd brought back from the hospital down to Madame Just. She was behind her window, peeling potatoes. As soon as she saw me, she stopped and opened the door, motioning me in.

"*Merci mille fois*, thank you so much," I said, presenting her with the bouquet.

She studied the flowers. "The chrysanthemums look reasonable for this time of year."

Without another word, she took them to her sink, filled up a bowl with water, and submerged the flower stems. Then she took her sewing scissors and cut an inch or two off the stems.

"This is important. You must cut them underwater at an angle. That prevents air bubbles so they can drink the water."

"That is good to know, Madame Just. You are very wise," I said, marveling at her ability to avoid discussion about the real reason I was there.

She found a vase she liked, arranged them exactly so, and put them on the table. Only then did she sit down and look at me.

"So, Mademoiselle, was I also wise to tell you about that doctor? You are in *bon santé*, good health?"

"I will be. I came to thank you for cleaning up my room … and for Dr. Marcovici, yes. Although right now I feel sad."

"That will pass. Your friend François, he was upset when I told him you were in the hospital."

"Yes, but it's what he wanted. And that's what makes me sad."

"Don't be a silly girl. Never forget that it was you who first went to the doctor. And you were right to do so. Don't live your life for the other person. You will heal; you will survive. That is what is important."

She picked one of the flowers and handed it back to me.

"Listen to me. I would rather be a concierge my whole life than be with someone who was false."

I wanted to hug her, to comfort her. But she was done.

"Mademoiselle, go to bed and rest. I have dinner to cook."

In spite of her embarrassment, I gave her a quick peck on both cheeks and made the long climb back to my room. Madame Just had said I would survive, but could life ever be the same?

"The *grippe* was the worst," I explained to Monsieur Charpentier. "Fever, cough, upset stomach; I couldn't move. A prisoner in my bed for four days!"

"Better than if you infected the entire family," he said in his usual dry style. "You will make up your lessons this week."

And I did, although I was still weak and didn't do much else. I missed so many classes at the Sorbonne I stopped altogether. Walking the streets of Paris was my solace, diverting my mind from what I'd gone through, and what would never be. There were unexpected, wrenching moments—a mother pushing her baby in a carriage, a little boy with his parents sailing a boat in the Jardin de Luxembourg pond. Whenever I saw a pregnant woman touch her belly, my insides ached with emptiness.

On one of my walks, I passed by Shakespeare and Company, and George waved me up to the loft. Colin was lying on the faded blue bedspread, reading.

"Kate! Where have you been?"

"Out and about. Here and there," I said, embarrassed to tell him what happened. I changed the subject. "What are you reading?"

He lit up. "I've walked through Huxley's doors of perception into a new realm: Existentialism." He held up Sartre's book *The Age of Reason*. "Listen to this: 'I go away, I walk, I wander, and I wander to no purpose: everywhere I go I bear my shell with me.'"

I listened, inhaling the words. "Wow, that sounds like my last two weeks. I should read this," I said, taking the book from him and leafing through it.

"Sure, take it. It's about a man trying to find money for his girlfriend's abortion."

Instantly, my enthusiasm drained away. I closed the book and gave it back to him.

"Maybe not," I said, hoping he didn't notice the catch in my throat. But Colin knew me too well. He looked me straight on.

"Kate, what's wrong?"

I wiped away tears already dripping from my eye. "The problem that happens when you don't use rubbers. I had to fix it."

"That wanker." He took me in his arms and patted me on the back like a baby. The tender gesture broke open the floodgates.

I melted into his shoulder, finally letting go, the torrent wetting his thick wool sweater.

After I quieted, he wiped my tears, smoothed my hair, and lifted my chin so he could look me in the eyes.

"But you're okay now?"

I gave him a shaky smile. "I found a doctor to help me."

Colin waited to hear more. But I wasn't ready to go into details of the horrible mess. I gathered myself together. "Got to get back to my tutoring. Just wanted to say hello before you left for India."

"Despite my British heritage," he said, buttoning my coat, "I'm not a believer in stiff upper lips. C'mon, take the trip with me. Who knows, we might keep going around the world."

"Colin, you're sweet, but I haven't canceled Berkeley grad school yet. If that 'wanker' doesn't come to his senses, I'll bury my sorrow in Modern European history."

"Boring Books in Berkeley, hey? I urge you to reconsider Very Brilliant in Bombay. Much better ring to it."

As I started down the stairs, I heard his low voice, almost as if talking to himself. "I care about you, Kate."

I pretended I didn't hear. "*Bon voyage, mon chèr ami,*" I called back.

And then, a change. François had been leaving notes for me with Madame Just, and even phoned several times to the Charpentiers', but each time I made excuses not to see or talk to him. Madame Just's wise words echoed in my head--I didn't need someone who was false, who simply pretended they cared.

But when François began showing up after my tutoring session several times a week, refusing to listen to my excuses, and whisking me away to dinner, a movie, or even a Sunday outing—what could I do? He was his old irresistible self, but more important, he seemed truly concerned about my health.

As I healed and was able to look outside myself, I began to sense that he too had been shaken by the abortion. But when I tried to talk about it, the sadness of it, what it meant for our relationship, he would always shy away.

One Sunday François took me to Chartres Cathedral, where we basked in the beauty of its famed blue stained-glass windows—I in the artistic grandeur; he in his religious devotion. As I watched him pray, I wondered if he was still struggling with his decision about the abortion and what he had allowed to happen.

As we left the cathedral, he put his arm around me and held me close. "I have prayed for God's mercy and forgiveness. He understands that none of us are perfect." He kissed me softly. Then the crooked smile. "My dear Kate, we go on with our lives."

I hugged him back, hoping that his beliefs could this time help, not hinder us. Was it possible? Could we become a team again that had gone through the worst, and survived?

Christmas approached, and François invited me home to spend the holiday. I was pleased but surprised. Wasn't he worried that his mother would somehow suspect what had happened?

"Eiem dreeming of ze white Chreestmas," François sang in his off-key, charmingly accented English. Snow had begun to fall as we drove out to Villeneuve-le-Roi for Midnight Mass. By the time we arrived, it looked like a storybook village inside a snow globe.

When Mass was over and Father Xavier bade us a *Joyeux Noel*, I searched the priest's eyes for a sign that François had confessed, that he'd spilled the beans about how he, the former altar boy, had been tempted into sin. But the priest only smiled and welcomed me to this holy night.

We took Madame Granier back with us to the old stone house. François's big brother Philippe, his wife Sylvie, and their seven-year-old twins, Daniel and André, were already seated around the dining room table. François grandly pulled out a chair for me next to Sylvie and gave us both a hug.

"Isn't 1:00 a.m. a little late for dinner?" I asked.

"It's not dinner, it's the best meal of the year, *Le Réveillon*. How we welcome Christmas!"

Course followed festive course. Incredibly rich, melt-in-your-mouth foie gras accompanied by champagne; Coquilles St. Jacques with a crisp Chardonnay, roast goose served with the Pommard wine François had brought. There was much talking and laughing and telling of stories. His brother wanted to know all about Hollywood, and the children had a thousand questions about Disneyland.

I was an exotic alien in the Granier world, and although they treated me with warmth and friendship, I wondered if I'd always be the foreigner, outside looking in. By my third glass of wine I was imagining what would happen if, after Sylvie commented on her difficult childbirth, I shared that I got pregnant and had to start my own abortion. I came to my senses and buried the shameful thoughts I would never say.

Madame Granier decided that François and I would bunk in the living room. It was beyond her comprehension that we would do anything to violate her trust in us. I was assigned to the couch by the fireplace, and François to a cot at the other end of the room.

While François was in the W.C., I quickly changed into my long flannel nightgown and scurried under the quilt as he entered dressed in his old pajamas.

We were alone for the first time since the church service. I had to ask.

"François? It's your business only, but I couldn't help wondering if the priest … uh, you know, have you gone to confession?"

"Some things are private to only you and me."

Once again, the subject was closed. I watched his shadowy form get out of bed and walk over to the old armoire. He opened a large drawer and rummaged around. "Ah, *voilà*," he said as he took out a packet and brought it over to me.

As I made room for him on the couch, he switched on a small lamp, and took out photos he'd taken of the Algerian villagers when he was in the army. He stopped at the photo of a young woman in an embroidered coat, draped in layers of silver necklaces, a stack of silver bracelets going up her arm.

"This is Djamila in her wedding dress. I took photos of her marriage feast, and to thank me, she gave me one of the bracelets she had worn that day. Said I should give it to a special girl." He squeezed my hand, then fished out a small red silk pouch and gave it to me. "I want you to have it."

Inside the pouch was the handcrafted silver bangle, evocative of Arab weddings and harem nights. I slipped it on as if François had given me a diamond ring. With this gift, any remaining doubts about François vanished into the pre-dawn air. This bracelet must be his way of saying that he wanted us to be together; that our love would triumph.

"It's beautiful, François." We kissed tenderly, chastely, not wanting to arouse our desires. We'd already sworn we would not repeat the past.

I snuggled into the quilt, holding onto the bracelet encircling my wrist. For now, this special evening hung suspended in a universe of its own, where our story might have a happy ending after all.

By New Year's Eve, Paris had become a winter fairyland. We drove up winding rue Mouffetard, past the shuttered food shops to Place de Contrescarpe, where lights sparkled in the bare trees, and the fountain's water was frozen into arching icicles. We were to meet his friends at La Coupole to toast the New Year, but first we'd have supper at a romantic bistro.

As the maître d' led us past huge mirrors framed by graceful Art Nouveau molding, I glimpsed our reflection: the perfect image of a young French couple in love. I'd been daydreaming all day about our future. We would rent one of those old apartments in Saint Germain with parquet floors and lots of light. François would become a famous television director. I would find a job at the U.S. Embassy or that fabulous new UNESCO building.

Perhaps in a few years, a baby. I could imagine it all, because there was no doubt in my mind François would ask me to stay in Paris, and he would do it at the stroke of midnight.

Seated at a tufted leather banquette, sipping our champagne cocktails, I basked in the warm glow of romance as François held my hand and touched the silver bangle he'd given me, holding it up to reflect the candlelight.

"You will be the only one of your friends back in America to have a true Arabian bracelet," he said with a touch of pride.

Back in America? I struggled to process his words. Didn't he want me to stay?

"François, I don't have to leave. I'll cash in my plane ticket and postpone graduate school." I touched his cheek and looked into his eyes. "Isn't that a good idea?"

He smiled as if we were having one of our conversations on the philosophy of life. "Kate, so much has happened. At home, you can see more clearly; you can recharge, start again. Then you can decide about Paris."

Decide about Paris? What about us?

A tear escaped down my cheek. Then another.

"What is it, Kate?" François handed me his handkerchief. "What's wrong?"

Didn't he know I loved him? For me, those three little words were sacred—once I said them, I would be exposed, vulnerable. But I had to tell him, even if it meant losing him. I pushed out the words that I'd never said to another, in English or in French.

"*Je t'aime.*"

The mask was off. The words hung in the air while I waited for them to be returned.

Averting his eyes, he spoke in a whisper. "Yes, I know."

His words echoed like a death knell to my heart. I went numb; I could feel only humiliation, rejection. But I was too proud to reveal my broken soul.

I excused myself, dried my tears, and came back with a smile plastered on my face. We had a lovely dinner, though I have no memory of it. Later, as the clock struck midnight at La Coupole, we toasted to 1965 with all his friends. François kissed me and I gave him a hug. But it was the public me that did that. There wasn't anything about 1965 I wanted to celebrate.

Two weeks later, we stood inside the café at Etoile, waiting for the airport bus. It was crowded and noisy, the last place on earth for a proper goodbye. But I insisted that François not drive me to the airport. I didn't want all that time alone with him. My small talk was used up.

"I will miss this," I said, taking in my last look at Paris: a crowded bar lined with Frenchmen adding sugar cubes to cups of coffee, the white-aproned waiters serving at tables with Ricard carafes and ashtrays. I would miss it all, even the blue hazy cigarette smoke hanging in the air.

As we made our way to the waiting bus, I grabbed François's hand as if to prove he was flesh and blood. Again, I felt the electric shock of recognition when our hands made contact.

A last hug, and I climbed the steps up into the bus, walking in a blur through the crowded, narrow aisle until I found a window seat. I struggled to slide open the window as he approached the bus from below. Leaning out, I stretched to touch hands once more.

"The Empire State Building. We will meet," he said, straining to smile.

"*Oui*," I managed to say, still wanting to believe that fantasy. Then the bus lurched forward, breaking our contact. I watched him grow smaller and smaller until the bus turned a corner, and he was no more.

chapter thirty

1977 September 26

How had a thirty-second phone call split my protective armor with such force? The wound I'd not allowed to heal for thirteen years was ripped apart, exposed, raw. While I waited for François to call back, I relived our roller-coaster romance—from the first days of passion to our final goodbye in Paris. Or what I'd thought was the end.

Soon after my return to California, there were letters from François. Lots of letters. Written in the English he was practicing for when we would meet at the Empire State Building.

> *My little Kate, since you are leaving*
> *there is a big empty. I did not think it so big.*
> *All of Paris call again me to you.*

François missed me! He realized how much I meant to him.

It might not be easy, but nothing would stop us from being together.

I kiss many you and I kiss everywhere you.

Once again, I took the bait. This time, it had to be true. I planned my trip to New York, with an open-ended leave of absence from graduate school so I could return to France with him.

Then after several months, his letters stopped. And my letters to him were returned unopened.

Should I have gone to France, tracked him down? I could not get back on his roller-coaster. I could not risk another rejection.

It was over, I told myself. But always there, the mystery. Not knowing why. Unfinished.

Thirteen years later, he had done it to me again.

After a sleepless weekend, I couldn't wait any longer for his call. I went to work as usual, sitting mutely by Annette as she edited, my insides in turmoil, my mind on the empty apartment, imagining the phone ringing and ringing with no answering machine to pick up. François would finally give up calling, and the black void would remain forever.

The afternoon of the third day, Annette paused the Steenbeck, the image of Andy Warhol in the Deauville casino froze, and she turned to me, rubbing her neck.

"I need a break."

She stood up, stretching, poured two cups of hot water from her plug-in pitcher, dumped in two teabags and, as they brewed, paced the room. She glared at me, accusing. "What's wrong? You have barely made a sound the last few days. A few grunts yes or no. You are useless to me."

She reached behind the Steenbeck and retrieved a bottle of Rémy Martin, poured a splash into each of the mugs and handed me one.

"What you need for your malady. I can use it too, after sitting with you all day."

I sipped the steaming cognac-laced tea, its warmth spreading through me.

A few moments of silence, then Annette went for it: "Must be a problem of the heart. Jean-Claude Renaud?"

I almost gagged as I swallowed, laughing at the idea of being lovesick over Jean-Claude. "No," I said as soon as I could talk, "we've been having fun. I can't complain."

"Then what? We must, how you say, get to the point?" she warned curtly. "We need to work."

Annette was always straightforward. But she usually tempered her advice with empathy and humor. Not this afternoon. She was acting less like a fairy godmother and more like a drill sergeant. I caved.

"When I was a student in Paris, there was a young man," I said, as if I were narrating a documentary, the fewer words the better. "It ended badly. Thirteen years later, I'm back here, and I wrote him a short note. He finally called me. Then, after a few seconds, he hung up."

"That's it?"

"He never called back." In my mind, this devastating crisis was obvious.

Apparently not to Annette. "He's an idiot," she said. "*C'est tout,* that's all."

Annette's laser-like perception pierced through my bullshit. We ran through the possible scenarios of why François hadn't called back: He was too busy, too scared, or heard my voice and freaked out. We even considered the ultimate scenario: he dropped dead before he could call back. Annette liked that one the best. But did it even matter? Whatever the reason, the result was the same.

He was gone.

Just like that, she yanked off thirteen years of fantasy, longing, and what-ifs as if they were an adhesive bandage. I saw myself with sudden clarity: a thirty-five-year-old ruled by lovesick thoughts more suited to a teenager.

Now that the festering wound of my youth was exposed to the light of day, there was hope for it to heal. After all, Annette had always seen me as a grown-up, and with a little magic from the green dress, so could I.

I turned the Steenbeck back on and let out a sigh of relief. "Time to work."

A souvenir from Milan to make up for my absence. So wrote Jean-Claude on a package the concierge left in front of my apartment door. Perhaps a reproduction of da Vinci's The Last Supper, the city's greatest claim to fame? Nope. When I tore off the plain brown wrapping, I saw a box labeled Armani.

Wow. Armani was the hot menswear designer, but he'd lately added women's fashions to his collection. I guessed Jean-Claude was having Armani design the wardrobe for his new film. Whatever the reason, this was no small gift. Nestled inside the layers of tissue paper was a meticulously fashioned pants suit. Another note was in the breast pocket: *The Hôtel Ritz, Bar Hemmingway. 10:00 p.m.*

I took a quick shower and slipped on the low-cut silk camisole, the fine virgin wool beige jacket and pants. How could Jean-Claude have known it would fit me perfectly? With its graceful, flowing lines, the outfit signaled sensuality as well as power.

An Armani suit demanded a cab. "The Ritz, 15 Place Vendôme," I casually told the driver, as if I were headed to my neighborhood bar. Not quite. The classic 18th-century Place Vendôme was the jewel box of Paris, and its biggest diamond was the Hôtel Ritz. The hotel's swank style had actually inspired the word "ritzy." It was so ritzy that jeans were not allowed. Not to worry in my Armani suit.

The doorman greeted me like an honored guest.

For one of the most famous bars in Paris, the wood-paneled Hemingway was a surprisingly small and intimate room. Jean-Claude hadn't arrived yet, so I sat in one of the neoclassic green leather chairs and ordered Hemingway's favorite cocktail, chilled and extra-dry.

Sipping my martini, I studied the writer's memorabilia throughout the bar: trophy antlers, photos of exotic places and famous friends. Jean-Claude said the hotel was Hemingway's favorite place to stay. Legend had it that at the war's end, he rushed back to Paris and "liberated the Ritz" from the German Luftwaffe. Apocryphal or not, it must have been one helluva party.

I was toasting to my own liberation when Jean-Claude entered the bar. I smiled and waved, but he didn't acknowledge me, taking a place at the bar as if I were a complete stranger.

He'd already started a game. This was going to be fun.

Only after he received his J&B on the rocks and took a sip did Jean-Claude turn away from the bar, surveying the room. When at last he glanced my way, I was staring at him over the rim of my martini glass, my free hand slowly gliding down my neck, fingertips caressing the top of the camisole, slipping down to lightly brush my breast. He raised his glass and took a swallow of whisky. I discreetly moistened my lips with my tongue, then sucked the martini's onion off its toothpick and into my mouth. He got off his bar stool and approached. He was also wearing Armani.

"May I join you?" he asked.

I nodded to the empty chair. "Do I know you? Please introduce yourself," I said.

He sat down, took my hand, and kissed it. "No names. But I promise to reveal much more than that." For a split second, he grinned and I stifled a giggle. Then we were back in character.

"A beautiful suit," he noted, caressing the fabric. "And a classic fit. An Armani?"

"Yes, a gift from a friend. He was supposed to meet me here, but it seems he's indisposed."

"His loss. Perhaps my gain?"

"A rhetorical question needs no answer," I said. "What brings you to Bar Hemingway?"

"Returning from a business trip to Milan. I am in textiles." He fingered my jacket again. "I always stay at the Ritz on the way back to my home in Lille."

"I see you agree with Ernest," I noted, pointing to a Hemingway quote on the bar menu.

When I dream of afterlife in heaven,
the action always takes place in the Paris Ritz.

"But how could he have written that?" Jean-Claude purred. "He never looked into your eyes."

Another classic line. Jean-Claude was the epitome of French *savoir faire.* Not like American men with their jeans and T-shirts, who said what they thought and put their cards on the table face-up. Boring. Jean-Claude had a silver tongue, a civilized brain, and oodles of charm, even if I never quite knew what he was up to.

He told me about his trip as if he were selling fabric instead of making film agreements. I related my evening with Memphis Slim as if I were a powerful record executive. It was after eleven o'clock when he stood up and took my hand.

"You are captivating, but I have an early train. Please, stay at the bar and have another drink on me." As he shook my hand, he pressed a key into it.

"Perhaps one night we will meet again."

"*On ne sait jamais,*" one never knows, I said.

As he left, he motioned to the waiter to bring me another martini.

Alone again, I sipped my second martini, playing out this new game in my head. I was the stylish, powerful businesswoman who erupts with volcanic passion for one unforgettable evening and is never seen again. He was the traveling salesman with whom I'd have my way. I relished this fantasy of strangers in the night, a game that engaged both mind and body. I drained the martini and stood up. Dessert was ready to be served.

I turned the key in the lock of room 416 and stealthily entered the softly lit room. Jean-Claude was already in the huge brass bed, his eyes closed, a *petit* smile on his face.

I took off my shoes, tiptoeing past the sitting area that bore a striking resemblance to the queen's antechamber at Versailles. Carefully laid my jacket and pants on the gilt-edged chair next to the bed. Then, in my camisole and panties, I leaned over Jean-Claude, his eyes closed.

"Playtime, *mon chèri*," I whispered, kissing him lightly on the forehead. He opened his eyes and I smiled into them.

"*Quelle surprise*, my beautiful woman of mystery," he said.

Strangers in the night carried no baggage. No expectations; no disappointments. Not the past with its ruined dreams and broken hearts. Not the future with its worries about what might be. There was only now.

"What is beautiful about me?" I asked Jean-Claude. "My mouth?" I lightly brushed his lips with mine. "Or my tongue?" And I gave him a deep kiss, my tongue darting, teasing. I was so into the role I was exciting myself. A thought invaded my mind. Maybe it wasn't playacting; maybe it was who I always was but never allowed myself to be.

I took off my camisole, my braless breasts aching with desire. "Or my *poitrine*?"

He placed his hands on my breasts and drew them to his mouth. Yes, they were small. But they were just right.

"I love your breasts," Jean-Claude murmured.

"And *mes cuisses*? What about my thighs?" I said, running my hands down my long legs. "And this, how do you say, *ma petite chatte*?" I said, lightly rubbing myself.

"I love it all," Jean-Claude responded, as I planted kisses down his body. My *petite chatte* turned into a lioness, arching, undulating, performing my own dance of seduction. Feeling heat build inside me. Yes, Dr. Engler, with your red-hot thermographs, you are so right. Sex is fun. Sex is good. So good.

If Annette had helped me see the light, my night with Jean-Claude closed out the François chapter and freed up my life. A good thing, too, because we were down to the wire on Deauville.

For the next three weeks, I practically lived with Annette in her editing room. In an inspired moment, I asked her to edit a scene in the *Star Wars* press reception from the POV of aging starlet Bunny Banks, and in a coup de grâce, Harrison Ford's reaction to her. He was the Hollywood dream on the way up; she was the nightmare on the way down. I was sure Patrice would like it.

"The scene is funny," Annette said, rubbing her neck. "But it makes jokes of film people. Cinema is serious! How about a scene of David Lynch's *Eraserhead*? That says something important about life and death. About fear."

"Annette, You're a genius editor, but I'm responsible for the cut. *Eraserhead* is just too weird. We're keeping Bunny and Harrison."

I hated to see Annette like this, wanting to include something so strangely morbid. My vision was for the inspired merging of art, show biz, and fantasy. And I needed to show Patrice I had the chops to direct *New Americans in Paris*.

Annette was still fuming, so I changed the subject. "How's your neck? Too many hours in front of the Steenbeck?"

"Kate, how do you say? You are the pain in the neck." She smiled curtly at her own joke, swallowed an aspirin, and focused on the screen in front of her.

Best to give her some alone time. I grabbed a chocolate bar from our editing room stash and went to my office to write narration. On top of my desk, I found a letter from Sydney Pollack's office with his signed release. I really had Susan to thank, and I hadn't heard from her since Deauville. Time for me to be the generous one and call her. I checked my watch. It was nine in the morning in Bel-Air. I took a bite of chocolate and dialed.

"Hello?"

"*Bonjour*, Susan."

"Kate! How did you know?"

"Know what?"

"I've made reservations to fly to London for the kids' annual grandparent visit. My soon-to-be ex is simply too busy with his movie star whore, so I volunteered to take the trip, especially since after I deposit them —"

I knew what she was going to say. Why wasn't I thrilled?

"I'll come to Paris! And this time I will stay with you."

Please, Susan, not now! All those times I wanted to see you and you weren't there for me. And now you want me to drop everything for you.

"I'd love that more than anything," I said, hoping to politely discourage her, "except I'm on deadline, and well, remember Jean-Claude Renaud from Deauville?"

"The producer with the Porsche? Of course! Don't worry," Susan said, oblivious to my concerns. "I won't stay long. After a week, the fish Gramps leaves on the kitchen table starts to smell, and that's my signal to get the kids out."

"Sounds wonderful," I said, resigned to the inevitable.

"Oops," Susan interrupted. "The little one discovered how to throw peas on the floor. Think there's a TV episode in it? I'll send you my plane schedule. Bye!"

I was glad she'd cut me off. I almost told her about Memphis Slim and *New Americans in Paris*. Best to get Slim locked in before I said anything.

Rob could help. We'd had a great day together and even seemed on the same wavelength. Not to mention he looked pretty cute in his green corduroy jacket. I shook myself out of the daydream, broke off another square of chocolate, and dialed.

A receptionist answered. "Good morning, Seaboard Records. How may I direct your call?"

"Rob Greene, please." A pause while I swallowed. "Paris calling."

"One moment."

Then, his voice. "Hey Paris, I thought of you last night as I made an omelet in my new pan."

"I'm glad! That means the stove's working." *And that you're thinking of me.* "And *merci* Monsieur, for the omelet lesson. Rob, your stories about Memphis Slim—they're amazing! I've got some great ideas—"

"So does my boss," Rob interrupted. "He's finalized the album deal with Eddie Barclay!"

"Superb! That's why I'm calling. I'd like to set up an interview with Slim, if that's okay with you?"

"Sure, you're working with France-Nouvelle, right?"

I fudged. "I'm sure they'll be on board, but the first interview is for research. We'll shoot later."

Annette was walking past my cubicle, impatiently motioning me back to work.

"Hmm," Rob said. "That sounds ..."

"I'd love to talk more to you about Slim, but I've got to go," I interrupted Rob. "Give Lucy a hug for me and have fun with the stove!"

I hung up, biting down on the last chunk of chocolate. Who knows? Maybe Rob and I might actually work together.

Back in the editing room, Patrice was giving Annette a neck and shoulder rub as he viewed a clip from *An American in Paris*. When he saw me, Patrice reached over and paused the Steenbeck. "You are working my brilliant editor too hard, Kate."

"But we've still got that scene with Harrison Ford and ....."

Patrice cut me off with a piercing look. *What was going on? Did they have a fight?*

After they'd gone, I sat down at the Steenbeck and turned off the lights.

Yes, I would do this. With or without Patrice. I'd find real stories of *New Americans in Paris* for my own documentary. In the dark, by the flickering light of Gene Kelly dancing, I lost myself in my new passion.

chapter thirty-one

1977 October 14

"How many times have I screened a film here? I know where I'm going," Patrice said with utter confidence as I followed him down the hallways of the cavernous Buttes Chaumont TV studios, vainly searching for its screening room.

The picture was locked. It was now titled *Deauville: L'Invasion Américain*, and it was time for Antenne 2's approval. Patrice usually went alone to these network screenings to take all the credit, but I'd talked him into letting me come along so I could learn about French TV. My hidden agenda was to meet network executive, Jaqueline Joubert, so I could contact her later about my own project. I'd even worn my new Armani suit as a talisman of power.

"We must be on the wrong floor; these are production studios," I told Patrice as we walked past open doors that led to huge sound stages. One stage looked like a variety show set, quite cheesy by

American standards. It was altogether different at the next stage I peeked into, where a man with a clipboard was supervising a crew putting up an elaborate drawing room set.

"Over here, Kate!" Patrice waved his can of 16mm film to me from down the hall, below a sign that said *salle de projection*. "Don't make us late!"

Just like a man, wandering the halls for fifteen minutes, then blaming me if we were late. I hurried to catch up to him even as a delayed reaction sparked in my brain: That man with the clipboard. Something about him … no, it couldn't be. François must have left Antenne 2 years ago for his utopian community. By now he was in the French countryside decorating a cave or painting a barn.

I was glad I'd worn my Armani when Jacqueline Joubert greeted us with her coiffed blonde hair, pearls, and tailored suit. We chatted about American television, then I snuck in a comment about the great American singers and musicians living in France. Planting the seed.

The room soon darkened, and we sat down to watch *Deauville*. I gazed at the screen, but I couldn't get my mind off the man with the clipboard I'd seen in that last studio. *Merde*, was I condemned to think about François whenever I saw someone who bore a passing resemblance?

"Bravo," Joubert clapped as the lights came up. "Patrice, your film will attract both our younger audience and the more sophisticated *cineaste*. It will be a privilege to present it." Then she turned to me.

"Patrice's films always have an interesting take," she said, "but the idea that cinema can inspire our dreams and change reality—do I detect a woman's touch?"

I glanced at Patrice, not wanting to upstage him, but he grinned and nodded. "I love women helping me with my programs, isn't that right, Kate?"

Patrice knew how to turn anything to his favor. I would do the same.

"Madame Joubert, your comments mean so much to me. You are truly a pioneer; I remember watching you on TV when I was a student at the Sorbonne."

Joubert began talking about the old days at Antenne 2. I nodded and smiled, about to bring up my idea for *New Americans in Paris*, but the image of the man with the clipboard buzzed inside my head like a fly trapped against a closed window. I had to swat the pest.

"A friend of mine worked here back then," I said. "A young set designer. It was so long ago; I'm sure he's left Paris. His name was François Granier."

"*Mais oui,*" she said, her eyes lighting in recognition. "François is our art director. He designs my sets."

The pit of my stomach fell as fast as a high-speed elevator, then bounced back with a sudden surge of adrenaline. I didn't want to see him. I had to see him. I was going to be sick.

"At the moment," she continued, "he's installing a set down the hall. The second soundstage on the left. You can find him there."

My face froze in its professional smile. Inside, panic. "Thank you, but we have to get back to the office."

Patrice's radar switched on, eyebrows raised. "Kate, we can meet later back at the office." Flicking a speck of dust off my shoulder, he whispered in my ear. "Do it. Be whoever you want to be."

I walked down the hallway, my footsteps echoing, my mind frozen. I opened the door to the soundstage and peeked in. After thirteen years of longing and obsessing, imagining a thousand scenarios in my mind, I had no idea what I was going to say.

Just walk away, Kate. Forget it.

About to leave, I nervously adjusted my jacket and remembered I was not the girl with a lovesick dream. I was a woman who wore

Armani; a curious woman with questions I wanted answered. Why had he stopped writing to me so long ago? What had become of him?

Yes, I could do this. I would do this.

The man with the clipboard was sitting in a tall director's chair, head down, making notes. I walked over and stood in front of him, waiting for him to look up. When he did, I saw his eyes were the same warm brown, but they were tired. There were creases in his face, shadows underneath his eyes, thinning hair. His lithe body had grown thicker with the years; a bit of a belly protruded over his jeans. But he was François.

It was sad to see him like this; but it was also easier.

"*Oui?*" he asked. "*Je vous peux aider?*" He smiled at me, the same smile he had when he saw something he liked.

I shook my head in mock disbelief. "You really don't know who I am?"

Startled, he peered at me through the fog of years.

"*Oui, c'est moi*, it's Kate," I said.

His face turned pale. "*Mon Dieu!* But how is it you are here? You are so beautiful!"

I could not say the same for him, so I stuck to the facts. "I'm working on a documentary for France-Nouvelle, and we were screening it for Jacqueline Joubert," I said in a measured tone. "You would've known that if you had called me back."

He was flustered, but since I was maintaining my cool, I seized the moment. "It was a shock. You barely said hello before you hung up … and then didn't call back. Why?"

"*Je m'excuse.* I was so busy, time escaped me."

So I hadn't missed his call. As Annette had speculated, he was an idiot.

I limited my response to a small smile. I wanted my questions answered. But not with excuses. I needed the truth.

He stood up and gave me the French cheek kisses. "It is good to see you," he said.

I doubted that. But I plunged ahead.

"I was surprised you're still here. I thought you would have left for your *communauté* long ago."

First came the Gallic shrug, then the pushing back of that stubborn lock of hair that fell over his eye. The crew had stopped working; they were looking at us, probably wondering who I was. François picked up his leather jacket. Was he embarrassed to have them see me, afraid they might ask who I was? One of them, holding a large painting, approached.

"Where do you want this, François? It's too big for the fireplace."

"We'll find a place later. I've got a meeting," he said. "Keep working; I'll return shortly."

"Okay, boss."

"Ah, 'boss.' English has invaded *le langue Français*," I said, trying to break some ice. But François took me by the elbow, guiding me, not listening.

"This is no place to talk. We will have a drink." He hurried me out of the soundstage, down a corridor and through the front door of the building. There was a café on the corner, but he didn't stop, as if someone he knew might see him.

As if he wanted to deny my existence.

The studio was near Butte Chaumont Park, but the surrounding streets were clearly blue-collar. François walked briskly down the block, ignoring me, until we turned down a small side street and entered a neighborhood bar with rickety chairs and Formica tables. Tobacco smoke hung heavy in the air. Ads for cigarettes, beer, and lottery numbers plastered the walls.

"*Un carafe rouge*," he told the bartender, and led me to a table in the back.

We sat down on a banquette with rips in the worn leatherette.

I was calm, steady. But didn't try very hard to hide my sarcasm.

"I think you'll be safe here."

No response. Our wine arrived. I sipped, he gulped.

"Really, I can't believe it. Kate, you look *superbe*. What's become of you?"

I kept calm. I wanted him to feel like he'd been but a blip on the radar screen of my life.

"I tried graduate school, don't you remember? Hated it. Wanted to come back to France. But you stopped writing. Didn't answer my letters. You disappeared. Why was that, François?"

I waited for an answer. None.

"I ended up working in television. *Une coïncidence, n'est-ce pas?* Patrice Carrière hired me to produce *Cahiers de Californie*. It airs on Antenne 2."

He nodded in recognition, impressed.

"And you?"

François shrugged. "Antenne 2, never left. I wanted to start *La Famille Communauté*, but …"

He fell silent. He looked like a stranger, he talked like one. Where was his sparkle and passion? I touched his limp hand. No electricity. There was a ring on his third finger. If he noticed I was not wearing a wedding band, he didn't mention it.

I thought of the times I'd been afraid that he'd reject me. There was nothing to be afraid of anymore. And I wanted answers. I heard my own voice, still low, but more insistent.

"François, two weeks ago you called, talked to me for less than a minute, hung up, and didn't call back. After thirteen years! Why?"

"I told you I was *occupé*," he said, eyes averted.

This approach wasn't working. Frustration broke through my patience. Without realizing it, I found my voice.

"Fuck it; don't tell me your excuses. I'll tell you the truth. And you're going to listen. Thirteen years ago, you charmed me, you romanced me, and yes, we made love. It was wonderful."

He looked into my eyes for the first time as I spewed out the words I needed to say.

"I loved your passion, your vision. Your humor. And yes, your body. But also your faith. Except for what you called a sin. It wasn't a sin. It was protection!"

He winced but stayed silent. We both knew where I was going.

"You said we'd have a baby if I got pregnant. When it happened, you asked if the doctor could 'take care of it.' Afterwards, you didn't want to talk about it, and then you told me I should go home! François, I felt so alone"

I felt a tear sliding down my cheek. But it was okay. Holding it in was worse..

"Maybe we weren't meant to be together," I said, now going to the heart of it. "It was the right decision not to have a baby; but it wasn't the right way to make that decision. We could have helped each other through it. Whether or not we ended up together, we would have healed."

Tears were streaming down my cheeks. I'd never felt stronger.

"The worst part was you stopped answering my letters after I got home. And now, the same thing on the phone. How could you have left me hanging like that? Both times!"

He was struggling to keep his stone face, but it began to crack. I'd finally provoked him enough to talk.

"Kate, enough!" His face was flushed, contorted. "You want to know? I will tell you. But you must listen, too." He took a cigarette. "This conversation is why I didn't call you back two weeks ago. When I heard your voice, I knew you would want to know; you would want to talk." He was like a cornered animal trying to defend himself.

"Yes, I want to talk. I deserve it. Why did you send me home? Why did you stop answering my letters?"

He saw it was hopeless; I wouldn't let him escape.

"I knew you would be better off without me."

"That's bullshit."

"Okay, okay, I didn't know how you would be," he confessed. "But you would be home with your family, you would get over me."

"Yes, get rid of me, then you could pretend it never happened."

"I hoped. But no," he said. "That night you left, I met friends at the café you and I went to on rue St. Jacques. We celebrated my freedom, but as I drank, it was like trying to fill up a leaking vessel. I realized Paris was empty without you. I was empty without you."

Memories of love mixed with pain opened inside me.

"I remember your letters. How you missed me. How we'd meet in New York. But that was bullshit too. If it was true, why did you stop writing? Why?"

"It was true, Kate." He was holding on, but I could see the hurt in his eyes. "I remember too well. I wish I could forget."

He tapped his cigarette lighter on the table, nervously snapping it up and down. Unbelievable. It was the Zippo I had given him thirteen years ago. If he wanted to forget me, why was he still using it?

I thought of the handmade silver bracelet he had given me that long-ago Christmas Eve. I'd worn it for years, long after he left my life, hanging on to the crazy hope that he'd given it to me out of love. I wore it until the bracelet broke in two. Even then, I'd kept the tarnished pieces, a symbol of a connection I couldn't let go.

He lit another cigarette. "And this is what I wish I could forget the most: my mother."

"Your mother! She was so *sympa*, so gracious. I loved your mother."

Anger lit up his face. "That's it. I'm done. I don't have to tell you anything. It was over a long time ago."

"Over? I've lived with it for years, that black hole inside of me.

Hating you. Loving you. The misery of not knowing. God knows I want it to be over."

"Then accept it. I have. I'm sorry I called you. I'm sorry I hurt you."

He stood up and put money on the table. "Let's go. I'll walk you back to the metro."

He was doing it again. Running away, not giving me answers. I did not have another decade to obsess over this.

I pushed him back down. "Don't you dare!" I yelled. "Don't you dare not tell me what happened. You, you … *Salaud*, you son of a bitch!"

He looked around to see who was in the bar, who was watching. Grabbing my hand, he half-dragged me out onto the sidewalk.

"*Calme-toi*. Be quiet for God's sake," he said, hissing at me. "I work near here. This is a public place." He hurried me down the street. "Don't you think I thought about this for thirteen years too? Don't you think I wondered about you, regretted what happened? But we must live with it. We must live with the sins we committed; our liaison of the flesh."

I refused to feel that sickness in my stomach, that bottomless pit yawning open. I found my center. I controlled my voice.

"Liaison of the flesh? How dare you say that's all it was! When will you realize we didn't do anything wrong? Don't you even know that abortion is now legal in France?"

"It may be legal, but it will never be right."

We'd reached Buttes Chaumont Park. He led me down a quiet path until he found a secluded bench where we could sit. We were both exhausted.

"You cannot make it right, Kate." His voice was weary; he gave up against my onslaught. "Do you know why I stopped writing? I'll tell you everything. I waited for God's forgiveness. But all I felt was the guilt that kept growing. I did penance, sleeping without heat for months. In that freezing room, I prayed and prayed. I stopped drinking. Nothing helped. I couldn't talk to anyone. I couldn't go to confession. It got so bad I couldn't enter the church."

I listened, shocked to learn of the depths he'd taken himself to.

"I went home to see my mother. She made dinner for me. It was coq au vin, my favorite, but it tasted like cardboard. My mother and I, we talked about the week. She criticized me for something; I don't remember what. I talked back to her. It got worse, and before I knew it, I screamed at her the meanest thing I could think of. What we had done. The abortion. She slapped my face as hard as she could."

He held his hand up to his face as if it were still stinging. "You are an imbecile,' she shouted at me. 'Have you so little self-control, so little discipline, that you must give in to your base instincts?'"

I was stunned. "Why did you tell her? What good would it have done?"

"I was sick, Kate, sick with guilt, and the sicker I became, the more I had to punish myself; to punish everyone around me. My mother especially. She was so hurt and angry, I thought she was lost to me."

Of course, it would have been Maman who delivered the fatal blow. François would have been too ashamed to ever see me again. I had no tears, only an ineluctable sadness for us and the burden we each had carried alone.

"Oh, François. Why didn't you write and tell me?"

He wasn't hearing me. He had more to confess.

"I didn't stop you. Maman said that was my sin. I was the man. I should've stopped you."

"That was all I wanted you to do: to stop me."

"But you were so strong, so independent; you didn't need me."

I couldn't believe what I was hearing.

"I wasn't strong, I was miserable. I don't know how you saw me like that."

"You wanted to discuss ideas, philosophy, find purpose. You were not like the other women I knew. And you were American. Jewish. Kate, you were a strong young woman."

"The answer was to shut me out of your life?"

"I was afraid to love you, Kate. You were too much for me."

He was silent, twisting the ring around his finger.

"And your wife?" I asked. I didn't want to know. I had to know.

"After that night with my mother, I pushed everyone away. I swore to live my life alone. But there was this girl, Denise, who worked on the stage crew. She had a baby. How do you say? *Un enfant d'amour*? Not married—there was no father. Denise would not let me alone. She brought her little boy to work. She invited me for dinner."

I knew the answer before I asked. "You got her pregnant?"

He sighed. "We married in September. Our son was born five months later."

The last piece of the puzzle. François, guilt-ridden, wanting to make things right. And this young woman with an illegitimate child gave him the way out: spend the rest of his life doing penance.

I had my answers. "You atoned, François," I said quietly. "You did the 'right' thing."

He looked at me, this time without shame or guilt. This time with regret.

"I was afraid to see you, and now that I have, I know why. Yes, I was scared to face you, to feel the guilt again. But more than that, I knew deep inside I would feel that connection to you."

He took my hand. In his eyes, I saw the hope that he could once again work his magic.

For thirteen years, I'd been locked in my past, yearning beyond reason for this moment when his touch might heal that wound of loss and rejection. But it was a stranger's hand: no connection, only a chasm impossible to bridge.

With his crooked smile, he waited for my response. To say what? That I still loved him?

Looking at him, I shuddered at the thought. It was all about him. His remorse. His shame.

I let my silence hang in front of him like a question mark. Then I said, "I know," as he had said to me that New Year's Eve when I declared my love to him.

I was done.

chapter thirty-two

1977 October 17

"Dump them anywhere," Susan instructed the cabbie stumbling into my apartment carrying her mountain of luggage. At 9:30 p.m., two hours after she was supposed to arrive, Susan made her grand entrance, still sporting the blonde wig to hide her massacred hair and wearing a Carnaby Street miniskirt and boots. Yes, no matter how busy she'd been depositing her kids with Trevor's parents, she'd managed to get in some shopping.

"Oh, damn," she said, flinging herself down on the sofa. "Forgot to call you. Got hung up in Soho and took a later flight."

Susan had always been the one who led the parade. I wanted to make this time different. I'd even canceled my dates with Jean-Claude so she and I could take the week to reconnect. And though I'd lost my 8:30 p.m. reservation at the two-star Michelin restaurant with the Eiffel Tower view, I was determined to salvage the evening.

I brought out a chilled bottle of champagne, popped the cork, and poured us two glasses.

"To friendship!" I toasted. "There's a terrific little bistro down the street; I think it's still open. Steak frites, coq au vin? Then we can take a walk along the Seine—"

"Dancing, I want to go dancing," she interrupted, "to celebrate my freedom!"

Denying Susan had never been an option, but she did come up with some good ideas.

I casually displayed my Paris hipness. "Shall I take you to the hottest disco in town?"

"Give me ten minutes!"

She rifled through one of her suitcases, flinging clothes on the floor until she found tight black spandex pants, an off-the-shoulder silky white T-shirt, and high platform pumps. I changed into one of my Monoprix specials—flared bell-bottom jeans, tight in the ass, topped by a plunging red tank top with spaghetti straps.

We were ready.

For the rich and famous, Le Sept was the spot to be seen. It was also the gayest, which only made it more *en vogue*. I talked my way past the long line and into the restaurant, thus ensuring an *entrée* to the underground disco. Waiting for the action to start after midnight, we lingered over our very expensive Coquille St. Jacques and carafe of wine. I tried to begin our reconnecting process--sharing long-ago memories of dancing our first night in Paris--but Susan would have none of it.

"Those days are dead and buried, like I'm going to bury that viper of a husband."

Somehow the discussion always came back to Trevor, and how she'd been so terribly wronged. Finally, when even she was bored with her story, she fluffed her blonde curls and swallowed the last of her wine.

"I'm done with the fucker. Let's dance!"

The dance floor was crowded and noisy. Young men dancing with perfect partners--their own mirrored reflections. Susan and I danced together, we danced alone, we danced with groups of gay men. Once in a while, a straight man (or so he seemed) approached one of us, hoping for a *pas de deux*. We waved them away. We were flying fish that didn't want to be caught. Neither one of us needed romance; we needed to dance.

When the DJ segued into R&B soul, we slowed down enough to people-watch. I pointed out Rudolph Nureyev dancing his own funky ballet, and spied Mick Jagger himself. Damn, he was with a new girlfriend.

It was way past 2:00 a.m. when Andy Warhol made his entrance onto the dance floor, a ghostly presence drifting through the haze of cigarette smoke. With his impassive white face and lank platinum hair, he stood like a silent totem, his entourage swirling around him in a sycophantic dance. Then, to the strains of Marvin Gaye's "Let's Get It On," he took the hand of a glittering drag queen in sequined miniskirt and peacock-feathered cape, and the royal couple climbed up the stairs and disappeared.

"I wonder where King Andy's taking his queen," I shouted in Susan's ear.

"Let's find out," Susan said, propelling me to the exit to follow them.

Out on the street, I was suddenly bone tired, ready to call it a night. But when Warhol told his cab driver, "Castel," Susan flagged down the next cab, shouting to the driver, "Castel, *si'l vous plaît!*"

"Castel's a private club," I warned Susan as I followed her into the taxi. "The only way we'll get in is if I mention Jean-Claude's name. And if he's there, I don't want to bother him."

"If he's there, we'll sneak out," Susan said. "Castel," she repeated to the cab driver, "Fast, uh, *vite!*" She turned to me, triumphant. "See, I remember some French!"

We arrived at No. 15 rue Princess in time to see Warhol and his queen disappear behind the red door. I paid the taxi driver and followed Susan to the unmarked entrance.

"*Bonsoir*, Hugette," I said to the gatekeeper, as if we were best friends. "I was here with Jean-Claude Renaud …"

"*Mais oui, la petite amie Américaine*," she said. "Wait here. He's in the disco, I'll tell him you're here."

"How, how … nice," I stammered, with visions of me crashing one of Jean-Claude's business events, or worse, a private *tête à tête*. Susan came to the rescue.

"I'm feeling sick; we have to go," she said, starting to gag as if she were about to throw up in front of the door.

"Another night, Hugette," I said as Susan dragged me away. "Please say nothing to Jean-Claude, I don't want to worry him."

"*Je comprend*, I hope your friend feels better," and the door shut. We ran across the street, laughing as if we'd pulled off the world's narrowest escape.

"We do have a rhythm together," I announced. "Once again, your timing is impeccable."

"Timing, my ass. I'm really going to puke."

We were in front of Birdland. I peeked into the jazz bar; the crowd had thinned out, and a pianist was playing smooth and cool. Susan ran to *la toilette*, while I got us a table and ordered cognacs. When she reappeared, she was smiling.

"Whew, that's better," she said, taking a couple of deep breaths. "Got a second wind. We can start all over again," she said, swirling the brandy in its snifter. She took a sip, looking at me with x-ray eyes over the rim of the glass. "Why didn't you want to see Jean-Claude? Are you afraid he's with someone else?"

"He keeps his business stuff separate."

Jean-Claude was not who I wanted to talk about. This evening was supposed to be about Susan and me. About our friendship.

Yet Susan persisted. "We could have stayed separate from him on the dance floor."

How to explain my sex life with Jean-Claude without sounding like a jerk? "He might want to play games. And I'm not in a game-playing mood."

"Games?" she asked, eyes agleam. "What kind of games? Might you be referring to fucking games? Where does he like to do it? On the dance floor, in the *toilette*?"

I suddenly had an urgent need to elevate my relationship with Jean-Claude to higher ground. "Jean-Claude's very creative in his scenarios. He's, well ..."

"He's rich and powerful," she cut me short. "It's okay, Kate. You don't have to be in love to go after the Horowitz diamond."

"What the hell is that?"

"Listen, and you shall learn," she smiled playfully. "On the plane, I sat across the aisle from a woman—*très chic* if you like Chanel, teased hair, and a figure you wouldn't believe. I'd guess over forty, way over, in that well-preserved facelift, boob-job sort of way. She was also sporting a diamond that'd be at home in Elizabeth Taylor's jewelry box. At least ten carats, maybe fifteen."

Another one of Susan's Hollywood stories?

"The diamond was casting a giant reflection on the seat in front of me. I told her how beautiful it was."

"And?"

"The woman moved her hand closer, practically blinding me. 'It's the Horowitz Diamond,' she said. 'Top-grade. Flawless. But it comes with a curse.' What kind of curse? I asked her. With a straight face, she said, 'It comes with Horowitz.'"

"Yes?" I looked at her, waiting for a punchline.

"Kate, don't you get it? Her name was Mrs. Pamela Horowitz. Married to the cursed Leonard Horowitz," Susan laughed wildly, then stopped abruptly as the piano player took a break and her laugh blasted through the bar. She clicked her brandy snifter to mine, now sotto voce.

"A toast to the 'Jean-Claude Diamond' in your future!"

How dare she! My games with Jean-Claude were nothing like the Horowitz Diamond … were they? I couldn't ignore her innuendo and deflected the accusation back to her. "Well, you certainly got the Trevor Diamond."

Susan snorted. "When I met him, he didn't have money for a rhinestone. But he was cute." She stopped, looking for reassurance. "Wasn't he cute?"

"Yes, he was. But you'd only known Trevor for a day before you left Paris with him. C'mon, be honest. Did you marry him because he was a great person? Or because he had a ticket to Hollywood?"

"*Our* tickets," she corrected me. "He had wide coattails, and I was smart enough to hang on. What's wrong with that?"

She herself had put the mirror up to the truth. Trevor's coattails had become her prison.

"Nothing's wrong, if you don't mind a curse. Trevor got you what you wanted. But then you had to live his life."

I finally hit a nerve. Susan exploded, desperate to validate herself.

"Trevor and I were a Golden Couple. You would have done the same, Ms. Holier Than Thou." Shaking, she downed her cognac and called for another.

So much for camaraderie. What was under the surface for so long was finally erupting. And I fanned the flames.

"You think I wanted someone like Trevor? Look at what he did to you! Susan, you paid too high a price for what you got."

"You bitch!" she cried in a desperate attempt to defend her life. "He's an artist. He's the father of my children." Susan was bawling. "He's an Oscar nominee!"

She collapsed, sniveling like a toddler who'd dropped her ice cream cone. I dug into my purse and handed her a tissue.

"*Calme-toi*, don't beat yourself up. You were young, in Paris. It took a while to see the truth. The same for me."

She wiped her eyes and blew her nose.

"What do you mean? My life is in ruins, but you had that affair with … what's his name." She wiped her face, catching her breath in big gulps. She never remembered his name. "You know, that Frenchman I got you a job with? Have you looked him up? Or are you still running from your failure?"

I had wanted to tell her about seeing François, but the old anger charged back. *If you hadn't abandoned me in Paris, I wouldn't have been left alone to butcher myself. At least you had Trevor; I only had heartache.*

I was about to strike back, spill the poison out, when I realized I had kept my own guilt and fear inside all these years, unable to face my truth. I had to blame someone for what I'd done with my life. I'd blamed Susan and the life she'd chosen. I'd been blaming her for thirteen years.

"Susan, you have no idea what happened between François and me. What I went through." I paused; it was still so hard to get the word out.

"Abortion," I muttered, but Susan was lost in her own angry thoughts, avoiding my gaze.

"Abortion," I forced myself to speak up. Still no reaction.

"ABORTION," I said again, this time loud enough to get her attention, as well as the two remaining waiters. She looked at me, curious.

"What? Who said anything about abortion?"

"I did." The tears were about to come. Let them come. At this point I didn't give a shit what Susan thought of me. If it meant the end of the friendship, if she thought I was a fuckup, so be it. She looked at me, this time intently, trying to understand.

"You mean you had an abortion? Because of François?"

I took the last swallow of my cognac. I could do this; it was just a word. "Yes, I had an abortion. I had to start it myself. I thought I was going to die."

Susan was wide-eyed, in shock. She put her hand on my arm. "Oh, Kate. I'm so sorry. Why didn't you tell me?"

Thirteen years too late, at four in the morning in an empty jazz bar, I told Susan about the rubbers and François's refusal to wear them, about Dr. Marcovici and his Gauloises cigarettes, about Madame Just, about that whole hellish night. Even how I blamed Susan for leaving me. As I talked, the heavy burden, the shame I'd carried for so long began to lighten. I was even able to muster a smile about Oscar Wilde, me, and wallpaper. I shared how I'd shut down for so long, so wary of commitment. Susan listened and did not speak until I was finished. When I was done, she leaned over the table and hugged me.

"That was a shitty thing to go through. But weren't you lucky you didn't get the 'François Diamond.'"

I imagined myself stuck in Villeneuve-Le-Roi; no career, my days spent alone with Maman and the children, church on Sunday, forever carrying the weight of François's guilt.

Could I at last admit it? It sounded awful.

"The François Diamond had a lot of flaws," I said. "In fact, it wasn't even a diamond. Yeah, I went to Paris and all I got was a lousy abortion."

At that moment it seemed very funny, and I started laughing, big gulps of black humor relief at the ridiculousness of the sad reality that had gobbled up my young Paris dream. Susan joined in, and we laughed and laughed at the absurdity of life, at the mistakes we'd made, at the fact that we were together again in Paris, crying over men.

Susan dug in her purse, pulling out her lipstick, passport, papers, and finally an envelope she waved at me. She threw it on the table.

"Go ahead. Open it up," she told me.

Inside were two airplane tickets to Morocco.

"It's still summer in Marrakesh," she said. "We can ride camels in the desert. Have spa treatments at the hamam. Go to the casbah. Stay as long as we want."

"*We?*" As cool as it sounded, she had kids, and well, she had kids.

"Kate, I need you. I can't take it anymore. The fighting, the lawyers—did I tell you? Trevor's attorney said I have to be out of the house in two weeks."

"Susie, don't panic. You'll move. You'll fight him. You've still got your kids."

Susan was silent. She opened her wallet, still lying on the table, and looked at the photos of her darling children. Then she jammed them back into her purse.

"I can't take it anymore, Kate. I'm leaving."

"What do you mean? You've got to pick up your kids in London in a week."

"No, I can't. I can't." She started crying. "Where is my life? The kids come back from seeing Trevor, and all they talk about are the presents from Daddy and his whore. Excuse me, Darlene. And what do I give them? Kate, they take my soul. There's nothing left of me." Her face hardened. "Let Daddy pick them up for a change; let him be the responsible one."

"You don't know what you're saying. Don't make any decisions now," I urged her. "Stay in Paris with me for the week, then pick them up. You'll feel better. You'll be all right."

Susan was calm, no longer hysterical. Which made it scarier.

"No, I won't be all right. I don't know who I am anymore." She shook her head. Then as quickly as she had broken down, she went back to being Susan, taking charge. "Come with me to Marrakesh."

How could I say no to Susan? I never had before. I realized that everything I'd done with her was me following in her footsteps. She won the lead in the high school play; I played a walk-on.

Police hosed her down the City Hall steps at a sit-in, while I took notes for the *Daily Cal.*

Hadn't I wanted this for so long? Susan to need me?

But I needed myself more.

"Susan, I can't go to Morocco. I've got my own life now; I've found something I really want to do. A documentary of my own."

She jammed the tickets back in her purse, annoyed by my response. "The reason you don't want to go with me to Marrakesh is because of your glamorous job, your Jean-Claude waiting in the wings. Don't tell me it's because of some little documentary."

There was nothing to say. Because I finally understood. It was so simple, really. I didn't want to be Susan. If having her golden life meant living inside Susan's head, I didn't want it. The compromises she'd made, the false world she created, the constant struggle to "be someone." I felt a delightful twinge of "Kate-ness." I was glad I was me. I would be jealous no more.

"Susie," I said, "I don't want to argue. I see now that even if you hadn't left Paris, we were bound to go in different directions. But all those dreams we shared when we were growing up; we'll always have that."

It was almost 5:00 a.m., closing time. I wrapped her coat around her shoulders and led her out of the bar, ignoring the bartender's offer to call us a taxi.

Gathering herself together, she murmured, "It's Marrakesh with or without you."

"Okay, go visit the sultans. But tonight, let's have our Paris."

We walked through the empty Parisian streets. Not speaking, and yet communicating in the way of friends who knew our true selves before life muddied up our dreams. By the golden light of the old lamplights, the mystery of the past came alive, and Paris was ours. It belonged to us, this beauty of a city.

There was a brief moment when the lamplights dimmed and all

was black. Then slowly, our eyes saw the city in the first light of dawn. We made it to the Seine as a patch of pale pink sky appeared over Place St. Michel.

Impossibly, a cab pulled up at the taxi station. He sped us down the *quai* and back to No. 1 L'Abbé-Roussel, to the warm cocoon of my apartment. We drank a cup of tea and went to bed as the sun pushed away the remnants of black night.

Susan would never understand my dream, my passion. But it was mine.

I was ready to face Paris on my own terms.

chapter thirty-three

1977 November 1

It was already November, and the games with Jean-Claude had continued with well-executed invention and clever improvisation. But it was Jean-Claude's intellect and zest for life that intrigued me. What turned me on the most were our spontaneous late-night trips to Le Drugstore.

Paris was having a love affair with all things American. One of the hot discos was called Nashville where everyone wore Frye boots and danced to country rock. Mother Earth was a health-food restaurant where you ordered a whole-grain wheat sandwich with alfalfa sprouts and avocado. And you went to Le Drugstore on the Champs Élysée if you wanted anything from aspirin to cosmetics to books to the best hamburgers in Paris.

While Jean-Claude and I devoured those burgers with a good *vin rouge*, he held forth on everything from his latest business deals to juicy gossip about French movie stars. He'd been reading Sun Tzu's *The Art of War* and gifted me with an aphorism from The Art of Jean-Claude: "Life is playacting. Write your own script, then make it come true."

The opportunity to put Jean-Claude's guerilla strategy into action came sooner than I expected, with a party invitation from record mogul Eddie Barclay. The word was that Barclay gave great parties, extravagant soirées with elaborately designed themes. This party was to be a private, intimate cruise on the Seine for 150 of his special friends. Jean-Claude was one of those friends. And I was a friend of Jean-Claude.

Wearing my Armani (what else?), I arrived at the Bateau Mouche embarkation to find a lively cocktail party already in progress. I was waved onto the boat and into a fantasy of red, white, and blue.

The theme for the night's event was a celebration of friendship between the U.S. and France. American and French flags were everywhere in sight; mini flags even waved from toothpicks on the hors d'oeuvres. Travel posters of Saint-Tropez and Santa Monica lined the deck, and Hollywood was the destination on a mock metro sign. I was surprised Barclay hadn't asked Andy Warhol to paint a can of Franco-American spaghetti.

I heard the faint sound of good old American blues, and followed the music into the cabin lounge, where Memphis Slim was at the piano, and with him, of all people, my tenant, Rob Greene.

My first thought: What arrangements had Rob made for Lucy's care? My second thought: Who was the pretty young blonde in a tight minidress he had his arm around? I elbowed my way through the crowd toward the piano when Jean-Claude materialized in front of me.

"Who are you? Have we met before?" Jean-Claude asked with our now familiar greeting, kissing me on both cheeks.

"I'm not sure," I responded in kind. "Perhaps at the Ritz?"

"No, no, Le Drugstore. Burgers and Beaujolais. Remember, this is French-American night. Barclay made a deal with Seaboard Records. The Memphis Slim album is their first joint project."

"I was on my way to see Slim. I was at the recording session," I said, subtly reminding him that I too was a player on the power field. *Write your own script, then make it come true.* "Didn't I tell you Slim is a major part of my documentary, *New Americans in Paris*? Barclay's going to want some of my footage," I said.

"You are learning," Jean-Claude said. "Take advantage of business when you can. I also have a *petit* meeting; we'll rendezvous for dinner. No game tonight, but we'll make the evening profitable." And he was off through the crowd.

I walked over to the piano, not wanting to interrupt Slim, when Rob caught sight of me. My tenant looked as surprised to see me as I had been to see him. He whispered something to the mini-skirted blond and turned to me.

"Of all the gin joints in all the towns, in all the world, she walks into mine," he said in a passable Bogie impression. "I've always wanted to say that," he said, grinning in that ambiguous way I hadn't yet figured out. I played along.

"Then I hope you've already asked Slim to play 'As Time Goes By'?"

"Good idea. Maybe later." He switched characters, wiggling his eyebrows and an imaginary cigar à la Groucho. "Don't worry, little girl, Lucy is in good hands with neighbor Linda. And what brings you here?"

This was a new Rob, the showbiz party animal. It wasn't so much that he looked different. Suede jacket and designer jeans must be a record producer's uniform. But he was definitely not the guy who'd cooked omelets in my apartment. Had he jazzed up his personality for the job, or for the blonde? Could I be the teeniest bit jealous? Nah, he was my tenant.

"My friend Jean-Claude is a buddy of Eddie Barclay," I said. "I had no idea this was a party for Memphis Slim and his record. Imagine my surprise. And you?"

"I would have called you, but last minute, my boss wanted help with the record release, and I flew in today. Although he seems to be doing okay on his own." He gestured to a long-haired man in his fifties with wide bell-bottoms, tight shirt, and a heavy gold chain peeking through abundant chest hair. The over-the-hill swinger had his arm around a young woman in a skimpy minidress.

"Looks like he's ready for *his* release," I noted.

"Which is the reason he made the record deal. Any excuse for a party in Paris."

"Don't let me stop you from doing the same," I said, glancing at the blonde who was now leaning over the piano, all the better to show off her bosom. "Nothing wrong with having a Paris dream as well as a California dream, *n'est ce-pas?*"

"And where is your friend?" he inquired, evading my question.

"Jean-Claude's always got a business deal going; I'm meeting him for dinner. Anyway, I wanted to say hello to Slim."

"Look, the boat's moving," Rob said, pointing out the window. "You can see Slim later. Let's go out on the deck where we can talk."

I was stuck. If I wanted to shift Rob into a business contact as well as a tenant, I had to be friendly. We zigzagged our way through the crowd to stand at the railing. I waited for my straight-shooting tenant with the open face and funny impressions to say something. Anything.

But Rob was silent, staring at the illuminated reflections in the river.

Everyone has an agenda, or so Jean-Claude said. What was Rob's? He was clearly a player in the sandbox of dating. I wondered for a moment if he wanted to play in mine. The silence was interrupted by Eddie Barclay's voice blasting out of the loudspeaker.

"*Bienvenue,* welcome! Tonight, we celebrate our partnership with Seaboard Records, we celebrate our new record of the great blues artist Memphis Slim, and since we are French, we celebrate with dinner! Please join us inside."

"Let's talk later," Rob said. "I've got to sit with my boss and his friends. Glad you're here, Kate." He gave me an awkward pat on the shoulder and rushed back inside.

I went in search of Jean-Claude, deciding to stop enroute at *la toilette.* I was walking toward the WC when the door opened, and a beautiful woman walked out, smoothing her *très chic* scarlet satin dress, patting her shining black chignon into place. Right behind her, buttoning his jacket and straightening his tie, was Jean-Claude. I was processing this information when he waved me over, unfazed by the sight he knew I'd witnessed.

"Kate, I want you to meet Claire Berger. She's Eddie Barclay's PR rep."

Claire shook my hand, quickly assuming her business demeanor.

"*Bonsoir,*" I said, maintaining my cool. "This is quite an evening."

"*Merci.* Very nice to meet you. Please excuse me, but I must attend to the dinner," and she hurried down the passageway.

Jean-Claude guided me into the dining room, ebullient. "I think you will like Claire. We will get together later, the three of us."

I took a tissue out of my purse and rubbed lipstick off the side of his cheek.

"I thought you said no games tonight," I said, not sure how to respond to the sickening sensation in my gut.

"Spontaneity, my dear Kate, is exciting. This is a game not to be passed up, no?"

"But dinner always comes first," I said, avoiding a response.

"*Oui, ma chérie.* I enjoy your enthusiastic appetite in all things."

The fact is I wasn't that surprised at Jean-Claude's behavior. And I certainly wasn't going to let it get in the way of my dinner. We had our choice of foie gras or shrimp cocktail, barbecue ribs or frog legs; French fries or … French fries. While I mulled over Jean-Claude's proposition, I ate well and drank more champagne. By the time we were offered *éclair au chocolat* or apple pie ("a little of both, please"), I knew exactly what I wanted to do about this new game.

While exploring sex from A to Z with Jean-Claude, I had found myself developing a scientific detachment. How many positions could the human body put itself into in the name of fucking? The list was growing, but as much as a *ménage à trois* might add to my sexual repertoire, in my heart I didn't want to play this game. There'd been a real intimacy between me and Jean-Claude. We'd shared ideas as well as bodies. Without that, I had no interest. But there was something I did want to know.

"Jean-Claude," I said as we were served our *café noir*, "did you have a chance to hear Memphis Slim tonight? His music, his story-telling, his life—I'm excited about the possibilities for my program. I'm positioning it for the huge variety show audience. What do you think?"

"Yes, it's an interesting thought, Kate. I'm sure Claire would have some good ideas; we'll talk to her later."

"Talk to her while we're having sex?" I asked, going straight to the bottom line.

"*Ah, ma chérie,*" he said, surprised by my bluntness. "Afterwards, when we feel like talking."

"And if I don't want to have a threesome?"

"You would be missing a wonderful game."

"And the possibility of your interest in my TV program?"

He put his hand beneath the table, caressing me where it always felt so good. I took his hand away.

"Jean-Claude, I want to talk about a real business opportunity, and you'd rather turn me on?" I continued with a smile. "Sure, you're a great business mentor and I know we're friends. But could you ever see me as an equal associate? Excuse the expression," I ended on a light note, "but like most men, you want to be on top."

He again put his hand under the table, trying to make my words about something else. "Kate, I remember a delectable time when you were on top. Perhaps you are jealous of Claire?"

I smiled and put his hand back on the table. "No, Jean-Claude, I'm not jealous." I didn't have to defend, analyze my attitude, or wonder if I was a prude. The only thing that counted was that I didn't want to do it. Not just a game with Claire, but any of it.

However, I did have an option in mind. I gave him my most winning smile. "I'd like to propose a new game. We'll go for the big time."

He was intrigued. "Kate, you are so creative. Tell me what you have in mind."

"A business deal," I said.

Taken aback, he opened his mouth to speak, but I touched his lips and shook my head.

"Don't say anything. I know you don't mix business and sex, so I'm taking away that obstacle. Think about it. I'll schedule a meeting with your office to present my plan for *New Americans in Paris*."

"But Kate—"

I remained cool, betting he would love me taking charge. "I'm going out on the deck now. Feel free to rendezvous with Claire on your own."

As I hoped, he'd instantly assessed the situation and recovered nicely. "But of course, *ma chérie*. Enjoy yourself."

The *bateau mouche* was crossing under the last bridge before returning to the Eiffel Tower, when it hit me. I'd gambled my Jean-Claude game "winnings" for a chance to remain friends on a business level. I knew Jean-Claude loved being my Pygmalion, but his pupil was ready to graduate. I hoped I hadn't screwed myself.

As the boat came out the other side of the bridge, Rob appeared on deck.

"Thought I'd see the last leg from the best seat in the house."

Startled by a loud woosh and a bang, we looked up to see fireworks exploding off the boat's top level. A spectacular display of Fourth of July and Bastille Day rolled into one. I started to sing "Le Marseillaise" in salute to my freedom, when Rob interrupted.

"Was that man I saw you with your Parisian dream?"

"*Pas du tout*," I responded, my face a smiley mask. "He's a friend, a possible business associate."

After a knowing look, Rob politely changed the subject, giving me that wide American grin. "Hey, speaking of business, I've been working on an idea you might be interested in. I wanted to talk about it earlier, but I just got the green light."

"What is it?"

"At dinner, as Slim was putting on a show for us, I reminded my boss of all the great R&B artists out there who are still recording." Rob paused dramatically, then rushed to get it all out.

"It's official! We're going to use the Memphis Slim record to launch an R&B label for Seaboard. A big part of the PR could be a documentary about Slim and the other artists. I'd like to talk to you about it. That is, if you haven't committed to another company yet."

I was stunned. Rob had offered me an incredible opportunity and I was flying—until I remembered all the other opportunities that had turned into disappointments. I had to play this cautiously.

"It could be a good fit. Let's do lunch," I said, the Hollywood reply that meant absolutely nothing. The ball was back in his court.

"Hmm," he said, "Paris or L.A.? Crêpes or burgers? I'll be in touch." He hugged me goodbye and went inside the cabin. I watched him through the windows as the pretty blonde French woman straightened his collar and kissed him. Rob had his California dream girls and his new Parisienne girlfriend. A good sign he didn't need another woman around, unless it was business. Just as well, I told myself.

It was time to get Patrice and France-Nouvelle involved.

The next morning, I found Patrice alone in his office, staring into space. There was a bottle of scotch on his desk, an empty glass beside it. A blank notepad was in front of him, but he wasn't writing, just tapping his pen in time to whatever was going on in his head. His shirt and jacket were rumpled as if he'd been wearing them for two days. He did not look happy—I hoped he and Annette were okay. She had still been acting rather strange. He gathered himself together as I plopped down in a chair and placed a bulging file on his desk.

"Kate, what are you doing here?"

"Last-minute clean-up. Here's the show file, including releases, contracts, paid bills, licenses. I've filed the script drafts and music and production notes in my office."

"As always, you are a pro." He glanced through the folder and smiled weakly. Maybe it was postpartum blues: *Deauville* was airing that night. The deadly quiet of the empty TV department must be depressing. He needed a new project to wrap his head around, and I'd give it to him.

"You're going to love this. Remember the project I told you about earlier, *New Americans in Paris?* I've found my main character and he could be the pilot for an entire miniseries. What a story! Not to mention I've got possible co-funding with an American company."

I waited for him to show interest, but Patrice was silent. Finally, he roused himself.

"I have news, too, Kate. I've put a hold on pre-production and development. I'm leaving France-Nouvelle. No more TV. At least for a while."

It was a bomb of nuclear proportion.

"What the hell? You going somewhere else? I don't understand."

"It's a private matter."

This was not the Patrice I knew. What could it be? Now I was angry, and I was not about to let it go. "Is that all you can say?"

He closed the folder. "Annette hasn't wanted to talk about it until she was certain, but yes, you deserve to know. Those neck pains?"

"Yes, I know she's been difficult, but the film's finished. She can rest."

"It wasn't a strain. The cancer is back. It's in her bones, and it's spreading fast."

"No! That can't be," I cried. "There's always some treatment …"

He shook his head. "I had to fight with her to accept chemo. Last night she shouted and shouted; but I wouldn't let her give up." He mustered a small smile. "It was impressive, her growing list of swear words."

The shock waves penetrated deep inside me. How could I have been so blind? Annette was difficult in the editing room because the cancer was back, and I had only made it worse.

"Annette's done her first chemo, and she wants to be alone. She's going to her family house in Normandy. She doesn't want anyone to see her like this. Correction. She doesn't want me to see her sick."

"I'm so sorry."

"Don't be." His impassive face was now beginning to crumble. "I can't let her be alone. I'm going with her. She can't stop me. I'll stay until …" He stopped, unable to continue.

"What about your wife? You always told me you would never leave her."

"I'm not leaving her. Unless she wants me to. I don't want to hurt Christine, but I've told her what I must do. That it won't be for long. She's angry now, but I think she'll understand. And if she doesn't, I'll deal with it later."

Patrice, always so cavalier, able to jump in and out of bed with equal joy and speed, was acting completely out of character.

"You're in love with Annette, aren't you?"

"You cannot believe it, can you?" There was the hint of an ironic smile. "Yes, Kate, I love her. And she must have love while she makes this journey."

I was numb. I'd heard the words, but they would not sink in. My dear friend Annette, dying. Patrice changing his life to be with her.

I sat there, unable to move. I'd learned how to be the confident woman I wanted to be; how to play the part, to know the rules of the game.

In a flash, all the rules were broken.

PART FOUR

"*If you are lucky enough
to have lived in Paris as a young man,
then wherever you go for the rest of your life,
it stays with you, for Paris is a moveable feast.*"

—Ernest Hemingway

chapter thirty-four

**1977 November 11
Normandy**

"We'll have fun," Annette said on the phone, inviting me for the weekend to Normandy. It had been almost two weeks since she and Patrice left Paris, but she seemed the same Annette, her voice steady and lightly teasing. "If I can't get rid of Patrice, at least you'll be a buffer."

Although I longed to see Annette, I was afraid I couldn't mask my sadness. But there was no excuse not to go. Certainly not work. I hadn't found a new job, and my *New Americans in Paris* project had slid into a glacial holding pattern.

"Of course, I'll come," I promised. The next day I was on the train, staring out the window at the Normande cows grazing in their pastures, not a care in the world. Every day, their prized milk was turned into the finest butter and cheese. Definite job security.

Oh, to be a placid cow, chewing my cud, constantly in demand.

I had dreaded seeing Annette looking sick and in pain, but when I got off the train at the tiny Carentan station, there she was, glowing—from the sun, the wind … and dare I say, from Patrice's comforting arm holding her close. Her colorful scarf was so artfully wrapped around her head, I couldn't tell if it protected her hair from the wind or covered the effects of chemo.

We piled into an old Peugeot and Patrice drove along a winding country road through a scattered collection of farmhouses, at last turning down a long gravel driveway lined with trees. We stopped in front of an imposing stone manor with a mansard roof and round castle keep. My guess was 16th century.

"It's been in my family for generations. My cousin Marguerite lives here most of the year," said Annette as she unlocked the huge carved wooden door and we walked into what must have been an early Renaissance baronial hall, now a living room with leaded pane windows and Persian carpets scattered on stone floors. The comfy sofas and chairs were the only concession to the 20th century.

Annette sank into the wingback chair by the massive stone fireplace. "I've made a deal with Marguerite. First chill in the air, she's off to the south of France, and I have the place to myself. I love the fall in Normandy. I can breathe here."

"Stay there, *ma petite* heiress, I'll get the *aperitifs*." Patrice kissed her, then went in search of libation.

Annette sighed in resignation. "I insisted Patrice not come," she said. "You can see how much good that did."

"I can see he loves being here with you."

"As long as I don't look sick. But we'll see." She winced and put her hand to her neck, turning it from side to side, as if she could stop the pain by stretching. Glancing around to make sure we were alone, her cheerful demeanor disappeared, and the reality of her condition shone through. "I don't want Patrice to see me waste away. I want him to remember me as I was. I wasn't going to do chemo. Why go through that again? But here I am, back on treatments. He couldn't stand me giving up."

"He couldn't stand the thought of losing you."

"That may be, but my hair is falling out. I'm tired, weak, wanting to vomit half the time. I don't want to take pain pills; they make me *stupide*. I told Patrice he could stay only if he kept me in marijuana."

I smiled, but my heart was breaking.

She took my hand. "Kate, can I give you a job? Keep Patrice busy, away from me so I can rest. I don't want him to know how I feel." She looked me square in the eye with a wry smile that recognized the folly of attempting to outwit nature.

"I heard the church tower strike five o'clock, cocktail hour," Patrice said in a booming voice, as he entered the room carrying a large silver tray holding a bottle of champagne, glasses, and cups of crackers, peanuts, and olives.

We drank, munched, and smoked a joint from Patrice's weed stash. Patrice and I told Annette about our filming adventures with *Le Cahiers de Californie*. She laughed at the screwball mix of our stories: singing telegrams, nudist apartments, roller-skating discos, and of course, Dr. Engler's study of the human orgasm. Annette declared that she would come to L.A. for our next shoot, but only if she could participate in another Engler study. Patrice flexed his lean muscles and said that he was available that night for auditions.

Who was this Patrice? I knew the man who eagerly dove into L.A.'s hot tub scene, who separated love and sex, who claimed he'd never divorce his wife because he wanted someone to grow old with. What happened to that Patrice?

Annette, that's what.

The next day, despite the weed party, Annette wasn't feeling well, and "remembered" that she had to look over paperwork concerning the manor. Patrice said we would stay home with her, but Annette insisted that he take me sightseeing.

"Take her to our most important site, the American Cemetery. It's her history as well."

He made a face. "Too morbid. Kate doesn't want to do that."

Au contraire. If I got Patrice to the cemetery, I could sell him on the French D-Day documentary that I'd pitched in Deauville. Then I'd have a job while I researched *New Americans in Paris.*

"I'm told my uncle is buried there," I said wistfully. "Perhaps I can find his grave." End of discussion. Annette would never forgive him if he didn't take me.

Twenty minutes later, Annette had packed a wicker basket of ham and cheese sandwiches, tucked in a bottle of Perrier, a good red wine, two wine glasses, and even a chocolate bar. She thrust it into my hands and pushed us out the door.

I tried to enjoy the trip through the idyllic Norman countryside, but Patrice was seething.

"Kate, you are now my boss? You knew I didn't want to go to this cemetery, this devastating reminder of war! I bet you don't even have an uncle buried there."

"There's over a hundred Stars of David at the cemetery. I'm sure to find a relative."

Lined up straight in a vast field, row upon row as far as the eye could see, were white crosses, with a few Stars of David mixed in. We watched a young woman walking down a row of crosses with a bunch of chrysanthemums until she knelt and placed her bouquet in front of one of them.

"I've heard the local townspeople adopt a dead soldier to make sure he is not forgotten," Patrice said, shaking his head. "Why don't these people want to forget? What good does it do to remember the carnage, the suffering?

"I was so excited when I became a war correspondent in Vietnam. I was going to capture bravery in battle. But there is nothing heroic about war."

He fell silent. I looked into his haunted eyes; his anguish was real. I realized now why he didn't want anything to do with war. He still lived with its horror.

He shook his head as if he might bury the memories again. "Let's go. Enough."

My heart went out to him—he needed to feel it was safe to talk about war; that I would listen and not judge.

"I researched a program on Vietnam vets. The U.S. military is looking into PTSD. Post-Traumatic Stress Disorder."

"Yes, we'll do a sequence on our next *Cahiers de Californie.* C'mon, let's go."

I had to let him know he wasn't alone. "Lots of vets try to bury their memories inside. They fester into nightmares, and the PTSD can ruin their lives."

"You think I ruined my life?" He was instantly indignant; how dare I put him in that category.

I held my ground. "No, but you saw the same terrors the soldiers did."

He looked at me, steely-eyed. "How do you know, Mademoiselle Kate? You and your very safe life. What ever happened to you that gives you memories that never stop haunting you?"

I was silent, but inside I was reliving that night in my chambre de bonne: the pain, the fear, the waiting for death. Only now was I beginning to free myself by letting out my secret, by exposing it to the light of day.

"None of us are immune from the nightmares of the past," I said, "but they don't go away unless we talk about them."

Gazing out at the ocean, he collected himself, determined to prove he wasn't hurting because of Vietnam. "You want to hear my war story? Then you'll stop bothering me?" His voice grew flat, the words chillingly dispassionate.

"I was in a squad camped out in the jungle. This kid, Danny, was special. A Black kid from Chicago. He wouldn't take *merde* from anyone, so of course we connected. I showed him how to take still photos with my Nikon.

"One night I was covering a six-man patrol, and Danny was sneaking photos, when BOOM, a mine exploded. The three guys in front of me were screaming from the shrapnel that hit them. Danny, well, Danny's legs were mangled below the knee. The butchery was unimaginable. I almost passed out."

Patrice took a breath, then his voice lowered, and he pushed the last words out. "But I did my job; I kept filming while we waited for the choppers to arrive. Danny hurt like hell, except for his legs; he couldn't feel his legs. I shot the medics doing triage on Danny, loading him onto the chopper... ."

"Danny?" I asked, afraid to say more.

"I don't know what happened to Danny," Patrice whispered, a look of pure despair on his face. He lit a cigarette and took a long drag, unable to meet my eyes. "The truth is the chopper pilot said I could help take Danny to the hospital, but I made an excuse to stay behind." He had to force the next words out. "I couldn't face seeing him suffer. Maybe die. That's the worst part of the nightmare. I didn't have the guts to stay until the end. I couldn't help him through it."

He finally looked at me. "That's the memory I live with, Kate. Most of the time it's buried; but it never goes away, waiting for something to trigger it. Could be a helicopter, a walk through a cemetery ... and I hear Danny screaming for me as they put him on the chopper."

It was out. The shame, the guilt, the what-ifs that fed Patrice's nightmare until it had become his own personal monster.

He ferociously ground out the cigarette. "I've been so worried about my Annette. Whether I can be strong enough to watch her suffer, to stay to the end, to love and support her."

I took his hand and we stayed quiet, until the gray clouds took over, the rain began to fall, and we ran to the cover of our car.

The next day Annette appeared at breakfast smiling under a jaunty fisherman's cap, wearing one of those blue and white striped French sailor shirts. She looked radiant, claiming last week's chemo was gone from her system. Not to mention, she'd also smoked a joint.

"Today is for Kate and me," she announced. "*Le* shopping!"

Annette had driven those narrow curving roads since she was a teenager, and we whizzed into Ste. Mère Église, a town made famous as a D-Day landing site for U.S. paratroopers, its shop windows still displaying *Merci* signs to the American GIs. In one boutique, she bought a pair of golden hoop earrings to go with her gypsy scarf. She even looked through next spring's fashions; either she felt she'd live long enough to enjoy them, or money didn't mean anything now and she might as well enjoy spending it. She was fearless, but she was also tired. I needed to find her a place to rest.

"I'm starved. How about lunch?" I asked.

"Yes, let's go to Café Matilde's down the street. It's been here since I was a child."

The tiny café was already crowded with locals and tourists. Matilde, the owner, an apron barely covering her buxom body, recognized Annette, hugged her vigorously, and took us to one of the wooden tables by the window, removing the RESERVÉ card and planting it on a less favorable table.

"Don't even look at the menu," Annette said. "We are eating à la *Normandaise* today. The only question is, galette or crépe?"

"And the difference is?"

"The Galette Complète is made of buckwheat, grated cheese, a slice of ham and an egg on top. *Delicieux!*"

"Then it's the Galette Complète for me."

"For dessert, the crêpe with apples, crème fraîche, calvados." She kissed her fingers. "Heaven."

Without asking, Matilde brought us two large mugs, and Annette ordered lunch.

"It's cider," Annette explained, as she took a good swallow. "Not like any you have ever tasted." She clinked her mug against mine. "I am happy today. I can eat … and drink!"

I took my own swig of the freshest, crispest apple in a liquid form. Endowed with enough alcohol to make me feel very, very good.

"It's great to see you like this," I said. "How are you feeling?"

"I am happy today, but the chemo has been *dégueulasse,* or as you say in proper English, it sucks. I did it only for Patrice. We had such a fight about it!"

Annette would rather live in the moment, be happy. She was still teaching me.

The Galettes Complète arrived and we savored every mouthful of egg, crépe, and ham. Only then did she tell me why she was feeling so good.

"I cannot bear the chemo. I must listen to my own voice. I'm stopping." Annette waited while I digested the dire meaning of her decision.

My heart was breaking. But how could I know what I would do in such a situation? It was her choice.

"The doctor called yesterday when you were out with Patrice," she explained. "The latest test results were worse. I could keep up the treatments, maybe have four or five more months living with this shitty feeling … or stop the poison and have some good days."

"Maybe get a second opinion?"

"I've had a second opinion, and third as well. It's the same."

It was her life; her decision.

I responded calmly, as if we were discussing having a tooth pulled. "And Patrice? You've told him?"

"Yes, last night." She shrugged. A tear appeared in her eye.

"Annette, remember, you were my confessor. Let me return the favor. I won't tell him anything. I swear."

"No, it's not like that. I am crying because he listened to me. For the first time, he didn't try to change my mind. I told him he should go back to Paris. I warned him I would look terrible. He said I would always be beautiful to him. That he wanted to stay."

Tears were running down her cheeks.

I handed her a tissue. "I'm glad. There may still be some hope for him."

She wiped away the tears. "What did you two talk about yesterday? He seems different."

I shrugged. "Oh, the usual. A lot of spirited discussion."

Annette sniffed the apple crêpe, letting its Normandaise aroma infuse her spirit. "I'm so glad you came, Kate. *Bon appetit!*"

Sleep did not come easily that night. At 3 a.m., I wrapped a quilt around my shoulders and went down to the drawing room, looking for a cognac to settle me. Patrice was in the wingback chair, stoking the fireplace. I poured us both a Courvoisier.

"She told you about the chemo?" he asked.

"Yes. I sensed she'd stop, just not so soon." I gave him his cognac and sat on the sofa next to him.

"I don't want to lose her, Kate. But I'd rather face my sadness with her than without her."

"Now you see what love does."

"I always knew what love does. That's why I avoided it."

He threw a couple more logs on the fire. "You've changed. You seem stronger. To get me to talk about Vietnam, it took courage. You wouldn't have said those things to me back in L.A. . . ."

"No? You forget too soon. How about that night at Greenblatt's? Eating cheesecake?"

He laughed at the memory. "The cheesecake. I love that cheesecake."

He lit a cigarette and offered me one. What the hell, I took it.

He blew one of his fancy smoke rings. "Yes, I remember our chat as well as the cheesecake. Sex versus love, wasn't it?"

"Yes, and will you not agree with me that what you have with Annette is worth more than a million nights of casual sex?"

"Yes, Annette has become my guiding star; I will follow her until I can no more. But Kate, there is no right answer. If you have no one like Annette in your life, you must still live, enjoy the moment. Don't forget that."

"Patrice," I said, "I am only speaking theoretically, but my research of the last couple of months proves your argument is sound. However, I've decided I prefer the combo: love and sex together."

"In the meantime, don't starve. Have fun." He smiled his wicked, impish grin.

Back in my room I turned off the lamp, and in the darkness I looked out the window. A million stars sparkled in the sky. Were there more stars in France than in California? More choices, more inspiration? Or were they merely easier to see?

The next morning as I boarded the train back to Paris, I hugged Annette goodbye. "I'll miss you."

"I know. Me too," she replied.

We both knew what we were saying. As the train pulled away from the station, I took photographs with my mind, concentrating on how I would remember her—wearing the gold hoop earrings dangling below her headscarf, blowing me a kiss. Was that a wink as she waved to me? I was too far away to be sure, but I'd remember it that way; a cosmic wink at life, how we always want more as soon as we can't have it.

The last image I saw as the train went around the bend was Patrice hugging her. He'd be facing his biggest challenge: how to love someone you had to lose.

Poor Patrice. Lucky Patrice.

It began to rain. Sheets of water slammed the train windows, obscuring the view. I pulled out the book Patrice had given me that had been gathering dust on the manor's bookshelves: *The Myth of Sisyphus*. During my young dark days in Paris, looking for meaning and a purpose, I'd read the book. But I couldn't understand how Sisyphus could keep pushing that damn rock up the hill, only to have it fall back down over and over again. Condemned to failure, destined to live without a higher purpose, without hope. Thirteen years ago, I'd slammed the book shut, certain there must be more to life than that.

As I reread the chapter on Sisyphus, I again imagined carrying a rock up the mountain. But this time my rock was polished, sculpted to my design. As I walked, I'd enjoy spring weather and the bucolic view of the valley below. Knowing me, I'd trip on a gnarly root or a slippery pebble, too proud to ask for help, ashamed of appearing weak. I'd struggle to get back on my feet. But once I shared with fellow hikers, their support made it easier. Arriving at the summit, I'd set my rock down in triumph. Only to watch it slide right back down the mountain.

I closed the book and stared out the window as the rain tapered off. I thought of all the challenges I'd already faced hauling my "rock" up a mountain filled with obstacles: returning to Paris to face my past, struggling to make my own film, confronting François, even my time with Jean-Claude. Each climb had given me a new taste of life, whether or not I'd reached a destination. Could it be … was it possible … that the meaning was in the journey itself?

chapter thirty-five

1977 November 14
Paris

What a sight he was in his three-piece pinstriped suit and bowler hat. Jauntily waving his walking stick, Memphis Slim stepped out of his Silver Shadow Rolls-Royce on boulevard Montparnasse and sauntered into La Coupole.

Fitzgerald and Hemingway had done their share of drinking at this legendary brasserie. Now it was Slim who had his favorite table.

For hours that afternoon, Slim and I drank Johnnie Walker Red in the restaurant's Bar *Américain* and talked about the blues and life in Paris. We had such different backgrounds, but we were on the same wavelength: We had both found *liberté*, égalité, *fraternité* in this city. As darkness fell and Paris turned on its bright lights, Slim swallowed the last drop of his scotch, and took a Mont Blanc fountain pen out of his breast pocket. He picked up a paper napkin, scribbled something and handed it to me with a flourish.

I give Kate Miller exclusive rights to film me in a documentary!
Signed, Peter Chatman aka Memphis Slim

"That's my promise, Kate. "We'll get going on this as soon I get back from my European tour in April."

I was thrilled. My bubble was riding high, but how did I keep it afloat until April?

My only work offer was Patrice's under-the-table job translating France-Nouvelle photo captions. I tried it, I was good at it, and for eight hours I silently screamed with boredom. This was not the Sisyphean rock I wanted to push up the mountain for a day, let alone eternity.

My short-term lease at No. 1 L'Abbé-Roussel was almost up. The rental agent promised to find me another apartment, but everything he showed me was dark and dreary.

I considered my options. One: A mind-numbing workday followed by a depressing evening in an ugly apartment. Two: A trip home to regroup. Within six months, Patrice could be back at France-Nouvelle, ready to have me develop documentaries on the French D-Day and *New Americans in Paris*. Meanwhile, my best chance of finding seed money was in L.A., especially if Rob Greene got Seaboard Records involved with Memphis Slim. I could pick up freelance jobs, work on the *New Americans* proposal, and take meetings. It was hard to leave Paris, but the thought of returning soon to France made the decision easier. Besides, I would be with my beloved Lucy.

Life was promising once more.

I called Rob and gave him notice on the house. He was surprised to hear I was coming home, but as always, pleasant and friendly.

"Too bad I didn't have more time in Paris; we could have eaten more oysters."

"*C'est la vie*," I said. "You were busy with your friend."

"The blonde? Nah, she was one of my boss's party girls. Although I did learn a few more words of French."

"A little pillow talk is the best way to learn another language," I said, the words popping out of my mouth.

He came back at me. "*Oui*, I suppose your French has improved."

Be pleasant, Kate, stick to business. "Yes, I even spoke French with Memphis Slim. We drank scotch together at La Coupole, and he's signed on …"

"Damn," he interrupted, "I've got a call from TR Melville. Got to go, but don't worry, I'll find a place to live. Give me a couple of weeks."

"I'll extend your lease if you need the time," I assured him.

"A good businesswoman is irresistible," he laughed. "*A bientôt*."

For a guy with an open all-American face, Rob was as much a mystery as ever. But we'd had fun in Paris, and if I was lucky, he'd help me with Memphis Slim.

I called my parents, who were thrilled with the news and offered their guest bedroom until Rob moved out of my house. "Can't wait to have some of your meatloaf," I told Mom, and this time I meant it.

The returning French diplomat who owned my apartment was fortuitously delayed in Teheran, which gave me time to wrap things up. I spoke often with Patrice and Annette. They were playing card games, watching TV, cuddling and eating chocolate. Enjoying each day.

I invited Jean-Claude for a drink at the Ritz. I'm sure he thought I had a new *sexe sportif* game to play. Instead, while he enjoyed his J&B, I pitched my proposal for *New Americans in Paris*. He listened with interest, and even complimented my persistence.

"Kate, it's a great idea, but Eddie Barclay wants *me* to do a special on Memphis Slim. Imagine that!"

I really loved this new game. "Sorry, Jean-Claude, but I've got an exclusive with Slim."

Jean-Claude's suave, debonair demeanor flinched. But business was business, and he was now facing a worthy adversary.

"Perhaps we could discuss some French participation," he said.

Life was still full of surprises.

On my last day in Paris, the Eiffel Tower was lost in fog and the Seine a murky black. No matter, my mission was clear. I found a flower stand at the Montparnasse Train Station, bought a budding white azalea plant, and walked down Rue de Rennes to No. 149.

Her hair was gray and she wore reading glasses, but Madame Just was still sitting at her table, cutting vegetables. She looked up at me, knowing instantly who I was. Had I come to see the Charpentiers? They had moved, she said, after the children left home.

"*Mais non*, Madame Just," I told her. "I came to visit you."

She shook her head as if she could not understand why I would go out of my way to see her, but she accepted the azalea plant. "They need a special kind of soil to grow. I will take care of it."

I smiled. "As you took care of me, Madame Just." I thanked her again, but she only smiled curtly and cut me off. I wished her well and left, knowing we had truly understood each other.

I took my last metro ride to boulevard St. Michel and hurried through the cold into the coziness of Shakespeare and Company. As always, George Whitman was behind his desk. I asked him if he remembered Colin, the Brit who wrote poetry back in 1964.

"Colin?" He studied my face. "Ah, you were Colin's friend."

I nodded. "Do you know what happened to him?"

"He disappeared to India. But then a few years ago, out of the blue, I got a shipment of his book of poetry. He gave a reading and signed them. Then gone again. Don't know where."

"He wrote a book!" I said. "Do you have any left? I'd like to buy one."

George reached behind his desk and handed me a dog-eared book with a ripped cover. "It was in our lending library. Got some use," he apologized.

"Even better."

Flipping through *Knickers in a Twist*, I stopped at a page with a short poem titled "Training the Shrew." It was Colin's offering to me during the dark times of that other Paris.

> *A small tree,*
> *helpless,*
> *needs only a support,*
> *which by being there*
> *strengthens,*
> *and the tree grows straight.*

"Take the book; a present," George offered, seeing my obvious attachment to it.

"No, no, I have to pay for it. I must." I gave him 20 francs.

As I exited the bookstore, I noticed a faint glimmer of sunlight behind Notre-Dame. As if pulled by a magnet, I crossed the bridge and entered the cathedral. Noisy tourists were milling about, and the stained-glass windows were as dull as the weather. But none of that mattered. I walked down a side aisle lined with statues of saints and stopped at the one with the most burning candles. Digging out some coins, I deposited them in the box and lit a candle for Annette, with a wish that she would find peace.

I'm not sure what inspired me, but I lit a second one. A just-in-case, covering-all-the-bases candle. This one for the few biological cells that had once been in my body, cells that came from François and me. I stood in front of the candle, watching the flame take hold and burn brightly. I was about to leave when I saw a choir boy in front of the altar, and knew I needed one more candle.

For François. In forgiveness.

It was almost Thanksgiving. This year, I would be home.

chapter thirty-six

1977 November 26
North Hollywood

North Hollywood definitely wasn't Paris, but there were shady trees and friendly neighbors. Not to mention it was Thanksgiving weekend and I was wearing only a light T-shirt, sandals, and jeans. I squinted against the sun as I knocked on my own front door. Rob had a few days left on his lease, but I couldn't wait to see Lucy. When Rob opened the door, I was kneeling on the porch, braced for her onslaught of love.

Instead she stopped short at the front door, uncertain. A few months must have been like years to her.

"Lucy, my love!" I cried, reaching out to hug her, to bury my face in her fur.

"She was eating her breakfast," Rob explained. "Welcome back. Come in!"

I entered an episode of *The Twilight Zone*. It was my house, but not my home. Kate clutter disappeared, and strange alien objects had invaded. Boxes of promo records next to my stereo. On the coffee table, a pipe rack, ashtray, *Rolling Stone* and *New Yorker*. A racquetball glove and racquet propped against the wall. Even a new fern on the dining room table.

I was the uncomfortable guest; Rob, the gracious host. He brought me a cup of coffee, offered a chair and sat down on the sofa. Lucy had followed him into the living room and took her place at Rob's feet.

"I see who's the boss," I said, sipping the freshly brewed coffee.

Rob patted Lucy on the back. "She's a good girl. We've had a great time." He straightened the magazines on the table, brushing away a few stray Lucy hairs. "I've loved being here. I told you in Paris that I was getting to know you through this house; you seemed to be everywhere." He motioned vaguely in the air. "But now that you're here, I'm not quite sure what to do with you." He laughed at the absurdity of the situation.

"Hey, I'm the guest today," I reassured him. "I see you've added some homey touches. I especially like the pipe rack."

He picked up the ashtray that sat next to it and handed it to me. It was one of those French ashtrays advertising Ricard Anisette.

"I lifted this off the *bateau mouche* in Paris. It's for you."

"That's sweet, but you should keep it. Impress all the California girls with your international flair."

He shrugged, a slight smile on his face. "Remember when you came to my office to sign the lease?" he asked.

"Sure," I said. "Best business deal I made this year."

He laughed. "I gave you cash. After you left, my assistant said you were cute."

"How nice of him."

"No. I mean, yes. What I mean is right now, you look cute.

Well, maybe not cute," he backtracked, "but you look right. You look like you belong here."

"Well, it is my house." I smiled.

He scratched his beard. "That was the problem. Every time I had a girl over, I'd think of you being here. And now that you're here, I understand why. It's your personal touches that made it such a great house."

"When I go back to Paris in six months, you can move back in," I offered.

"No, no, I see now, this very second, that you need to be here; this house is you. Anyway, I've rented a house up in Laurel Canyon with a swimming pool and a year's lease. In fact, Kate, it's a good thing the landlord is an old man who's moving to a retirement home." He paused, as if there was something else on his mind. "When girls saw your photo, you almost ruined a few evenings."

"'Almost' is the operative word, I believe."

He laughed out loud. "That's what I mean. You make me laugh. You cook a good omelet. I want to talk about music and books with you. I want to know what you thought of *Tik-Tok of Oz*. We really should be friends. I bet we know a lot of people in common."

"Don't forget the pooch in common," I said. "She's going to be very upset when you leave."

"Would you consider visiting privileges for Uncle Rob?" he asked. As if to add her vote, Lucy presented her rear end to him, and he vigorously patted her on the fanny.

"Sure, permission granted," I said, knowing that after a few weeks he'd be on to his new life, and Lucy would simply be one more female he'd loved and left.

"She can stay until I move out," he said. "Don't want to confuse her more than necessary."

"Oh, Lucy, you're going to be so discombobulated, I'll have to get you a therapist." I got down on Lucy's level and gave her a big hug. This time she accepted it, rolling over on her back, inviting us to scratch her tummy. I felt a sudden rush of togetherness with Lucy and Rob; all three of us with the common objective of getting her tummy rubbed. What had this dog gotten me into?

"I'll be out by Sunday noon," Rob said. "Lucy will be inside and the key under the mat."

He was clearly back to business, and I pushed any thoughts of togetherness away.

"How's the Memphis Slim record coming along?" I asked him.

"Cross your fingers. It's being released in a few days. I'll bring over an album. If it sells, I'll have the leverage to bring you in for a meeting about that documentary."

With these words, I at last solved the mystery of Rob Greene's motives. He was a friend. Truly interested in my filmmaking skills; not giving me the kind of vague promise that usually led to a casting couch. Professional. The way it should be.

And I left, thinking, how cool, I was going to get a free record.

Two weeks later, I was settled back in the house, Lucy had returned to normal, and I'd found a freelance job locating stock footage for an African wildlife documentary. I was paying my bills and keeping my furry baby in kibble. I even started working on a Memphis Slim budget. The *New Americans* proposal was almost finished. Life was good.

But the house felt empty.

Late at night, before I went to bed, I'd walk through the rooms, trying to see it through Rob's eyes. What was so special about it? As far as I could see, it was just a house. But when I hung my green dress and Armani suit in the hall closet, I found a tuxedo and a fringed suede jacket hanging there, clothes he'd left behind. The next day, mixed in with my records, I came across some of his albums: Miles Davis, Hall & Oates, Steely Dan.

Had his spirit blended in with mine? No, I was sure Rob Greene was already on to his next California dream. Besides, I had my own dreams to realize. I was truly happy by myself.

When I took Lucy for walks, she tried to sniff at a poodle who ignored her. "Lucy, you'll find another dog who wants to play," I assured her, reflecting on complications that come with relationships. Anyway, who needed them? I'd been saved from a lifetime of challenges with François.

Susan and Trevor—they deserved each other. Jean-Claude and his ex-wife? Had they even had a relationship? And then of course, Patrice and Annette. Their love was beautiful, but it came with heartbreak. If I was ever going to accept love's complications, it better be with a partner who saw the value in helping each other push our rocks up the mountain.

So why did the house seem empty? Why did Lucy curl up at the front door, as if waiting for someone's footsteps on the walk? I decided we both needed time to readjust. I knew that one day soon I would have a reason to put on the Armani suit or the green dress, and I would be back at the banquet. Until then, everything was fine.

Almost a month after I'd moved back in, I hadn't received the album Rob had promised me, and besides, a few of his clothes and records were still in the house. I called him.

"Not that your tux doesn't look great in my closet," I said, "but some day you might want to wear it. Besides, I'd love to hear the Memphis Slim album." Hint, hint.

He was his ever-pleasant self. He'd been meaning to call, but he'd been frantic with work, especially with the new R&B label. He'd drop over on his way home from work.

At 7:00 p.m., Lucy perked up her ears and started barking. She ran to the door before the bell even rang.

"Lucy, calm down. I'm sure it's just Rob."

I opened the door. Yes, there was Rob in a TR Melville baseball jacket, a Steely Dan T-shirt, and jeans. He looked down as Lucy ran out on the porch to welcome him.

"Lucy, I'm home," he said, in his best Ricky Ricardo voice, happy to be back from work at his Cuban nightclub.

I burst out laughing, and he followed suit. But as he looked up at me, he grew more serious. He took a deep breath.

"Kate, it took me awhile, but guess what I figured out?"

I shrugged. "You've got a career as a celebrity impressionist?"

He almost laughed again but stopped himself. "No, there's only one way to say this to you," he said. "As the real Rob Greene." He took another deep breath. "Try as one might, you can't plan your life. It simply happens."

What did that mean?

"Yes?" I asked.

"I tried to ignore it. It's useless. You, Ms. Kate Miller, are not my landlady anymore. But I think you are my real California dream."

I stared at him, speechless, trying to understand. That's when Lucy jumped up and humped his leg, and I understood everything.

Because in one hand, Rob Greene held the album … in the other, a single red rose.

Epilogue

*"The art of life is not controlling
what happens to us,
but using what happens."*

--Gloria Steinem

2022 May 14
Los Angeles
The Women's March

Pink, pink, everywhere pink. I ride the frothy wave of women in knitted pink pussy hats jamming into L.A.'s Pershing Square. I'm to meet Susan in front of Starbucks, but she texts that she's trying to find Jane Fonda and pitch a movie idea. Knowing Susan, she'll make it happen. That's okay, because I'm exactly where I need to be, in this sea of pink surging forward to claim women's rights—no, *human* rights.

I fall in with the crowd, take out my phone, and start shooting video. I feel hope rising inside of me. I love this new generation. They understand that no one will be free until everyone is free and in charge of their own body, regardless of gender, color, origin.

Everywhere I point my camera, I'm getting great shots. A bare-breasted woman (kitty decals strategically placed) holds high her sign: *I am woman: hear my pussy roar.* Another young woman in boxer shorts and gloves shouts her truth to power: *We are not ovary-acting!*

Two rows ahead of me a tall marcher sports a toy kitty atop a bright pink pussy hat. Suddenly the kitty hat turns around: surprise, it's a young man wearing the hat. I notice other men marching with us, supporting women. But aren't there always good men who understand what equality and reproductive rights mean?

It took a few men before I found the right one. No, we found each other. Memories with Rob invade my mind—adventures and challenges, but also quiet pleasures and feisty arguments. Through it all, I made my documentaries and Rob put them to music. We worked together. We loved together. We had a kid together. We've enjoyed life's banquet, but we also help each other carry our rocks up the hill, over and over.

The crowd is growing, friendly yet determined. I'm taking a shot when a young woman walking in front of me turns around, waving her poster: *Never Going Back.*

There's a twisted coat hanger dangling from it.

I turn off the camera and reach out to hug her.

I feel an inexplicable but fierce desire to tell her what it was like back then. In a different world, a different country. But still the same.

This young woman is me. Past and present, we are one. As we fall in step, I begin to share. My heart is aching, because she is about to find out what's past is prologue.

There's another fight ahead.

ACKNOWLEDGMENTS

While it was sometimes a rocky road to the birth of my first novel, I was blessed with amazing support along the way.

My heartful thanks to:

-- Authors and teachers Eduardo Santiago and Mark Sarvas, whose UCLA Extension Writers' classes enlightened me from page one.

-- Classmates and writers groups: We struggled and saluted the joys of creating while we critiqued and inspired each other to keep going, chapter by chapter. A special thank you to Annette Bethers, who was always ready to read a new draft and urge me on.

-- Writers Guild members and friends: Much gratitude to Gary Goldstein, Peter Lefcourt, Robin Schiff, Larry Wilmore, Nicole Yorkin, and Mary Alice Kier, who helped me through the hurdles of publishing. And not least, to my oldest friend, author Dyanne Asimow who since the 5th grade has generously dispensed writerly advice and listened in sympathy throughout my uneven journey of novel-making.

-- Editors extraordinaire: Coralee Hunter, Dana Isaacson and Kate Ankofski not only showed me the difference between writing documentaries and novels, but made my story better.

-- Allison Mann, CEO of Hadleigh House Publishing: She has taken me step by careful step through the publishing process. Here is the absolute truth: I could not have done it without her.

-- Paris and its Parisians: Merci for giving me the stories to write this novel.

-- And above all, to my husband Mark, who has always been there for me. To support me ... to love me ... and who now speaks French better than me.

About the author

Joan Meyerson is an award-winning writer/director/producer of documentaries and television programs, including the *PBS National Memorial Day Concert*, for which she won two Writers Guild of America awards. The dramatic accounts she wrote about vets and military families reconfirmed her belief that the best stories come from real life, a belief she has followed in writing such varied programs as *Zoolife with Jack Hanna* (TV series), and *Children of Japan* (Disney). Having told the stories of others, she now tells one of her own, inspired by the two times she lived in Paris. A native of Los Angeles, Joan is busy finding more stories in her Valley Village neighborhood. *Who Needs Paris?* is her first novel.